THE
RACONTEUR'S
COMMONPLACE BOOK

THE RACONTEUR'S COMMONPLACE BOOK

by Phineas Amalgam

Edited by
KATE MILFORD

with illustrations by
NICOLE WONG

CLARION BOOKS
HOUGHTON MIFFLIN HARCOURT   BOSTON   NEW YORK

Clarion Books

3 Park Avenue

New York, New York 10016

Copyright © 2021 by Kate Milford

Illustrations copyright © 2021 by Nicole Wong

Clarion Books is an imprint of Houghton Mifflin Harcourt Publishing Company.

hmhbooks.com

The text was set in Bulmer MT Std.

Jacket art by Jaime Zollars

Jacket design by Sharismar Rodriguez

Interior design by Sharismar Rodriguez

Library of Congress Cataloging-in-Publication Data is available.

ISBN 978-1-328-46690-7

Manufactured in the United States of America

DOC 10 9 8 7 6 5 4 3 2 1

4500817298

To Lynne, who makes every story shine,
and to Tess, Griffin, and Nathan,
because every story is for you.

CONTENTS

ONE

THE BLUE VEIN TAVERN

THE RAIN HAD NOT STOPPED for a week, and the roads that led to the inn were little better than rivers of muck. This, at least, is what Captain Frost said when he tramped indoors, coated in the yellow mud peculiar to that part of the city, before hollering for his breakfast. The rest of the guests sighed. Perhaps today, they had thought. Perhaps today, their unnatural captivity would end. But the bellowing man calling for eggs and burnt toast meant that, for another day at least, fifteen people would remain prisoners of the river Skidwrack, and the new rivers that had once been roads, and the rain.

They passed the day much as they had passed the day before, and the day before that. Eventually, Mr. Haypotten, the innkeeper, announced supper in half an hour; he apologized for the state of the meals and the flickering lights, but without real worry. The Haypottens might run out of provisions eventually, but they had not kept this inn and tavern on the Skidwrack for a quarter of a century and more without seeing a flood or two, and they were well prepared for the whims of the river and the rain. The electricity might flicker and the hot water heating system, bought by the previous owners off an itinerant salesman when Mr. Haypotten was still in short pants, had never worked properly, but since the inn's fireplaces never went dark, its rooms never went particularly cold. Nobody would freeze, nobody would starve, and as for the rising water: "See that?" Mr. Haypotten would say, opening one of the windows in the lounge barroom against the cold and wet and pointing across the porch that wrapped halfway around the inn to indicate a blue step in the stairway leading down to the river. "That's where the river came back in 'fifteen. She doesn't dare come nearer than that. Water won't rise past a blue stair. Isn't that so, Captain?"

"That's so, Marcus," Captain Frost agreed today as he had every day, because Mr. Haypotten kept the captain in very good sherry. But when Mr. Haypotten left the lounge to go help his wife and the kitchen maid finish preparing supper, the captain sang a different tune. Captain Frost's eyes were deep-lined, his face tanned to mahogany, and his hair and beard bleached to a yellowed bone color from his decades at sea. He felt himself, not inaccurately, to be somewhat an expert in weather lore, and when the innkeeper was out of earshot, he muttered that he'd never heard such doss before in his life o' years at sea, and if painting a thing blue were all it took to put water in its place, then how was it every ship in the harbor wasn't sky-colored? Then he finished his very good sherry, pulled on his coat, and stomped into the hall and back out to check the weather and the roads yet again, as he did at every turn of the cracked half-hour glass he tended as religiously as if he were still aboard ship. It was never far from his elbow when he was inside the house, though it meant rearranging the place settings a bit at meals.

He left four guests behind in the lounge. Jessamy Butcher got up from her chair by the window, where she could see how very close the water was actually coming to the much-discussed blue stair, went around the bar, and found the captain's bottle of sherry. She poured herself a glass, then held the bottle up in one thin, gloved hand, offering it silently to the rest of the room. The tattooed young man named Negret declined and went back to the pages he had taken from the pockets of his tweed vest and was stacking together on the bar top: a mismatched collection of liquor labels, scraps of newsprint, wallpaper, remnants of the long, match-like twists of paper called spills that the maid kept in vases in each room for lighting the lamps and fires around the inn, and other scavenged oddments. When he had them where he wanted them, he took a sharp, round-handled awl from a roll of tools that lay open on the countertop before him and, pressing the pages flat with his palm, began to poke holes along one edge.

But his brother, Reever, nodded in response to Jessamy's offer and murmured his thanks as she reached across the bar to pass him a glass. Jessamy tried once again to decide whether or not the pale, brick-haired Colophon brothers were identical under their facial decorations. It was impossible to say. The tattoos were very similar but not quite the same, plus Negret wore his hair long and floppy, while Reever kept his short-cropped and cowlicky. And one didn't like to be rude by looking too long. Jessamy turned to the fourth person in the room. "Mr. Tesserian?"

At his table across the lounge, Al Tesserian looked up from his half-built castle of playing cards. "Dear God, yes. No, my dear, don't bother," he said as Jessamy made a motion to come around the bar. "Be . . . right . . . there." He placed a card and got up. The other three held a collective breath—but Tesserian's castles didn't dare fall until he gave them permission, which was generally done by calling Maisie, the youngest guest, to do the honors. Then and only then, when Maisie had pulled away a queen or gusted a sharp breath onto an ace, they toppled spectacularly, cards flying in all directions as if the laws of physics held no sway in the realm to which they truly belonged.

Tesserian accepted his glass with a bow, then returned to his architecture. He paused on his way to look at Negret's handiwork. "Binding another book?"

Negret nodded as he lifted the stack of papers and held the edge he'd perforated up to the light, checking to be sure the holes were lined up the way he wanted.

"It needs covers," Tesserian observed. He felt inside one sleeve, frowned, then took off the battered and narrow-brimmed porkpie hat he wore at all times except meals. From inside the lining, he produced a pair of aces and tossed them on the bar. "Will those do?"

Negret added the cards to his stack, one on top and one on the bottom. "Perfectly, if you can spare them."

Tesserian laughed. "An old gambler always has a couple of spare aces someplace."

Elsewhere in the inn, Petra, the guest who had been there the longest, borrowed from the maid a key to one of the countless glass cases that occupied walls and corners all around the inn so that she and Maisie could take down one of Mrs. Haypotten's music boxes, very carefully wind it, and dance for a bit.

Maisie Cerrajero was young and had been traveling alone to meet the aunt who was taking her in, with no luggage but an old ditty bag that held everything she owned. Each day someone said something along the lines of, "Won't your auntie be relieved when she gets here and sees that you're safe?" Most often that someone was Mrs. Haypotten, who had a habit of misplacing her spectacles or her ring of keys or her best little sewing scissors and was never quite sure what, other than "Thank you," she ought to say when Maisie inevitably found them for her, no matter in what unlikely place they'd been left. Flummoxed, she always came out with something like, "Won't your auntie be so happy to see what a nice, polite, helpful girl you are when she gets here, dear?"

Petra, however, never said anything like that, not even when Maisie found the dragonfly-shaped hair clip she had lost at breakfast two days before, half-hidden by the hem of one of the dining room curtains. Petra instead went for a key and a music box, because the unspoken truth was that, given the volume of rain and the slope of the hills, if Auntie had been on the roads at the wrong time, she was never coming — and Maisie was a girl, not a fool. But when that girl danced, sending her short sleek dark hair fluttering and the pleated skirt of her jumper frock swishing around her knees, her face lost its fear. And Mrs. Haypotten had an improbable collection of music boxes — forty-one that Petra and Maisie had managed to count — no two of which, as far as they could determine, played the same song.

Today, with the dragonfly back in its customary place among Petra's dark bobbed curls, they picked one from the tall cabinet in the parlor, which, like the lounge, looked out over the river-front. The cabinet had the thick, bubble-pocked green glass that was the only sort that could be made from Nagspeake sand, and Mrs. Haypotten had told them it held some of her favorite pieces, so they took extra care. Maisie chose a music box shaped like a kite with a terrifyingly delicate-looking ceramic key. She wound it gently, the eggshell-colored winder stark against the brown of her fingers. When she set it down and lifted the lid, it took a few notes before the tune resolved itself into "Riverward." Maisie hummed along as she spun in a wide-armed circle, swirling her shawl behind her as she turned, making the embroidered chrysanthemums upon it float in the air.

Sullivan, the young man who'd been sitting in a chair facing the fire, his eyes glazing over as they stared up at the big antique map that hung above the mantel, shoved himself abruptly to his feet and hurried out, briefly grasping Petra's wrist in apology as he stumbled past. That was unusual enough to make Petra look after him curiously. In the seven days since he'd arrived, Petra had never seen Sullivan do anything without an almost eerie sort of grace. He was so implausibly elegant when he moved and so bloody good-looking to boot that it was hard to believe he wasn't a hallucination. Petra had had to stop herself more than once from sticking him with a pin as he crossed a room just to see if then, finally, he'd make a misstep.

But apparently all it took was "Riverward." Interesting.

The old woman in the corner, thinner even than Jessamy Butcher, rocked her chair gently in time with the song as the music box wound down. Her skin, like Maisie's and Petra's both, was dark, but ruddy here and grayish there, uneven and slightly pocked, while Maisie had the clear and perfect skin of a child and Petra the kind of faultless complexion it would've taken a motion-picture actress an hour in makeup to achieve. The lady they all called Madame Grisaille spoke little, but she hummed as she rocked. It wasn't a loud sound — if the hot water coils in the cast iron case mounted on the wall across the room happened to be sizzling at the same time a wind rattled the windows, the hum was almost impossible to hear — but Petra and Maisie could feel it like a thrum in their bones as they danced, as if Madame's tune flowed through her and into the very boards, the very nails in the floor, and back up through their feet, so that it could sway with them.

"Madame is a dancer," Maisie had whispered to Petra the first time she had noticed this.

"When she was younger, you think?" Petra had whispered back. This had been three days ago, one evening when they were all on their way into the dining room, where Madame was always seated first out of unspoken respect for — for what? For her age, perhaps, or for her stateliness. If watching Sullivan was like watching a mirage that was too beautiful to be real, watching Madame was like watching a queen trying badly to disguise what she was, too regal for her sham ordinariness to be believed.

"No," Maisie had replied softly. "Not just when she was younger. Now. She's a dancer. She wants to dance when we do, but she holds herself back."

"Why would she do that?"

"I don't know." But the girl's eyes had begun to glow. "Maybe it's a secret."

"That she's a dancer is a secret?"

"No . . ." Maisie had looked thoughtfully at Madame as she followed Petra to the sideboard, where a buffet supper had been laid out and where Maisie had found a tortoiseshell button that had gone missing from Mrs. Haypotten's housedress earlier that day. "But she *has* a secret, so she doesn't dance. Because you can't dance and hide who you are."

Petra had thought that this was a very wise observation, and said so. She had also thought that if dancing showed one for who she was, Maisie danced like someone with no secrets to keep. That idea made her smile. But she hadn't wanted to make Maisie feel self-conscious, and sometimes the girl's dancing revealed as plainly as tears that she was carrying something that, when she remembered it, made her very, very sad. So Petra kept her thoughts to herself.

Today Madame Grisaille hummed along with "Riverward," and then "Gaslight," which was the tune plinked out by Maisie's favorite music box, a chrysanthemum-shaped one that nearly matched the flowers on her shawl. Then, another new thing, as if Sullivan tripping over himself hadn't been strange enough: as the sun began to set across the river and the chrysanthemum played its last, slow notes, Madame stopped rocking. She reached into the white fur hand muff she always carried with her, even indoors, and took a new music box out of it.

This one was plainer at first glance, just a round box of gold and ceramic with a scene painted on the lid. She raised one finger to her lips and then began to wind it. There was something so secretive about the motion, Petra instinctively checked to be sure both the parlor door and the French doors to the porch were closed and that the three of them were alone.

"This one is from my room upstairs," Madame murmured in a voice gravelly with age. "I don't know that Mrs. Haypotten would be comfortable with my carrying it about, so we shall keep this between ourselves. But it plays a remarkable song."

She finished winding, held it out on one spread hand, and lifted the lid. Maisie turned her head sideways, trying to make sense of the now-upside-down painting on the lid—two people sitting at a fingerpost, perhaps?—but only for a second, because when the song began, it was everything the girl's dancer's heart could have wished for from a piece of music. It was joy and love and exquisite pain; it was danger and the thrill of adventure and the certainty of failure and the thrum of hope. It was dream and nightmare; it was flight; it was winter and summer and water and stone and metal and fire and earth, and Maisie danced as she had never imagined dancing before.

After a moment, Madame handed the music box to Petra, and at last, perhaps because it was only the three of them in the room, the old woman joined the young girl and they danced together hand in hand, and suddenly Maisie understood why Madame had refused to dance before. And she knew what the old woman's secret was, too, and she understood the knowledge for the gift it was and wrapped her arms around it, concealing it in swirling embroidered chrysanthemums as the two of them whirled together, both dancing now like people with no secrets to keep as the sunset over the river painted them in golden light, orange light, crimson light. Madame caught Petra's eye over the girl's head, and the two women smiled at each other.

Perhaps the notes found their way out through cracks in the windows, drifted on the rainy wind along the length of the porch facing the Skidwrack, and snuck back into the house through another chipped pane of glass in a different room altogether. Perhaps they had other ways of making themselves heard. Either way, beyond the hall, beyond the stairs, two people in the lounge heard the song too.

Negret Colophon, stitching an elaborate binding into his scrap-paper book, dropped his needle in surprise, then quickly picked it up again and pretended not to have heard anything.

Jessamy Butcher, who had been deep in conversation with Reever Colophon a short way down the bar, was less subtle. Her head turned so quickly in the direction of the music that several joints in her neck and shoulders cracked. The popping might even have been audible had her gloved fingers not at the same moment crushed her sherry glass to fragments and powder.

Reever, who had been debating just then whether it was time to invite Miss Butcher to continue their conversation in a more private corner of the inn, jerked back as glass and liquor flew. Jessamy did not appear to have noticed what she had done. "Remarkable," she said in tones of quiet wonder, ignoring his stare, along with those of Negret from a few seats away and Tesserian from the table with the card castle.

"What is?" Reever asked.

"That song." Jessamy breathed out, a strange huff that wasn't quite a sigh.

Reever looked back down at the bar top between them and saw that she still clutched pieces of the glass she had destroyed. He took her hands in his and gently uncurled her fingers. One by one he removed the shards carefully from her palms, where small spots of blood had begun to seep through her pristine pink gloves. Then he held her hand for a moment when he had finished, watching her face.

She did not appear to notice any of this, and he could hear no song.

After a moment, Jessamy took her hands back and got to her feet. Self-consciously she tucked a stray bit of hair into place and smoothed it back with her palm, a gesture that left a small rose-tinted streak among the pale blond finger waves over her ear. She walked out of the lounge and across the hall, then slipped into the parlor. Petra and Madame looked over sharply, but when Jessamy closed the door behind her, they relaxed.

The song, improbably, had not yet begun to slow. "Do you want to dance too?" Maisie asked, reaching for the newcomer's hand, ignoring the blood that marked Jessamy's gloved palm like stigmata.

Jessamy spun Maisie around by the fingers that held hers, but her feet stood firm on the floor as she shook her head. "I don't dance," she said with a smile. "But I know that song well. I tried to play it once, but it's more difficult than it sounds. I was a musician, you know. Long ago, back in another lifetime."

Musician or not, Miss Butcher is a dancer too, thought Maisie, who could always tell. *I wonder what* her *secret is.*

There were six other people at the Blue Vein. The Haypottens, of course, and Sorcha, the maid, who was sixteen, plump and black-eyed, and utterly smitten with Negret Colophon, a thing that had shocked everyone who'd realized it, because in the same inn there was Sullivan, whose face was so perfect it would've been blinding except for that tiny scar he wore under one eye. But Sorcha, like Maisie, was a girl, not a fool, and she sensed unerringly that there was danger in that much beauty. And even though he wasn't precisely what you'd call handsome, there was something about Mr. Negret, with his face obscured by the swirling pattern of dotted tattoos, that made her need to look closer, and to sneak surreptitious glances whenever she came across him looking through the books on the shelves in the lounge, or the atlases on the mantel in the parlor, or the decades' accumulation of assorted bound material that stuffed the corner bookcase where the stairs turned midway between the first and second floors. Not to mention that when he thought no one was paying attention, he sang under his breath as he pieced his paper scraps together into hand-stitched tomes or stood at a window, reading by whatever light managed to filter in through the rain.

But of course, in an inn, the maid, at least, is almost always listening, and more than once when she went around at night to bank the inn's fires after everyone else had gone to sleep, Sorcha had caught herself singing the words of the firekeeping prayer she'd learned from her mother's father to the tune she'd gotten from Negret.

The last three guests were in the public bar at the front of the inn, where they were allowed to smoke. There was Antony Masseter, a tall traveling merchant whose right eye was green as a cat's and whose left was hidden by a rust-colored patch. Mr. Masseter had a round, dappled scar like a firework on one palm and appeared to suffer from insomnia that drove him to wander the halls of the inn at night. Between his light footsteps and the rain, he was almost soundless, but Sorcha and one or two of the others had caught glimpses of him, when nightmares or thirst or the need for a bathroom or the fear of the fires going out or something else had driven them out into the halls in the darkling hours.

Three nights ago, when Petra had caught him at it, Mr. Masseter had given himself away with music. As she'd been returning to her room, she'd caught a faraway, barely audible spill of tiny notes from somewhere down on the first floor of the inn: "High Away," the song played by a red casket on the bottom shelf of the glass cabinet in the parlor. Petra had paused at her door, trying to remember whether she had given the key back to Sorcha after she and Maisie had finished with the music boxes in that cabinet earlier in the evening. She glanced over her shoulder to where Sullivan was frowning in his own doorway. Their eyes met. "Masseter," he had whispered so quietly that only the sibilants were audible. "He's always up late." He nodded to the door of the next chamber down the hall to the right. "I hear him go out." Then he'd touched his fingers to his lips, not quite a blown kiss, and disappeared into his room.

Sullivan, as Sorcha could have told everyone, did not sleep either. She'd heard him later that same night pacing in his chamber when she passed on her way from her own tiny room to the kitchen to sing the firekeeping prayer as she checked the stove to be sure it hadn't gone out.

Sorcha usually slept soundly, but something about all this rain gave her nightmares. The peddler who'd sold the hot watter system half a century ago hadn't had the parts on hand to heat every room in the inn and he'd never come back in all those years to finish the job; not to mention the system had to be stoked up every morning anyhow to sizzle and knock what heat it did give to the rooms that had coils. Sorcha's banked fires kept well overnight, but lately she woke up twice, sometimes three times a night in a panic about the fires, so twice, sometimes three times a night, she tied her apron over her nightgown and went around the inn, checking every stove and fireplace she could get to without disturbing a sleeping guest. No, Sullivan did not sleep, but at least he stayed in his room — unlike Mr. Masseter, who had scared her half out of her skin the first time she'd come upon him staring into one of Mrs. Haypotten's hallway display cases as if he couldn't remember how he'd gotten there. Now she knew to expect him in the corridors, but that didn't make it any less shocking when she came across him suddenly in the dead of the night. He walked like a cat.

In the light of day, however — even at sunset — Masseter was ordinary. Today, after Haypotten popped into the public bar to announce supper and popped out again, the traveling merchant offered a pocket box of small cigars to the other two men sharing the room: Phineas Amalgam, a freckled and salt-and-red-pepper-haired neighbor of the Haypottens who'd come the day the rain had started just to borrow a box of matches and had wound up stuck there along with the travelers; and an artisan printmaker called Gregory Sangwin with darker gray hair and skin the color of a wash of good walnut ink on fine Creswick paper, an acquaintance of Amalgam's who had come to stay at the inn on his recommendation.

Sangwin's usual work was printing delicate, detailed pictures and illustrations from carved wooden blocks, and he amused himself by crafting small animals out of wood that found their way to Maisie every night at dinner. This had become a joint effort between himself and Sorcha, who saved all the small-ish bits of firewood she came across and passed them to Mr. Sangwin, who, once he'd magicked them into beasts and birds with his inlaid whittling knife, passed them back to the maid. At supper the creatures turned up on Maisie's plate, in her napkin, even in her soup on the day Mr. Sangwin had turned a longish splinter into a swimming dragon.

Today the printmaker squinted through his pince-nez at a tiny seabird with outstretched wings that he was busy carving from a scrap of pearwood. Maisie's animal, a river otter, already sat finished beside his cup. The bird was meant as a thank-you to his co-conspirator. He looked up, blinked, and accepted one of Masseter's cigars. "Thanks."

"Albatross?" Masseter guessed.

Sangwin nodded. "For the maid. She's a good sport, passing along the little girl's critters." The cigar temporarily forgotten, he lifted the bird, squinted at it, and touched the point of his knife to a tiny hole in one wing to cut away a nearly invisible splinter. "Perhaps Mrs. Haypotten will have a spare bit of ribbon it can hang from."

Phineas Amalgam stood staring down at a small card house that Al Tesserian had built on one of the bar tables the night before and that was somehow still standing. He accepted a cigar but tucked it in his vest pocket rather than lighting it. "I'll go ask her, shall I?"

"Good of you, Mr. A.," said Sangwin.

"Think nothing of it," Amalgam said. "Sorcha's a good egg. Known her since she was a tot." He nodded his thanks to Masseter and left the parlor. Later, as they all drifted into the dining room, he passed a length of blue velvet ribbon to Sangwin.

Mrs. Haypotten, bustling through a moment later, paused to squeeze the printmaker's elbow and murmur, "So kind." And as everyone else was smiling at Maisie's delight at discovering the river otter peeking out of a bread roll, Sangwin tucked the albatross on its ribbon into the maid's hand.

After supper, as they had done every other night, the guests moved into the parlor for coffee and tea beside one of Sorcha's well-kept fires. It was Phineas Amalgam who, on the evening of that seventh day of floods, suggested the stories.

"In more civilized places, when travelers find themselves sharing a fire and a bottle of wine, they sometimes choose to share something of themselves, too," Phin told them as he settled into his favorite chair, one of three that stood before the hearth. "And then, wonder of wonders, no strangers remain. Only companions, sharing a hearth and a bottle."

Mr. Haypotten, laying out the coffee on the sideboard, winked at his wife, who held the teapot. Amalgam, a folklorist, made his living collecting tales and putting them into books, so perhaps the innkeeper was thinking that his neighbor's suggestion had a bit of self-service to it. And it might have been that he was right. Still, it was a way to pass the time.

The wind and rain rattled the windowpanes and the French doors as the folks gathered in the parlor looked from one to the next: the young girl in her embroidered silk stole; the twin gentlemen with the tattooed faces; the gaunt woman with her nervous gloved hands constantly moving; the other woman, gaunter still and hidden beneath two layers of voluminous shawls, whose red-brown skin showed in small flashes when her wraps did not quite move along with her. The gambler in his old porkpie hat, building a castle on the floor before the fire with a pocketful of dice and at least six decks of cards, not counting the strays planted here and there about his person. The captain, lurking by the sideboard, where he'd stowed the half-hour glass and was itching to turn it but was also thinking it would be rude to interrupt Amalgam or get in the way of the Haypottens as they worked. The printmaker, smoking Masseter's cigar by one of the windows overlooking the river. The young man with the perfection and the scar, and the young woman with the dragonfly in her dark curly hair sitting just far enough from him on the sofa that the arm he had stretched out along the top of it did not touch her shoulder; and the gap between them, where Maisie had been before she had gone to sit beside Tesserian on the floor to help build the castle. The maid beside the door to the hallway, who must be counted here because no one who sings prayers set to stolen music when she works at a fire can be left as mere set-dressing in a tale; and the merchant, leaning on the mantel, toying with the filigree on the big music box that lived there: a case the size of a loaf of bread, which stood open to reveal a beautiful tree wrought of several kinds of metal, with roots entangled among the device's gears.

"If you will listen," Phineas Amalgam said, swirling his glass, "I will tell the first tale. Then perhaps, if you find it worth the trade, you will give me one of yours."

"Hear, hear." Mr. Haypotten passed Amalgam a cup of coffee. "Let's have a good one, Phin."

"Could you tell the one about the house in the pines?" Petra asked. Amalgam glanced at her, surprised. "I read it in one of your books," she explained.

"Oh." The folklorist had collected hundreds of stories into books. It was perhaps not terribly surprising that he did not immediately remember that the story Petra had asked for was not actually in any of them. "Yes, I suppose I could tell that one."

It can be hard to keep one's stories straight.

"Thank you," said Petra.

Unable to restrain himself any longer, Captain Frost turned the half-hour glass, and Phineas Amalgam said again, "Listen."

TWO

THE GAME OF MAPS

The Folklorist's Tale

*L*ISTEN.

There was a city that could not be mapped, and inside it a house that could not be drawn. It stood at the bottom of a hill on a street called Fellwool, a lane with broken pavement that had been overgrown and mostly hidden by ancient, knotty pines. It was the kind of house that, in simpler times, might have been called *enchanted* or *haunted* or *cursed*. These houses appear now and then in towns and cities that will tolerate them. Sometimes they survive. Sometimes they do not.

This house, the house in which this tale takes place, had survived for many, many years. It had copper pipes that reached down into the earth like roots; its woodwork had taught its stonework how to breathe in exchange for lessons in strength; and the ironwork that chased the eaves and climbed the walls and curled along the windows danced in the sunset. It allowed its rooms to roam like cats. It had permitted residents now and then, when the endless march of the years got lonely, but it never kept them long. It was a crafty dwelling, and it had ways of regaining its solitude when visitors overstayed their welcome.

A truth I have noticed — I believe it's a truth, at any rate — is that the extraordinary calls to the extraordinary. Over time, little by little, spoon by spoon and cup by clock, one cupboard and one key and one battered hat at a time, this singular house collected things to it: things remarkable and peculiar and marvelous and uncanny. When the house was occupied, this led to occasional ... let us call them *adventures,* although by *adventures* I don't mean only the cheerful and happily ending sort of occurrences. When it was empty, the house and its collection of wonderful and terrible furnishings whispered to one another. *What happened this time? Well, I'll tell you. It was wonderful.* Or, *It was terrible.*

Sometimes people ventured in uninvited. The house and its denizens dealt with this in different ways, depending. Much of that community was inclined to be more curious than annoyed, but some of the rooms were antisocial or easily insulted or worse, and some of the furnishings had questionable senses of humor or were inclined toward troublemaking or were simply malicious. The house itself came to dislike visitors simply because they caused so many tensions between the spaces and items the structure contained. Eventually it began to really discourage intruders, both for their own good and to keep the peace.

And to limit the amount of damage. Sometimes there was fallout when the more malevolent rooms and objects really got going, and the tools and brooms and mops in the house resented being made to clean up everyone else's messes.

One autumn, a man came to town. Though he was a peddler by trade, he was in town that year not to sell, but to acquire. The peddler had lost a thing belonging to his employer, and he had been tasked with the almost impossible duty of replacing the mechanism in question. The first of the many arcane pieces the reconstruction required was among the most important: a keyhole. Not a key, not a lock, but the actual keyway belonging to a particular sort of cabinet—the sort that formed an *adit-gate,* which is a technical term for what you might otherwise call a *portal.* And not just any portal, but the sort of portal that could bridge space and time, for the mechanism the peddler was attempting to build had to be able to manipulate both.

The peddler had traveled widely, and in his travels he'd read tales of this sort of portal: adit-gates hidden in wardrobes, and in looking-glasses; in clocks, in wells, in bedknobs. But it wasn't every building that would tolerate the presence of border furniture within its walls; buildings, after all, are mostly meant to keep the world *out,* not let other worlds *in.* And though he was a foreigner, he knew the city of Nagspeake well, and he suspected that if such a thing as an adit-gate was to be found there at all, it would be found in the peculiar house on the pine-choked street.

So the peddler went in search of a child, because while it is very difficult for an adult to pass through an adit-gate or even find one in the first place, *children* — especially the right sort of children — fall through them into other worlds all the time.

It wasn't long before he happened upon a small boy being ganged up on by a group of bigger boys who, conveniently, were giving him hell for being gutless. The peddler didn't catch what the boy called Pantin had done to deserve this, but he wasted no time in coming to the child's defense. "I bet he's braver than you," the peddler said, hauling the loudest of the bullies away by his collar. "Let him prove he's not a coward."

"How?" the bully snarled, trying unsuccessfully to twist out of the peddler's grip.

"Yes, how?" Pantin asked, curious.

The peddler thrust the bully away. "Let him stay a night in the house on Fellwool Street. I'll wager none of the rest of you would dare it."

They all shrank back at this suggestion; everyone knew the house on Fellwool was cursed. But poor Pantin was trapped. If he refused, he would be shown to be a coward, provably and perpetually. On the other hand, if he did it, he would be a *legend*. And so he agreed, because while small children are all prone to beastliness to some degree or other, they are also all capable of moments of most extraordinary courage.

That night, Pantin snuck out of his house with a lantern and a satchel full of supplies, and he met the other boys at the end of Fellwool Street. They walked over the broken pavement and through the twisted trees to the house, with Pantin, who figured he'd better start looking for his courage now, leading the way. Soon they saw lights in the thick darkness up ahead: candles glowing in the windows of the house. They found the peddler waiting on the porch. One side of the French front door was open, and through it they could see a cluster of lamps and candlesticks standing on a table in the center of the room beyond.

The other boys hung back, leaving Pantin to climb the porch stairs alone. "I thought I could offer some help, since it was I who got you into this," the peddler said. "A night is a long stretch, unless you have some way to pass the time."

"What sort of way?" Pantin asked, entranced by the dancing shadows inside the house.

"A treasure hunt," the peddler said, and Pantin looked at him at last. His eyes were blue and cold, even in the darkness. "And if you find the treasure and bring it out to me when your night is up, I'll pay you for it."

The boy's knees knocked. "What's the treasure, then?"

"Inside this house," the peddler said, "there will be an adit-gate. A . . . let's say a sort of *cabinet* that, when opened, shows you something *other than the inside of it.* That is the adit-gate. It might be part of any sort of cabinet, big or small, old or new. It might be locked, in which case, you may try this." And from his pocket he took a skeleton key. "Take care not to drop it."

Pantin took it carefully. It was pale where it wasn't marred by red and orange rust streaks, and it was rough to the touch, like unglazed china.

"When you find the right cabinet," the peddler continued,

"do not go into it, no matter what you might see. The treasure I want is the keyhole from that cabinet." He handed Pantin a rolled piece of oilcloth, inside of which the boy felt long, thin shapes. "These might be useful. Or then again, they might not."

Pantin stowed the peddler's skeleton key and the rolled cloth inside his pack, took a deep, deep breath, and stepped past the peddler and across the threshold. "Thank you for lighting the candles."

The man's cold confidence wavered. "I didn't light them."

The door swung shut between them before the boy could reply. The moment it banged closed, all the lights — the ones on the table as well as the candle in Pantin's own lantern — flared a deep blue. Then they blinked out, and he was swallowed by the dark.

He fumbled in his bag for matches as he lurched across the room. He struck a light and reached for the nearest candle, only to find his little flame casting its meager glow onto an empty table thick with dust that didn't look as though it had been disturbed in a very long time.

He still had his lantern, of course, and it lit without trouble, burning a perfectly ordinary flame. Pantin swallowed his nerves, lifted the lamp with an unsteady hand, and set out to explore the house and find the peddler's mysterious cabinet.

From somewhere in the darkness came the ticking of clocks, but there was no furniture in the big foyer except the dusty table. Opposite the front door, a sweeping curved staircase led up to the next floor. There was a single doorway in each wall: the front door he'd come in through and three wide entrances leading to rooms to his right, to his left, and straight ahead, the last of which was tucked under the curve of the big stair. Through the half-open pocket door to the left, he could just make out the vague shapes of furniture. That room, he thought, might also contain the source of the ticking. Through the arch that gave into the room on the right, Pantin's straining eyes, beginning to adjust, picked out the shadows of large, unmoving animal forms. He bolted instinctively for the arch under the stairs.

This led him through a dining room to a swinging door that deposited him into a hallway, which, in turn, took him to the kitchens. There, at last, the boy found cupboards to try. Some were empty and some were not, but everything he found inside each of the cabinets — cutlery, glassware, mismatched china — seemed ordinary. Even the empty ones seemed only ordinarily empty.

The kitchen had three other doors in it. Pantin chose a set of narrow, paired shutters that he thought probably led into a larder. He opened one . . . and found himself looking into the foyer again, *as if through the front door.* There before him was the dusty table, and beyond that, the big curved stair and the arch to the dining room below it.

This should have been impossible, and yet there he was. Pantin glanced back over his shoulder. If he *was* by some weird miracle now looking through the front door, then the driveway and Fellwool Street ought to be just as weirdly and miraculously behind him. But no: there was the kitchen, right where he'd left it.

Flummoxed, he stepped through into the foyer and closed the door behind him. He turned to open it again, and, instead of the kitchen, there was the outdoors and the dark circular drive. Out in the middle of it, the other boys had built a fire. Pantin shut the door with a shaking hand and leaned against the wood, breathing heavily. Was it possible he had found the cabinet the peddler had told him of so quickly? He didn't remember having seen a keyhole on the shutter doors, but then he hadn't been looking for one.

He ran across the foyer again and through the room behind the stairs. But this time, the back hallway beyond the dining room took him not to the kitchen but to a narrow set of steep steps that seemed as if it couldn't possibly exist without intersecting with the big sweeping staircase opposite the front door. And, just as unsettlingly, there was light up there. Pantin retraced his steps and found himself in a billiard room where the dining room had been.

The boy dropped to his haunches and covered his face with his hands. Then he started to laugh. Did every door in this place lead to something other than what logically ought to be behind it? If so, did he just need to find any keyhole at all? The laugh trailed off after a moment, and Pantin whispered, "Cabinets," into his palms. The peddler had asked for the keyhole from a cabinet, and anyway, Pantin had all night. He stood up and wiped his face.

Now that this space was a game room, there were cabinets to try: a sideboard with dusty bottles, a shallow case on the wall that hid a dartboard, a box of dry and flaking cigars and another of fragrant matches; but none of them turned up anything interesting. And there was a set of double doors covered by curtains. "Onward, then," Pantin murmured, stepping through into a towering, glass-ceilinged solarium full of dead and decomposing plants.

There was a barrister bookcase, its shelves protected by glass, but it held no surprises—just gardening tools, folded paper envelopes of dried seeds, a pair of notebooks, and a broken pencil. A cuckoo clock hung on the wall beside the door. Pantin dragged a chair over, took it down, and opened the back. He jumped as a live bird, red and green, hopped out, stretched its wings, and fluttered away to disappear down the hall. This was odd, certainly, and just as oddly, the clock was empty of workings. But the inside of the case was square and wooden and perfectly matched to the outside, and anyhow there was no lock or keyhole on it, just a simple hook-shaped latch.

He rehung the clock and climbed down, then picked his way through wicker furniture and broken plant pots to the glass-paned French doors across the room. He cleaned a grimy pane with spit and his sleeve and peered out. There, beyond the hedges enclosing an overgrown garden, he saw the drive that led to Fellwool Street again, which didn't make sense because the solarium hadn't been visible from the lane. Logically, then, the solarium ought to have been at the *back* of the house, not the front. But there were the boys, sitting around their fire, and farther on, a smaller glow flared and dimmed: a cigarillo, perhaps, in the hands of the peddler with the cold blue eyes.

Pantin went to the bookcase for the writing supplies he'd seen earlier. One of the notebooks had barely been used. He flipped past a few sketches of plants and accompanying notes to a blank page and, in a halfhearted attempt to make sense of the confusion of rooms and doors, tried to draw the layout of the house. But there was no way, on the two-dimensional surface of the paper, that he could puzzle together a logical arrangement of the spaces he'd passed through so far.

He gave up on that and began making rough drawings of each room, each on its own page, along with each entrance and exit he'd seen and where they'd taken him. Then he tucked notebook and pencil into his satchel, returned to the doors that had shown him the back garden with its overgrown hedges, and walked through them. Instead of stepping outside, he arrived in the kitchen by way of the paired pantry doors. And so the night passed.

Pantin was never certain that he explored the whole of the first floor. He looked through whatever space he found himself in: a library, a salon stuffed with taxidermied animals both familiar and strange, a music room, a parlor full of ticking clocks that asserted, ridiculously but with perfectly synchronized chimes, that he'd been in the house for less than fifteen minutes. In each room, he opened everything that would open: instrument cases, Davenport desks, chifforobes, curios, tea chests, case clocks. He sketched each room in the gardener's notebook. Sometimes the red-and-green bird appeared, fluttering overhead and disappearing through a doorway. Sometimes, instead of a new room, the house deposited him into the hallway that ended at the bottom of the narrow staircase with a spill of light at the top.

But at last Pantin began to notice a pattern: different kinds of entrances led to others that were similar. If he went through a set of French doors, he would emerge through French doors, so from the solarium he could get to the kitchen by way of the pantry, the game room by way of its curtained doors, or the foyer by way of the front entryway. Open entrances led to other open entrances, so he could get from the foyer to any room that also had at least one open, doorless entryway. Pocket doors led only to rooms that also had pocket doors — though that category appeared to include any kind of sliding panel, which Pantin discovered by leaving the music room through a pocket door only to find himself tumbling out of a dumbwaiter into a bedroom whose window, when he looked out of it, peered down on the solarium from an upper floor.

That bedroom in turn deposited him back on the first floor when he tried to leave through its door. Therefore, the boy concluded, what floor a room was on mattered less than what kind of doors it possessed.

Nine times out of ten, any entrance he passed through

took him somewhere he didn't expect. The peddler had said he wanted the keyhole of a cabinet, but would a keyhole from a door suffice? But no — none of the interior doors appeared to have any locking mechanisms at all.

Pantin began to notice something else, too. If he stopped to listen at a door before going through it, he could make a guess as to what room lay behind it. The parlor full of clocks was the easiest one, but each room, he found, had a sort of voice. The music room's old-house creaks sometimes came with accompanying tones, but out of tune, as if the instruments were settling as well. The solarium had a rattle of loose glass panes. The swinging door in the kitchen creaked on its hinges, moving with shifting air currents. Between hearing those sounds and knowing what types of doors each room had, Pantin was able to predict with increasing accuracy which room he'd be walking into, provided it was one he'd already visited.

Listening to the house and keeping detailed notes helped him navigate — or at least anticipate where the house was likely to take him — but Pantin never did make sense of how time passed in that place. Still, time *was* passing, and he began to feel the effects of exhaustion and nerves. For a long time, though, as the night wore on, the constant strangeness kept him awake and alert, which was good because sometimes there were unlikely accidents.

In the taxidermy salon, just as Pantin was opening a firearms closet of burnished wood, a mounted head fell off the wall, and only the open closet door saved him from being skewered by a spiraling antelope horn. In the music room, a wire in the open-topped grand piano snapped and whipped out with a discordant *ploing*. It missed lashing him right across the neck only because he happened just then to be holding up his lantern for a better look at an unfamiliar brass instrument on a nearby chair. The impact when the wire hit the metal edge of the light was enough to send a crack snaking through the glass on one side.

Only once, in all the rooms he explored, did he find anything that wouldn't open easily at a touch: a terrarium shaped like a small glass church that he discovered in the clock parlor, in which a little porcelain rabbit wearing a clerical collar and clutching a tiny glass bauble in its paws crouched among a collection of sad-looking flora. When he couldn't raise the lid, Pantin lifted the terrarium carefully from the mantel and set it on a coffee table. He touched the streaked key in his pack, but there was no lock holding the delicate glass structure closed, just a rusty hasp at one roof edge. Pantin took out the peddler's tools and carefully worked a small screwdriver between the rusted bits until he felt the hasp give.

He lifted the lid and peered down into exactly the same scene he'd seen through the dusty glass from the outside, though now he could see that the glass bauble contained a single flower woven of hair, and the plants, through some miracle of glass and humidity, looked like they might still be clinging to life. He opened his canteen and poured a trickle of water into the soil at the bottom of the terrarium, then closed the lid. The minute bell in the glass belfry chimed once as he put the little church back into its place.

Not long after that, Pantin found the map room.

He was in the hallway, having just turned away from the narrow staircase for the umpteenth time, and was about to step out into the foyer. The room through the right-hand arch had changed again. And, although he couldn't make out the source, there was light in that room — enough to lie tantalizingly across part of a strange chest with an assortment of drawers of various shapes and sizes, and to glance along one edge of a framed map on the wall above a leather chair just right for curling up in to take a very short catnap. The room called. The light all but beckoned.

He stepped out of the hallway and into the foyer, and the house dumped him right back into the hallway, as if the entire world around him had pivoted 180 degrees. Pantin turned and tried to go through again, and the same thing happened. He grabbed unsteadily at the wall for a moment before trying once more to leave the corridor, but the second his foot stepped across the threshold, the house shifted again. For whatever reason, it did not want him going into the room with the chair and the map.

He tried for a few more minutes to find a way to it, despite the house's efforts to keep him out. The map room had a doorless arch, so he consulted his notebooks and tried every open entry he could find, but the house just kept throwing the narrow staircase at him, over and over — the one with the light at the top, which had not at first seemed like it could possibly fit where it was without running into the curved foyer stair.

Evidently the house had decided it was time for him to climb these particular steps, so although he longed for the welcoming light of the map room, Pantin went up.

He emerged on a landing, where a bare bulb in a wall sconce threw dim bluish light into a cramped hallway with a green baize door midway down its length. Pantin opened the door and looked out into a wide gallery with a red carpet. A carved marble balustrade ran the length of the gallery on the other side, broken only by the opening that marked the top of the grand foyer staircase.

From where he stood, Pantin could see a little way into each of the rooms below. The room with the map on the wall was still there, with its warm, glowing, come-this-way light. From that angle, the top of the cabinet was visible. Upon it sat a collection of globes in varying sizes and a single, partly unrolled chart that showed blue water.

Abruptly the green baize door swung shut, whacking him right in the nose and flinging him back against the wall of the corridor lit by the flickering bluish bulb. When he shoved it open again, the red-floored gallery was gone, replaced by a different one with a blue carpet. Instead of looking down into the foyer, this gallery overlooked the solarium through a wall of green-tinged, many-paned windows. Pantin crept across the space, held up his lantern, and looked through the glass. The bird from the cuckoo clock fluttered past on the other side, singing.

The boy didn't know it, but the house had done him a kindness, just as it had when it had refused to let him into the foyer once the map room had appeared. Possibly this was the influence of the parlor, where Pantin's own act of kindness in watering the terrarium had not gone unnoticed. But what is certain is that the gallery where the curved stair landed was one of those spaces within the house that had a tendency toward violence.

What looked like a russet-and-red paisley pattern in the carpet was actually an array of bloodstains of varying ages that had dried to a range of rusty tones. It wasn't a very imaginative space —it was home to a collection of grudge-holding suits of armor carrying a variety of edged weapons, most of which were a bit anachronistic for the armor they'd been paired with. But those weapons had impossibly sharp edges, and the suits moved preternaturally fast for collections of plate metal. In fact, the only more vicious space in the house on Fellwool was the map room, which used its enchanting light as an anglerfish uses its lure.

And now, of course, Pantin could think of nothing but getting to that very room, with its tantalizing cabinet full of drawers and that light that made each of the globes atop the cabinet seem to wear a sort of halo. And, logically, it seemed that the shortest way there would be through the red-carpeted gallery. But the house did not seem to want to allow him into it.

Pantin slumped against the wall that faced the solarium and tried to work out how to use what he'd learned about the house so far to find his way to the map room, tiredly watching the bird flap its way around and around the domed, green-glass-paned ceiling.

Was this a joyful flight, a celebration of having been let out of the clock? Or was it a desperate flight, a doomed effort to find a way out of this new, larger, glass cage? Was the sky beyond the solarium beginning to lighten, or had Pantin's eyes managed to adjust at last to the constantly changing darkness in this place? And if the sky *was* beginning to lighten, did that mean morning was really on its way, or was it only daybreak here, in the blue-carpeted gallery? The timepieces in the clock parlor had been tolling behind a door just down the hall only minutes ago, and Pantin had counted only two chimes. He watched the bird flapping in its endless circles and tried not to feel quite so much of a connection to it.

He took out his notebook, leaned down into the glow of his lamp, and began to sketch the red-carpeted gallery, but he hadn't seen much of it before the door had slammed in his face, so he didn't get far. After that, Pantin sat there for what felt like a long time, trying to figure out how to reach the map room. It wasn't just the problem of the spaces moving around; for whatever reason, the house didn't want him going into the chamber with the glowing light. And gradually Pantin convinced himself that this was because the thing he'd been looking for, the cabinet with something else on the inside, was there.

The house made old-house noises around him, subtle creaks and squeaks that seemed almost like a voice. "Let me into the map room," Pantin said quietly. Then louder: "Let me into that room! Why won't you let me into that room?" He thought he knew why, of course, but it wouldn't do to confirm it. Not if the house was really listening.

A new sound overlay the creak-and-squeak: a sort of slither of wood against wood, accompanied by the ticking of many clocks. Pantin didn't have to open the notebook to know that the parlor now lurked behind the nearest door in the wall he was still leaning against, the one he had come through to arrive here, overlooking the solarium.

"I know you're keeping me out of that room," he said. "I don't know how to convince you to let me go there." Then, in a fit of total honesty, "I think I might go mad if I can't go in." *Or perhaps I've gone mad already,* he thought helplessly, *believing I can talk to a . . . a moving parlor.*

For a long moment, there was nothing: no new sounds and no movement other than the circling bird on the other side of the glass. Then the air around him shifted, and somehow the gallery shifted too, in a way Pantin could understand only as a sort of sigh. The wood-on-wood slither came again, taking the clock-ticking away with it. Pantin took a deep breath and opened his notebook to the page with this gallery on it. He turned the page and looked down at the sketch he had begun of the *other* gallery, the one with the rust-colored carpet.

Now, I don't know why the house's answer to Pantin's asking for access to its most vicious chamber was to make him pass through another similarly malevolent space first. Perhaps the house or the clock parlor or whatever entity had the most influence at that moment decided that it had better show Pantin what he was asking for. Perhaps the house figured if the boy couldn't manage the bloody gallery, he certainly couldn't survive the map room. Perhaps it decided the boy must have some sort of death wish, in which case the house was fully within its rights to decide to set his inevitable end in the gallery, where the carpet was already spoiled beyond fixing and blood splatter didn't particularly show up against the flocked red wallpaper.

Who can know these things, really? We spend our lives passing through spaces, not wondering what they think of us or what logic they possess, other than the logic we imposed on them as builders or occupants, which is nothing more than a reflection. Surely places, if they survive for long, develop their own logic. Their own personalities. Their own senses of strategy.

In any case, Pantin grabbed his lantern, scrambled to his feet, opened the door, and flung himself into the red gallery without a clue as to what he was in for. It's possible the house did him one last favor on his way through the doorway, because his foot caught on something right at the threshold and he landed on his hands and knees. His light rolled away and went out, flashing its last flicker on the sharpened, moving blade of a pikestaff. The blade, which had been in motion since just before the boy had opened the door, missed his head by inches and embedded itself in the door frame hard enough to send splinters flying. One of those splinters nicked Pantin's ear as he rolled sideways screaming and saw the suit of armor motionless by the door, bent into an unnatural curve with one end of the pole clutched in its gauntlets and the blade still stuck where it had landed.

He spotted the second suit of armor moving in the dimness out of the corner of his eye, but the moment he looked straight at it, it stopped. At a sound behind him, he whirled to find the suit with the pike motionless, but its blade was now free of the door frame. Another wheeze of scraping metal yanked his head around to see a third suit standing stock-still in the middle of the gallery, right between Pantin and the curving staircase that led to the foyer. A fourth suit behind the third had frozen in the act of stepping away from the wall opposite the balustrade.

More sounds behind him, and Pantin spun again. The second suit was much closer now, and it carried a huge, gleaming battle-axe. But in pivoting, Pantin had turned his back to Three and Four, and he could hear both of them moving. He turned to check on the first one, and not a moment too soon. Number One froze with the pikestaff over its shoulder, and it's likely that with even a second more, it would have swung for Pantin's head, and that would've been the end of this story.

The underlying geometry of the house might've been incomprehensible, but the logic behind the suits of armor was crystal clear to Pantin, who had played Stop and Go in the schoolyard plenty of times and who had no problem accepting the idea that otherwise-inanimate objects might be able to move when one wasn't looking. He scrambled backwards across the gallery until his shoulders touched the balustrade, turning his head rapidly from left to right to try to keep an eye on all four suits. He couldn't quite do it; the suits had been at this for a good hundred years, and they knew where all the sightlines were. And they were *fast* — they didn't fail to take advantage of every half-second Pantin's eyes were elsewhere.

By the time the boy was on his feet again with his back to the railing, Number One was halfway across the gallery with its pike ready to strike and Numbers Two and Three had made some good progress toward him from the opposite ends of the space. Behind Three, Number Four had taken up a sentry position at the top of the stairs. Pantin suspected that was a bit of a bluff, since he was pretty sure all he'd have to do to keep the suit immobile was walk up to it, looking right at it, and keep his eyes on it until he was safely down on the first floor. But it hardly mattered, because he'd also have to pass Three to do that, and once he was past, he'd have to keep his back to Three in order to keep his eyes on Four. Not to mention if he kept watch on Three and Four for any extended period of time, he'd have his back to Two, and Number One was a yard away with its very long weapon at the ready and needed only a few seconds' worth of inattention to strike.

So, with his eyes on Number One, the closest suit of armor to him, Pantin reached for the banister at his back and hoisted himself carefully up onto it. When he was sitting and stable, he shifted and swung first one leg and then the other over, finding toeholds between the uprights and staring at the blade of Number One's glinting pike. He could see all three of the others peripherally now, but just barely.

Pantin began to edge his way along the outside of the banister toward the stairs, feeling blindly for places to put his feet. He could feel a thrumming energy, as if all four suits were coiled animals waiting to strike the second he blinked.

Finally, when he thought he was out of reach of the pike, he transferred his stare over to Three and Four, keeping Number One just barely in the corner of his eye. But now Number Two was out of eyeshot, and free. Pantin forced himself not to look as Two clanked to life, because now he was even with Number Three, who held a short, gleaming sword at the ready.

Number Two flashed into the same peripheral space as Number One and froze dead.

Pantin exhaled and kept edging along. He passed Three and reached the place where the banister curved to meet the stairs and angled down. He stepped onto the first stair, climbed over *that* banister, then backed down three steps more until he could see all four suits of armor.

He walked rearwards all the way down, just in case, then experimentally turned his head when he was at the bottom. He heard clanking and turned to find all four suits of armor standing in a sentry line at the top of the stairs. But they didn't try to follow him down, nor did they attempt to throw their weapons after him.

Pantin's legs gave out. He sagged to his haunches and crouched there for what felt like an hour, until his pounding heart began to calm and the numb, shocked tingling in his body began to dissipate. He raised his fingers to his neck where the splinter had cut him, and winced.

As if to get his attention, a clock he hadn't heard before tolled, and Pantin, still crouched on the floor, turned to his left to look through the open doorway into the map room. The light spilling from it was gentle and warm and welcoming. He walked over the threshold.

It was the most captivating chamber he'd ever been in, full of carpets in rich, vivid tones and deep, sink-right-into-it furniture in leather and velvet. The bookcases had glass fronts, and the desks had curved, carved legs. Every surface held something fascinating: navigational instruments, globes, boxes of expensive-looking drafting equipment. The walls were papered in a pattern that called to mind gentle, rolling waves, and framed maps and assorted bits of cartography hung everywhere. Some were as small as a book page. Others were bigger than Pantin himself.

He walked up to one of the smaller pieces on the wall, a beautiful collection of the sorts of monsters that he had only ever before seen cavorting at the edges of maps. Some of them here were peeking out from behind a hand-drawn square of rope enclosing the word *LEGEND*. Inside the rope, under *LEGEND*, was a handful of symbols meant to help a reader interpret the map.

Most of the creatures surrounding the rope stared eastward, as if the whole group were tracking something beguiling just out of view beyond the dark wood of the frame. One, however, leaned over the top of the symbol box, its claws hooked into the *E*s in *LEGEND,* and stared straight out of the picture at the viewer.

It wasn't quite a dragon, and it wasn't quite a tiger, and it wasn't quite a goat. Its horns curled almost all the way from its forehead to the corners of its wide, fanged mouth, and Pantin couldn't decide if the tendrils framing its head were tufts of hair or tentacles. He leaned in, suddenly fascinated with figuring out what those waving bits were meant to be. Closer and closer, until only a hair's breadth separated his nose from the glass over the creature.

A puff of warmth gusted gently past his cheeks.

Pantin bent nearer still, staring at the tendrils and trying to work out whether he was seeing suckers or just stains on the paper. Another puff of warm air feathered his face, this one carrying a whiff of salt water and rotting meat. Enthralled, Pantin barely registered it. Up close, the tendrils seemed almost to wave as the creature's head loomed larger, taking up more and more of the boy's field of vision.

Another balmy puff of sea and carrion ruffled Pantin's hair. He didn't notice.

There was no glass. He didn't notice that, either, nor the fact that his hands now gripped the frame like a windowsill as the top half of his body angled through it. In fact, he might have been halfway down the thing's gullet before he noticed *anything,* if not for the fact that the creature, which was capable of holding itself still for truly stupefying lengths of time but which hadn't had a fresh meal in years, couldn't stop itself from drooling.

A single tepid drop fell onto Pantin's hand. He glanced down, the spell of the creature's waving tentacles broken, and frowned at the spot of damp between his knuckles. Only then did he register that his top half appeared to be leaning through a window and into perilous proximity of a monster.

Pantin flung himself backwards as the creature's mouth snapped shut. The world warped, and as he fell on his backside onto one of the map room's beautiful rugs, the aperture that had somehow opened up between himself and the marginal monster became nothing more than a bit of a map in a mahogany frame again.

It's a measure of how accustomed Pantin was becoming to witnessing the impossible (or perhaps just how exhausted he was) that his first thought wasn't *This room will kill me if I let it* —that thought came later—but instead *That's it! That's what I've been looking for! The thing whose inside is different from its outside!*

But no, he realized as he approached the map again, cautiously. There was no lock here. Something about this picture or its frame held a portal, which was miraculous, certainly—but the peddler hadn't wanted a portal. He didn't want just any old miracle. He wanted a keyhole. A ... what had he called it? An *adit-gate.*

Pantin sighed and turned back to the rest of the beautiful room. *Well,* he thought, *there are plenty of cabinets here to try. But this room will kill me if I let it.* And he began opening things. Rolled maps, flat maps, decaying maps and incomplete maps and unfinished maps. Cartography fashioned of lines, of dots, of yarn and sticks, of shaped wood and linen and skulls, of gloves and spheres. And the map room held itself still and waited.

Now and then, one of the pages he unrolled made his fingers tingle strangely or felt oddly chilled, as if it had just been brought in from the cold. Once, he slipped as he climbed up onto a table to reach a portable lap desk on a shelf and found himself tumbling to the floor. This was a near miss: there had been a map already unrolled on the table's surface, and what had felt like a bit of odd clumsiness had, in actuality, been Pantin's left leg falling into the painted landscape. Only because he'd been leaning to the right to reach the portable desk had he merely fallen off the table rather than tumbling into the map, in which the legendary carnivorous beast that prowled the prairie could actually be seen by anyone who looked closely enough. Or at least, the paths it trailed through the waving watercolor grasses could be seen, but then, anyone who looked that closely was probably already falling in, and this beast didn't always wait as patiently as the tentacled monster did.

Pantin had picked himself up and glared down at the map on the table. "No, you don't." He swept it to one side and moved on. But after that, he was a bit more careful as he passed in the shadows of more maps and more marginal monsters and occasionally unrolled more doorways into the habitats of terrible things. All around him, the room waited. *Soon, soon,* it whispered silently to its cartographic bestiary. *Soon. Be patient.*

At last, Pantin reached the side of the room opposite the arched entrance and paused. He looked around for anything that could be opened that he hadn't already tried. On the wall behind him, the largest framed map hung at a slight angle from the bent nail and frayed twine that supported it, its top edge tilting a few inches away from the rolling-wave wallpaper and looming into the room. Pantin had deliberately kept himself at a safe distance from this particular piece, which was a darkly beautiful representation of a forested hinterland. Or at least, it had *seemed* like a safe distance.

Without warning, the twine broke and the map crashed to the floor, where it stood up on its lower edge for a fraction of a second before falling forward into the room. Pantin half turned, but he barely had time to raise his hands before the map toppled right over him. And then, in the space of two breaths, he found himself crouching in a dense, cold forest, and for some reason holding a decomposing, lichen-rimed tree branch in both upturned hands.

Now the thought was clear as a bell: *This room will kill me if it gets the chance.* Except he wasn't in the room with the soft, warm light anymore. Now he was in the dark and the cold amid sharp tangles of undergrowth, and there were noises of large bodies in the bracken and not enough light to see beyond the nearest overhanging trees.

Instinctively his hands uncurled to let go of the branch;

some part of his brain had noted that it was damp and rotted and wouldn't make much of a weapon, and given the sounds coming through the trees, Pantin was going to need one. But just in time, the boy stopped himself. In the cold dark, there was one faint source of light: a narrow trickle painting the downturned backs of his hands. The light under the branch was different from the illumination above and around it.

The noises got louder and closer, and the unseen things began to shriek at one another. Desperately, he raised the branch, which he realized was much heavier than it seemed it should've been, and just as if he'd raised a shutter covering a window, the map room became visible before him. Pantin flung himself under the branch and through the opening, feeling his body roll across carpet instead of forest floor.

Behind him, the top edge of the map fell to the ground with a puff of old-room dust and forest-scent.

Pantin scrambled backwards until he collided with the chair by the desk. Then he leaped away from that, terrified the rolled maps on the surface might tumble off and catch him. He stood, thought he might fall again, and reached for a low bookcase, the nearest piece of furniture without maps either on or hanging above it.

This room will kill me if it can, he thought for the third time.

"Enough," he said aloud through chattering teeth. If it wasn't daylight outside yet, if the other boys were still out there waiting, and if they tried to hassle him about coming out early, Pantin decided he felt perfectly up to throwing a few punches.

The peddler would have to contain his disappointment too. Pantin had evaded murderous suits of armor and animate cartography. He was done being intimidated by mere humans. And he was done with the house on Fellwool Street . . . assuming the house would deign to let him leave so easily.

At that moment, Pantin made an accidental discovery. As he waited for his breathing to return to normal, he looked down at the top of the bookcase he was leaning on. The only things on it besides his shaking hand were five books sandwiched between two bookends shaped like the bow and stern of a ship. Because he couldn't quite bring himself to try to stand on his own yet, Pantin let his eyes roll over the spines. One of the titles leaped out at him: *Bournefont's Cartography: Legends and Keys.*

Keys. And then he remembered having seen the word *Legend* inked inside the symbol box on the map fragment with the monster that had attempted to eat him only a few minutes ago.

Pantin took the book cautiously from its place and began turning pages. It was illustrated with pages upon pages of cartographic symbols and their meanings. In some examples taken from actual maps, the symbol charts were labeled *Legend* as they had been in the fragment with the mesmerizing monster. In others, they were labeled *Key.*

Inside this house, there will be an adit-gate, the peddler had said. *Let's say a sort of cabinet that, when opened, shows you something other than the inside of it.*

Maybe you couldn't call a map a *cabinet,* but Pantin thought these particular ones fit the spirit of the peddler's request nonetheless. And now that he knew the word *key* could be applied to cartography, too . . .

Pantin set the book down, returned to the map fragment with the horned and tentacled creature, and examined the legend beneath its curling claws. There, under the icons for train tracks, caves, roads, and rivers, was a symbol that looked a bit like a slice of pie topped by a circle. It was a keyhole, and it was labeled *PASSAGE*.

He hurried around the room, looking at the legends and keys of any map he thought was too small to carry him away. The keyhole was there almost every time, sometimes shaped differently, sometimes labeled *transit* or *departure* or *strait,* but always recognizably a keyhole. At last he came back to the one on the desk that he'd nearly fallen into. Yes, there was the little keyhole in its legend, labeled *aditum.*

"Adit-gate." Pantin laughed, a bizarre, out-of-control sort of giggle. "Aditum." Then, abruptly, he stopped laughing. He folded up the map and shoved it unceremoniously into his pack.

Immediately he could feel the fury of the room around him. He didn't wait to see what other uncanny traps it had at its disposal. Pantin sprinted for the arched entryway that, by all appearances, gave into the foyer. He leaped through it headfirst, sprawled onto tile, and came to rest with a thud against the big center table.

The front door was open again, and thin gray light sifted through the trees beyond the drive out front. A tall figure stepped into the opening and lifted a glowing cheroot to its mouth.

"Morning," said the peddler, exhaling smoke.

Pantin got to his feet and marched across the foyer to the door, not entirely certain where he'd wind up when he crossed the threshold. Apparently the peddler had the same idea, or something like it, because although he very carefully did not step in, he reached one hand through into the house. Pantin took it, gripping the gloved palm as hard as he could, and let the peddler pull him outside.

And then . . . he was outside.

The peddler looked down at the shaking, exhausted child. "How'd you do?" he asked, puffing on the cheroot.

Pantin reached into his pack and passed him the map.

The peddler unfolded the page and stared down at it. "What the hell is this?"

Pantin looked around, his bleary eyes landing on the remnants of the fire the boys had built the night before and the sleeping bodies lumped around it. From the looks of things, only two of them had stayed. "The map key," Pantin muttered. "That's what you want." Then he stumped down the porch stairs and kicked the nearest sleeper in the gut. "Hey!" he snarled as the boy jerked upright. "Where'd the rest of the cowards go?"

Then he fell over in a dead faint. But when the story was told later, as it was again and again over the years by the students of Pantin's school and beyond, it was reckoned that nobody could fault him for that. After spending a night in Fellwool House, the boy had earned his rest.

THE ROOM APPLAUDED politely, all except Captain Frost, who tapped the last few grains of sand down from the top of the glass, turned it over on the sideboard, and hurried out of the parlor. A moment later, a gust of air and a rattling of the window-panes told them the captain had gone outside by the front door. When the breeze had stilled, Tesserian riffled through one of his decks and handed Maisie two of the knaves: the black knave of keys and the red knave of caskets, to finish a peaked window.

Phineas Amalgam sat back and drained the dregs of his coffee. Then he looked at Petra. "Was that the one you meant?"

"That was it."

"Ah." He nodded his thanks to Sorcha as she refilled his cup. "That story isn't in any of my books yet, you know."

Petra frowned. "Certainly it is."

"It isn't. When I was telling the bit about the suits of armor, I remembered. It's meant to go into my next collection, but I hadn't decided which of two versions of the story to include. There's one where it's not suits of armor in that hallway, but instead the floor is lava and the house has a much better sense of humor."

"Well, I must've heard it somewhere, mustn't I?" Petra asked breezily. "I assumed it was from one of your books, but perhaps it wasn't. Or perhaps I was thinking of a different peddler tale after all. There are so many."

"Peddlers always get short shrift in folklore," Masseter complained from where he stood beside the mantel with his arms folded. "They're always villains."

"Was this peddler a villain?" Tesserian asked thoughtfully. He glanced at Maisie. "What do you say, miss? Was the peddler a villain?"

Maisie considered. "I think—"

Mrs. Haypotten tsked as she bustled over with the teapot to refill Tesserian's cup. "Sending a child into that sort of danger? Certainly he was." She patted Maisie on the shoulder and bustled off again in a flurry of blue polka-dotted crepe. Maisie, whose face was safely hidden from standing adults by virtue of her being seated on the floor, rolled her eyes.

"You see?" Masseter shook his head and took one of the little cigars from his pocket. "Villains, even when they're not villains," he said, plucking a spill from a vase of long paper matches that stood on the mantel, matches that Sorcha had fashioned so that they looked not like sticks of twisted newspaper but like tall, thin, sculpted paper flowers.

"No smoking in here," Mrs. Haypotten said briskly as she left the room to refill the empty teapot. Masseter glanced sharply at Sangwin, who tossed the end of his cigar out the window.

"They're not *always* villains," Amalgam said mildly. "I can think of plenty of tales where they're not."

"*You* can." Masseter deposited the flower-shaped spill back in its vase, then dropped into an empty chair beside the fire. "You sift stories for a living. But can anyone else?" He looked around the room. This turned out to be a bit of a challenge. Silence fell. Captain Frost came back, his shoes and beard wet from the rain, and took up his cup, and still no one could think of a tale in which the peddlers were not the villains.

At length, in the chair in the corner, Madame Grisaille spoke from the depths of her wrap. Her voice gravelly as ever, she inquired, "Can you think of one, Mr. Masseter?"

Masseter closed his eye and pressed a finger in the space over his nose between it and the patch. "I am a peddler of a kind," he observed, "and I've heard it said that every man believes himself to be the hero of his own tale. So perhaps this is a more difficult question than I thought when I first asked it."

Reever Colophon had been sitting in one of the three high-backed chairs before the fire with his legs thrown out long and careless before him. "I know one," he said, stretching his arms overhead. "I'll tell the next tale, if you like, and you lot can say if the peddlers are the villains in it or not."

THREE

THE WHALEBONE SPRING

The First Twin's Tale

THERE WAS A PORT TOWN that crouched between a bay and a hill; you may have heard of it.

If you have, understand that this was long before the days of the pirates who in later times became the runners of rotgut whiskey and Cuban cigars, endangered butterflies and irises that bloomed in illicit colors. It was before the ancestors of men like John Deadlock and Carrick Bend, who for a while turned smuggling into a way to rebel during one of the city's darkest times. These were earlier, more innocent days, and the port was a small and simple place that relied on ships and traveling merchants for news of the world over the hill and beyond the bay.

One morning at the opening of market season, a Yankee peddler came to town on a wagon drawn by a black nag. He stopped in the square, unhitched the pony, and with a few jerks of a crowbar and a few swings of a hammer, converted the wagon into a stall. He began to set out his wares: sundials and water clocks, chronometers and pocket watches, mantel clocks, candle clocks, tide clocks. Clocks that announced the hours with chimes, with internal pin-cylinder music boxes, with ingenious wooden figurines that clacked tiny rosewood claves or rang miniature glass bell trees. Last of all he hung out a shingle that read ALPHONSUS LUNG, CLOCKMAKER.

The next morning, another Yankee peddler arrived in a wagon, this one drawn by a long-eared mule. He, too, drove into the market square, and with a few adjustments, he turned the wagon into a stall selling tin: tin pans, tin soldiers, tin whistles and flutes and pipes, tin lanterns and flatware, even tin fences that unfolded like a row of figures cut from creased paper. His shingle read CASSITERIDES BONE, TINSMITH.

The day after that, a third Yankee peddler drove a wagon drawn by a pied pony into the square and set up his stall under a shingle that announced him as IGNIS BLISTER, PYROTECHNICIAN. He filled his shelves with things that flared and flamed and burst: candles, fireworks, fusees, black powder, flash powder, rushlights, repeating matches and friction matches and foxfire torches.

The fourth Yankee peddler to arrive drove a pair of tall red horses, and in his wagon he carried three ebony coffers wrapped in bands of brass. They seemed the sorts of chests that could hold only treasure, or saints' relics, or the heads of kings. The fourth peddler took one coffer down carefully, and the curious citizens jostled and pushed for a glimpse within as he lifted the lid.

Inside, there was only paper.

The first three Yankee peddlers scoffed. The fourth fixed them with a faint smile as he unpacked sheaves of paper that had been stitched into pamphlets. "You laugh, brothers. What do you sell?"

The first Yankee peddler nodded up at his shingle. "Clocks and watches, brother. I am called Lung."

"Tinware," sniffed the second, clipping patterns into a lantern with a pair of shears. "My name is Bone."

The third lit a cigar with a cedar match that flared green. "Blister," he said. "Infernal devices and sources of light."

The fourth Yankee peddler tipped his hat to the other three and went on laying his pamphlets out upon the counter of his stall. "And I am Drogam Nerve."

"But what do you sell?" Cassiterides Bone inquired.

Alphonsus Lung picked up one of the pamphlets and flipped through it. "These poor things? What sort of pathetic bookmonger are you?"

"I am no mere bookmonger, and those are not merely books," Nerve retorted. He plucked the pamphlet from Bone's fingers. "I am a catalog merchant. I don't sell these. I sell what's *in* them."

"And what's in them?" Ignis Blister asked over folded arms.

Drogam Nerve smiled again and pitched his voice so that

everyone in the square could hear his answer—which, on this market day, was a lot of people. "Everything, my friends. These are catalogs, and with them you can find and order anything and everything imaginable." And he bowed to the assembled people of the town.

Well, this was something new. The citizens pored over Nerve's catalogs with their woodcut illustrations and discovered astounding goods they hadn't even known existed. For some things, Nerve sold blueprints the purchaser could follow to build a house, a train station, a carriage; for others, he took orders and promised delivery of the actual item within a fortnight.

But the peddler called Nerve was not the only one to arrive that day. A ship docked, carrying news of coming danger: invaders from up the coast and over the hills were headed south. There was only one enemy likely to come from that direction, and it was the only enemy capable of striking fear into the town on the bay. An impromptu community meeting came together in the market square to discuss what should be done.

"That's easy," said the Yankee peddler called Lung. "You will need timepieces in order to coordinate your defense, and a great clock whose tolling can be heard throughout the town, so that all will know the hour of the attack." And he opened his cart and showed them small pocket chronometers and enormous timepieces with bells that pealed like alarms. "I have heard tell of these people," he warned. "You must not be caught unawares."

"No," said the Yankee peddler called Bone. "What good will knowing the hour do if you can't defend yourself? What you need is fortification: a great and powerful perimeter strung from hilltop to hilltop to keep the invaders at bay. I, too, have heard of these people, and you must at all costs keep them from entering your town." And he displayed lengths of fence and barbed wire with edges sharp as a razor's.

"Those won't work," argued the third Yankee peddler, the one called Blister. "You need more than clocks and fences. I *know* these people. You must destroy them outright, or you haven't a chance of survival. You must arm yourselves." And Blister showed them weapons: cheirosiphons, fire lances, firepots packed with glittering incendiary powders, and bottles of Greek fire.

The fourth Yankee peddler waited until his fellows had finished. At last, the people of the town turned to look at him. He shook his head slowly.

"You may announce the hour of their coming with one of Brother Lung's clocks," he said. "You may hold them at bay for a while with Brother Bone's fortifications, and you may even kill some with Brother Blister's handiwork. But it will serve only to delay the inevitable. In the end, they will win, and they will take your city because they outnumber you and because they are stronger, rougher, madder than you. In the end, if anything can best them, it will not be you — you will all be gone, either fled or killed. Only the city itself will remain. In the end, only the city can stop them."

"How can a city do this?" the mayor asked. "Do you know a way?"

Drogam Nerve took a catalog from his stall, opened it, and showed the mayor the page he had selected. "You must build this." *This* was a sequence of designs that would turn the city itself into something like a combination of a clock, a fence, and a bomb all wrapped into one.

"How much?" the mayor asked.

Drogam Nerve smiled and pointed to the price printed in the bottom corner.

The city hurried to raise the money, bought the plans for Nerve's device, and began to build. It was an infinitely complicated design. Some of the components — escapements and flashpans and fuses and assorted bits of metalwork — could be had from Lung, Bone, and Blister, but the design also required pieces the likes of which had never been seen in the town on the bay. These had to be ordered from Nerve as well, who hired the fastest riders to be found to undertake the journey to the warehouse of his partner, Octavian Deacon.

Piece by piece, the city was turned into an infernal device.

Finally, the time came to put the last part into place: a great steel spring. "Pass the word for the mainspring," went the call through the town, but among the parts that had been ordered, there was no giant steel mainspring. "Pass the word for the mainspring," went the call again, but the local engineers had no springs big enough to power the city-turned-weapon.

Time grew short. The mayor went to the Yankee peddlers. He found them sitting in the market square, playing cards. "Mr.

Nerve," he said, "we seem to have forgotten the mainspring, and we haven't steel enough to make one."

Nerve went for his catalogs, but the mayor shook his head. "There is no time," he protested. "Our enemies will be here in a matter of days, surely."

Alphonsus Lung looked up from his cards. "You have no steel, but what about whalebone?"

"Of course," the mayor snapped. "Half of our citizens are whalers. But what good does that do?"

"Among my clocks," Lung said, "there is one from China that uses a mainspring of whalebone. If you have enough whalebone, you can fashion your spring from that."

The mayor looked to Nerve, who consulted the plans. "Well," he said, "I wouldn't be able to tell you how it might affect the mechanism."

"You mean it might not work?" the mayor asked.

"Oh, it'll *work*," Nerve replied. "The question is, will it work in the same *way?* When you change the construction of a device, you often change the manner in which it operates. You are proposing to alter the very heart of the machine. Certainly it will make a difference."

At that moment, a deep explosion like the firing of a cannon echoed through the landscape, and saffron clouds spewed into the sky over the hill. "That is one of my incendiaries," Blister said, eyeing the haze. "They have reached the head of the river."

The city was out of time. No one had any better solution,

so the mayor ordered the town's engineers to craft a mainspring from whalebone as fast as they could. In a matter of hours, the giant whalebone spring was finished and placed where it belonged, at the heart of the mechanism that turned the city into a snare. The device was wound by a dozen men circling around a huge capstan. The trap was set.

Then a far-off sound like the shearing of giant scissors tore through the air. "That's one of my fortifications," Bone said, peering westward through a spyglass. "They are only a few miles away." The time had come to evacuate.

So they left the city: the citizens piled into ships, and the Yankee peddlers hitched their ponies and horses and mules to their wagons. The mayor invited them to watch the battle unfold from the vessels out beyond the harbor, but the Yankee peddlers shook their heads, and one by one they started up the winding road that had carried them into town in the first place.

The city was deserted when the invaders swarmed into it. A cry of triumph rose from its streets as they discovered that they had conquered without even having to fight. Meanwhile, out on the vessels in the bay, half the citizens watched the city through spyglasses while the other half counted down the minutes on an assortment of timepieces purchased from Alphonsus Lung, until at last the time had come for the trap they had made of their city to spring on the invaders.

And then the assorted clocks on the ships sounded their varied alarms.

Nothing happened.

The citizens shook their timepieces. They stared across the bay. They waited. Still nothing happened, and nothing continued to happen as the conquerors took possession of the port.

The city did not spring the trap it had become. Something was wrong, either with Drogam Nerve's plans or with the way they had been executed, or perhaps with the whalebone spring itself.

Out on the bay, the mayor and the engineers argued over what had gone awry, and the citizens wailed and blamed and despaired. In the end, only one thing was certain: Nerve had said the device would work with a whalebone mainspring, but he had definitely been concerned that this makeshift heart might change *how* it worked. Perhaps changing the spring had changed its timing.

So the newly exiled townsfolk watched their city fall — the city they had built, and loved, and then turned into a giant infernal device and left to defend itself. They watched, and still they waited for the whalebone spring to release its force. And still, nothing happened.

In the city, the conquerors celebrated as they took possession, unaware that all around them a hidden weapon lay coiled: a weapon in the shape of a city, its whalebone heart winding slowly, slowly down. And it winds down still, all around us, as the city waits and bides its time.

Which leaves this problem for all who hear my tale to solve:

Who are you descended from—the townsfolk or the invaders? And are you, even now, living in the middle of a trap that continues winding down to the moment in which it will finally spring?

Ticking? I hear no ticking.

Reever told his tale without getting up from his chair, with the fire alternately casting him in shadow and gilding his cowlicks with reflected shades of red and gold. He spoke almost without moving.

Maisie, staring up at him from the floor, gave a shiver, barely noticing as she accepted the four aces that Tesserian handed her. The Blue Vein Tavern was in a port town between a bay and a hill. *Had* something been ticking? Other than, of course, the case clock between the vase of matches and the big music box above the fire? She glanced at Petra, who gave her a wink as she clapped for Reever's performance.

"Delightful." Jessamy Butcher stood and crossed from a shadowy little table in one corner of the parlor to pour herself more coffee at the sideboard.

"I'm delighted you think so," Reever said with a lazy smile. "Will you be telling one yourself?"

"You've been wondering what kind of tale I'd tell, haven't you?" Jessamy's voice was light as she stirred sugar into her coffee, but Reever Colophon saw her fingers twitch on the cup, and he wondered fleetingly if she was about to crush it the way she'd crushed her sherry glass.

He watched her hands, watched her face, noted the reddish

stain still darkening one swish of pale gold hair. "For days." There was nothing lazy in his expression now, or in his voice.

The room held its breath. *If there were music, he would ask her to dance,* Maisie thought with a pang. And then she realized that this amounted to exactly the same thing; perhaps it was just as impossible to keep secrets when you told a tale as it was when you danced. Others in the room looked in amusement, wonder, envy at the young man who had, with a mere two words, laid so much out in the open. Sorcha, trying to imagine saying such things out loud herself, glanced almost involuntarily at Negret, who'd taken a chair beside the glass display case full of music boxes in the corner nearest the hallway door. She was the only one who saw the flash of sadness cross the other Colophon twin's face.

Jessamy met Reever's eyes at last, and the rest of the room might as well have vanished around them. "I think you know the kind of story it would be." Her empty hand closed around the stains in the palm of the glove it wore as the rust-streaked lock of hair fell down over her temple again.

He forced his own hand not to reach for her clenched fist or smooth back the fallen curl, but instead to lie still on the arm of his chair. "I don't care. It would be yours."

A beat, then two; then Jessamy tore her eyes away from him and pushed her hair back into order. "Someone else," she said abruptly, and took her coffee back to the table in the corner.

The room exhaled. Reever closed his eyes, opened them again.

From the chair by the glass cabinet, his brother spoke up. "I've thought of another one, Masseter. A story where the peddler isn't the villain."

"O rarest of lore," Masseter said archly. "Would you share it?"

"I will. And as it happens, it's doubly rare, being a story in which—well. Let me just tell it." Negret smiled at Maisie, who, truth be told, was still feeling a bit unsettled by Reever's tale. "I think you might like this one."

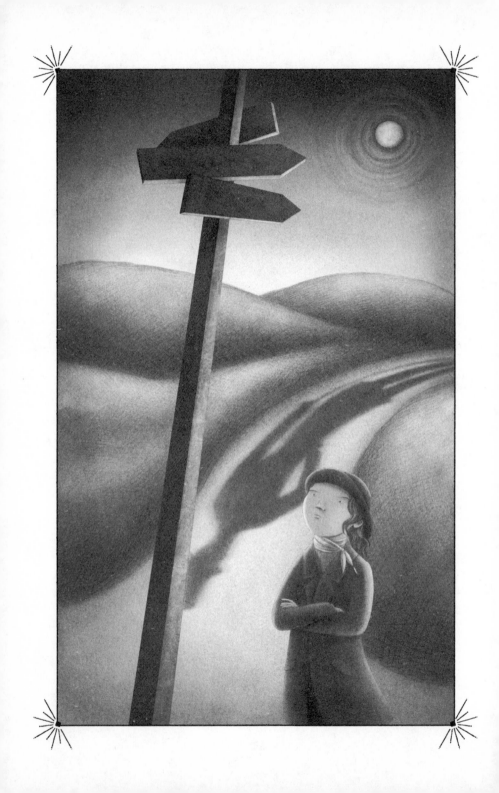

FOUR

THE DEVIL AND THE SCAVENGER

The Second Twin's Tale

IF YOU BEAT THE DEVIL, you can win your heart's desire. Everyone knows that, and some foolish folks probably think they could do it, too. But the Devil is a master gambler, and he makes his living off that sort of fool. It takes arrogance to dream of challenging him, but arrogance rarely helps anyone win, and the Devil, who is not usually arrogant, almost never loses.

Still, it's happened, though it's a rare and peculiar thing when it does. This is the tale of one of those occurrences, when the Devil got the worse of a deal. And this encounter was special right off the bat because it isn't often the Devil encounters something he wants. Usually, deals with the Devil begin with someone wanting something from *him*. Folks don't have much — other than their souls — to tempt the Devil. Not usually.

On the road between two remote towns, the Devil was

walking alone at twilight when he came to a crossing of ways. And there, stopped under the fingerpost, was a scavenger's wagon.

Now, the scavengers in this part of the country had a certain reputation, and as the Devil approached for a closer look at the rag-and-bone fellow peering up at the signs with a frown, he was reminded of stories he'd heard. It was said that the scavengers in these parts were all descended from one or another of the legendary Yankee peddlers of old. It was said they could work near-magical feats with the things they collected, and if they could not make a thing they needed from what they had or could find, they simply changed their minds about needing that thing. And while you might think someone whose work is picking through cast-off things and rubbish would be considered the lowest of the low, the way I understand it is that among the chapmen of those parts — the many sorts of itinerant peddlers on the roads and in the towns — the scavengers were first in precedence, and therefore in any gathering of peddlers, the scavengers were honored most highly.

As the Devil strolled nearer, it occurred to him that this scavenger was a bit on the small side. Then, as the Devil's shadow fell across the ground before the stranger and announced his diabolic presence, the small figure turned, and the Devil noticed two things. First, the scavenger had eyes the silver-gray of half-dollars or the full moon on the right kind of night. Second, the scavenger was small because it was a child — and not only a child, but also a girl.

The girl and the Devil greeted each other the way solitary strangers do: friendly, but wary-like. Well, the Devil wasn't precisely wary; you don't have to be wary when you're the Devil. But he was curious.

"Lost?" he asked.

"Nope," the girl said easily, "just deciding. You?"

"Nope," the Devil replied, "just intrigued." And he admitted that he had never encountered one of the famous scavengers of these parts.

"Well, then." The child beamed, trotted past the stamping mule at the front of her wagon, and began to turn a crank on the side, near the front wheel. The crank was nearly as big as she was, and as she rotated it, the side of the wagon unfolded creakily, gaping wide like the lid of a music box until the whole thing had converted itself into an open-fronted shop topped by a patchwork awning.

The scavenger leaned on the crank and waved at the shop front. "Be my guest," she invited in a voice that whistled slightly as she spoke. The Devil tapped the brim of his hat, climbed a set of stairs made from bolted-together pieces of mismatched metal, and took a look around.

Most everything was in a drawer or a chest or a box. There was a trunk of colorful rag scraps and another of white ones. There was a crate of furry dead critters that were probably waiting to be skinned and rendered down, and another of critters with scales. There was a chest of paper fragments: wallpaper, newspaper, printed broadsides and used postcards, torn crepe paper crowns from expended Christmas crackers. A wooden cask of teaspoons sat under a shelf full of the jars of flitting goldfish the scavengers traded to children for household oddments. And hanging from the ceiling on threadbare lengths of faded satin ribbon were a dozen or so clocks of all sorts: cuckoo clocks and pocket watches and spring-wound tin alarm clocks, all ticking together: *tick, tick, tick, tick, tick.*

There were other things, of course, but the Devil was vaguely disappointed. It was more or less the same bunch of stuff scavengers everywhere carried. Even the clocks; the fact that they were so perfectly synchronized was a little unsettling, but they all looked like perfectly ordinary timepieces as they whispered together: *tick, tick, tick, tick, tick.*

The girl was watching him closely with her odd silver eyes. "Don't see what you're looking for?" she inquired in her whistling lisp. The Devil got the uncomfortable feeling that she knew what he had been thinking.

"Just don't see anything I particularly need," he said carelessly.

"What do you need, I wonder?" The little scavenger looked at him thoughtfully.

"I don't need anything," the Devil said. It was true.

She nodded. "It would have to be something very special, then. Something you want."

The Devil grinned and allowed that he couldn't really imagine what that might be. But to himself, he admitted again that he was curious. And again, as soon as he'd had the thought, he wondered if the scavenger knew it somehow.

"Let me think." She zipped past him and began opening drawers. The first item she held out was a molded black thing, roughly oval and carved to look like a long-necked bird with its head resting on its feet. "It's an inkstick made from soot collected after a martyr was burned at the stake. You grind a bit against a stone and mix it with water to make writing ink."

"How on earth could you know where the soot came from?" asked the Devil, skeptical.

"I know because I gathered the soot and made the inkstick myself," she retorted. "I can show you the mold I formed it in."

The Devil assured her that he believed her, but all the same, he didn't feel he simply had to have the inkstick, even if it had been made from a martyr.

"Here's a knife made from iron extracted from a saint's blood," the scavenger said, opening another drawer and removing a blade. "Perhaps that is the sort of thing you're looking for?"

"How did you happen to find a thing like this picking through garbage?" the Devil asked, looking at the knife. It was very beautiful; the space just above the cutting edge on both sides had been etched with a creeping pattern of lilies of the valley. "And how could you possibly be certain about where the iron came from?"

"I didn't scavenge the knife," the girl said with a grim smile. "I scavenged the blood. I extracted the iron myself. That's how I know what I say is true."

But the Devil had caught sight of something more interesting than the martyr's ink or the saint's iron. When the scavenger had begun hunting for something to tempt him with, she'd looked through a big drawer whose contents had clattered hollowly as she'd shoved it mostly closed again. Mostly, but not totally — the Devil could still see what it held. It was full of white and off-white and gray and pale-brown bits and pieces. Bones. All sorts and all sizes of bones. And one of them was very interesting.

It was a short, thick, squat bone engraved all over with a pattern of neat hatch marks stained with brown ochre ink. Where there weren't hatch marks, there were curling rows of cursive words in a language the Devil recognized and yet couldn't quite bring the name of to mind.

"It's a pastern bone," the scavenger said, unerringly spotting the item that had captured his attention. "Part of a set for playing knucklebones, I suspect. You need five to play the game, but I only have that one." She plucked it from among the rest and held it out. "Here."

The Devil turned the pastern bone over, and even up close, the shapes carved into it taunted him. He knew every language ever invented, and he knew this one, too, but it had been so long since he'd encountered it, he couldn't remember where he'd seen it or when, let alone how to make sense of the writing. It was as if he had the words of a song stuck in his head, but the name of that song was hovering just out of his memory's reach.

In the end, that was the thing that made him want the bone. "How much?" he asked as casually as he could.

The scavenger considered. "One tooth," she said at last. "Your tooth." She tapped her lip where it hid one of her canines. "This one. The sharp one."

Whatever the Devil had been expecting her to request, it wasn't a tooth. "What for?"

She shrugged. "You never know when something like that might come in handy." She opened another drawer and took out an ugly contraption that looked like an oversize house key with a little claw at one end and a turning crank at the other. "I can pop it right out myself, right this minute. Won't even hurt. Well, not much. Not for long. Probably not, anyway."

Not exactly a confident statement, but that hardly mattered. It wasn't that the Devil was concerned about pain, and it wasn't as if having one tooth gone would be any kind of inconvenience. Still, in this wagon he'd seen ink made from a martyr and a knife made from a saint, and he couldn't help but wonder what this young scavenger would do with one of his eyeteeth. But he was sure she wouldn't tell him to what sort of use it might be put, and he just didn't like the idea of making a deal he couldn't clearly see both sides of.

And yet, there was that engraved bone, and the more he thought about it, and the more he tried to remember how to read the language carved upon it, the more he wanted it. Certainly a mystery like that would be worth one tooth.

And yet.

Overhead the clocks whispered on: *tick, tick, tick, tick, tick.*

Well, the Devil decided to handle this the way he handled

every bargain he made. "Tell you what," he said. "I'll play you for it. If you win, I'll trade you for the tooth and I'll give you a favor as well, with no strings attached to it. If I win, you give me the bone, and your soul, too."

The scavenger scratched her head as if she was thinking, but her silver eyes were sharp. "Do I get to choose the game?"

"Certainly," the Devil said in his most gentlemanly voice.

"Two teeth, then. And keep your favor."

"Done," the Devil snapped, only a little surprised. "What's the game?"

"Not a game," the scavenger corrected. "A challenge. If you can guess what I plan to do with your tooth, you win and I lose. If you can't guess"—here she paused to look thoughtfully up at the clocks tick-tick-ticking away— "in sixty seconds, then I win."

"How many guesses do I get?" the Devil asked.

The scavenger smiled thinly. "As many as you have time for." And she reached up for the lowest-hanging of the clocks, a large pocket watch, and untied it from its faded blue ribbon. She held it high so that the Devil could see its face, and the two of them watched the second hand as it climbed toward the twelve: *tick, tick, tick, tick, tick.*

"Begin," said the little scavenger.

The Devil, of course, had already been racking his brains to remember everything he knew that could be done with teeth. He figured he had a clue in that he'd seen what the silver-eyed girl had done with the saint's blood and the martyr's ashes, so he tried to think about what could be done with the hard bits of a body.

"You'll make it into porcelain," he suggested.

The scavenger shook her head.

"You'll use it to make a cupel to separate silver from ore, or some other alchemical thing."

"No."

"You'll make some sort of bone oil from it, something to burn in a lamp or to poison a well."

"No."

"I don't suppose you'd use it for something as simple as scrimshaw, or making needles or awls with, or that sort of thing?"

The scavenger shook her head again. "I have plenty of bones I can use if I want to do that."

Tick, tick, tick, tick, tick. Twenty seconds left. The Devil was starting to get frustrated.

"You'll make it into baking powder. You'll make it into neat's-foot oil for getting rid of scales. You'll bury it and hope it grows into something interesting, a dragon, or some sort of warrior prince. You'll . . ." No more ideas came. Now the Devil was completely at a loss.

Tick, tick, tick, tick, tick.

"Time," the scavenger sang. The Devil grabbed the watch, but of course the girl had no need to lie. A minute is a minute — usually, anyway — and the Devil's minute was up.

"Bad luck for you. You came up with some good ideas,

though." With one hand the scavenger took a wooden stool from where it hung on the wall, and with the other she pushed the Devil out of the wagon into the night.

She put the stool on the ground, and the Devil sat, because what other choice did he have? He'd made a deal and he'd lost. All he could do was look up and try to focus on the stars while the little silver-eyed scavenger girl put her dental key into his mouth, tightened the claw around one of his canines, and wrenched it out by slow turns.

She'd lied about how badly it would hurt.

The other one she took was a molar from the back, and when it was all over, she packed the holes in his mouth with cotton soaked in moonshine liquor and handed over the carved pastern bone the Devil had bought with his pain and his teeth. Somehow he couldn't quite look at it now, so he just tucked it right into his pocket as he stood up to make himself scarce.

Before he left, though, the Devil turned back to the scavenger. "What's the answer?" he asked indistinctly through his mouthful of cotton and firewater.

The scavenger rattled his bloody teeth in her palm, looking like she was deciding whether or not she thought he deserved an answer. At last she simply smiled, pulling up her lip with one little finger, and all at once everything, including the lisping tone of her voice, made perfect sense.

There was a gap right where her left eyetooth ought to have been.

"I needed it to replace one I lost," she said. "Although you sure came up with some good ideas, and I'm plenty glad I asked for two teeth instead of one."

You can imagine the Devil got out of there as fast as he could manage without *looking* like he was trying to get out of there as fast as he could.

And that's how a scavenger girl with a missing tooth beat the Devil.

NEGRET WAS RIGHT: Maisie liked that story a lot. She applauded energetically along with the others. "So usually the Devil wins?" she asked as Tesserian tugged up the hem of his right trouser leg to retrieve a queen of signs and a two of points from inside the ankle of his sock.

Negret's smile twitched. "Usually."

Maisie made a steeple of the two cards and looked up again. "Are there many of those stories?"

"Of the Devil making bets?" Negret glanced from her to Amalgam, whose chair almost directly overlooked the castle construction. "Rather a whole mess of them, yes?"

"I believe I've heard Phin tell one or two of those," Mr. Haypotten said, rubbing his balding head. "I seem to recall something about a guitar player." He brushed a few crumbs from the sideboard into his pocket.

"There are, in fact, a mess of them," Amalgam confirmed. "And more than a few with musicians. When it's a musical challenge, it's called a duel, or a headcutting. The Devil almost always wins those. I've heard there's one song and one song only that beats the Devil, but it's a beast to play. Not just anyone can do it." He stirred his coffee and tapped the spoon on the lip of his cup once, twice. Then he looked at Jessamy Butcher.

The gloved woman had still been seated at the corner table at the start of Negret's tale, but during the telling she'd strayed closer to the fireplace. Now she faced the flames, her own cup and saucer abandoned on the mantelpiece. "Have you thought of a story yet, Miss Butcher?" Amalgam asked gently.

"Not yet." Jessamy's tucked shoulders straightened sharply, awkwardly. "Whose go is it next?" she asked, too brightly. She twirled to survey the room, looking for the next teller with a strange light in her eye — perhaps just a reflection from Sorcha's well-kept fire; perhaps not — and with that single action, she told her secret to Maisie. Just one twirl, just one rotation, but there was an entire terrible dance within it, to eyes for which motion was its own kind of storytelling.

Jessamy had come in to listen to the song that was everything, the song that even Madame Grisaille could not fail to dance to. But Jessamy had refused to dance. *I know that song well. I tried to play it once, but it's more difficult than it sounds. I was a musician once upon a time, you know.*

Maisie choked back a sound as she found the secret and knew the tale without needing to hear it.

Mrs. Haypotten, seeing the girl's stricken face, misunderstood. "Come, now, we've had enough of these dark stories," she announced. "Enough of peddlers and devils and their shenanigans. Hasn't anyone got a cheery tale?" She took what passed for the center of the room and looked around it, then clapped her hands together. "Well, then I'll go next." She leaned between Reever's and Amalgam's chairs and over the card castle to ruffle Maisie's hair. "You'll like this one, young lady. Nothing terrible in it at all."

FIVE

THE QUEEN OF FOG

The Collector's Tale

THERE WAS ONCE A TOWN—no, a kingdom, by the sea. And it was just full of all the things that children like: unicorns, fairies, lollipops, and . . . well, I'm sure I don't see any reason for making that face, Phin. It was just full of lovely things, this town—kingdom—was. And in it was a gir—no, a *queen*. Let's just call her . . . what shall we call her, love? Let's call her Queen Maisie. Sounds just right, I think.

Queen Maisie lived with her auntie, Lady Dorcas, which is a lovely name too, being also my sister's name, as it happens. (Not the "Lady" bit, of course, just the "Dorcas.") Anyhow, one day Lady Dorcas sent Maisie—Queen Maisie, that was—out to the seashore to collect up some pretty shells—well, of course, Phin, yes, I suppose it was somewhat irregular, the lady telling the queen what to do. Yes, of course there was a reason. I'm just getting to it, if you'll let me tell the story.

Lady Dorcas, as I was saying, *gently suggested* one day that Queen Maisie go out of doors and collect up some pretty shells, which, the kingdom being right there on the coast, it was full of, and beautiful shells they were, too, conch and whelk and horseshoe crab and all of them bright as mother-of-pearl in the right light — Yes, even the horseshoe crab, Phin — which of course there always was, since in that kingdom there was only sunshine and never ra — Phineas Amalgam, if you don't stop interrup — yes, I suppose it *would* make things difficult for the farmers, but aren't you always saying stories can't tell every single detail or they'd go on forever and lose the plot? So what do you want to hear, how agriculture worked in that place, why the lady sent the queen out, or all the lovely things that happened when the queen went to the beach?

Well, I don't personally see them as plot holes, you monstrous old know-it-all, I see them as *editorial choices,* which I've often heard you speak of. So let's move on, shall we? Or are you telling this story and not I?

Now, where had I got in the tale? On the beach, I think. Queen Maisie rode her pet unico — well, that look on our miss Maisie's face reminds me that perhaps the queen didn't have a pet unicorn after all. Instead she had a . . . a . . . well, all right, Miss Maisie, I suppose we'll go with that. She had a three-headed donkey, and its name was Fred-Morty-Tucker, same as my brothers, who, come to think of it, are not unlike a three-headed jackass themselves.

So Queen Maisie and Fred-Morty-Tucker went out to the

beach below the castle, and the queen had a nice little basket with her in just exactly the queen's favorite color, which was what, Miss Maisie? What was the queen's favorite color, Miss Maisie? Miss . . . well, anyway, let's say it was a pretty orangey color like those daisies on your shawl. Or are they dahlias? Oh, *chrysanthemums.* Of course, exactly what I meant. But just that color. And the queen hopped off Fred-Morty-Tucker and took off her shoes in the sunshine and walked across the sand, which was not at all hot on her toes — Now you listen to me, Phin, of *course* you can have a sunny day and not also have toe-scorching sand. And anyhow, that's not the point. What is — THE QUEEN TOOK HER BASKET AND COLLECTED SOME SHELLS, YOU OBNOXIOUS OLD FOOL. THAT IS THE POINT. And then she collected Fred-Morty-Tucker, who had wandered off to eat some tasty nettles, and they rode home. And it had been a lovely day at the beach for all.

The — WILL YOU STOP INTERR — oh, excuse me, miss, just say that again? Er . . . well, no, no, of course that isn't the end. I was just going to tell about all the different kinds of pretty shells that — but I suppose I can skip that part, if you'd rather hear . . . because yes, of course, you're right, something else must happen. Let me just remember what it was. Not because I don't know what happens next, you understand. I'm accustomed to doing the shells first, you see. Trips me up a bit, telling it out of order. But as you wish. Let me think.

Just a moment more, it's right on the tip of my brain.

What was that, Sorcha?

Yes, I believe you're right. Thank you for reminding me.

Queen Maisie was just on her way back to where Fred-Morty-Tucker was chomping at the nettles, when she spotted — what did you say, Sorcha? — a washerwoman by the sea. And when Queen Maisie introduced herself, the woman looked up and said, "Of course I recognize our sweet, good, kind queen, Your Majesty! You surprised me, is all. My name is" — what was it, Sorcha? Oh, yes — "Bean-Knee," said the washerwoman.

Bean-Knee, Sorcha? Really? What on earth sort of name is Bean-Knee?

. . . Oh, my. Really? Good Lord, that's dreadful. Never mind. I've just remembered it wasn't Bean-Knee that Queen Maisie met there at the water's edge. It was —

What's that, Miss Maisie?

You'd *like* for the queen to meet Bean-Knee?

But — but my dear, did you hear who Bean-Knee *is?* What it means for the queen to meet her?

You did?

And you'd still like sweet, good, kind Queen Maisie to meet her there by the sea?

Good Lord. Children are macabre little beasts, aren't you?

I had really meant to end the story with a birthday party, you know. Candles and fireworks and cake with the queen's name in icing of that pretty orangey color, or any color you like, if you'd rather a different. Presents and games and so forth, with the queen winning a special prize of . . . of a *new frock!* A new frock with a . . . a *matching hat!* And both of them made of . . . of the feathers of a bird that *grants wishes!* Doesn't that sound nice? That, of course, was why Lady Dorcas had sent her out. Because it was going to be a surprise, you see, which obviously I couldn't have said at the beginning, or it might have spoiled everything, *Phin.* Sometimes the plot holes are there strategic-like, so endings don't get spoiled.

Except now we're going to have to ditch all that, if Queen Maisie really meets Bean-Knee. Are you sure you wouldn't prefer the party, dear? They could bob for apples.

No?

Fine.

Queen Maisie walked up to Bean-Knee, and it was a good thing for her that she'd spotted Bean-Knee before the washerwoman spotted her, because if Bean-Knee spots you first, all sorts of awfulness can happen to you. But as it happened—What sorts of . . . ? Well, really, Miss Maisie! I wonder at you, wanting to hear all these dreadful things. You'll have nightmares.

You have them already?

Oh.

Well, then I suppose I can tell you that if Bean-Knee had spotted the queen first, the queen would have lost the use of her limbs, for one thing, and fallen over helpless into the surf, where perhaps she might have drowned, or a sea creature might have come and carried her off. I'm sure you're about to ask what sorts of sea creatures, and I suppose no friendly mermaids or sea cows will do, so you might as well know that the waters off the coast of the queen's land were simply infested with golevants.

You've never heard of golevants?

That's funny; I thought everyone knew about those. There was a rhyme when I was a girl that people used to say. I think the idea was to keep us off the rocks out at Morrawhick Point, for it was at least once a season that someone lost a child or a best friend on those rocks or the waters below them. Anyhow, it went:

> *The rocks are tall, the rocks are slick;*
> *Don't climb up at Morrawhick,*
> *For in the waters off that shoal,*
> *The golevants will eat you whole.*

Except, of course, it isn't terrible enough, the idea of monsters eating one whole, is it? Because then you might survive in their bellies until someone came along to get you out with a strategic sneeze or bit of vomiting or a good sharp fillet knife, like Red Riding Hood or Pinocchio and Geppetto or Jonah. No, there was a second verse, if I recall, one that explained in detail that by "eat you whole" the writer didn't mean you'd be guzzled down in one gulp, but rather chomped slowly to pieces, the whole of you, beginning with the toes and ending with your screaming head. It didn't say precisely what a golevant looked like, though, now I think of it. I always thought of them as — well. Never mind.

The point is, the queen saw Bean-Knee first, and called out her hello, so then Bean-Knee had to reply, bound as she was by tradition and the laws of politeness, which apply doubly to uncanny things. Let it be a lesson, Miss Maisie. Always be polite, for a hello-how-are-you is as good as a salt ring to many a supernatural creature. Also good manners is good manners, no matter where you go.

Well, Bean-Knee replied politely enough, but she immediately began folding up her washing. And Queen Maisie was such a good, kind girl that when she saw this, she immediately reached down for a piece of cloth to help the washerwoman finish her work. And from that moment on, Bean-Knee couldn't leave until such time as the queen handed that piece of laundry back. You see? Politeness and manners pays, because if Bean-Knee had run off, Queen Maisie might never have learned a secret that would change her life.

She was folding that one bit of cloth when Queen Maisie realized it was just exactly the double of her favorite nightgown, only stained all over in rust-colored patches, and raggedy holes all over, too. "I say," said she, "this looks just like one of mine. How funny. How did it get ruined so?"

Bean-Knee sighed. Because, you see, since Queen Maisie had spotted her first and since she held a piece of the washerwoman's cloth, Bean-Knee was bound to answer truthfully. And so she said, reluctantly but honestly, "It *is* yours, Your Majesty, and it came that way because that is how yours will look in the morning, after Lady Dorcas has had you killed and taken your crown."

Oh, dear. That took a rather morbid turn. But I warned you, didn't I? Sorcha said Bean-Knee washes the shrouds of the dead, and I offered you a birthday party instead. But here we are: golevants in the water and murder in the castle.

Queen Maisie took this very much in stride. "I suppose that's why she sent me out for shells, isn't it?" she asked.

"No," the washerwoman answered. "She sent you out for shells because she is going to throw you the best-ever birthday party, with cake and presents and games and apple-bobbing and fireworks, and she's busy setting it up. Just the very best party you could have wished for. Then she'll kill you after, when you're sleeping off all the sugar you've eaten."

Queen Maisie hugged the bloody nightgown to her chest. "Is there nothing I can do?"

The washerwoman pointed to the nightgown. "If you had not caught me before I finished washing that, there would be nothing. But you have, and so you may be able to stop it."

"How?" the queen asked.

Bean-Knee shook her head. "I am obliged to answer only three questions, and that question makes four. But you're a kind girl, and I appreciate that you tried to help me with the folding." She turned and rummaged in a work basket full of bottles that sat beside her on the beach and took one out.

Now, here I am going to tell you exactly what Bean-Knee said when she gave this bottle to Queen Maisie. I don't say that I agree with it, but it's what the washerwoman said, and I will relay it faithfully, because the alternative is lollipops, and you've rejected those.

I suppose really you're a bit too old to be satisfied with lollipops. I apologize.

The washerwoman said, "You're a good, kind, sweet girl.

And goodness and kindness will take you a long way on the right sort of day, and if I could make one wish for you, Your Majesty, and for all of your friends, it would be that you never meet anyone undeserving of your noble heart. But the truth is, there are people out there who will throw you a birthday party in the afternoon and kill you in the evening, and that's a sad fact of this terrible world. You cannot save yourself unless you can become a different sort of person when you need to."

"Become a different sort of person?" Queen Maisie repeated, and she was fearful. "Will I turn back afterward?"

The washerwoman smiled sadly. "That's your fifth question, and I'm not obligated to answer it. But surely you understand that whether you succeed or fail, you will never again be a girl who no one has tried to kill."

For a moment, Queen Maisie cried, and I think we can forgive her for that.

The washerwoman put a hand on her shoulder. "But I suspect," she said quite gently, "if you succeed — if you survive — you will discover something new about yourself that you will be glad to know. You will find that you are brave. And not because you had to *become* brave, but because you were brave all along. So there is that, if it is a consolation." And here she put the bottle from her basket into Queen Maisie's hand.

Queen Maisie examined the bottle. Inside was something like a swirling mist, gray-blue and shifting. Maisie began to ask what was in it, but of course that would have been her sixth question, and she didn't want to push her luck. Fortunately there was a label pasted to the glass, and the one word written on it was *FOG*.

Now, of course you can be sure that questions seven, eight, and nine were also on the tip of the queen's tongue as she looked at the washerwoman's bottle. But Bean-Knee was not obliged to answer any more, so the queen didn't ask.

"By your leave, Your Majesty," Bean-Knee said, because one doesn't take one's leave from royalty without you get their say-so, and also because, since Queen Maisie was still holding that ruined nightgown, the washerwoman couldn't just go anyhow, not without being granted permission.

"Yes, of course," Queen Maisie said, and she held out the nightgown.

"Oh, you mustn't give that back to me," Bean-Knee told her. "If you give it back, I must wash it, and then all hope is lost. Not to mention," she said with a wink, "who's to say it won't come in useful?"

So the queen and the washerwoman parted ways. Queen Maisie put the bottle of fog and the nightgown into the bottom of her sunset-colored basket, and then she piled shells on top of it. Then she went back to the nettle patch where Fred-Morty-Tucker was still munching.

"That was odd, no?" asked Fred.

"Could've knocked me over with a nettle," said Morty.

"What's our plan?" asked Tucker, who was the pragmatic one.

"I'm not sure," said Queen Maisie as she mounted up. "But anyhow, let's go get this stupid party over with."

And it was no easy feat, pretending to care about the cake and games and apples and the basket-colored frock. It had even occurred to Queen Maisie that the dress might be poisoned—such things happened, after all, out there in the world—but then she remembered the state of the nightgown she'd gotten from Bean-Knee, which certainly looked more like the aftermath of a stabbing, and anyhow, if the plan was for the new dress to kill her, she'd never have been wearing the nightgown to die in. So when Lady Dorcas suggested she go and try it on, Queen Maisie agreed. She had been told about the wishing-bird feather-trimmings, so as she put on the frock and hat, she tried desperately to wish the whole situation different—but of course nothing happened. You can't pluck a magic bird for a dress and still expect it to grant wishes for you. So Maisie sat in that dress out on the balcony with her dearest friends as the sun went down and fireworks exploded over the sea, which I don't need to tell you drove the golevants positively out of their minds, so that the fireworks reflected off of waters as choppy as Queen Maisie's heart and mind. She still had not figured out what to do with the bottle of fog, and it was nearly bedtime.

Then, at last, the fireworks were done, and the lights went out over the choppy, monster-infested sea. Queen Maisie hugged each of her friends and kissed them goodbye. And then she thanked each of the retainers and servants and cooks and washers of dishes, all of whom had come out to see the fireworks and celebrate their queen. She thanked each one by name, and she gave them each one of the shells she had gathered that day.

Yes, Phin, she collected that many shells. They were small.

No, Phin, the fog and the nightgown weren't still in the basket. May I proceed?

"Bedtime, Your Majesty, wouldn't you say?" asked Lady Dorcas, her voice sugary as a boiled sweet, with the same hardness under its gloss.

"Yes, Aunt," said Queen Maisie, matching Lady Dorcas's honey tone. And she hugged her auntie and kissed her cheek, and no one who saw the lady and the queen in that moment would have guessed that one was about to try to murder the other and that the intended victim knew it perfectly well.

The queen went up to her bedroom and closed herself in. She had finally come up with a plan, and she wasted no time in setting it up. She took one of her unspoiled nightgowns, stuffed it full of bedclothes, and thumped the lot into the shape of a girl. Then she tucked it into her big four-poster bed, pulling her quilt right up to its chin. The hat made of wishing-bird feathers stood in for her own head, and partly covered by a pillow, it looked right convincing, especially after Queen Maisie had closed the bed-curtains and made it dark inside. Then she took the ruined nightgown with the stains and tears from where she had hidden it behind a potted plant, and put it on. It made her shudder a bit to do it, but a girl can't let shudders get in the way of saving her own life, now, can she?

Next, the queen doused all the lights in the room and opened up the doors to her balcony to let in the moonlight. Then, still dressed in her tattered nightgown with the bottle of fog clutched in her hands, she crept behind a tapestry by her bedroom door to let her eyes adjust to the dark and wait for what would happen next.

The palace clocks chimed ten, then half-past, then eleven, then half-past that. And then came a new sound, but a familiar one: Queen Maisie's door opening slowly. Then footsteps, also familiar, and just one set of them. Lady Dorcas had come to do the job herself.

Queen Maisie waited until her aunt had crossed the room; then she slipped out from behind the tapestry just in time to see Lady Dorcas lean through the curtains. *Thump, thump, thump, thump, thump!* Five thumps, to match the five tears in the ruined nightgown she wore. Just as Queen Maisie had guessed, her aunt had not looked too closely at the shape of the girl under the bed-clothes. But she might check to be sure her knife had done its work before leaving, and that would spoil the effect. There was no time to hesitate.

Queen Maisie uncorked the bottle of fog and poured some out at her feet, hiding the bottle in her nightgown pocket. (Another lesson, Miss Maisie: A girl always ought to have pockets in everything, even nightgowns.) And then, with the fog swirling about her like all the mystery of the underworld, Queen Maisie stepped forward in her bloodstained nightgown and spoke. "Why have you killed me, Aunt?" she demanded.

Well. You may imagine for yourself how shocked Lady Dorcas was. She jumped back away from what she had taken to be the girl's body in her bed and dropped the long, thin knife she'd been holding. At first she thought she'd made some sort of mistake, but then, of course, she saw the rips and the stains: five, to match the five blows she'd just delivered. Not to mention there was that fog pooling about Queen Maisie's ankles. A right ghost she looked.

And then the ghostly queen stepped forward again. "Five times you stabbed me, Aunt," she said.

And Lady Dorcas backed away, of course. "I . . . I didn't!" she protested, the wicked liar.

Queen Maisie took another step toward her, and the fog followed. "It was not hard to lie to the child-queen of this land when she was alive and there was nothing but sunshine," she said in a singy sort of voice. "But now I am the Queen of Fog, and you will not lie to me again."

And she took another step. And Dorcas backed away faster this time, four steps that carried her right to the door to the balcony. "Your Majesty," Lady Dorcas protested desperately, "forgive me."

"Five blows, and you dare to ask my forgiveness?" Queen Maisie took another step. "The Queen of Fog has not given you leave to speak. But I will give you a choice, since for many years I thought you loved me."

"What kind of choice?" Lady Dorcas barely got the words out, her teeth were chattering so hard.

"The fog, or the sea," said Queen Maisie.

"I don't understand," Lady Dorcas managed.

"Come with me into the fog"—and here the queen brought the fog swirling up between them with a flick of her wrist—"or take your chances in the sea." And she pointed at the balcony behind her aunt. "The fog or the sea, Aunt. Which will it be?" And then, because, of course, only one of those choices would really do, Queen Maisie flicked her wrist again and sent the fog lunging obediently after her aunt.

And that was all it took. Lady Dorcas screamed, turned, and leaped over the balcony rail.

Now, had she jumped from any other balcony in the castle, she would've been dashed to death on the rocks. But Queen Maisie's window was the only one that fell straightaway down into blue sea. Or at least, it might have been blue sea on any other night, when an hour of explosions in the sky had not driven the golevants into a frenzy that, hours later, still had not calmed.

There was a splash, and then there were screams. Queen Maisie dropped into a chair by the window. She didn't look. A girl should never hesitate about saving her own life, but that doesn't mean she has to watch a hundred ravenous sea creatures tearing her assassin of an aunt to shreds if she doesn't feel up to it. And Queen Maisie was exhausted. Before the screams died down, she was asleep, and the fog tucked itself right around her like a blanket, around that girl in her stained and tattered night-gown, and it wasn't cold and clammy at all, but soft and woolly, like you'd imagine a cloud might be if you could pluck it down from the sky and use it for a pillow.

They found her there in the morning, and of course at first, seeing the nightgown and the knife tossed where Lady Dorcas had dropped it, and that fog still swirling about like mystery, the queen's lady's maid thought her mistress had been murdered in her chair. But then Queen Maisie opened her eyes and stretched, and it was as if she'd come back from the dead right there before her maid's eyes.

And I can tell you that the fog stayed and followed her like a train from that day forward. She was in many ways the same kind, sweet, good queen she had always been, but she would never again be a girl no one had tried to kill. Still, she knew she was strong, and she knew she was brave, and she knew she was clever, and on days when the memory of that night came back, she reminded herself of all the things she was, until she was not afraid anymore.

From that day on, her people, when they weren't calling her a miracle, called her by the name she had given herself on that fateful night: they called her the Queen of Fog.

There. Not the story I meant to tell, but perhaps . . .

Did you?

Did you really?

Well, then I'm very pleased to have told it, even if it wasn't what I'd planned.

Shall I get you another cup of chocolate, miss?

MAISIE ACCEPTED her refilled cup of chocolate and turned, satisfied, back to the castle of cards. Tesserian handed her the queen of caskets and the queen of knots.

In the corner rocking chair, where she had been sitting nearly motionless, her body silently enfolded in her mass of wraps, Madame Grisaille stirred. The shifting satin might as well have been a soft voice whispering *Shhh*. The room fell utterly silent.

"That was a good tale," Madame said, her voice thrumming. "I think, although it was not the story you wanted to tell, Mrs. Haypotten, you did well. As did you," she said, smiling and taking one of her thin dark hands from the white fur muff to gesture briefly at Sorcha. "And now I will try to do as well." She looked thoughtfully at the folklorist in his chair before the fire. "I do not think you have heard this one, Mr. Amalgam; however, I suspect the masters Colophon might know it." Her dark eyes turned toward the twins, lighting first on Reever, to Amalgam's left, and then on Negret, by the display cabinet. "Please correct me if I get anything wrong. My memory occasionally suffers a touch of rust."

Reever grinned and Negret guffawed, and as she was appreciating the way the laugh lit up Negret Colophon's face under his floppy hair, Sorcha blinked in surprise, noticing the glint of what looked like a second row of teeth behind the first.

Don't be ridiculous, she thought. *Nobody has two sets of teeth.*

"Just a moment," Captain Frost said, turning his glass. He hurried from the room, the windows rattled, and then his sharp, heavy footfalls returned. He settled himself into a chair between the sideboard and one of the river-facing windows. "Please continue, madam."

"Very well."

SIX

THE ROAMER IN THE NETTLES

The Old Lady's Tale

NETTLES GROW TALLER over the place where a body is buried. Or so I am told. Despite what people believe about very old folk, I am an expert in neither death nor gardening.

There was once a boy. I like the name from your story, Phin, so let us call this boy Pantin, too. Perhaps it's even the same child. Who can say?

Pantin lived in a house of red stone, beside a garden ringed by crumbling stone walls and full of nettles that grew taller than his own head. In fact, though it had been decades since the last oldster who knew the truth had passed, the garden beside Pantin's house was no garden at all. It was a very old, very secret, very private cemetery; a cemetery that had been built for one grave alone. That grave had never had a marker of any kind, other than the garden that was planted above it and the nettles that quickly overcame everything.

There are many such secret graves in Nagspeake. This one belonged to a hero. Most of them do.

This man under the soil — or what was left of him — had not only been a hero; he had been what is sometimes called a *roamer.* It is difficult to convey the many, many things that word means, particularly since roamers come in all sorts. Most of them spend at least part of their lives in wandering, but not all; some were once human, but over long years and a life of uncanny experiences, they became something subtly different; others had never been human for even a moment. Some do great things with their time, which can be very long indeed. Others walk and watch. To an outside observer, some would seem to be heroes, like the man under the nettles, and others villains. But all of them have at least a whiff of the otherworldly about them.

This particular man, our roamer-hero, had been buried clutching a box. I don't know what was in it. I never opened it. But the box itself was a thing of artistry, the kind of box meant to hold miracles, or magic, or perhaps even a single miraculous, magical memory. It's important to know, at the outset, that the box was there, in the dirt and the decay beneath the nettles. But Pantin didn't know it; he hadn't so much as an inkling that the grave itself was there, much less that in the grave — or what was left of it — the bones of a hero held a maybe-miraculous box.

The thief didn't know it either — not at first. But that's getting a bit ahead of the story.

Another thing they say — those mysterious voices that say things that get retold in tales like this — they say that iron behaves badly in a graveyard. And of course, when they say this, they mean not just any iron, but the old, wild kind, the sort that can change its shape when you're not looking. The kind that, sometimes, at sunset, doesn't care whether you're looking or not. In those moments, if you are looking, you can see the old iron dance in the last warmth of the day. But of course, you've all seen that before. Except possibly Mr. Tesserian — you're not from Nagspeake, are you?

No, I thought not. Anyhow.

They say that old iron behaves badly in the gardens of the dead. I think the truth is more complicated. Still, it is true, at least, that Nagspeake does not build graveyards where old iron is to be found in abundance. However, people looking to hide graves do not always have options for where to put them. The hero's grave wasn't in a place that spilled over with old iron, like the Quayside Harbors, or Shantytown, but the iron was there, for eyes that knew how to look for it. Pantin's red house stood at the edge of a wood, and the wood was peppered throughout with lampposts and lanterns in places where there was not so much as a trail needing light. Sometimes, in the evenings, the lamps and lanterns would open up and let their lights out to roam like feral creatures. Some nights, the woods were thick with wandering will-o'-the-wisps.

Pantin and his neighbors called them bonelights. I do not think they ever learned where they came from. But you, Maisie — I would like you to know that, should you ever find yourself lost in the woods, and should you encounter one of those lights, you may say to it, "You once showed a lost boy back to the road. Would you please help me find my way?" For the lights did once help Pantin when he was very lost in the woods, though that is a different tale.

Yes, there was a good deal of iron in the woods. Even the red house was not entirely empty of it. The house was tall and narrow, of a sort that would've looked much more at home in a town than at the edge of a wood. Perhaps there had been a bit of town there once. Or perhaps, Pantin sometimes thought, the town was coming, and his house had simply gotten there first. It had old iron in its walls and its foundations, and there was an iron rain gutter that ran all the way around the roof, with a spout at the corner nearest Pantin's own window. That corner also had an iron gargoyle that changed its shape every few nights. Ever since he had been very, very small—much smaller than you, Maisie —Pantin had thought of it as his particular friend and confidant.

Which is another thing you might do well to remember, Maisie. Old iron listens when you speak to it. Old iron hears.

Three families lived in the house. On the first floor was the old man who played a guitar and lived with a dog named Joy; on the second, a mother and her twin daughters, Poppy and Tulip; and on the top floor, Pantin and his parents. And, of course, beside the house was that very old, very crumbly wall with its garden full of very tall nettles.

One day, a thief came.

He came first, as they so often do, in the guise of—oh, dear, I'm terribly sorry, Mr. Masseter, but I'm bound to say that he came to the door in the guise of a peddler. One rather like that Drogam Nerve in your story, Master Colophon, bearing books full of things that could be bought unseen and delivered later. I do seem to remember that this particular man had catalogs from a company called Morvengarde, though perhaps I'm mistaken. I imagine those names — *Morvengarde* and *Drogam Nerve* — look much the same on paper, and my eyes have never been sharp.

I am trying to recall the name the thief used. It reminded me of mathematics, somehow. Trigonometry? No. *Trigemine.* That was it. Shocking blue eyes, he had. I recall that well. But now I'm losing the thread.

The thief came to the front door and went up the stairs, knocking on the door to each flat. And at each door, when it was opened, he showed his books full of things to wish for. Then he explained that his job was not simply to sell, but also to buy.

"To buy what?" the man with the dog asked.

"Oh, all sorts of things," the thief said. Trigemine's master would pay good money for objects of value, and many things were more valuable than people realized.

"How valuable?" asked the mother of the girls named after flowers. Her job did not pay well, I think, and she often came up a bit short of money.

"Well, it depends on the object," the thief replied, taking a single round brass jeweler's loupe from his waistcoat pocket. How would it be if he had a look about, to find an example?

"All right," Pantin said curiously. He was alone in his family's flat, and he was certainly old enough to know one oughtn't open the door to strangers, and I expect his parents gave him a good talking-to afterward. But he opened the door for the thief called Trigemine, and stood aside. The visitor put the glass into one eye and stepped in, already looking around, just as he had in the two flats below Pantin's. And just as he had done in each of his previous stops, he paid particular attention to *boxes*.

In Pantin's apartment, there weren't many. In the parlor, there was a group of three little trinket boxes Pantin's mother had collected as a girl; in the kitchen, there was a box that held the sugar and a box that held comfits and a box that held patent pills. Trigemine barged right into the boy's parents' room without so much as a by-your-leave and spent a moment examining a music box that had belonged to Pantin's grandmother. In Pantin's own room, there was a small cigar box that had been repurposed to hold treasures. The thief gave that the longest look of all. But at last he set it back on the bedside table and sighed.

"Nothing?" Pantin asked. "Nothing we have is worth anything?"

The thief looked down at him thoughtfully. "You have many valuable things here," he said at last, "but not the thing I was hoping to find."

"What were you hoping to find?" Pantin asked.

The thief hesitated. People often make the mistake of telling children too much, with the idea that they won't understand what they're being told—not the true meaning or value of it. This man had made that mistake before and paid dearly for the error. On the other hand, he also knew well that children often know more than they seem to. So he weighed the risks carefully, and then he answered, "I am looking for a coffret. It's a very special sort of box, or casket."

"Casket?" Pantin repeated. "You mean, like a *coffin?*"

The thief laughed. "A coffin is a type of casket," he said, "but not all caskets are coffins. In any case, the sort I'm looking for isn't here."

And then he chanced to peer out Pantin's window, which looked out on the garden grave of the dead hero.

This man was no more an expert in death and gardening than I am, but he, too, was a roamer. He had roamed long and far in both space and time, and he knew more lore than can be accumulated in the span of a single life. In a matter of seconds, he had taken in the crumbling old wall, the nettles that had filled the space inside the perimeter, and the terrible heights to which the prickly plants had grown. And, with Pantin's question about caskets and coffins fresh in his mind, he understood immediately what he was looking for, and what he was looking *at.*

Heroes, you see, are rarely buried without tribute of some kind, and treasure — even if it is merely a trove of memories — is rarely put into the ground without a container to hold it.

The thief doffed his hat, thanked Pantin for his time, and left as quickly as he could, the heels of his well-shined boots drumming neatly on the stairs as he left the red house and went in search of digging and prying tools.

He came back to the house once more before nightfall, bringing three bottles of sherbet with him — not the shaved-ice sort, but the drink made with fruit-and-flower arrack—and he delivered a bottle to each home as a thank-you for letting him have a look around, beginning with the one on the top floor. Pantin, however, was not allowed to have any, even after supper, as punishment for having let a stranger into the flat. This is how he happened to be wide awake, talking to his friend the old iron gargoyle and not drugged asleep like everyone else was, when Trigemine returned with his digging tools in the dead of night and began to exhume the hero's grave that no one had known was there.

Pantin had trouble sleeping in those days. He had been having nightmares about the time a month or so before when he had fallen through a sinkhole into an old abandoned tunnel that had been built for a pneumatic railway. And Maisie, I will tell you that if you ever find yourself suddenly falling into a tunnel anyplace belowground in Nagspeake, the thing to do is in two parts. Firstly, feel the rails to see if a train is coming. Secondly—do this part quickly if you do feel a vibration—say quite loudly, "You once showed a lost boy back to the surface. Would you please help me find my way?" For the iron in the below did once help Pantin when he was very lost in the tunnels, though that, too, is a different tale. Never forget, Maisie: Old iron hears. Old iron pays attention.

Anyhow, Pantin was awake. He sat with his back against the wall below his bedroom window, which he had opened in order to let in his gargoyle friend. Pantin called the gargoyle Troublewit after a sort of bendy folded paper toy for children and magicians, because a troublewit can take any number of forms, and the iron creature reconfigured its own shape so often. That night, Pantin was whispering to Troublewit about the injustice of not being allowed to drink any sherbet. The gargoyle didn't reply, but it did occasionally move its mouth and flex its iron-taloned feet in sympathy. Suddenly, there was a curse from down below in the garden and a quick flash of light. The thief had begun the process of wading into the nettle sea.

Pantin peered over the windowsill. "That's Mr. Trigonometry," he whispered, for he couldn't remember the thief's name any better than I could.

He and the gargoyle Troublewit watched as the thief pulled on a pair of gloves, fought his way to the place where the nettles were tallest, took a shovel from his wrapped bundle of tools and dropped the rest, and began to dig by lantern light. "What's he doing down there?" Pantin asked.

The gargoyle tried to convey its answer simply by means of nodding and talon-wiggling. When this didn't work, it hunkered down and reconfigured itself into something less solid, something with empty places within that could resonate, and paper-thin places that could vibrate or collapse and swell like a bellows to pump air. It had done this before, but rarely, for it was elaborate, hard, and detailed work every time. "He is digging up the hero," Troublewit said at last, his voice gravelly as the scraping of the shovel below, and masked perfectly by it too.

Pantin took his friend's new voice in stride. "What hero?"

Troublewit shrugged. "I don't know them all. There are

scores of them; I can't keep track. But this may be one of the great ones. He has been there many, many years. Longer than you. Longer than the house. There is the hero, and he is in a box, and he holds another box in his hands. Or that's what there was when they put him in the ground. Things change over time. You know."

"I know," Pantin agreed. Then he remembered the conversation he'd had with the thief earlier in the day. "He said he was looking for a coffret — a box or casket of some kind. He couldn't have thought he'd find the hero's coffin in one of our flats, so it must be the box the hero is holding that the peddler wants."

Troublewit looked at him. "Shall I go get it? Before the peddler finds it?"

"Can you?"

Troublewit shrugged again. "Of course. I am everywhere in Nagspeake. I can go everywhere iron is, or goes, or can get. I can take the coffret and put it out of the thief's reach."

"All right, then."

The gargoyle looked at the iron rainspout. As the man in the garden toiled with his shovel, the metal spout stretched, drawing itself out into a long, thin iron vine, and slithered silently down the corner of the house to plunge into the earth below, leaving a length of itself twisted like a climbing creeper against the corner where the gargoyle crouched, unmoving.

After a moment, Troublewit spoke up again. "I see no coffin any longer, only the bones of the hero held below where the earth has tumbled them. But there is also the small box."

But Pantin was watching the digging peddler, who swore now and again as the nettles tore at his sleeves. Perhaps, if this was the same child as in Mr. Amalgam's tale, the boy was realizing he had met this man before, and wondering if anyone who would go to so much trouble to have the things he sought as to search for them in cursed houses and nettle-choked grave gardens would give up the hunt for this coffret simply because he didn't find it in the first place he looked.

Troublewit glanced sideways at its friend. "I have taken the box deep underground. Don't worry. I'll bring it up the rainspout when the thief is gone."

"It's not that I'm worried about," Pantin whispered. He ducked down behind his windowsill. "I think it's possible he knows the box is somewhere nearby. If he doesn't find it there, he may come back here again to look for it. Unless . . ." But the boy shook his head.

"Unless what?" the gargoyle asked. "Unless he can be convinced not to?"

Pantin nodded. "But I don't know how we could do that." Could the thief be scared away? Would that be enough? Doubtful. It would be better if they could somehow convince him the box he sought had never been here.

Surely the peddler with the mathematical-sounding name would never believe a boy who wasn't even sure what the man was after. Yes, Pantin knew, because the thief had told him, that the thief was after a box. But why? What was it about this box?

Abruptly Pantin remembered that his parents were sleeping

one room away. They would know what to do. He left Troublewit crouched in the window and darted into their bedroom. There, of course, he found them sleeping peacefully, but he could not wake them. Terrified, he headed for the door of his flat, meaning to wake the mother with the twins. But then he saw the empty bottle that had held the sherbet, and he remembered that, when the peddler had delivered his gift to Pantin's parents, he had had two bottles more meant for the neighbors. Pantin realized that he might well be the only person awake in the entire house.

It was up to him to get rid of the peddler-thief for good. But how? How could one boy alone manage that?

But then, crossing the flat to return to his room, he remembered that he wasn't alone. He had Troublewit. And the two of them had someone else, too. They had the original owner of the box the thief was after. They had the hero.

Or his bones, at least.

"I have an idea," Pantin whispered to the gargoyle. "It involves the hero."

Troublewit's iron gargoyle's mouth stretched into an O of understanding. "Humans are afraid of bones, aren't they?"

"Sometimes," Pantin said. "But I don't think this man will be. The hero will have to do more than just scare him. The hero will have to speak."

"I can manage that." The gargoyle nodded. "I think I know how the bones go together, but it won't be less frightening if they aren't exactly right, will it?"

"No, it'll be *worse*," Pantin replied in ghastly delight.

"As I thought." Troublewit's gargoyle face grinned back. "The thief's digging will go faster if the hero also digs."

Pantin shivered and leaned his forearms on the windowsill. He couldn't quite see how it began, but after another couple of swings with the shovel, the thief paused. He tilted his head. He bent low, his lantern casting strange shadows from among the nettles. Then he straightened abruptly and staggered backwards, tripping over barbed weeds and his own feet to land on his backside and his palms. He screamed in pain, or perhaps in fear, or both. He felt around among the nettles for his shovel, still shouting obscenities, as he stared with horror at the hole he'd been digging.

Painted garishly by the light of the lantern and the shadows of the snarled weeds, the mortal remains of the hero climbed out of the hole and faced the thief.

There wasn't much left, just old, old bone and rags, which the iron had restored to a mostly human shape, wired together in much the same way that scientists do with the skeletons that are displayed in museums. But the iron had done more than just piece the bones together; it had given the long-dead hero a bellows and paper-thin vibrating places and hollow resonating places inside the remnants of his ribs and skull, connected by delicate throat pipes.

The hero of iron and bone made a sound of rasping metal, like a sigh and a cough and a grinding all forged into one. Then, still cast in black nettle-shadow and shards of lantern light, it spoke. "Why have you desecrated my grave?"

It was enough to make Pantin shudder. But if the thief quailed, the boy couldn't see it. Just as he'd feared, now that he was past the initial shock, Trigemine held his ground. "I am here for the coffret that was buried with you, my lord."

"It is long gone, and I have promised curses for any that disturb so much as the weeds that cover my resting place." The hero raised a bone-and-metal hand and pointed a finger at the thief. "Go."

"I will go." But the thief tilted his head and looked at the hero thoughtfully. "How did it come to be gone, then, my lord? Who disturbed your rest before I came? And how long ago? Perhaps I can avenge the theft for you."

Pantin and Troublewit looked at each other. "Oh, dear," Troublewit said softly. "I should have had the hero say that it was never here at all. How shall I have him reply now?"

Pantin thought fast, but before either of them could come up with an answer, the bones of the hero below gave a strange shake. As the boy and the gargoyle stared down into the grave garden, the creature Troublewit had constructed began to move. Not merely move: it began to *change*. It was a bit like watching someone who had been sitting or standing for too long suddenly straighten up and shift around to work out the kinks — if, in working out the kinks, that person also had to actually put some of its body parts back in the right places. Joints that the iron had connected at slightly wrong angles twitched themselves true. A scapula that had been installed backwards stretched up and out like a wing, reversed itself, and folded back into place. The hero's left hand plucked one finger from its right, the iron filaments that had been holding it in place instantly letting go as the hero tugged it. Then, as he held it over an empty spot on his left hand, the filaments there reached out and wired the finger securely in.

"Are you doing that?" Pantin asked, confused.

"I am . . . not," Troublewit whispered. "I don't understand this at all."

Then, his bones in the right places now and standing taller than before, the hero began again to talk.

"I will speak for myself now." The voice was subtly different this time. The reorganized body did not look up at the window, but both boy and gargoyle were immediately certain it was aware of their presence and that the statement was meant for the two of them.

Trigemine, meanwhile, simply inclined his head. "As you say, my lord."

"And you will drop that spade." The hero nodded its skull at the shovel the peddler-thief grasped. "You hold it like a weapon."

The thief hesitated only a second, then plunged the shovel's tip into the weedy earth so that it stood vertically, handle within reach. "As you command, my lord."

"Your politeness is a farce," the hero said. "You are a thief. A robber of graves. But you are too late. The iron has taken my coffret. It has taken it down, deep into the earth, below the tunnels under the city, below the land that lies beneath the tunnels. It is out of your reach."

"Is there no way to retrieve it? I would happily do whatever's required to bring it back to you, my lord. I have no interest in what it holds. I would ask only the box itself in payment."

"There is no way at all," the hero said, "unless you can convince the iron to return it. I rather think, however, that the iron would return the box to me anyhow if I were to ask it. But I do not propose to do that."

Trigemine looked at the iron-and-bone revenant for a moment. Then he kicked a foot out savagely at the shovel, and he swore.

"So much for your sham politeness," the hero said in a tone of dark amusement as the shovel flew across the tiny cemetery and struck against the old wall. "Go now, before you do any more damage to my garden." He stretched out his arms, flexed his composite fingers. "For I believe I could do a good deal of damage with this body if I chose to."

The thief swore again, collected his tools and his shovel, and fought his way through the nettles and out into the night. He did not take his lantern, because the hero stood in the way.

When the thief had gone, the hero turned up to the window. "Come down, please."

Pantin and Troublewit looked at each other. "All right," the gargoyle said, and Troublewit scrambled easily down the stone of the wall. Pantin leaned out the window and saw the metal of the rainspout change its shape again, this time into a perfectly serviceable ladder that stretched all the way from the boy's window to the stone wall of the grave garden below it. He followed Troublewit down. As they stood on the wall, the nettles that choked the garden parted, clearing a path from Pantin and his friend to the hero of iron and bone. Heart pounding, the boy and the gargoyle approached.

"M-my lord?" Pantin said experimentally.

At that, the hero actually laughed, and the sound was truly bizarre as it resonated through the ironworks that made up its insides. "Don't be ridiculous, child. No one called me that, even when I had breath, blood, and a proper body." He looked down at the form Troublewit had built of his remains. "I think I understand why you have done this," he said to the gargoyle. "Did you also plan to take the coffret?"

Pantin glanced at Troublewit. "We hadn't thought that far ahead," the boy admitted. "Mainly we wanted to stop the thief from taking it, though I couldn't tell you why—other than that he had clearly come to steal it."

"That is reason enough. Do you know what is in it?" the hero asked, looking from one to the other.

"No," Troublewit said. It was not of iron. I could not have looked inside without opening it.

"The thief wanted only the box," the hero said thoughtfully. "That is interesting."

Pantin nodded, but of course he was thinking, perhaps

as you are, that it was the *least* interesting thing to him at the moment. One of the great heroes of the city, or perhaps his ghost, had taken possession of this strange, partly human body and was now speaking to the boy and the metal gargoyle as if it was all perfectly normal. Pantin couldn't quite bring himself to care right then about why a thief might want a box.

"I would like to borrow this frame," the hero said at last, looking at Troublewit. "The parts of it that aren't mine, that is. Will the iron permit me — that is, would the iron that now holds me together consent to travel with me, for a time?" His voice had a curious note of reverence to it as he spoke to the gargoyle, and for the first time, Pantin thought about the fact that the friend he called Troublewit was more than a mere decoration someone had built into the red stone house. Troublewit was part of something no one in Nagspeake quite understood, something *huge*. His friend Troublewit was a mere projection, in the way that some kinds of mushrooms are merely a small, visible part of a huge network that stretches, unseen, for miles in the soil.

"Yes," Troublewit said at last. "The iron will travel with you for as long as you choose."

Pantin eyed the rags that were the revenant's only garments. "If you will stay a minute more," he said, "I can give you one of my father's old coats."

The hero nodded, and Pantin hurried back up the ladder and through his sleeping flat to the cupboard where his family hung their cold-weather things. He returned with an old tarpaulin coat and a felt hat.

The hero pulled on the coat, and his strange body adjusted again, lengthening and narrowing to approximately the proportions of Pantin's father until the garment fit perfectly.

"Thank you," the hero said, looking at Troublewit and Pantin from under the brim of the hat. "As a token of my thanks, you may keep the coffret and what is inside it." Even as he spoke, a film of iron, thin as paper, spread over the planes of his skull, layering a face of dark metal over the bone.

"Thank you," said Troublewit.

"Thank you," said Pantin.

The hero nodded, and the nettles parted again, this time to give him a path to the overgrown main gate of the grave garden. When he reached it, the vines tangled in the hinges flexed their green fingers to pull the door open ahead of him.

He did not take Trigemine's lantern, but as he walked toward the trees at the edge of the woods, he bent to pick up a branch from the ground. At the timberline, one of the strange, roaming bonelights that Pantin had often caught glimpses of came drifting through the darkness. The hero held up his branch as if it were an unlit torch, and the bonelight landed atop it like a tame parrot.

Thus illuminated, the hero disappeared into the woods, leaving the two friends to ponder what had happened, and what this strange gift they had been given might turn out to be. Pantin, of course, was young and had many wonders left to see; Troublewit was — or was at least part of — something older than the stones of the house, older than the river itself, and it was a wonder simply to discover that there were surprises left in the world for it to encounter.

Did they find the coffret again?

Of course, for there is no place in Nagspeake where the iron cannot go if it cares to.

What was inside it, that beautiful box made to hold something just the size of a miracle or a memory?

As I told you, I never looked inside. Pantin did—but that's the beginning of another story for another time, and this is the end of the story I set out to tell.

Or nearly the end. Perhaps . . . yes, now that I think of it, I suppose it is just possible that this sort of thing—raising the dead, wiring them up like museum specimens, and setting them loose in the city—this sort of thing could be precisely why people say old iron behaves badly in a graveyard.

INTERLUDE

THE ASSEMBLED LISTENERS applauded. Tesserian and Maisie added a balcony to their card castle, made of the king of knots, the knave of bottles, the two of spades, and the ace of caskets, though the gambler had to hunt for the ace for a moment before Maisie herself spotted the corner of the card peeking up from behind the band on his hat.

"I am sorry, Mr. Masseter," Madame said with a nod to the man in the chair to her right. "But you see, in this story, it wasn't so much a peddler as a robber posing as one."

"I do see the distinction," Masseter said, sounding mildly annoyed nonetheless.

Petra looked thoughtfully at him as she slipped her stocking feet out of her shoes and folded them up underneath her on the sofa. "I have been thinking of your question of peddlers, and I have remembered another tale in which the peddler is not the villain." The dragonfly in her hair caught the firelight as she turned and glanced over her shoulder at Sangwin, the print-maker, who had stayed by the window overlooking the river from which he'd chucked his cigar. "It's the one you mentioned, the day you arrived."

"I don't recall." Then Sangwin's face shifted through quick realization into discomfort, and then confusion. He frowned sharply at Petra, the lines on his face blending with the shadows cast by the rain on the window beside him. "But . . ."

"Yes, you do," she said, ignoring the printmaker's disquiet. "You remember. It was Phineas's tale of the uncommon keyway that brought it to mind, but I've been hesitating because I confess I wasn't sure whether I might offend Mr. Masseter by telling it. Then it popped into my thoughts again with Madame's story of the miraculous box. It was a tale you did the illustrations for, I think you said."

"Why would it offend me?" Masseter asked. "You've just said the peddler in this story isn't a villain."

"It isn't that the fellow in question is a peddler," Sangwin said cautiously, still looking at Petra. "It's that he loses an eye. And of course, yes, there *is* a peddler in it, but that's a different character."

A strange shifting passed around the room as each person within it tried with varying degrees of success not to look directly at the russet-colored patch that covered Masseter's left eye. All except Petra, who laughed. "Oh, I had thought they were both peddlers. You must tell it. Clearly I'd get it all wrong."

Sangwin looked dubiously from Petra to Masseter.

"Put your mind to rest, Sangwin." The peddler smiled thinly. "Does the fellow in your tale at least lose his eye in a spectacular fashion?"

Sangwin considered. "It's somewhat the point of the story, the losing of the eye, and yet I don't know if I can answer that question."

"Tell it, then," suggested the still-smiling peddler, "and we shall decide."

The printmaker inclined his head. "Then I will." One last curious flick of his dark eyes at Petra, then he glanced at Maisie, who sat with her knees drawn up to her chest watching the two of them with open curiosity. "Do you know what is a hollow-way, young lady?" he asked.

Maisie shook her head.

"It is a passage through trees," Sangwin said. "But a hollow-way is more than that, too. A hollow-way is a sunken road, a place where the track has been worn down so that it lies below the level of the land around it, and the trees on all sides form something like a canopy overhead. To pass along a hollow-way is much like traveling through a sort of forest tunnel." He glanced out the window at the drowning woods on the far shore of the rising Skidwrack. "They are very old ways, and old ways often lie differently on the landscape, leading to places other than where you think they ought to if you merely look at them on a map. Strange things can happen on roads such as these."

He turned to face the room, leaned his back against the windowsill, and laced his brown fingers together before him. "Of course, I can picture the woodcuts I made for the pictures perfectly well," he murmured, looking up at the blackened exposed beams in the ceiling. "It was forty years ago now at least—one of my first journeyman projects. I made so many versions—with different trees in the drawings, different woods for the printing blocks, then different inks made from more trees still. The *words*, though . . . but of course, it's a poem. Let me just remember the first line, and I ought to be able to recite the rest."

On the floor by the fire, Tesserian handed Maisie a knave with a single visible eye.

SEVEN

THE HOLLOW-WARE MAN

The Carver's Tale

THE SUN doesn't fall on the hollow-way, not even when
branches are bare.

The trees knot and tangle around it;
the bracken and vines curl about it;
the leaves whirl and crackle all through it —
it's always deep twilight in there.
Folk hereabouts shun the hollow-way if another road
    might do as well.
They say that it's more than just dark there,
that uncanny creatures oft walk there,
and good folk who chance it get lost there,
and find themselves halfway to hell.
So it's mostly deserted, this pathway; we avoid it
    whenever we can.
Except every autumn emerges

a figure from out of the birches.
From the mouth of the hollow he lurches:
the traveling hollow-ware man.

The hollow-ware man is a peddler, his wares an
    assortment of tin.
And kettles and teapots he'll sell you
of copper and nickel and brass, too;
buckets and silver-plate cups, too:
all things that are empty within.
Now, the hollow-ware man is a strange one, but his wares,
    they are wondrously good.
He peddles such strikingly sweet things,
gleaming and bright filigreed things,
uncommonly well-made and neat things
that hold more than you think that they should.
And other things, too, he will sell you, whatever you can't
    do without.
The rarest of things you can get here —
uncanny and wondrous things had here —
miraculous things can be bought here
when the hollow-ware man is about.
Unbelievable hollow-ware wonders he crafts with his
    hammer and flame
that he only will sell in the hollow-way,
on his way out of town, in the hollow-way.

But they come at a cost in the hollow-way:
not everyone comes back the same.

One day into town came a stranger, a man with such cold
eyes of blue.
He said, "I've come in search of a box, here,
a particular, finely wrought box here,
a box I can fit to this lock here,"
and he showed us the lock he had, too.
The lock was no everyday gadget, and anyone looking
could see.
So we sent him the way of the hollow-ware man;
we sent him straight after the hollow-ware man.
He'd only just left, had the hollow-ware man —
there was only one place he could be.

So the man vanished into the hollow-way; what happened
next, we never knew.
But he came back that night walking slowly;
he trudged into town, undone wholly;
and when he looked up at us coldly,
his left eye was tin and not blue.
For the hollow-ware man takes strange payments
in exchange for his goods so divine.
He'd asked a high price for the right box;
one cold blue eye for the right box;

and then he'd installed that bizarre lock
and a replacement hollow-ware eye.
The stranger he left us that evening, 'fore the blood even
    dried on his cheek.
Of the box that had cost him so dearly,
that had blinded him halfway (or nearly),
of the lock that it fitted so queerly —
the stranger refused to speak.

‿— INTERLUDE —‿

A MOMENTARY SILENCE FELL. "And so?" Mr. Sangwin asked, his voice uncomfortable and artificially light as he picked up his glass from the windowsill. "Is our peddler here a villain or no?"

Masseter made a thoughtful, humming sound. "What do you think, young lady?" he asked, glancing down at Maisie. "After all, the box was clearly worth an eye to the man who bought it. Whether or not he was pleased to pay that much, he chose to do it. He could have walked back out again when he'd heard the hollow-ware man's price."

Jessamy spoke up from the other side of the fireplace. "Maybe he didn't feel he had that choice." Her voice was quiet but hard. "Just because a fellow *can* charge an eye doesn't necessarily mean he ought to."

"I don't think people should charge eyes," Maisie said decisively, her own eyes locked on Tesserian's cards as he picked out the king of caskets and the knave of lenses.

Mrs. Haypotten tutted. "Honestly, you lot with your grim tales. Who's next? Hasn't anyone got a cheerful story?"

"I'll tell one." Everyone turned to the beautiful man with the scar below his eye who lounged at the opposite end of the sofa from Petra, his outstretched arm still just barely not reaching her shoulder. "It's a love story. And in deference to your wish for more cheerful yarns, Mrs. H., it's even got a happy ending."

"Oh, my." Mrs. Haypotten blushed. "Well. That's very nice of you, dear."

"It ends well," Sullivan said, "but it begins in the dark, and in the cold."

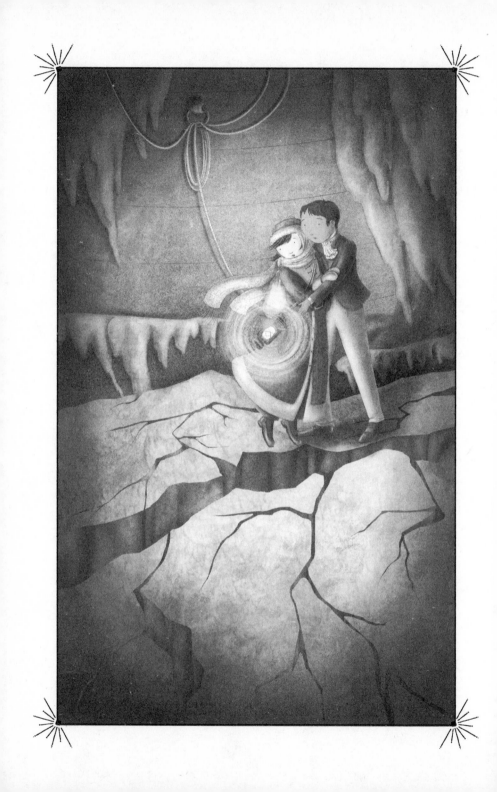

EIGHT

THE COLDWAY

The Scarred Man's Tale

HERE IS A WINTER PLACE, if you like: when the
river Skidwrack freezes, a whole world comes into being in the
city of Nagspeake that wasn't there before, a sort of neither-here-
nor-there-land above the river but below the district called Flotilla.

Flotilla is the island district. Some of it is built on pilings
that were sunk, Venice-style, into the muck at the bottom of the
river long, long ago. Some is built of boats lashed to the landed
bits (such as they are) and to one another. There are bulkheads
that ring the whole, but sunken mechanisms move them when
the district needs moving about. They say that once, in order
to protect a legendary ship and its crew, every single one of the
component vessels cast off and scattered into the Skidwrack,
causing the entire district to vanish in a matter of hours, leaving
nothing but those old oaken posts, left behind like fragments of
an incomplete skeleton.

So there is the river, and there is the district of Flotilla upon it. When the river freezes, there comes the Coldway: a warren of tunnels with the frozen river underfoot, where the curved sides of boats of all sorts form the walls and a ceiling arched like a cathedral, where the bows and gunwales of the vessels nestle up against one another to form the roof. In some places it's high-ceilinged like a cathedral too; in others the tunnels scarcely have height enough for an adult to walk upright in them. Because the makeup of Flotilla changes so often, the Coldway is never the same place twice. And yet, for all that the shape of the route changes and for all that it is temporary, I am reminded of something Mr. Sangwin said about the old ways that traverse the landscape; the Coldway, too, is, at its heart, a route just as great and powerful as any of the other noble old roads that cross the world, and a map of the Coldway shows a realm in which strange things often happen.

And, like any great and old and strange place, there is a great and old and strange tale about it: that the Coldway is no mere path of ice, but the back of one of the mysterious creatures of the Skidwrack River: the blue-and-green serpent known as the *caldnicker.*

The caldnicker spends much of the year lying at the bottom of the riverbed. Mostly it sleeps, though now and again it stirs in its rest, shifting the inlets of the Skidwrack with it. The caldnicker dreams almost ceaselessly, but sadly the majority of its dreams dissolve in the river before they make it to the surface. All of this changes, though, when the first winter frost begins to settle on the riverbank. Then the creature rouses itself from its dreams and makes its way downriver to Flotilla, where it winds itself among the hulls, twining in and about and throughout the spaces under and between the structures, and then falls asleep again until springtime.

This, of course, is why the floor of the Coldway is made of such dark ice, and why it freezes in unusual patterns that resemble frost-rimed scales. It's also how the oldsters of Flotilla explain the peculiar lights and sounds that are so often to be found in the tunnels: When the caldnicker sleeps on the surface of the river, the dreams that in the underwater slumbers of warmer seasons merely dissolved into the Skidwrack are borne instead into the freezing air of the Coldway. There they solidify, and there they walk, roaming the paths formed by the body of their still-sleeping dreamer and haunting the Coldway like ghosts until the thaw. And then, like the frost and the ice and the winter, they vanish.

These are old stories, of course, and there isn't much talk of the caldnicker outside of Flotilla in these modern times. But to this day, the people of Flotilla call the annual freeze of the waterways beneath their city the *nick* — as in, *There's no Coldway until after the nick settles in properly*. And, of course, while the explanations for them have changed over time, the nick still brings with it the peculiar sounds and lights that have always haunted the ice-floored tunnels below Flotilla.

And speaking of the changes time brings: Because the Coldway is, of course, never the same place twice, each winter when the river freezes, someone quite intrepid has to go into the tunnels and map them. Because without a map, it doesn't do to venture into the Coldway. It's frigid, of course, and precious few are the places where the vaulted bow-and-gunwale ceilings part to reveal open sky. Voices carry there, but not up to the surface. If you get lost in the Coldway, you will freeze before you are found, if you are found at all. Most likely your body will keep in the cold until the river-ice melts and the Coldway disappears, and then it will sink into the Skidwrack, never to be seen again.

The people of Flotilla keep those maps to themselves: the Coldway and its route are their secret. And here is the secret of the secret: To this day, the intrepid surveyors of that in-between place are almost always children, because they can venture down onto the ice before it's thick and strong enough to hold an adult. In addition to being reckoned a great adventure (and one that logically ought to be forbidden on the grounds of danger), it can be lucrative. Good surveys of the Coldway fetch high prices.

One winter, at midnight on the coldest night yet, a girl called Mair dressed in her warmest clothes, packed a bag of matches and candles, a canteen and some bread and cheese and a chunk of cake, some artist's pastels, a staff, and a long rope with hooks at either end, and snuck out of her bedroom window into the frigid night. It was the first night she thought the ice might've been sturdy enough to dare walking on, and if she hurried, she thought she might well be one of the first surveyors to venture out, which meant a generous bounty if she was also quickest to get her survey to the cartographer who would make that year's map.

For an hour or so, nothing outside the ordinary happened. The cavern was gold and green in the light of her lantern, and the ice floor had frozen in the same uncommon pattern of frost-edged scales it always did. The walls and roof were a curving patchwork made up of scores of boat hulls in a rainbow of chipped and faded colors. Thick icicles hung from them, along with knotted lengths of cordage, which, by long-standing tradition, were always lowered down from the houses and ships by their owners and masters for the aid of anyone using the passages below. Mair knew to stay close to the hull walls, where there were handholds and where the ice was thicker. She walked with one end of the hooked rope tethered to her belt and the other end clutched in the hand that also held her pencil as she noted the twists and turns of the labyrinth. She knew how to test the floor's thickness before she put her weight on it, and she knew the particular, peculiar sounds the ice made in that space, and how those creaks were different from the sound of the ice splintering.

There were other sounds in the cold and the dark too: she was not alone. But that was no surprise; she'd known she wouldn't be the only child who snuck out of her room that night. And although they were all technically competing for the first-survey reward, they also all knew that it was much better not to be alone down there when the nick was still settling in.

And then the inevitable happened. Distracted momentarily by the reflection on the ice of something moving up ahead, Mair put a foot down where she hadn't tested the floor. The ice squealed in protest, a sound so like a scream that Mair dropped her staff in shock. But she recovered herself in a heartbeat and jabbed an iron hook through the nearest hanging loop of rope just as the floor under her feet cracked to pieces. The tether at the other end of the rope was secure on her belt, so she knew she wouldn't fall far, but she braced herself for the stabbing pain of freezing-wet feet and ankles.

She felt the ice go, felt the beginning of the short fall. But the stabbing cold-wet didn't come. Instead, her feet scrambled on the crumbling floor and she felt herself yanked hard by the belt toward the nearer of the hull walls. She grabbed for handholds and found herself clinging not to a bumper or a length of cordage or any other bit of boat hardware, but to a boy with wide, terrified eyes. He wrapped his arms around her and held her as tightly as she had ever been held as the floor behind them splintered and reached out with its webwork of cracks in all directions, as if the ice itself knew Mair was still there and it still wanted to see her fall.

With his back to the wall, the boy whistled three discordant notes, and instantly the splintering stopped just shy of the surface directly under her feet.

"How did you do that?" Mair whispered, turning her head to stare over her shoulder and down at the fractured floor of the tunnel.

Instead of answering, the boy asked, "Are you all right?" He looked at the rope that still tethered her to the loop of cordage overhead. "Oh, I see. You were fine all along."

"Well, you did save me from wet feet and a lot of maneuvering," Mair said. They were still holding fast to each other, but neither moved to release the other. It makes for a very romantic image, but for her part Mair was occupied with working out the safest way to let go, and the safest direction in which to move when she did. Also, she'd dropped her staff, which she would need in order to disengage the tether hook from the loop it hung from, directly over the center of the radiating cracks — along with her drawing pad, which there was no way she was leaving without.

That is, she was *mostly* occupied with all that. Because she had never held anyone so closely or for so long, there was a small collection of synapses in her brain that could not fail to notice that out of the corner of her right eye she could see the boy's cheekbone, and a scattering of frost clinging to his curling dark sideburns. And as for the boy — well. For reasons that will shortly become evident, he was in a state where nearly everything he encountered made his heart ache with wonder and joy, and although he had acted on pure instinct when he'd pulled Mair out of the way of the splintering ice, now he was holding on simply because he didn't want to let go.

"I need my staff there," Mair said, nodding back toward the center of the tunnel. The boy had to lift his head to see over hers in order to follow the gesture, and for a moment Mair felt the skin just below his jaw press against her forehead.

Under different circumstances, she might have noticed that she ought to have felt his pulse there. Or then again, perhaps not.

In any case, she let go of the boy at last, reached past him to the hull at his back, and felt around until her fingers found an iron ring. Then she unhooked the end of the rope that was connected to her belt, and threaded the hook through the ring so that now a line ran from the wall to the loop of rope hanging down over the cracked ice.

The boy looked critically from the line to the compromised ice at the center of the tunnel. The staff lay between the two of them and the worst of the cracks. Reluctantly, he let go. "It will hold," he said. "At least, it will hold long enough."

"I think so," Mair agreed. She inched carefully out, both palms curled around the rope overhead, until she could reach the end of the staff with one foot and pull it toward herself. She let go of the rope with one hand, bent slowly, picked up the staff, and, after a moment's pause to make sure the fissures didn't seem to be spreading, she stretched her foot just a bit farther and caught the drawing pad she'd been using to map the tunnels with her toe. "Catch," she called over her shoulder, and kicked the pad back toward the boy.

"Got it."

"Thank you." Another pause, then she reached up with one end of the staff and nudged the iron hook out of the loop of cordage. She caught it as it fell, hung it from her belt, and eased herself back toward the hull wall where the other end of the rope still held fast. When she was safely back at the solid verge of the ice, she disconnected the second hook. Then she and the boy edged down the tunnel and away from the cracks, with Mair testing the floor all along the way. At last they came to thicker ice, and then some that was thicker still. Only then did the boy and the girl stop and face each other.

"I'm Mair," said the young surveyor.

The boy had no name, but he knew the terms for a number of cold things. "Hail," he said, choosing one at random and quite accidentally picking a word that is both a cold thing and, sometimes, a moniker.

"Hale," Mair repeated. "Thank you."

He handed back her drawing pad. "You're mapping the cold roads?"

"Yes." She permitted herself a long look at the strange boy. "You're not, are you?" His eyes were wide and black, with no visible line where the pupil ended and the iris began. Frost dusted his hair, and his eyelashes. He smelled like the cold, but when he had held her, the skin against her forehead had been warm as her own. Mair remembered the flicker of motion that had distracted her just before she had nearly fallen through the ice, and she realized she was talking to one of the caldnicker's dreams, though she wasn't sure how he would feel if she asked outright. Would he even know?

(As it happened, he did know — though not all dreams do comprehend that they're dreams, as you probably understand from your own experiences. And he recognized that Mair was not, but since she didn't mention it, neither did he.)

They explored the Coldway together for the rest of the night, and when finally Mair led the way back to her own home, they arranged to meet the following evening after she had submitted her survey.

The dream called Hale wandered in a daze until the agreed-upon time. The other dreams in the tunnels watched him with sympathy. It was easy to fall in love when the world was new and everything was wonder, and Mair was fearless and brilliant and resourceful and confident and they had no trouble understanding why Hale would be fascinated by her. But the older dreams — the ones the caldnicker dreamed over and over again, year after year — always warned the younger about contact with humans. *You will lose them with the thaw,* the recurring ones said. *There is no knowing if you will come back, or who and what you will be if you do, because dreams change; and if you do come back, no way to know whether the one you love will be waiting, because people change too. The only thing that is certain is that you will break their hearts, and the only thing that will prevent yours from breaking as well is that we dreams-of-the-caldnicker have slack water in place of hearts. Still, slack water can become a tide, if you're not careful.*

But Hale pretended not to hear, and the next night, he waited for her at a place near her home where a flight of old wooden steps descended from a bulkhead on the surface down into the Coldway. They went on meeting there each night after that, to avoid as much as possible the other human foot traffic in the tunnels, which dwindled to next to nothing when the sun went down. Mair always brought some sort of sweet from the district above, because Hale's delight at sweets made her laugh. Hale took Mair to places where the ice had frozen in the most interesting ways, because she loved to draw, and the subtle patterns and shiftings of color in the ice in the strange light of the tunnels fascinated her. Every night, when she first appeared on the stairs, he would reach up a hand to help her down, and every night she took it, even though they both knew she didn't need it. Sometimes he offered a hand when the floor was uneven underfoot too, and when he did, she took it again, even though they both knew she was surefooted as an arctic hare on the ice. Things like this happened more and more frequently as the winter wore on, until finally they dropped the pretense without discussion and simply held hands as they wandered the tunnels.

And then, one night, Mair stopped walking. She pulled on the hand she held and drew Hale close. He put his arms around her — the first time he had done that since the moment they'd met — and Mair kissed him, and Hale's heart-that-was-not-a-heart became a tide, just as the old recurring dreams had warned it would.

Winter passes, always.

When warmer currents begin to stir, so does the caldnicker under the ice, stretching its back in waves that send creaks throughout the Coldway. Mair began bringing the tether rope with its iron hooks down into the tunnels with her, and stepping more cautiously when she and Hale walked near the center of the ice. He whistled the cracks together when he could, but it got harder and harder to manage, requiring longer and longer stretches of song that left him breathless and slow afterward. There was no doubt about it: the Coldway was beginning to fail.

"What will happen?" Mair asked at last.

That night Hale had brought her to a place where ice and frost and lichen had made a picture like a landscape on one of the hulls, and they had been sitting on a blanket Mair had brought from home while she painted it with bits of chalky pastel crayon in the light of a lantern. Now and then they heard cracking from down the tunnels.

Hale hesitated. "The recurring ones say we sublimate. When the temperature warms enough, the conditions in the tunnels cause us to go directly from solid to vapor."

"And then you're gone?"

He nodded. "And then we're gone, unless we are dreamed again."

Mair put down her drawing. "There must be a way to keep that from happening."

During the hours when Mair lived her life above the tunnels, Hale had passed his time in asking this question of every dream he could find. None of them had an answer, though many had tried to find one. Now he shook his head. "If there is a way, no one knows it."

"Someone must know," Mair insisted. "What about the cald-nicker? Has anyone thought to ask it?"

"Yes," Hale said simply. "It's been thought of. But it can't be done."

"Why?" But Mair worked it out almost instantly. "Because the caldnicker stays submerged, and dreams dissolve in the Skidwrack. *You* can't ask it because you'd be gone before you could reach it. And even if it were to come up for a breath or a look around, it would be after the ice above it melts, and then it would be too late."

Hale nodded once. He did not like the emphasis she'd put on the word *you*. Ice creaked somewhere not far away. "Finish your drawing," he suggested. "It's getting late."

Mair gave him a considering look before she went back to her picture. But it wasn't long before she set down her pastels again. "Let's try it."

Hale shook his head again. "We can't," he said as resolutely as possible.

"*You* can't," Mair argued, "but I can. I'm a good swimmer, and I won't melt."

Hale knew her well enough by now to guess that if Mair said she was a good swimmer, she was probably excellent—but that didn't matter. All that mattered was the *second* thing she'd said. "You won't melt," he agreed. "But you'll freeze. Or you'd get stuck, lost under the ice."

She laughed. "No, I wouldn't. In the first place, the river is already warming up, or we wouldn't have this problem; and in the second place, I didn't spend all that time making a map of the routes down here just to get lost—not in them, and not under them. I know how to protect against the cold, and I know how to protect against getting stuck below. I can do it."

All of this had occurred to Hale days ago, the moment it had occurred to him to wonder if the caldnicker might know how to keep him from vanishing in the thaw: that he couldn't swim down to the creature, but possibly a human could; and that if there was anyone who could pull the thing off and come back alive, it was Mair. But he also knew that even *her* chances were slim, and he knew it was not a chance he was willing to have her take on his behalf.

"Don't you think," he asked quietly, "if the caldnicker knew how to make its dreams hold their reality — to make its dreams *come true* — don't you think it would have done it before now?"

"It's asleep," Mair said simply. "Maybe it would, or could, if someone only woke it up to ask the question."

Hale kissed her forehead. "The answer is no. Let's not waste the time we have."

But Mair could not stop thinking about the possibility. Later that night, when they stood at the bottom of the stairs that would take her back to the surface of Flotilla, she made her arguments for seeking out the caldnicker all over again, and those arguments were devastatingly simple.

"I can do it," she said. "I bet I can even work out exactly where to look for its head." She put a hand under Hale's jaw and, with fingers stained by chalky colors, touched the place where she had once felt no pulse. But now that he had a tide instead of slack water where his heart should have been, there was a beat there. "I love you," Mair said, and she kissed him again. "Let me try to save you."

Hale had known this was coming, and he had his answer ready. He didn't say, "I don't want you to do that for me," because then Mair might have told him, "But *I* want to do it for you." He didn't say, "I can't ask that of you," because that left room for Mair to reply, "You don't have to ask." He didn't say, "I couldn't bear it if something went wrong and you didn't come back," because then she might have said, "Nothing will go wrong," or she might've even gone so far as to point out that if anything *did* go wrong, Hale wouldn't be around to feel anything about it. He didn't say, "I can't let you," because they both would have known he couldn't possibly stop her. There were so many potential wrong answers, and he had already worked through them all.

So he said, "Mair, I love you," because it was the true answer. And then he said, "No," because it was the right answer.

Mair stared at him in disbelief. "Just . . . no?"

"I believe in you," he said, lowering his nose to hers so they were exactly eye to eye. "But I'm asking you not to try."

She held his gaze, unblinking. "If you love me, you'll let me."

"If you love me," he said, ignoring the hurt in her voice, "you won't."

They looked at each other for a long time, each wanting badly to kiss the other again but neither knowing whether it would help or hurt their respective arguments and both sensing that, help or hurt, it would've been unfair.

And then, something miraculous happened. Mair's face, which had been looking mutinous and angry and wounded, wiped itself clear and reconfigured itself into an expression of resolve. "Then we'll find another way."

He smiled, relieved. "You could stick me in an icebox, I suppose."

"Then I'd better start looking for one that's big enough." With no reason not to any longer, they kissed again, and then Mair went reluctantly up into the dawning daylight.

That day in the tunnels, in between asking despairing questions of every dream he could find, Hale whistled the ice together wherever he could, trying desperately to extend the life of the Coldway. Up above, the morning dawned frigid — much colder than it had been for the last week. Somehow this felt like a good omen, and Mair set aside every other task she had and threw herself into the search for a way to save the boy she had fallen in love with. Truth be told, if the stakes had not been so high and the time so short, she would have relished the challenge. Mair was an adventurer at heart, and she was young enough and fearless enough that so far, she had not really come up against her own limitations — all reasons why Hale was desperately lucky to have her on his side, and all reasons why he had been desperate to convince her not to venture under the ice.

First she went to the library and looked up every tale of the caldnicker that she could find. Hours passed while she pored over the stories, but nothing she read suggested any solutions to the problem she wanted to solve. She allowed herself ten minutes of panic and desperation while she figured out what to do next, and then she went to the cartographer who made each year's map of the Coldway. After all, the cartographer was the first one to hear the accounts of the surveyors who ventured into the tunnels every winter. Surely, Mair thought, she wasn't the only one who had come back with tales of the caldnicker's wandering dreams. Surely the mapmaker had heard some of those tales over the years.

The cartographer's apprentice welcomed her when she knocked at the studio door. "Mr. Oronti is out," he said apologetically. "Is there anything I can help you with, Mair?"

Mair sat down at the apprentice's desk and made herself comfortable. "Tell me everything you know about the dreams in the Coldway."

The apprentice laughed, then changed his mind. "All right."

He began to speak, and it turned out that Mair had been right: Nearly every year, he and the the cartographer heard at least one tale of a Flotillan encountering one of the caldnicker's wandering dreams. Some of those tales were love stories; none of them ended happily, and at least one surveyor had never been heard from since. Both apprentice and master suspected that fellow had done exactly what Mair had proposed: he had ventured under the ice, looking for the head of the caldnicker in order to wake it and ask how to bring its dreams properly to life; but he had failed, and the cold river had taken him.

"The only thing I can tell you that might help you," the apprentice said at last, "is that if you've read the folklore, you know that the caldnicker's dreams are said to sublimate in the thaw." He hesitated, and when he spoke again, his voice was reluctant. "Do you know what it means for a substance to sublimate?"

"It means to go directly from solid to vapor," Mair said, remembering Hale's words.

The apprentice nodded. "That is one meaning. But that doesn't have to be the end of the process." He took a piece of paper and a pencil and made a quick sketch of two beakers connected by a tube: one with fire below it, one with ice. In the beaker over the fire, he drew a lump. "A substance can be heated until it evaporates, then moved rapidly into a very cold chamber, where it condenses again." He drew an arrow from the lump up through the tube and into the empty beaker over the ice, where he drew a handful of dots on the sides. "Chemists frequently do this to filter out impurities; alchemists do it to initiate transitions."

"So even after a thing has been changed to vapor, that doesn't mean it's gone?" Mair demanded. "It can be made solid again? Whole?"

The apprentice put up a warning hand. "Solid again, yes. Whole again, no — the whole point of sublimation is that something is left behind. In alchemy, the point of sublimation was often to reduce the physical to the spiritual — that's the solid-to-vapor part, if you follow — and then reconstitute the spiritual as a more perfect solid." He smiled sadly. "A lot of alchemy sounds like allegory when you say it out loud."

Mair's excitement faltered. It did sound like allegory, but not like an allegory for anything she wanted to think about in connection with Hale.

Silence fell for a moment. "You've thought about this a lot," Mair said to the apprentice. He nodded, and his face was grim. "Why?"

"Because I used to survey the Coldway too, when I was

younger and lighter," he said at length. "And because I couldn't figure out how to save the dream I met on the ice. And I have never been able to bring myself to go back."

The hand that held the pencil shook. Mair took it and held it until it stopped twitching. Then she tapped the drawing. "Did you try something like this?"

The apprentice shook his head. "I was too afraid. The whole thing depends on letting them go to vapor, you see. I couldn't bear to suggest it."

And even if it works, Mair thought, *something will be left behind.*

The clock on the mantel chimed. The sun was going down. "Thank you," Mair said, and she left.

She didn't wait for nightfall to go to the Coldway. She went straight from the cartographer's studio to the place where she and Hale always met. During the day, public-safety officials monitored the entrances and exits to the tunnels, especially as it got closer to spring, and one of them shouted a warning to Mair as she ran to the stairs. "Take care," he called, and his breath was visible in the air as he spoke. "Feels cold tonight, but it's treacherous below nonetheless."

"Thank you," she called, but she slowed only as much as she had to in order to keep from losing her footing on the frosty wood-plank steps.

He was not waiting there when she reached the bottom, but Mair didn't worry. It was earlier than they usually met. Still, the creaking of the ice floor and the shifting of hulls was audible right away, and it was coming from all directions. Mair hadn't stopped home between the cartographer and the Coldway, and she didn't have her safety equipment with her, so she gingerly tested the surface just below the stairs with the toe of one boot. It shifted. Not much, but enough. Her heart sank. The Coldway was failing.

She forced herself to wait there, and it was no easy feat. At last, she heard his whistle echoing through the tunnel as he approached. The melody sounded weaker than usual, and she wondered how much of the day Hale had spent trying to knit the ice back together all on his own.

But then he was there, and they fell into each other's arms. Mair could feel how hard he was breathing, and the beat of the tide in his chest pounded against her. All around them, the tunnels protested; the hulls, whose subtle movements were barely perceptible even in warm weather and came to a near standstill when the nick set in, had begun again to stir in the fragmenting ice. Hale was near collapse as well. He'd known this might be his last night in the Coldway. He'd spent himself trying to hold just the one stretch of tunnel nearest Mair's stairway together, and still it was crumbling. A shaft of sunset fell down the stairway, painting the girl he loved in colors he'd never seen before. He wanted to tell her she was beautiful, and he promised himself he would do that as soon as he could draw proper breath.

While she waited for Hale to get his wind back, Mair told him what she'd learned from the cartographer's apprentice. She explained the idea that had taken shape as she'd crossed the stretch of Flotilla between the studio and the stairs. Then, as his wheezing breath rasped against her chest and the tide-pulse in his throat thudded against her cheek, she told him the risks: all the ways she feared this vague new plan was likely to go wrong.

As Hale listened, his breath quieted, and the arms around her stopped shaking. By the time Mair was finished speaking, his body and breath were calm. His hands stroked her back, and Mair realized she was crying.

He was silent for a moment, and then, in a voice very close to his normal one, Hale said, "These are acceptable risks."

Mair punched him in the arm. "Have you been listening to me at all?" she exploded. "I just explained that you have to allow yourself to be reduced to vapor to so much as *try* this, and even if it's successful, some part of you will still be lost! How are those acceptable risks?"

"They're acceptable risks because they're mine," he said simply. "My answer is yes."

"I don't know if I can do it," Mair said.

Hale smiled. "I can't ask this of you."

She smiled forlornly back. "You don't have to ask." Together they looked up into the red rays of the sunset. "Do you think that bit of sun and daylight will be enough?" Mair wondered.

"I think anything other than the freeze of the Coldway will be enough," Hale said. "As long as you can get where you need to be quickly. I don't imagine you'll have much time."

She swallowed and nodded shakily. "I know where to go."

"Then take me there." He took her hand, and together they

walked up into the shaft of sunlight. As soon as they were fully above ground, Hale could feel something change: something elemental inside him began to rearrange itself. "Hurry," he whispered.

Mair exhaled as much air as she could as he pulled her into his arms and she, in turn, pulled his face as close to hers as she could. And then the girl inhaled, breathing the waking dream in as he came apart and turned to mist in the sunset. He smelled of all the cold of the river, and when her lungs were full, she held her breath, though she wanted to sob, and she raced from the bulkhead by the stairs to the nearest frosty window shaded from the sunlight. She leaned in until her nose was a hair's width from the glass, and she exhaled until there was no breath left in her.

As she leaned back again with a gasp, the frost on the window changed, warmed, faded, recrystallized before her eyes. Layer by layer, an image painted itself over the glass in a starry rime of cold condensate. As Mair watched, a boy's face took shape. The details were hazy — the effect reminded her of working with her chalky pastels: you had to look at her paintings from a bit of a distance to really see the picture. But she was adept at looking at things that way, and so she had no trouble. Especially when the frost boy smiled at her. A hand resolved itself, pressing against the glass.

There was a bucket full of half-frozen water below the window. Mair took off her gloves, bent, and pressed her own hands to the freezing surface to chill them. When her fingers began to tingle with numbness, she straightened and put one palm to the glass where Hale's frost hand was. She held her breath.

Five freezing-cold fingers curled away from the glass and intertwined with hers, and carefully, slowly, Mair pulled Hale away from the window: first his hand, then his arm, then one shoulder, then his face and head emerged. One foot, leg, and hip climbed over the windowsill, and then the other, and then there he stood, free of the glass, shaking with cold, but solid, and mostly stable.

He was never not cold from that day forward, but the chill was manageable; he was never completely stable, either, but then again, no *human* is ever completely stable, and it seems unfair to hold a dream to higher standards. Sometimes he felt that there were differences between a small tide and a heart, but those, too, could be worked through.

Neither he nor Mair was ever completely certain what was left behind in the sublimation. Whatever it was, in the long years of their life together that followed that winter, neither of them missed it.

And every year after, from that one to this, they have haunted the Coldway together from nick to thaw: Mair surveying and painting with her pastels, Hale whistling at her side. Now and then they come across another of the caldnicker's roaming dreams down in the tunnels, and when they do, they are happy to share what they know of how dreams come true.

INTERLUDE

T**HE ROOM EXHALED** again, and Captain Frost got to his feet. It was time to turn the glass. "You know," he said as he lifted the sand clock and rotated it, "I rather thought, when you said you would tell a love story, that I knew which one you were going to tell. Or what sort, anyway," he amended. He set down the glass, picked up his sherry, and said in a tone of mild surprise, "I was wrong."

"What sort were you expecting?" Sullivan asked, nodding thanks to Sorcha as she refilled his glass of whiskey.

The chair Frost had occupied in between trips out into the rain was positioned by the window a few feet behind the sofa, which was nearer the center of the room. Rather than returning to it now, he crossed the room with his drink and his half-hour glass to the empty chair beside Negret near the display case, from which he could sit and face the young man sitting beside Petra on the couch.

"I rather thought," said the captain slowly, "that you might tell a tale of the seiche." At the word *seiche,* around the room, heads that had been turned toward the captain swiveled back to look at Sullivan with curiosity. Frost took another sip. "But damn me if you didn't tell exactly the opposite of a seiche yarn."

"What's seiche?" Maisie asked, eyes on the handful of court cards, all hearts, that she was using to add a little pergola before the castle.

"You've never heard of the seiche?" Captain Frost barked a laugh as he set both his liquor glass and his half-hour glass on the small table between himself and Negret. "What this world is coming to, I don't know."

"It's all right, Miss Maisie," Tesserian said, taking a fresh deck from his pocket. "I've never heard of it either."

"It's no 'it,'" the captain retorted. "It's a 'they.'" He glanced at Sullivan. "Do you want to field the question, or shall I do it?"

Sullivan's preternatural poise didn't so much as flicker. "Go right ahead. I imagine you know the legends better than I."

Frost gave him a long look. "I don't think that's true." He cleared his throat. "I'll explain, but I'm saving my turn to tell a proper story for something else, so I shall try to make it brief." He pointed to the huge map on the wall above the mantelpiece. "Have a look, young lady: a good, close look."

Maisie got to her feet and, carefully avoiding the card castle, stepped onto the hearth. She stretched up on her toes to grip the mantelpiece and peer over it. Sorcha hurried over to carefully lift the music box with the filigree tree out of the way, passing it gently to Mrs. Haypotten, and then going back to move the case clock, the vase of paper spills, and a small stack of books, too.

"The captain will be wanting you to see the creatures at the edges," Sorcha said to Maisie when she had finished. "Shall I give you a boost?"

"Thank you," Maisie said, feeling a bit awkward to be the center of all this unexpected fuss.

Sorcha gave her a wink. "It's good to know about the seiche, just in case you ever find yourself meeting one." She knelt on a knee on the hearth and offered her hand to help Maisie step up onto her other, bent leg.

The map showed the Skidwrack and its inlets. It was old, with the green-brown of the river and the green-blue of the pine woods on the riverbank painted by hand. The compass rose had been drawn in ink, and to eyes that knew the city well, it was clearly meant to look like old iron. In one corner was the usual warning always found on maps of Nagspeake waterways (which, whether due to a restless caldnicker or for some other reason, could never be trusted): THIS MAP IS NOT MEANT TO BE USED FOR NAVIGATION. And at the farthest inland reaches of the river, where the Skidwrack and its offshoots disappeared off the page, the words HIC ABUNDANT SEPIAE were enclosed in an oval formed by the curving bodies of two sleek river otters very much like the one that had been hidden in her napkin at dinner.

"Otters?" Maisie asked. She turned and looked from Frost to Sullivan. "What's so terrible about otters?"

Frost crossed himself as he picked up his drink again and took a long pull from it. It looked rather as though he was fortifying himself for a task he didn't particularly care for.

"I've never yet found anyone who could tell me how the two things came to be associated with each other," Sullivan said, observing Frost's hesitation, "but for as long as any oldster on the Skidwrack can remember, superstitious folk have always crossed themselves when they see river otters, for fear of the seiche. Except, of course, for the odd foolish romantic who actually thinks he wants to meet one. The seiche are supposed to be beautiful, after all."

"I thought you didn't want to tell the thing," Frost snapped.

"The silence was threatening to become awkward," Sullivan retorted.

Sorcha stepped into the breach. "Not just beautiful," she corrected, helping Maisie back down. "Magnificent. Stunning. You hear them spoken of like mermaids or selkies. Perhaps it's the selkie lore that first tied them to the otters, the way selkies are tied to seals — but of course the seiche are no shape-shifters, nor is there any magic pelt that, hidden, will keep one from returning to the water."

The captain nodded his agreement. "Nor would there be any point in hiding it if there were. When a seiche girl comes ashore, it's because ashore is where she wants to be, and from the moment she shakes the water from her heel, her life becomes a search for the one thing that will allow her to remain on land: someone else who's willing to take her place."

"Take her place . . . in the river?" Tesserian asked.

"Aye." The captain affected a portentous tone. "For the water knows what belongs to its kingdom, and it keeps a close tally of its creatures, wherever they are. When one of its citizens tries to defect, the water demands an equal exchange, and until that exchange is properly completed, the water goes in search of what has left it."

Tesserian nodded and began to lay out the new, blue-backed

cards in a wavy pattern of overlapping scales before the castle and its handful of outbuildings, like a flat tide lapping at the worn floorboards. "I see."

Maisie looked from the captain to Sullivan as she sat cross-legged beside the card castle again. "I don't. Not exactly."

"In short," Sullivan said, his gaze on the encroaching paper sea, "when one of the seiche attempts to leave the water, the waters will rise in the wake of the leaving until either the seiche returns to it—a death sentence, for seiche lose the ability to breathe underwater once they've been ashore for a day—or someone else goes voluntarily to take its place, which is also a death sentence, for humans can't learn the trick of breathing underwater. And it must be voluntary," he repeated. "The sacrifice can't be made through trickery, or it doesn't work."

It was impossible for anyone in the room to fail to be aware of two things. The first was that outside, the waters were still rising. The second was that, although for the most part none of those who'd heard of the seiche could remember hearing of one in the shape of a man, if one *were* to imagine a seiche boy, Sullivan—tanned golden, his face lean and even under long-ish hair the brown-gray of wet stone, staring at the cards out of eyes the changeable color of the river—might well have fit the bill. He, too, was more than beautiful; he was magnificent, scar and all.

Maisie, fascinated and vaguely disconcerted, glanced quickly around the room to see if she ought to be worried some-how. At their posts by the sideboard, the Haypottens wore wary expressions, but everyone else seemed to be taking this strange possibility in stride, as if it were nothing more troubling than an awkward conversation they might have to redirect if it got too uncomfortable. Closest to her was Sorcha, her black eyes steady and her tiny wooden seabird hanging from the blue velvet ribbon around her neck. The maid's round face held a fascinating, unfathomable expression. There was a secret there, for certain.

It was harder to draw secrets out of stillness, but Maisie tried anyway, seeking clues in the tiny uptilt at the corner of Sorcha's mouth, the hardness of her eyes, the interlacing of her fingers. She held her hands that way a lot, but already Maisie understood that there were volumes to be read in the gesture, if you knew what to look for. How tight was the clasp? How white the knuckles? Were her hands clasped behind her or in front, and if in front, did her arms hang long and loose, or were her elbows bent so that they seemed to rest on her hips? Which thumb was uppermost, the left or the right, and was her middle right finger twitchy or still? How did her shoulders and chin tilt?

No, right now, Sorcha was placid, confident, even defiant. Whatever the others in the room were thinking or feeling or guessing, Sorcha *knew,* and Sorcha was not afraid. And with that realization, Maisie decided she needn't be afraid either.

Now Sullivan's changeable eyes flicked up at Captain Frost. "And you thought I was going to tell a seiche tale. Should we take that to mean you think there's a seiche in Nagspeake who hasn't found her sacrifice?" Sullivan smiled. His straight white teeth shone in the firelight. "If there is, you must hope she finds someone soon, or we shall all be washed away." His grin faded. "I confess I would find that supremely unfair."

"I don't suppose it isn't a *she,* but a *he?*" Frost asked harshly.

"He?" Sullivan grinned again. "What say you, Mr. Amalgam? What's the lore tell about that?"

The old folklorist shrugged. "Can't say I've encountered that variant in the tales I've come across, but logic says it must be possible."

Despite Sullivan's grin, a palpable tension had filled the space between the captain and the river-eyed man with the scar. "You came here looking for something, didn't you?" the captain asked.

"Of course I did. Why else does anyone go anywhere?"

"Did you find it?"

Sullivan leaned his elbows on his knees, his whiskey glass clasped in both hands between them. "Landsman, what I came looking for isn't here to find."

"Landsman?" Frost glared at him. "Captain for twenty years, commodore for ten, and you call me a landsman?"

"I do." The young man's teeth flashed again in what was just barely a smile and not a snarl. "You are. And if you really believe what you're hinting at, then you know that I, of anyone, have the right to say it."

Captain Frost shoved out of his chair, crossed the parlor in two strides, and yanked Sullivan to his feet, sloshing whiskey onto the younger man's battered leather shoes and his own old boots — otterskin boots, had anyone happened to looked closely at them. "Make it stop," he snarled into the young man's face. "You'll make it stop now, if I have to throw you into the maw of the river myself!"

The hot water coils in their iron case above the sideboard gave a sudden thudding rattle, and the room broke into commotion, but with a strange, reluctant delay, as if somehow everyone present had to remind themselves that this lurch from charged words into the physical wasn't just another bit of storytelling. The innkeeper was fastest. "Belay, there, Captain," Mr. Haypotten said quickly, hurrying forward with his hands fluttering in rapid and distressed gestures.

But the young man merely shook his head, and something about the motion was enough to halt Mr. Haypotten in his tracks. Sullivan passed his empty glass to Petra, then took hold of Frost's hands and pried his fingers from his lapels as easily as if he were peeling back the skin of an orange. "The water wants nothing from me, Captain," he said softly. "Nor has it these twenty years."

Ignoring the eyes staring at him, Sullivan turned and looked darkly out at the rain pelting the riverward windows. "My sacrifice was made."

When he turned back to the room, it was not Captain Frost to whom he spoke, but to the upraised face of Petra, who was still seated at the other end of the sofa.

"Once upon a time, I stood before a girl," he said, "and I told her, 'I don't want you to do that for me' and 'I can't ask that of you' and 'I can't let you.' And she answered 'But I want to do this for you' and 'You don't have to ask,' and then, finally, because we both knew I couldn't stop her — or rather, because she thought I couldn't stop her and I knew I wouldn't really try — she walked into the river. And it took her the way the river does. And here I am. I am this." He took a breath with a catch in it, and when he spoke again, though his eyes stayed on Petra, his voice was pitched to address the whole room. "No, Captain. That water is rising in the wake of some other, or perhaps for another reason entirely. And the river will not be fooled by a false sacrifice, so let's have no one in this room start thinking of walking out into the flood. It would do no good."

He turned to stare at Captain Frost, who glared back, clenching and unclenching his fists. Then Frost glanced at his half-hour glass, remembered that he had turned it but had not gone to check the weather, and stalked out of the room.

Maisie spoke up, tentatively. "She must have loved you so much, whoever she was."

At that, Sullivan snapped to attention. "No," he said sharply, pointing an emphatic finger at her. "Weren't you listening, Maisie? If you ever do read the seiche tales, you should know that this is where the lie comes into the lore. The stories are full of romance, and they make the sacrifice seem noble, even beautiful. But it's a seduction, and nothing more. What it *isn't* is *love.*"

"I know why the seiche are conflated with otters," Sorcha said, arms folded. "Because otters are sleek, handsome, playful creatures. You forget they're predators. They have a nasty bite, and they crack open the bodies of the creatures they eat with rocks."

Sullivan met her hard, black eyes, and a whole conversation passed rapidly between them.

Met one or two, have you?

Look at me. Look where I live. More than one, and I'm still standing.

Sullivan inclined his head. *Touché.* "You may be right. But seiche are worse than predators. True predators kill to live, and though it can be terrible to witness, every creature has the right to at least attempt to survive. But seiche demand their sacrifices simply out of a wish to change their own circumstances. They're not predators. They're monsters."

"But they'll die if they go back into the water," Maisie protested.

"They know that when they come ashore," Sullivan said shortly. "No seiche stumbles ashore and stays there until its gills fail by accident." He crossed to the girl seated on the floor by the castle and crouched before her, sitting on his haunches with his head lowered an inch or two so that he could look her in the eye. "Love can hurt. Love can be one-sided. And sometimes love requires sacrifices, too. But love is not predatory. Wherever you go from here, please be wary of anyone who demands to be given your heart rather than asking to be invited into it. Please."

The girl nodded, shivering, unable to look away from that river-colored gaze. "I will."

He held her eyes a moment longer, then pushed himself awkwardly up to his feet—Petra, watchful, observed, *That makes twice*—retrieved his glass, and went to the sideboard to refill it. Somehow, though he moved as if he were slightly drunk, he managed to avoid knocking over the card castle.

He set his glass down beside the bottles with a soft thump, and it was as if a bit of sorcery that had lain over the room, perhaps the same spell that had kept everyone from moving faster in the moment when Frost had grabbed Sullivan, burst like a bubble.

Mr. Haypotten cleared his throat and rubbed his scalp again as if brushing cobwebs from it. "Let's get these put back, then," he said, reaching for the case clock that Sorcha had set on the floor beside the hearth. "How's that coffee holding out, love?" he asked in a voice full of false blustery cheer. His wife checked the samovar, then clucked to herself and wheeled it out. "Perhaps some more biscuits, too," he called after her as the door shut. "Blast," he muttered, reaching for the tree music box, which Mrs. Haypotten had stowed on the corner table where Jessamy Butcher sat, half-hidden by shadow and tapping gloved fingers on the tabletop. "Don't imagine she heard." When the box was back in place, he went out after his wife.

Reever rose from his chair before the fire and stalked to the sideboard, where he gave Sullivan a brief, steadying clap on one shoulder. Then he filled two glasses with sherry and turned toward the table in the corner just as Jessamy got to her feet. "I believe I'll just take a quick turn up the stairs and back to stretch," she said quickly. "Sorcha, are there anything like lap blankets about?"

"I'll find some," the maid said, looking critically at the fire. "I didn't like to make it up too strong, not with the young lady and gentleman building their castle so near."

"I completely agree." Jessamy and Sorcha left the room together. Maisie muttered something about the water closet and darted after them.

Reever, still holding two glasses, watched them leave. Then he changed direction and went to join his brother, who sat in one of the chairs by the display case. Reever handed Negret a sherry and dropped into the empty chair Frost had temporarily taken over and then abandoned, along with the half-hour glass that still stood on the table between the chairs.

Madame Grisaille, who had been silent since finishing her tale, stood and reached out a long, thin hand to Sullivan. "I, too, could stand a bit of a stroll," she said in that voice that was so like the turning of stone grinding wheels. "Would you be so kind?"

Sullivan chuckled humorlessly. He finished the liquor in his glass, then crossed the room and took her hand. "Certainly, madam. Let's go make sure old Frost hasn't gone to try to stop the flood by main force."

As she swept from the room, both Colophon brothers touched their knuckles to their foreheads in a gesture Frost would've recognized as the same obeisance sailors made to captains aboard a ship. Madame acknowledged this with a small, amused twist of her mouth as she swept out in a rustle of skirt and shawl, leaving Reever and Negret, Antony Masseter, Tesserian, Sangwin, Phineas Amalgam, and Petra still in the parlor.

Tesserian got to his feet, muttering, "Stay," as he extricated himself from the card-built landscape on the floor. He looked around at the others. "Who's for a smoke, while there's a break?" The twins shook their heads, but Amalgam rose from his seat and Sangwin retrieved his glass from the windowsill. "Masseter?" Sangwin asked as he crossed the parlor. "I owe you for the cigar earlier."

The peddler nodded. "I'll meet you in there." As the others left for the public bar, Masseter strolled over to Petra, who had not moved from her corner of the sofa all night. "Have you decided on a tale, then?" he asked, his one green eye glittering in the light of the tall floor lamp just behind the sofa.

She smiled up at him. "Just deciding on the ending. I think I'll hold out to be last, if I can. What about you?"

He nodded. "I'll tell one, though I'm still deciding which. A traveling chapman gathers tales, but we've had so many peddler tales already. Peddlers, tricksters, gamblers, and lovers." He reached into his pocket and took out a small cigar and a folding knife. "I rather wish I could think of something completely different." Masseter opened the knife and cut a notch in the end of his cigar. "Any requests?" He raised his voice and turned to include the twins in the question.

Reever said nothing. "I'm sure you'll come up with something," Negret replied, flashing a grin with too many teeth in it and somehow still managing to keep the expression friendly. Masseter acknowledged this with a careless nod of his head and looked down at Petra again.

"Oh, ask Maisie," she said breezily. "I already had my story requests honored."

"Yes, you did, didn't you?" Masseter eyed her curiously. "Both of them. What made you ask for those, I wonder? The first one especially. And where did you hear it? Amalgam says it wasn't one of his."

Petra got to her feet. "He's mistaken. That, or he isn't actually responsible for every single piece of lore in Nagspeake. Excuse me."

As she walked out of the parlor, she paused beside the chair where Reever Colophon sat staring moodily at Frost's half-hour glass. A sympathetic glance passed between them.

"What is there to say?" Reever asked quietly.

"Nothing that would make a difference, perhaps," Petra said.

Negret spoke up. "But you're here, and so is she."

"For now," Reever said, his voice bleak.

"For now," Petra agreed. "It's not nothing." She crouched to watch the last few grains of sand fall from the top bulb of the glass, reached out, and turned it.

Masseter had strolled to the French doors during this exchange, the better to light his cigar near a window and politely ignore the conversation. When Petra had gone, he also departed, heading for the public bar, to which the other smokers had decamped, and leaving only a faint wisp of sweet smoke in his wake. The parlor fell quiet around the tattooed brothers, who were accustomed to silence and did not feel obligated to break it.

NINE

---◈---

THE TAVERN AT NIGHT

JESSAMY AND SORCHA went up to the attic, where Sorcha thought she'd most recently seen the collection of small blankets she'd made the year Mrs. Haypotten had taught her to knit. She could've gone to the linen cabinet for everyday quilts instead, but the attic had other useful things in it as well.

The maid pointed Jessamy toward the corner where she knew the chest of blankets full of uneven edges and slipped stitches to be, then took herself off to a different corner to rifle through a trunk that had been up there since before even the Haypottens had bought the tavern. She emerged a few minutes later and went to Jessamy on the far side of the attic with three pairs of antique but pristine gloves in her hand.

"Will these fit you, miss?" Sorcha asked. "See if they might, and I'll see what I can do about the stains on yours, if you like." She considered mentioning the bloodstained blond lock currently tucked behind Jessamy's ear and decided to wait until they were downstairs again and closer to a washbasin.

Jessamy took the proffered gloves wordlessly. Her pink-clad fingers roved over the offering as she searched for words. "I think they'll fit perfectly," she said at last. "But I'll wait to try them on until I'm certain the bleeding won't start again." She tucked the gloves very carefully into the pocket of her dress. "Thank you."

Outside, where the road met the river, Captain Frost stood with the toes of his sea boots at the water's edge. His eyes were closed under his tarpaulin hat, and he hummed an old shanty under his breath as the rain pounded down on him.

Sullivan, hands in his pockets and head unprotected from the weather, went to stand at his side. "Sometimes the rain is just the rain," the younger man said.

"Tell yourself that, do you?" There was still bite in the captain's tone, but it lacked the conviction it had carried before.

"Every day."

"And do you believe it?"

Sullivan shook his head. "No."

"At sea," the captain said after a moment, "weather always means something. To believe anything less is to put an entire ship at risk."

Sullivan said nothing. He sat on a rock beside the road, propped his elbows on his knees in the darkness and the downpour, and watched the captain with eyes that had no trouble finding enough light, even on a sodden and moonless night, to see the shifting expressions on the old mariner's face. And he waited.

"What did you come here looking for, if your sacrifice was made so long ago?" Frost asked at last.

"The same things I always look for," Sullivan said, blinking back the rain. "A way to live in the world after what I've done. A way to live among them. A way to pay. Atonement."

"I thought you might say 'forgiveness.'"

He shook his head. "The only person who could give that can't do it, and if she could, I wouldn't ask it. It isn't for her to make me feel better about what I did."

"They say all you need is to repent." The captain spoke bitterly.

Sullivan shook his head slowly. "That's for whatever lies beyond." He watched the old man carefully. "I looked it up, you know, 'repentance.' Trying to find out what I ought to do with the pain and the regret. And I kept finding the words 'turn' and 'return.' Turn from evil, return to the good. But the only way I could find to apply it all to me — the only things I could turn from and turn to — was to turn away from the banks and return to the river. And you see I haven't done that."

"Would it bring her back?"

Sullivan shook his head. "No more than it would stop this flood. If I thought it could, I would try. I wish there was a grand gesture to make that would mean something, but I think perhaps that would be too easy." The captain said nothing, but his stony face was damp despite the tarpaulin hat. Sullivan hesitated, then asked gently, "How many souls, Commodore?"

Frost's chin rose a fraction of an inch. "Two hundred, between the battle and the storm."

"How long ago?"

The captain looked at the young man at last. "Should that matter?" he asked curiously.

Sullivan tilted his head indifferently. "Some would say yes, but I imagine only the ones who've never been responsible for the death of another."

In the doorway of the tavern, Madame Grisaille stood under the cover of the inn's porch roof, watching the backs of the two men. She considered calling, debated going back to the kitchens for mugs of warm coffee or chocolate, and decided at last that time and solitude were what was wanted. She slid one thin, patchy hand from the white fur muff, then reached out and touched the twisted old iron lamppost beside the porch for a moment. A shivery vibration thrummed through the iron and into the ground. Then Grisaille watched as, down beside the road, camouflaged by night and rain and the old, old pain of the two men at the edge of the floodwater, stems of dark iron reached up out of the soil and stretched skyward into the torrent.

Unnoticed—or ignored—by Sullivan and Frost, the iron stems grew and branched and arched over their heads, fronds reaching for each other from either side of the lane and twining themselves together into a canopy wrought of irregular braided and knotted metal tendrils. Here and there broad iron leaves sprouted like roof tiles, diverting most of the rain away from the men below.

Madame Grisaille nodded, satisfied, and went back inside, where she found Maisie returning from the water closet. "A dance before bed," Madame said. "The telling is finished for tonight, I believe."

They returned to the parlor. Negret now lay sprawled on the sofa, humming to himself and gazing out into the rain with one hand tucked in his vest pocket and his glass of sherry forgotten in the other, but Reever, still staring moodily into the half-hour glass, had not moved from the chair by the music-box cabinet, and the castle, of course, stood precisely where Tesserian had told it to stay.

"I would hate to knock it over," Maisie said, eyeing the castle. "It's not finished."

"The beauty of castles made of cards is that they are temporary, meant to be built and rebuilt," Madame replied as she reached for the door of the cabinet. "But I do not think Mr. Tesserian's castles fall until they are ready."

"Shall I find Sorcha for the key?" Maisie asked.

At this, Reever roused himself enough to chuckle. "The lady needs no keys."

Maisie frowned. She had not realized that the twin gentlemen with the decorated faces had particularly noticed Madame at all, beyond holding doors for her and waiting, as they all did, for her to sit first at meals.

The old lady's body blocked the lock and handle from the girl, so Maisie couldn't see what she did to manipulate the mechanism—but she remembered Madame's secret, so she was able to guess. Sure enough, the door opened easily, and Madame took down a box shaped like a teapot. "No sad songs tonight." She wound the teapot and lifted the lid, and a joyful melody Maisie didn't know spilled from the spout like steam.

Madame offered Maisie her hands. The girl hesitated, glancing at Reever, the nearer of the twins. She beckoned the old lady close. "But they'll see," she whispered. "They'll know your secret."

"My dear, they already know," Madame whispered back. "They have been in Nagspeake longer than anyone. The city has no secrets from them." She smiled at Reever. "Only people confuse them these days."

Reever snorted. "Too much truth, my lady." He got to his feet. "Fine, then. No sad songs. You have always danced with us, so dance with me now." He held out his arms and, as Maisie laughed in delight, he and Madame Grisaille began to swirl around the room.

Then, "Come on," Negret said. He set down his drink and got to his feet, then reached for Maisie's hands and swung her around, following the other two. Madame and Reever danced like family who had not met in a long time; Negret and Maisie danced with sheer, silly abandon, the young man adding twirls and dips as often as possible to keep his partner laughing. Mr. Negret, Maisie thought in between flourishes, danced as if he had no secrets, or at least didn't care who might see the truth of them. And she was right, which was perhaps how he and Maisie managed to match their steps so perfectly and effortlessly to each other's.

The music began to slow to its inevitable halt. Then, before it had quite wound all the way down, the notes paused altogether for a moment. All four dancers glanced to the little table where Madame had set the teapot. Sorcha finished winding the box and set it down again, and the music picked up once more, faster than before. She opened her mouth to apologize and tell them all not to mind her, for she'd only come in to check the fire, unless anyone wanted a blanket?

At the same moment and without a word between them, Madame Grisaille extricated herself from Reever, who, in turn, spun Maisie easily away from his brother and commenced twirling her about in Madame's place. Suddenly, before she could speak a word, Sorcha found herself dancing with Negret Colophon, who murmured the words of the song as he danced, so quietly that she would not have been able to hear them if his lips had not been so close to her ear.

Jessamy stood just outside the door for a few minutes, out of sight but listening, with her arms full of the blankets she had insisted on taking from Sorcha before the maid had gone into the parlor to pretend to check the fire. Then she turned on her heel, dumped the blankets unceremoniously on a chair in the hall, and followed the scent of spicy-sweet cigar smoke into the public bar. Tesserian, Amalgam, Masseter, and Sangwin sat around a table against the far wall. This room was drafty by intention, so that the breezes off the Skidwrack could help waft away the smoke that accumulated there. But even as the panes rattled, at a table by the window overlooking the road the more modest house the gambler had built the day before was, improbably, still standing.

Jessamy pulled up a chair to join the four men. Masseter put away something small and glittering that he had been worrying against the scars in his palm, tucking it into his watch pocket. Then he took the box of little cigars from inside his vest, opened it, and held one up in an offering. Jessamy nodded and waited while the peddler notched the end with his knife. Tesserian lit a match for her, and the five of them sat smoking in silence for a few minutes. Then the gambler reached out again and took the cigar nimbly from Jessamy's gloved fingers as she crumpled, dropping her head into her hands on the tabletop, and began quietly to sob.

Her companions passed a silent conversation around between them. Amalgam, sitting to her left, put a hand tentatively on her shoulder. "I apologize."

Jessamy shook her head, hiccuped, and managed, "Not your fault."

She composed herself, and Tesserian passed her cigar back.

"May I ask what instrument you played?" Masseter asked, rubbing the scar in his palm with the thumb of his other hand.

"I can play them all," Jessamy said simply.

"Jack of all trades, master of none?" Sangwin guessed.

She looked at him for a moment. "Master of all of them, too, Mr. Sangwin. But it takes more than mastery. More than gifts." She drew on the cigar, exhaled. "I don't know what it takes, but on that night at least, the night when it mattered, I didn't have it."

Masseter tapped the ash from the smoldering end of his own cigar. His eyes rested on Jessamy's bloodstained pink gloves. "Do you know how long?"

"How long I have?" She lifted the hand that held the cigar and looked at the rust-colored marks on her palm. "No."

"If it were your last night . . ." Sangwin began thoughtfully.

"I begin every day with a similar thought," Jessamy interrupted coldly. "Respectfully, Mr. Sangwin, but forgive me if just once I waste an hour like everyone else."

The printmaker nodded. "Fair enough."

"Thank you." She took another pull on her cigar, then pushed herself to standing. "And thank you for this, Mr. Masseter," she added, setting the half-smoked cigar in the ashtray at the center of the table. "Good night, gentlemen."

"Pleasure," Masseter said as she left the room.

"I don't imagine she'll tell us," Tesserian said quietly as the cigar smoke swirled in Jessamy Butcher's wake, "but I'd wager it's a hell of a tale." Phineas Amalgam gave a mirthless chuckle. Tesserian shot him a glare. "Pun not intended."

Sangwin cleared his throat. "Speaking of tales . . . Masseter —"

The peddler waved his cigar. "Don't give it a second thought."

"Good of you." Sangwin frowned. "Thing is," he went on, troubled, "I really don't recall mentioning that tale to the young lady, Petra. I can't imagine I would have been so . . . so tactless."

Amalgam tapped ash into the dish. "Odd, isn't it?"

Masseter said nothing. He blew a series of smoke rings and watched them stretch, distort, and dissipate, looking for patterns.

Jessamy grabbed one of the blankets from where she'd abandoned them on the chair and fled up the stairs. She passed Petra coming down from her room, where from the window she had been watching the two figures under the iron arch in the road and wondering who would return and who would not. Wordlessly, without slowing their steps at all, each woman reached out and grasped the other's hand, a quick exchange of pressure. Each stood just a hair taller as she moved on.

When at last both Sullivan and Captain Frost climbed the stairs to the porch, Petra opened the door. She handed the larger of the blankets to the captain with one hand and reached up to take off his tarpaulin hat with the other. "The stories are finished for the night, I think," she said, hanging the hat on a peg by the door to dry. "But I saw Phin and the travelers in the bar, and

Masseter always seems to have a spare in that cigar box of his. I turned your glass at a quarter to ten, Captain. You have time."

"Thank you," Frost said. He wrapped the blanket about his shoulders. "I'll just see my way to some dry clothes first." He stomped down the hall and up the stairs, leaving Petra and the sopping Sullivan facing each other.

"You're a bit of a puppeteer, aren't you?" he observed.

She looked over her shoulder, toward the sounds of laughing from the dancers in the parlor and the scent of smoke from the men in the bar. "When circumstances require."

"And have you accomplished whatever it is you were after?"

"Not yet." But the words weren't meant for him, and she spoke so quietly that Sullivan almost didn't catch them.

Then Petra turned back toward him and hung the blanket she held on the peg beside the captain's hat. She reached up, and Sullivan tilted his face down nearer to hers. Neither of them blinked, or breathed, or looked away as she ran her fingers through the hair still streaming water down his neck, gathering it behind his head and wringing the rain gently from it. Then she took the blanket down from the peg and tucked it around his shoulders.

"Good night," Petra said.

Stay, he wanted to whisper. But with effort he managed, "Good night," instead.

She let go and backed away, and then she was gone. He counted to fifty in three different languages before he followed, just to be sure she would be safely locked away in her own room before he reached the hall they shared.

In the parlor, Maisie yawned for the third time and stumbled over her feet. Sorcha stepped out of her own dance and caught the girl before she could step on the card castle. "Come along, miss. Let's get you up to bed."

"Wait." Maisie pulled out of Sorcha's grip and crouched by the structure. She adjusted a single card, then allowed herself to be shooed out into the hall with Sorcha on her heels.

"Thank you for the dance," Negret called.

"Welcome," Sorcha's laughing voice shouted back from the hallway.

Reever put the teapot music box away, then helped Madame Grisaille, who had taken one of the chairs by the half-hour glass, to her feet. "I take it we stand with the woman, if it comes to that?"

"If it comes to it," Madame said. "If one of them would save the city and one of them would watch it drown, yes."

The brothers nodded. No more needed to be said. Reever and Madame Grisaille started for the door, but Negret held back. Before he left the room, he banked the fire, doing his best to copy the firekeeping ritual he'd seen Sorcha do over and over since his arrival at the Blue Vein, even singing the words she'd set to the song she'd borrowed from him.

On his way up to his room, after a moment's listening to be sure he was alone, Negret paused to examine the contents of the bottom shelf of the bookcase where the stairs turned. Then he stretched up on tiptoe and shifted the books on the top shelf, looking at each book and then peering into the space behind it. Finally, not finding what he wanted, he stretched his body another six inches taller so that he could reach one hand into the space between the top of the bookcase and the ceiling. He felt around with his left hand, then reached into the farthest corner with his right. Then he stepped back, empty-handed, and brushed dust and cobwebs from his many-pocketed tweed vest.

"Good grief," Reever muttered, appearing on the stairs above and trotting down to join his brother. "You're a giant."

Negret snorted as he relaxed back down to the twins' usual, just-shy-of-six-feet height. "They're all asleep. There's no one to see."

"They're never *all* asleep."

"No," Negret conceded. "That's very true."

The two of them stood for a moment, listening.

"Let it go," Reever said quietly. "This isn't why we're here." He tilted his head upward, toward the second floor. Negret nodded reluctantly, rubbed the last shadow of dust from his palms, and took the stairs two at a time, following his brother to their rooms.

A draft swirled through the parlor as the case clock on the mantelpiece chimed ten times. Captain Frost's half-hour glass continued to drain in a fine thread of sand. Not a card in the castle so much as stirred, not even when, much later that night, Antony Masseter, on one of his witching-hour perambulations, wandered in, effortlessly picked the lock of the display cabinet, and began winding music boxes one by one.

TEN

THE BLUE STAIR

WHEN THE SUN CAME UP, the rain had not stopped and the waters were still rising. The day that dawned was indistinguishable from the night before in all ways except for the difference in illumination and the height of the water.

Of course, some of the guests were not quite the same as they had been the day before, but those kinds of things are often harder to see in the light of morning, before the coffee has been brought.

From the front door, Petra could see the pebbly mud of the road washing in a brown slick down to the place where it met the vanguard edge of the flood tide creeping upward by agonizing degrees. Between the darkness of the sky and the rough gray curtain of the rain and the still-darker shadows of the blue pines that overhung everything, it felt more like twilight than morning. The threshold where runoff met flood was nothing but a vague and shifting line of frothy mire, but it was now well past the iron arch that had not been there the morning before. The road was going to the river, and the river was coming to the inn.

Gray morning became gray midday, and under occassionally flickering lights and the unpredicatable knocking and sizzling of the reluctant heating coils in their wall cases, the guests haunted the inn like uncertain ghosts. The exceptions were the Haypottens and Sorcha, who had an establishment to run and twelve guests to care for, and Maisie, for whom the Blue Vein and its denizens seemed newly painted in mystery after the previous night's stories. The innkeepers inventoried food and drink and planned meals and strung lines beside the two kitchen fireplaces and the potbellied stove in order to dry freshly washed linens that couldn't be hung outside. Maisie crept about the inn, looking for secrets and clues to secrets. And, frequently, finding them.

Sorcha passed from room to room seeing to fires, the little wooden albatross hanging from her neck on its bit of ribbon. After lunch she found Maisie in the parlor, looking adrift; the younger girl had followed one set of clues to what appeared to be a dead end and, stymied, was trying to figure out where she'd gone wrong and where to look for the next one.

Although ordinarily Sorcha was too observant to make this sort of error, she mistook Maisie's temporary confusion for boredom. She plunked the girl down at the corner table where Jessamy had been the night before and ordered, "Stay." Then she hurried to the tiny writing desk in her own bedroom, where in the single drawer she kept a stock of fancy papers saved from parcels and colored envelopes and the endpapers of books she'd found in the attic that were too old and broken to be saved. Then, hands full of scraps of gold and silver and scarlet and marbled stuff, Sorcha returned to the parlor.

She passed Negret on the stairs. Both Sorcha's step and Negret's faltered for a heartbeat, as if, having danced the night before, their feet couldn't bear to pass by each other so quickly. He stopped and glanced, curious, at the bounty she carried.

"I thought I'd make some fancy spills with Miss Maisie," Sorcha explained. Then, remembering the book he'd been stitching together the day before, she picked a nice piece of heavy stock swirled with blue and green and gold and held it out. "For your next bookbinding, Mr. Negret. I believe it came from a book of poetry."

He took it with a brief bow of his head, as if the receiving of the scrap was a great honor. "Would you use it, if I made one for you?"

Sorcha smiled. "I could find a use for a book, yes."

A different pair of people might have hesitated then, before moving on, but Sorcha had Maisie waiting below, and Negret was not the sort of person to feel he had to capitalize on a chance meeting on the stairs for anything if he thought there might be a better time for it later. So he nodded and murmured, "Thank you," and tucked the marbled paper carefully into his vest as he continued on up to the second floor. Sorcha continued on down, humming as she went.

In the parlor, she deposited the rest of the paper in front of

Maisie, who was waiting obediently but impatiently with her head lying sideways on the tabletop. Sorcha took a box from her apron pocket, and from that produced a pair of scissors she usually used for trimming wicks. Then she picked out a piece of gold paper, tore it into three strips, and cut a fringe into the long edge of one before rolling the paper tightly and at a slight angle into a long, narrow tube so that the frill spiraled elegantly up the outside.

"Now, watch," Sorcha said with a wink, and she took the tall, fringed tube over to the hearth and reached the end into the fire.

The spill caught, and the flame flickered slowly up to consume the rolled paper, with the gold fringe giving off greenish sparkles as it burned. Sorcha used it to light a candle on the table, then tossed the unburned remnant into the hearth, where the fire finished it off with a bursting pop and a little sizzle of jade sparks.

The two girls laughed, then got to work twisting more scraps into matches as the candle flickered on the table before them. Maisie cut and rolled her pieces into the spiraling fringe Sorcha had taught her, and Sorcha herself crafted ever more complicated spills from the pile of scraps and the occasional dab of melted wax. The first ones resembled long-stemmed flowers, then slender and branching trees. And then, twisting four or six or ten smaller pieces together, Sorcha produced a cavalcade of gaunt, long-legged, long-necked, or long-horned paper creatures. Since these wouldn't have fit in the spill vase on the mantel anyway, the girls lined them up on the hearth, and when the final twiggy, silver-paper hart stood under the last marbled green-and-white tree, Sorcha held out one of Maisie's fringed matches. Maisie reached past the menagerie to light it in the fire, then, at a nod from the older girl, began to set the parade aflame, one creature at a time.

The paper animals danced as they burned, as if the fire had endowed them with a literal spark of life, and Maisie watched in awe. So even fire had secrets. Who could have known?

Gray midday became gray twilight, and when dinner had been served, the guests found themselves once again gathering around the hearth while the storm rattled the old window-panes and the fire smoked as it worked on the damp logs. The dry wood had run low, and even Sorcha's careful firekeeping couldn't do anything about that—not if she wanted a normal blaze, anyhow.

Maisie dropped onto the floor next to Tesserian, emptied her pockets of the collection of wooden animals she'd brought down from her room, and began secreting them around the card castle so that they peeked out of windows or perched on balconies. This elicited a wince of concern from Mrs. Haypotten, who set a glass of juice at Maisie's knee just as the girl balanced the river otter on a tiny ledge that didn't look as though it could have possibly supported so much as a feather. But Tesserian merely grinned, scooped up the remaining beasts, and began passing them to Maisie one by one. When they were all in place, the two architects began building an addition on the castle, using a different set of cards printed with the likenesses of saints.

Madame Grisaille sat in her usual rocking chair to the left of the fireplace, swathed in her wraps, watching the construction with her hands tucked in her white fur muff. Amalgam, Sangwin, and Masseter sat in chairs drawn around the corner table to the right of the fire, where Jessamy had been the night before. From his waistcoat pocket, Sangwin took a piece of wood Sorcha had passed him earlier in the day, and he began to cut small, neat curls away from it. Periodically one or the other of the men shot curious looks at Petra, who had chosen a spot on the sofa again.

Sullivan entered and, discovering that she had not curled herself against the very farthest edge of the couch today but instead sat a bit closer to the center, decided to follow her cue and do the same. Jessamy swept through the room and took a seat on the hearth behind the two card architects. When Sorcha entered with another split log, Jessamy made a point of waving so that the maid would see she had switched her stained gloves for one of the pairs from the attic.

"They fit?"

"Perfectly. Thank you. I'll return the other two pairs."

Sorcha beamed. "Welcome, miss. But keep the others. I asked Mrs. Haypotten, and she agrees you ought to have some spares. Be sure to bring me your old ones, and I'll do my best with the stains."

Negret Colophon strolled in, looked around, and, since none of the three chairs by the fire had been taken, chose the one closest to the side of the room overlooking the Skidwrack, which had a small table between it and the chair to its right. From his pockets he took a small assortment of newly scavenged paper, including Sorcha's marbled endpaper. He set them out on the little tabletop, along with his sharp, round-handled awl. Mr. Haypotten gave him a wary look as he rolled in the beverage cart; punching holes in paper on the bar in the lounge was one thing, but his wife would take a dim view of any holes left in her parlor furniture. Having set out the paper and awl, however, Negret showed no inclination to do anything more with them. He stood again and went to pour himself a glass from one of the bottles on the sideboard.

Reever had followed his brother into the room, but before choosing a seat for himself, he paused to reach down and lift one of Jessamy's hands. She flinched but allowed him to examine the embroidery that covered the backs of the new gloves. "Interesting pattern. Reminds me of wrought iron," he said. "Beautiful." He stroked his thumb across her knuckles just before he let go. Then he dropped into the chair nearest Madame Grisaille in her corner.

Captain Frost with his half-hour glass was the last guest to join them as he returned from his habitual weather check, followed closely by Mrs. Haypotten with a glass plate full of biscuits in her hands.

The captain cleared his throat as the Haypottens and Sorcha moved around the room with drinks and edibles. "I caused rather an abrupt end to the telling last night," Frost said, carefully not looking at Sullivan as he set his glass on the table between the chairs by the display case. "To make up for it, I'd be glad to tell the first tale this evening."

"Any peddlers, tricksters, gamblers, or lovers?" Masseter asked lightly.

The captain considered. "No, but there is an uncanny sea," he said, looking out at the river. On this side of the inn, which was higher than the roadway out front, the water had risen only — but exactly — to the level of the blue stair. "I thought it might be appropriate."

ELEVEN

THE STORM BOTTLE

The Captain's Tale

THE TROUBLES BEGAN, as they almost always do at sea, with an omen. There is always an omen. The difficulty is spotting it and determining its meaning in time to anticipate whatever it is it happens to be foretelling.

The children of the captain of the schooner called the *Fate* often argued over omens. It seemed to the captain's young daughter, Melusine, that her still-younger brother, Lowe, had a very solid instinct for spotting them, but that he tended to get exactly wrong whether they were good or bad. Some of this might've been because Lowe and Melusine had different mothers and had been raised with different tales and traditions, and moreover Lowe hadn't been at sea for quite so long as Lucy had. Still, *everyone* knows that corposants coming down a mast are bad luck. Everyone except for Lowe, who staunchly insisted that it was when they moved *up* the mast that you were in for it. And he couldn't keep straight when you ought to whistle and when you shouldn't under any circumstances so much as *think* of it. Whistling might be permissible if, for instance, you needed a wind and had already stuck a knife in the mast and the sailing master was safely out of earshot, but you ought never to whistle at almost any other time aboard ship, ever, or that same sailing master would find some particularly unpleasant and probably smelly bit of busywork to occupy the rest of your natural life.

Then came the matter of Lowe and the storm bottle, and this time, for once, they were in complete agreement. Breaking the storm bottle was bad luck for certain, if for no other reason than it had belonged to the captain's steward and he would be furious, and he had the power to make certain Melusine and Lowe ate nothing but stewed millers for a month if that was the punishment he deemed fair. And if stew sounds nice enough, it might change your mind to know that *millers* is the polite way of referring to rats if you have to eat them, which is not an unheard-of thing aboard a ship after months at sea, or as proper punishment for a particularly grievous offense.

The steward, Garvett, had bought his storm bottle from a glassblower in Venice. It was a narrow vessel full of liquid and some pale fluffy stuff that got cloudy or snowy or formed crystals, apparently according to what weather was coming. He had taken a bit of ribbing from the rest of the crew, who had scoffed at the idea that any sailor worth his salt needed a flask of milky water to tell him what he ought to be able to deduce from the sky and the sea and the plenitude of other signs the Good Lord had given him for interpreting the world. But then one day the storm bottle predicted snow on a perfectly mild and pleasant day in latitudes where snow had no business falling. Everyone laughed, until the sky began to cloud over. The steward sat, smug and vindicated, as the snow began to come down from on high. After that, the bottle was treated with more respect — until Lowe broke it.

Lowe thought the stuff in the bottle was camphor, which was a substance he knew well, since Lowe had a passion for fireworks, and some fireworks call for it as an ingredient. And while no one else particularly cared how the bottle worked so long as it did, Lowe became obsessed with figuring out whether he was right, and if he was, how camphor could not only make fireworks more brilliant but also foretell a storm. The steward, who had the good sense to be wary of seven-year-olds toying with treasured glass objects, took to hiding the storm bottle. But you couldn't conceal things from Lowe for long. He was observant and curious, and he was small and light enough to climb anywhere. Nothing was safe. But the steward kept trying, finding new places to hide the bottle, only for Lowe to locate it anyway and then be caught because he could never quite get around to putting the bottle back before the steward returned from wherever he'd gone. This went on and on.

And then came the day the *Fate* put in for a brief stop at Valletta, which is a port town on the island of Malta. That very morning, Lowe came sprinting into Melusine's little cabin as she was preparing to go ashore, a look of panic on his face and two bits of broken glass in his hands. "What do we do?" he whispered.

Melusine gasped. "You didn't."

Lowe brightened. "I know what was in it now, at least. I was right. There was water and alcohol and camphor. I could make him another one."

Melusine looked down at the remnants of the beautiful Venetian glass bottle. "He'll know, Lowe."

"I'll make him a better one," Lowe insisted. "You find a bottle. I'll get what goes in it."

He dropped the broken glass on Melusine's tiny table and darted out again, leaving her to wonder how he'd managed so quickly and efficiently to make her an accessory to his crimes in addition to ruining her chances for going into Valletta that morning.

If they had anything going for them, it was that they had some time. A third of the hands had already gone ashore, and Melusine had seen the steward and the cook row away from the *Fate* with the purser. They had to replenish the ship's stores, and they wouldn't be back for hours. The surgeon had left with them too, which was convenient because Melusine thought he might have a bottle among his medicines that would do, even if it wouldn't be as pretty as the broken one.

She found a suitable flask and emptied it, glancing briefly at the label and hoping *paregoric* wasn't anything particularly important. Then she hurried back to her own cabin, nodding at the hands who tapped their foreheads in salute as she passed and trying to come up with a likely answer to give to the shipmate who would inevitably notice that she'd just come out of the surgeon's quarters and want to know was she feeling all right. Miraculously, however, no one stopped her.

In her cabin, she found Lowe waiting with two mugs sitting before him on her table. "There's a problem," he said. "We have no camphor, on account of I made that nice bunch of exploding stars, and that was about the same time Cook wanted camphor when he was practicing that lovely dessert he learned from that ship's cook from Goa, and then the surgeon took the last bit to make up some of that pear-gory stuff he uses when someone's belly goes off. We shall have to improvise." He took a jar from one pocket, handling it with unusual reverence. "Hard snow," he said.

"Hard snow?" Melusine repeated warily. "Is there such a thing? Is it to do with fireworks?"

"There is, but no, not for fireworks. And I haven't made it exactly in the proper way—really it's not the sort of thing you can just whip up in the powder magazine, but we don't have time to refine the stuff. Still, it has a bit of mercury in it, which is also in the ship's barometer, and the barometer does nearly the same thing as the storm bottle did. And it sounds like how the camphor crystals looked, so I thought it might do."

He took the surgeon's bottle and poured in the contents of the two mugs, which turned out to be water and rum, and then tipped in a spoonful of the stuff called hard snow, which was syrupy and vaguely metallic. He corked the surgeon's bottle, and Melusine helped him seal it with wax. At last they sat back and considered their handiwork. It didn't look like much: just a round, wide-mouthed medicine vial — nothing at all like the narrow and graceful Venetian storm bottle — with a lump of thickish stuff at the bottom and watery grog filling the rest of the bottle up to the top.

They stared at it for a moment. Nothing happened, of course. They kept watching. "How will we know if it works?" Lowe asked, twisting the end of his braided pigtail.

Melusine, who couldn't imagine how it possibly could, shrugged. "This is your commission, Lowe. I haven't got the foggiest idea." And then something stopped her cold.

The thickish stuff in the bottle was moving. And not settling down to the bottom the way, say, stray tea leaves or grounds of coffee might do. No, it was hard to see — it was happening slowly — but Lowe's hard snow was *climbing up the walls of the bottle.*

"What does that mean?" Melusine and Lowe asked each other at the same time, both jabbing index fingers at the bottle.

And then the wooden world around them rocked under their feet. It was a small motion, but the *Fate* had been Melusine's home for most of her life, and there was no shift, no change, no matter how small, that the ship could've made that she wouldn't have felt. She grabbed Lowe's hand and, with her brother in tow, ran for the companionway ladder that led up to the weather deck.

The world beyond the *Fate* had changed. Valletta Harbour

was gone, replaced by a shocking sight: a wide expanse of deep red sea.

"I've heard of waters like this," Melusine whispered. "I've heard sailors talk about them, but I've never seen one."

"Look." Lowe tugged her arm, and Melusine turned to follow his pointing finger across the expanse where, if Valletta had been where it ought to have been, the Mediterranean Sea would've met the Ionian. But Lowe was pointing not at whatever sea was there, but at what was creeping out across it toward them: a thick white fog, borne on a cold wind that told Melusine they were no longer anywhere near Malta. Lowe whispered, "I can hear it; can't you?" Melusine cocked her head into the silence and listened, and yes, she could hear it—or she could hear *something,* just barely, in the sea smoke: a rustling, clinking, almost like ice when it fell from the rigging. As if concealed within the fog were bits of solid matter that clinked and clattered quietly as the mass rolled across the red waters toward them.

This is when Melusine realized that, under normal circumstances, she should never have been able to hear anything so quiet, not at that distance. She could hear it only because the ship was silent. No voices, no footfalls, no whistles or bells. As far as Melusine knew, the *Fate* had not been empty of sailors since the day she'd been launched, and probably not even before that. There would never, not ever, be less than a skeleton crew aboard, and in any case, she could think of no circumstances under which their father, the captain, would have left the ship without passing word to her and Lowe. But Melusine knew, abruptly and certainly, that despite the impossibility, despite the fact that mere minutes before, there had been at least seventy-odd sailors aboard, somehow she and Lowe were now alone on the ship.

"What's happening?" she whispered, fighting down terror. The silent ship was more than she could process. Nothing else —not the disappearance of Valletta Harbour, nor the nightmar-ish color of the sea, nor the strange creaking and tinkling sea smoke—was as frightening as the sudden emptiness of the *Fate*.

Lowe lifted his storm bottle in both hands. Inside, the oily, metallic hard snow was weaving impossible, branching patterns like frost on a window as it climbed the sides of the glass. "I don't know," he whispered back. "I don't know what the bottle means to say."

"It's saying something, that's certain." Fear would get them nowhere, so Melusine folded hers up and mentally shoved it in a pocket. The cold sea smoke rolled closer. Lowe shuddered. "Go and get yourself a jacket," Melusine said. "And get Papa's glass from his desk."

Lowe nodded once and darted away. While she waited for him to return, Melusine walked the length of the vacant ship and back to the low rise at the stern that passed for a quarterdeck, and as she did, the mist reached the *Fate* and wrapped every-thing above the red sea in cold, pale gray. Somewhere out there, the crystalline tinkling was coming closer, too, but not quite at the same rate as the fog. Melusine leaned over the starboard rail and stared out, looking for . . . well, she wasn't sure what. For something. Anything.

Her brother came scrambling awkwardly up the ladder, with their father's spyglass under one arm and the homemade storm bottle still clutched in his fist. He had forgotten the jacket. "Papa's not there," he said softly. "Where have they all gone?"

Melusine said nothing. Her eyes had picked out a smudge of rose in the fog, something riding above the water and reflecting its scarlet color. She held out a hand, and Lowe put the glass into her palm. She stared through it, following the sound and searching—and *there.* There it was, and it was a ship. A xebec, she thought. In that case, perhaps they were still somewhere in the Mediterranean. Its hull was red, but everything else, from the gunwales to the tops of the masts, was shadow and shroud. And it carried no lights that Melusine could see, despite the thickness of the fog. She passed the glass to Lowe and pointed.

"A ship?"

"A xebec." Now she could see it without the glass, with its unusual forward-sloping mast and the strange angle of its bowsprit. And she could hear that the tinkling noise was definitely approaching with the xebec, as if the other ship was parting not water, but shards of ice. And yet she still could see no lights, and she could hear no voices.

She glanced down at Lowe's storm bottle, which he'd passed her when he'd taken the spyglass. The hard snow lay all over the inside of the glass in patterns like sharp-horned, haloed moons. Wind and rain, the sailors would say to that, if they'd been there. But what would they say about the strange ship? Melusine didn't really have to wonder. She knew.

Phantom. Ghost ship.

It came closer, and Lowe took the spyglass from his eye. "There's no one on her deck or in her rigging," he whispered. "She's empty as the *Fate* is."

Emptier, Melusine thought. *Because at least the* Fate *has Lowe and me.*

Her brother fiddled with the end of his pigtail. "Will she ram us?"

"Not unless the wind shifts quite a bit. Not that there's much we could do if it did."

"And perhaps she can't, anyhow," Lowe said.

"Perhaps."

They watched the ghostly ship approach, making as if to cross the stern. And then, just as it drew level with the *Fate,* the xebec drifted to a halt. The cold wind that had brought both it and the sea smoke toward them kept on blowing, but the sails of the xebec hung slack, as if the wind had suddenly discovered how to slide right through the canvas.

As Melusine was trying to work out how any of this was possible, Lowe tugged at her arm again. "Remember you told me once that a ship was meant to have a coin under the mast, so as to be able to pay a pilot if it had to cross a river to enter the courts of the dead?"

"A ferryman to cross the river Styx, yes."

"Well, what if they haven't got one?"

Lowe, in his practical little-boy fashion, had somehow moved past the question of whether it *was* a ghost ship to what they were supposed to do about it now that it was there, drifting just beyond the *Fate*'s stern. Melusine passed Lowe the storm bottle and took back the spyglass. Somehow looking through it didn't make the ship appear any larger.

"Well, I don't know the route to . . . what did you call it? The courts of the dead? I don't know what we can do about it."

"If you didn't have a pilot who knows the channel — a ferry-man, if that's the word —" He looked across the red water at the lightless ship. "You'd need a lamp, at least. To try to see where you were going."

They glanced at each other. Lowe held the storm bottle up between them. It was glimmering faintly now from within with violet light, the glow slipping out through the gaps in the pattern that had climbed the glass the way candlelight slips out the holes in a punched-tin lantern.

"How would you do it?" Melusine asked, and then, before Lowe could reply, she added, "Because you're not boarding her. Not for all the world."

Lowe shook his head. "I have an idea." And he disappeared down the companionway ladder again. When he came back this time, he had a folding stand under his arm and a firework in one hand. A small rocket, one of the many he made himself and was emphatically not allowed to shoot from the ship any longer.

But those were rules for worlds without red waters and tinkling-crystal sea smoke and ghost ships. "Carry on, then," Melusine said helplessly.

Lowe lashed the glowing storm bottle to his rocket and set

the rocket in the stand. He took a cylinder of homemade matches from his pocket, lit one, and whipped it across the fuse. The spark climbed the cotton line, and a moment later, the rocket burst from the deck of the *Fate* and shot skyward.

It sailed up and arced over the other ship's sloping foremast, and then, like a fly caught mid-flight in a spider's web, it stopped as if trapped at the top of the mainsail. It hovered there for a moment, and then it began to descend: a violet glow moving slowly down the vertical length of the mast. And as the plum-colored light from Lowe's storm bottle spilled out across the deck, Melusine saw them. She saw the shadows first, and then the men they belonged to: scores of sailors, on the deck and in the rigging, all of them ghostly, and all of them looking across at Melusine and Lowe.

Some bad omens—like, for instance, a whole crew of the dead—weren't hard to spot. Ordinarily Melusine would've reached out instinctively to scratch the nearest bit of rigging, but there was nothing right in reach, so without thinking, she hawked up a mouthful to spit for luck. But before she could do it, Lowe whacked her arm urgently. "Ghosts are afraid of human saliva," he whispered.

She swallowed. "What on earth are you talking about?"

"Everybody knows that," Lowe hissed. Melusine stared. "Or maybe that's just back home—back in my mother's homeland, I mean. But just in case, be polite."

"I don't want to be polite." But just in case he was

right — after all, dead or not, they had a full crew and Melusine didn't — she raised one hand in a shaky salute.

One by one, the ghostly crew returned the gesture.

"See?" Lowe said, pleased. "And I told you lights coming down the mast were good."

But the ship didn't move.

"Why aren't they going?" Melusine asked after a moment. "They have their light."

Lowe scratched his head. "Maybe I was wrong. Maybe they still need a pilot." He looked meaningfully from Melusine to the *Fate*'s tiller. "We could lead them."

"But *I* can't do it," Melusine sputtered. "I don't know where to go! I can't steer a ship this size! And anyhow, we have no crew!" But even as she said it, she heard her own thoughts from earlier playing again in her mind: Those were rules for worlds without red seas and tinkling-crystal sea smoke and ghost ships, and to be fair, in this place and at this moment, with only two children aboard, even their own schooner might be considered a ghost ship.

Lowe shrugged. "If they've been lost at sea for long, perhaps any harbor will do. What is the saying about harbors and weather?"

"Any port in a storm." Melusine looked across at the phantom crew, then back at Lowe. "I'll try."

She took the tiller in both hands, and to her surprise and endless relief, it felt real. Nothing else in this place, in this moment, was as it should be, but the vibration coming through the tiller, the hum of the *Fate* itself, felt right. Melusine and the ship that had been her companion for her entire life could still speak to each other — even, apparently, at the boundary between the lands of the living and the dead.

She hauled on the tiller, and miraculously, the *Fate* answered Melusine's request, and even without crew to work the sails, she came about and turned her bows toward Valletta, or at least toward the thick bank of sea smoke where, in the other world, Valletta Harbour had been. They sank into the fog.

"Is she with us?" Melusine asked, meaning the xebec. "There's not much light for them to see us by."

Lowe, standing at his sister's side but looking back over their shoulders, nodded. "I think so."

Melusine never knew how far they sailed, or how long it took. There seemed to be no time and no distance on that foggy red sea. But the xebec, with its glowing violet light, stayed with them the whole way, and the two ships sailed in company for what seemed like hours.

At long last, something changed. It took Melusine a while to figure out what that something was, but at last she realized it was the color of the water. The sea had gone from red to purple, and now it was darkening to a much more ordinary indigo. Something about the sea smoke had changed as well. The breeze was warmer, and it had a familiar tang to it, a scent Melusine's senses instantly identified as one of the base notes of the odor of any harbor anywhere. Up ahead there were shadows in the murk: the hills, spires, and masts of Valletta Harbour.

"Oh, thank heavens." Melusine sighed.

Lowe said, "Look." She turned and followed his pointing finger. The fog was melting away, and with it, the violet glow of the storm bottle in the rigging of the ship behind them was fading too. It dwindled as the final remnants of the cold wind carried the xebec into the harbor. The phantom crew saluted again as they drew abreast of the *Fate*. Melusine and Lowe stumble-ran forward the entire length of their ship as the xebec sailed on past to vanish into the much more ordinary mist that drifted across the waterfront.

They ran as far forward into the bows as they could, leaning over the gunwales to catch a last glimpse of the red-hulled ghost ship as it swirled into nothingness, a last glimpse of the storm bottle before it vanished. Then they looked at each other as they became aware of sounds on the deck behind them, rising out of the silence: the shouts of sailors and the slapping of bare feet on the floorboards, the flap of sails, and all the ordinary sounds of a ship at anchor in a harbor.

The *Fate*'s crew, wherever it had gone — well over a hundred souls — had come back, and everyone was going about his task as if nothing strange had happened at all. "Or did *we* come back?" Melusine murmured, confused.

Lowe, whether thanks to his age or to his ancestry, was much more comfortable with the miraculous and not inclined to waste time discussing matters of the uncanny when there were more pressing things to worry about. "Melusine!" He pointed across the harbor, and from the tremor in his voice, his sister half expected to see the xebec or some other ghostly craft pulling toward them again.

But no, it was only the cutter returning with the cook, the purser, and . . . oh, dear . . . the steward.

"What do we do?" Lowe fretted. "I haven't time to find more hard snow now."

"We?" Melusine shook her head decisively. "Lowe, I'll follow you to a ghost ship and back, but as far as telling Garvett his storm bottle's gone, you're positively on your own."

CAPTAIN FROST HARRUMPHED, blushing a bit through the applause that followed his tale, then turned his half-hour glass and hurried out of the parlor. Masseter, thoughtful, made as if to follow him, then seemed to remember the captain would be going out into the rain, and instead went to refill his glass.

Jessamy got up from her spot on the hearth to make room for Mr. Haypotten to slide a covered silver toasting dish under the fireplace grate. It had a perforated lid, but Sorcha's well-kept fires always seemed to know better than to let any ash drop into the toasted cheese.

Tesserian helped Maisie complete a cupola with four cards: two from his deck of saints (a woman holding a flat scepter and draped in a deep red robe, and a bearded, tonsured man cupping a square-rigged ship in his left hand) and two from a more standard deck (the queen of seas and the knave of candles). "The captain mentioned the coin that pays the ferryman upon the river Styx," he said, neatening the stack of remaining cards from the several decks they were using. "I know a story about a ferryman right here on the river Skidwrack, if that would be of interest and if no one minds my telling it." He nodded up to the big map over the mantel.

"On the Skidwrack?" Sangwin said, setting down his knife and wood and brushing the castoff curls from his whittling into a little pile on the table before him. "And you not from Nagspeake at all. Where did you come across a Skidwrack tale?"

"An occasion much like this one," Tesserian said, "only it wasn't a flood that kept us from leaving; it was a cheater we all badly wanted to catch in the act." He grinned at Maisie. "Do you like riddles?"

"Yes," she retorted, in a tone that added, *Who doesn't?*

Frost returned. The windowpanes rattled. Tesserian leaned back against the hearth and murmured, *"Jacta alea est."* *The die is cast.*

Really, though, it was cast long before this particular story.

TWELVE

THE FERRYMAN

The Gambler's Tale

I'VE HEARD — perhaps Captain Frost will confirm this for us — that the same sea can seem to be a different place from one day to the next. And I am not from Nagspeake, as Mr. Sangwin has rightly pointed out, so you can all tell me if I've got this wrong, but I've heard that the Skidwrack, though it's a mere river, is just as changeable as the sea. I heard it from a friend who's a Nagspeaker born and bred, and I had no trouble believing him. For there are rivers in the middle country that are like that too: they change their shapes when the fancy strikes them; they take tribute from those who work on 'em, and they cling to their dead; their waters run blue here and green there and brown over there and red farther down around the bend. They say it's thanks to the mud, but I don't know about that. I think there's something miraculous about a river. Any river. Always have.

And there's something about the crossing of a river that's

miraculous too. They are their own lands — only the opposite, if you get me. And almost every waterway requires its own special crossing. Some you can cross by a variety of means; others have just one route from one bank to the other. Some rivers, you want to cross 'em, you've got to do it without going through. The Missouri's like that, in places. Try to cross through it on your own power, and you'll likely never surface again. Over's the only way. But even going *over* a river can mean different things. If you bridge moving water and cross from bank to bank, never touching the surface, do you arrive at the same place in the end as if you were to row? And what of the rivers where rowing's nearly as dangerous as trying to swim? What bank, what strange land, would you reach if you could reach the other side alive?

I've often thought a river can be something like the adit-gate in Mr. Amalgam's tale, though I'd never heard the term before. Surely it's like Mr. Sangwin's hollow-way, lying strangely on the land. You may think you know what's on the other side, but some percentage of the time, when you get there, you'll be wrong.

I've spent a lot of time on rivers. Mostly playing cards on steamboats, but occasionally for other reasons. And I've come to understand that there are places that can be reached only by crossing waterways. They don't exist on any maps, and they can be reached only by traversing in a particular way: by securing the services of a Ferryman. Not a small-*f* ferryman. A *Ferryman*, capital *F*. Some people call them *psychopomps*, but I met a Ferryman once who thought that word gave all the wrong ideas.

"The Susquehanna River doesn't become the Styx just

because you cross it in my keelboat," he told me, though he had to repeat himself before I understood what he was saying, for the man was always talking over the buzzing of the bees that had made a hive of the bobcat skull he used for a figurehead. "And not every far bank is heaven or hell or Fiddler's Green or whatever you want to call that sort of place. But I can take you to shores an ordinary pilot can't, and that's a fact."

So a Ferryman is not like the keeper of any old workaday passage boat, and some rivers are stranger than others. Which brings me to my tale: I heard a story only a fortnight ago about a Ferryman on the river Skidwrack.

According to my Nagspeaker friend, the one who told me the tale I'm about to tell you, the Skidwrack is unpredictable in many ways, but not generally vicious — the occasional flooding aside, and I don't think you can really blame *only* the river for that. There is, however, one place where the water brooks no passage. It's supposed to be a little ways downriver from an old abandoned floating mill, so it's often called the Tailrace. It doesn't look like much, just a rocky, misty stretch, but try to go from one side to the other and you'll get very wet, very fast, and possibly very dead in the same span of time.

And I suspect this might be a related fact: If you do manage to ford the Skidwrack at the Tailrace, you won't find Nagspeake on the other side.

Where would you wind up if you *did* cross there? My friend couldn't say. Perhaps in Fiddler's Green; perhaps in the States, perhaps in someplace stranger yet. Perhaps it's different for every passage. Except, of course, you can't pass there. Not on your own. But for those who, for whatever reason, simply must find a way, there is a Ferryman.

This particular Ferryman piloted—or perhaps still does pilot—a boat called the *Inferus,* and for a while he had a first mate. This is the story of how that partnership came to be.

The Ferryman had once been a man called Isaac Knickpointe, and although he had never precisely been an average, common-place fellow—roamers never are—he'd come to this particular occupation late in life, and at the time our story begins, he was still adjusting to it. He'd taken the contract because he had wanted to retire somewhere and mess around with boats all day.

I do not know how he came across the job vacancy, though, or how the post came to be available. I'd like to find out some-time. Anyhow.

We've heard some tales of tricksters. Knickpointe the Ferry-man was, I suppose, a trickster as well—but a very reluctant one. Again, he'd been hoping for a quiet retirement, and hadn't taken the job for the sake of skinning would-be crossers out of their last coins. Still, it is a rule that crossings of this sort must be paid for. And while all rules *can* be broken (many, it must be said, *should* be broken, and as often as possible), some can't be broken without consequences.

In Nagspeake in those days, there was a shortage of metal money. But people didn't stop needing to navigate into the miraculous just because they couldn't pay for it. In fact, the Ferryman observed, it was just the opposite. Nagspeake in those days needed miracles more than usual, and although crossing the Skidwrack at the Tailrace didn't necessarily promise a miracle, it put you on the road to a place where you could perhaps begin the search for one.

The Ferryman was duty-bound not to allow passage without payment, though he was often tempted to bend that rule. For a while he tried a system of trade tokens — coins he made himself from bits of bone and driftwood, whatever he could find. But he couldn't simply make the coins and hand them to would-be travelers for them to hand right back; the river wasn't to be fooled by such a transparent gambit. So the Ferryman began to make his own rules for how travelers could win the tokens from him.

He listened to every person who came without means to pay, weighed their circumstances, then asked them to solve a riddle. If they succeeded, the Ferryman would hand them a token on one bank, to be paid back to him on the other side. The riddle was different each time; he would vary the difficulty depending on the traveler's circumstances. In this way, Isaac Knickpointe became a trickster Ferryman.

One evening he was moored on the Nagspeake side of the river, enjoying a moment of quiet and a chapter of his book, when a greenish light appeared in a lantern on the far side, summoning him across to pick up a fare.

This was unusual. It wasn't unheard of for someone to cross into Nagspeake from the far side of the Tailrace, but it was relatively uncommon. The Ferryman cast off his boat, punted through the mist with a pole that reached long talons into the ground to grasp the rocky riverbed at each stroke, and found himself looking at a young boy. I think he would've been about your age, Miss Maisie. Certainly not much older.

"I need to cross, please!" the boy shouted as the Ferryman approached. He barely waited for the older man to tie the *Inferus* up to the dock before he crouched as if to leap down onto the deck.

The Ferryman caught the boy by the collar before he could jump and, stepping off the boat himself, hauled him back onto the pier. "Belay a minute, there." He deposited the child on a bench on the dock and stuck his hands in his pockets. "Have you got payment?"

The boy frowned. "How much does it cost?"

"How much do you have?"

The boy emptied his pockets and held out three cracked acorn caps. "I have three. Will three do?"

The Ferryman sighed. "I don't take payment in acorns, much as I might like to."

He considered the kid through eyes that had gotten very accustomed to evaluating potential passengers. Usually he could work out the entire story of a crossing in a matter of heart-beats: someone fleeing a dangerous spouse, a parent trying to find a child, someone seeking answers or changes they thought couldn't be found without venturing into the deep unknown. There were endless variations, but those were all mostly motives for people crossing in the *opposite* direction, and they all involved

some measure of desperation. Folks crossing into Nagspeake —
or *back* into it, for that matter — were rare, and although he had
said *I need to cross* rather than *I want to cross,* there wasn't so
much as a whiff of anxiety about this kid. Eagerness, yes. Fear,
worry, or despair, no.

"I will give you a token," the Ferryman said at last, still puz-
zled, "but you'll have to answer a question first."

"What kind of question?" the boy asked with an air of anticipation.

"A riddle," the Ferryman said, trying to think of a suitably
easy one to ask.

"Oh, all right." The boy brightened. "I like riddles."

"Good." And he meant it. The Ferryman was generally in
favor of helping people get where they wanted to go, and though
he couldn't quite work out the particulars here the way he usually could, Knickpointe had no interest in making this crossing
difficult. "There is a gent who came to me; he whistled tunes to
pay his fee. With him aboard, I used no pole. Who is he?"

The boy's face fell, and the Ferryman rapidly worked out a
clue he could give the child to help him figure out the answer.
But when the kid spoke again, he replied in a voice that was confident but a little sullen, "The wind."

"Correct," the Ferryman said, confused about the boy's dissatisfaction but trying to sound grand about it all nonetheless as
he reached into the vest pocket where he kept his small supply of
trade tokens.

"I know. I thought it would be harder, is all." Still

looking mildly disgruntled, the boy held out a hand to receive the Ferryman's token.

"You're upset that you got the answer right on the first try?" the Ferryman inquired as he opened the lantern and blew out the light.

"I'm not upset," the boy retorted. Then he made a frustrated noise. "Can I please have another one?"

"Another token?" the Ferryman asked, looking down at the circle in the child's hand. It was a nice one, cut from a piece of very old, licheny driftwood. "A different one? It doesn't much matter to me, but you're only going to give it back once we're across."

"Not a different *token*," the child said, exasperated. "A different *riddle*. A harder one."

The Ferryman looked at him. "You want a harder riddle?"

"You went easy on me," the boy accused. "It wasn't fair."

Under the circumstances, there didn't seem to be much point in lying about it. "I did it so I could give you a token," the Ferryman said, feeling like this was stating the obvious. "What part of that, exactly, do you object to?"

"I like riddles, and I want to do the crossing properly," the boy said. "That can't be the only one you know."

"All right," the Ferryman said. "Come aboard. I'll think of another as we go."

"All right!" The kid leaped aboard. "But don't make it too easy this time."

The Ferryman cast off his boat and took up his punting pole again. As he began to maneuver the *Inferus* into the Tailrace, he mentally ran through the riddles he knew. They fell into three general categories: simple ones, for when he wished he didn't have to worry about taking payment at all; hard ones, for when he didn't particularly want to make life easy for the traveler but didn't feel it was his job to deny passage outright; and finally, a handful of riddles without answers, which he kept for special occasions. These last he used most often when the passenger was another roamer. Roamers generally knew better than to try to cross without payment, and could rustle up a coin from somewhere if they really needed it. But if the Ferryman had to find a way to give a roamer one of his tokens, he felt entitled to offer a special challenge.

Within each category, the level of difficulty of the riddles varied. *A not-too-simple simple one, then,* he thought, and aloud he said, "Another gent I came athwart; he shook me down to pay his part. After that, the boat, it sank. Who was he?" It was the same sort of conundrum as the last, but Knickpointe had met plenty of adults who'd had trouble with it.

The boy groaned. "A shoal."

"Still not thorny enough?"

"Nooooo." It was as much whine as word.

"Fine," the Ferryman said, then mentally switched baskets, and dug for a medium-difficult riddle. "Silver thimble with a tongue, might fit on a giant's thumb."

At this, the boy actually stamped his foot. "A church bell. Why are you making this so easy?" he demanded, grabbing the side of the boat as it lurched sideways.

"Good grief. Fine." The Ferryman gave up trying to pull his punches. "I saw a jackdaw all in black, with silver eye and heavy pack."

"A thief escaping with his haul." The boy's face was pink with frustration.

"Silver yarn a-fraying, eleven threads a-playing."

His cheeks went redder still. "The Skidwrack in the moonlight!"

"I trust it in a sangaree but never underfoot."

"THAT'S ICE!" the boy howled, clenching his hands at his sides.

Knickpointe ground his teeth at the noise. "And where has all the church plate gone?"

The kid didn't answer for a beat, but only because he paused to get his vexation under control. "With the thief to the bottom of the channel, where the ice wouldn't hold," he answered bitterly.

The Ferryman rolled his eyes, kept punting, and went on throwing riddle after riddle at the boy, enduring the rising tantrum as his passenger answered every one correctly, until they reached the Nagspeake side of the Tailrace.

When they arrived, the Ferryman fended the *Inferus* off the dock and whipped a line around the iron cleat in a neat hitch to make the boat fast. Then he turned to consider his small passenger. "Did you not actually want to cross at all?" he asked quietly.

A tear slipped down the boy's cheek. "I did, but only for the riddles."

The Ferryman looked at him in disbelief. "You only wanted to cross because you knew I would ask you riddles?"

The child nodded. "Nobody else I know is any good at them. I thought you might have some I hadn't heard before."

"What about your three acorn caps?"

He shrugged. "I thought I should offer something."

The Ferryman pointed at the Nagspeake shore. "And what were you going to do when we got here?"

"Ask to go back, and answer more riddles for passage," the boy replied, as if this ought to be obvious. Then a thought appeared to occur to him. "Are you very angry?"

"Why should I be angry?" the Ferryman asked.

"I thought you might feel this was a waste of your time. I didn't think of that before," his small passenger admitted.

The Ferryman sighed. "What's your name?"

"Caster. Cas for short." He looked at the dock, and the shore beyond. "I suppose I have to get out here."

The Ferryman nodded. "But first, your token." He held out a hand, and Cas put the carved driftwood coin into it. Then the boy climbed out of the *Inferus* and onto the dock. He and the Ferryman looked at each other.

"Will you still take me back home?" Cas asked.

"My job is to cross the river."

"But are those all the riddles you had?" The boy's voice wavered with all the frustration and injustice that only a child who wants something and is being given everything *but* that thing can possibly feel.

The Ferryman held out a token for the return trip, this one carved from a cross-section of an old stained antler. "Those were about a third of the riddles I have."

Cas took the coin and climbed back down into the boat. "You have more? Are they as easy as the other ones?"

"Half of the remaining ones are too easy. The others ..." The Ferryman smiled as he cast the *Inferus* off again. "Only you can say. They are riddles without answers."

The boy's eyes opened wide. "Without answers? Then how does anyone answer them?"

"I couldn't possibly tell you." The Ferryman pushed the boat away from the pier with one booted foot. "That's the whole trick."

Cas sat on one of the boat's benches, practically vibrating with anticipation. "I'm ready."

"Here goes, then. Take your time: Whisper and say where you find extra moons anytime you want them."

Finally, gratifyingly, Cas hesitated, and his brow furrowed. He tilted his head, then tilted it the other way, then dropped his elbows to his knees and his chin into his palms. The Ferryman watched this out of the corner of his eye as he navigated the rocks and the rapids of the Tailrace. About halfway across, Cas lifted his head, a look of delight on his face. "My fingernails," he said, remembering to speak softly.

The Ferryman considered, then nodded once. "I believe you're right."

Cas laughed. Then he frowned. "But that means it does have an answer."

"It means you gave it one," the Ferryman said. "That's different. It has an answer *now*."

"Can I . . . can I have another?" Cas asked. "Not because that one wasn't hard. Because it was fun."

They were passing the halfway point of the Tailrace. The Ferryman nodded. "You may. But only one more. We can't go through all the answerless riddles I've got, or when we're done, I won't have any left."

Cas nodded. "All right. One more."

"Very well. I startled a cardinal off of his lectern. What did he say?"

The boy settled into his thoughtful posture again and stayed hunkered down until just before the Ferryman brought the *Inferus* up to the dock.

"I have it," Cas announced. And by way of answer, he whistled four notes.

The Ferryman took a moment to evaluate the response, worked out its meaning, and grinned. "Well done." He held out his palm for the token.

The boy handed it over and climbed out, radiating reluctance. "Thank you for the passage, Mr. Ferryman."

The Ferryman finished tying up the boat and offered his hand. "The name's Isaac Knickpointe. And you're welcome, Cas."

A flicker of violet-blue came to life on the dock they'd just left: someone summoning the *Inferus* from the Nagspeake side. The mist separated just enough to show the shape of a tall man standing on the pier. A flash of lantern light glinted off something shiny in the vicinity of his left eye, and Knickpointe recognized a passenger he'd carried before.

The Ferryman sighed and started undoing the cleat hitch he'd just tied. Then he had an idea.

"Cas, what are your thoughts on *telling* riddles?" he asked. "Fun or boring?"

The boy sat up a little straighter, interested. "I don't know. I never thought about it."

"Think about it."

Cas scratched his head. His eyebrows knitted themselves together. Then he said rapidly, as if it had come to him all in a rush, "Silver sky, silver sea, silver road between the trees. But if you should hear a crack, silver death amid the wrack . . . I know they don't have to rhyme," he added, "but it sounds nice."

"It does, you know." Knickpointe nodded, pleased. "That's good." He aimed a thumb over his shoulder at the light on the opposite bank. "Want to try it out?"

"Absolutely, I do." And Cas hopped eagerly back aboard.

Rather to his surprise, Cas discovered that telling riddles was almost as much fun as answering them. He began to turn up at the ferry dock regularly after that, and Knickpointe found himself looking forward to seeing the emerald light flaring to life on the Fiddler's Green side of the Tailrace. The boy, it turned out, had a knack for inventing new riddles to tell, although sometimes when he wanted to solve a puzzle or two himself, he would change things up and ask potential passengers to tell him one. Like Knickpointe, he developed a system: if the passenger was someone whose crossing they wanted to help along, Cas merely asked to be told a certain number of riddles. If it was someone who required more of a challenge, Cas would demand a hard riddle from the passenger. Very rarely — usually only with the approval of the Ferryman — he would demand to be stumped.

The boy turned out to be a trickster of the first magnitude, in fact, but after that, it was never quite as easy to cross as it had been, for Cas loved riddles too much to tell an intentionally easy one as frequently as the Ferryman himself had done.

One morning, when they'd been at this for a few weeks, Knickpointe surprised Cas at the wharf with a peaked hat the Ferryman had stitched with the words FIRST MATE, and he offered it to the boy with much gravity and pomp. Cas, of course, accepted, first with a yelp of delight and then with a much soberer "Yes, sir; thank you, sir." And the two of them piloted the Tailrace ferry together for many years after that, the younger crewmate handling the riddles while at last the Ferryman got to do what he'd always wanted to: spend his retirement messing with his boat.

INTERLUDE

"I RATHER FEAR we're going to need a Ferryman ourselves just to get out of here," Jessamy said, kneeling beside Petra on the sofa and leaning over the back of it to face the windows that looked out over the river. Petra scooted just a tiny bit closer to the center to give her more room. Sullivan pretended not to notice. Tesserian and Maisie used a saint wearing a short tunic and holding a long sword and another with a miter-shaped hat and a curling, crooked staff to finish a new balcony. When it was completed, Maisie moved a wooden tiger from a lower perch up to this higher vantage.

"No, indeed," Mr. Haypotten said, taking the toasting dish from the fire by its ivory handle. "Water won't rise past a blue stair, after all. The rain'll stop overnight; you see if it doesn't." Blissfully unaware of Captain Frost's rolling eyes, the innkeeper wrapped one hand in his handkerchief and, thus protected, opened the perforated lid of the covered dish. "Done to a turn," he announced, relieved that it wasn't remotely possible to tell that he'd had to resort to slightly stale bread and the last, mixed shavings of cheddar and rind to make the toasted cheese. They weren't going to run out of things to eat, but the fresh stuff was nearly gone.

As he served portions around, along with crackers and a plate of sliced, slightly winy apples, Sorcha spoke up from the hearth, where she was tending a second toasting dish. "May I tell one, sir?" she asked, directing the question at the innkeeper.

He looked up, surprised. "Well, of course, my dear," he answered, his reply nearly drowned out by the voices of his wife and a handful of the guests, all saying variations of the same thing.

"Will it be a tale with fires?" Negret asked, his smile a flicker of brightness, like the first stick of kindling to catch.

Sorcha's cheeks flared, but sitting on the hearth as she was, she knew her face was already red, so she met his eyes despite the flush. "Perhaps. I can certainly think of more than one."

"You were raised with firekeeping traditions, weren't you?" Petra asked.

Sorcha nodded. "With old ones from my mother's ancestors in Scotland, and newer ones born here, passed down through my father's family, who were Nagspeakers from all the way back. We were raised to know all the fires that burn, all the ways to conjure them and keep them, to learn from them and to live with them as neighbors."

"And fires can do so much more than people understand," Petra said dreamily, tucking her feet up under her on the sofa and leaning back, almost but not quite into the hollow of Sullivan's shoulder. (In his chair before the fire, Reever Colophon, who knew without having to ask that he and Sullivan were experiencing similar difficulties of the heart, saw this and stifled a sympathetic groan.) "More than lighting, more than warming, more than protecting . . ." She looked up at the ceiling as if trying hard to call something to mind. "What am I thinking of?"

"Some sort of fire magic?" Sorcha suggested with a lift of her eyebrow. "Pyromancy, perhaps? People do lump that in with firekeeping."

"Something like that," Petra admitted, laughing. "But not pyromancy. That's fortunetelling, isn't it? No, I mean the other thing. Fire-cunning, perhaps? A sort of . . ." She made an exasperated noise. "A sort of *reckoning*, isn't it called?"

The maid gave Petra a long, strange look. "Yes. Fire-kenning, my father called it, though I've heard fire-cunning as well. More properly it's *fierekenia:* fire-reckoning." She paused, curious. "People do know of pyromancy and other sorts of divination, but there aren't many who I've ever heard talk of reckonings, by fire or otherwise."

"What's a reckoning?" Maisie asked, shuffling through the unused saints for any shown with fire and setting those aside.

Sorcha, still curious, nodded deferentially at Petra. "Oh, I couldn't possibly define it," Petra protested. "It's just a thing I ran across somewhere. Probably heard a story." She, in turn, looked to Phineas Amalgam. "Aren't there stories about reckonings, Mr. Amalgam?"

"Certainly," Amalgam said, wondering, as he had the night before, what the young woman was up to with her little manipulations. "Sorcha, am I right in saying a reckoning is basically a calculation?"

Sorcha nodded. "But more than that. A reckoning is a calculation of the impossible. Not divination, which is either a foretelling or the finding of an answer that cannot otherwise be brought to light, but a true working out of deeply complicated factors to arrive at . . . well, any number of things. Truth, sometimes; but more often potential truth, for there's often more than one kind."

She frowned, trying to work out how best to explain, and as she considered, one of her hands, apparently of its own volition and without Sorcha even particularly noticing, reached into the glowing cinders at the edge of the fire. Her fingers trailed through the embers the way a person might trail fingers through the fur of a sleeping cat, and apparently without a shred of pain. But her hand was blocked from the sight of most everyone in the room by the castle of cards that towered before the hearth, and only three people saw. Mrs. Haypotten, who had come to the hearth to take Sorcha's place tending the toasted cheese, clucked her tongue quietly, but she had seen plenty of stranger things where the maid and fire were concerned and knew she needn't really worry. Negret Colophon, who had seen and felt the marks of old, long-healed burns on Sorcha's hands when they danced the night before, now understood how they'd come to be there. Last of all, there was Maisie, whose eyes grew wide with shock but who thought it might be rude to interrupt Sorcha by pointing out that her fingers were about to catch fire. Then, of course, she realized she had noticed those scars too, and yet another secret dropped into Maisie's lap like a treasure.

Sorcha, meanwhile, had found the words she was looking for. "Probabilities?" she said experimentally. "The likely outcome of otherwise unmappable and incomparable factors that can't be combined and evaluated by any other means. These are wildly difficult calculations, and there are consequences to the mere act of attempting them. That is a reckoning."

The guests — half of them, anyway — listened to this in surprise. It was the most Sorcha had spoken at any time, for one thing, and for a second, as she spoke, her voice took on an authority that seemed at odds with the housemaid's usual deference. A few in the room, however, were not surprised at all. Negret, of course; and the Haypottens, to whom Sorcha was nearly like a daughter, exchanged glances of pride. Jessamy Butcher, who was not in the habit of underestimating anyone, had suspected Sorcha of having something wondrous in her background that she was keeping carefully hidden, concealed under a veneer of ordinariness like hot banked coals tucked away under cold ash. And Phineas Amalgam had known Sorcha for years and, steeped as he was in old, strange lore, had guessed long ago that she came from a line of conflagrationeers. Just then, however, he was more interested in Petra's ongoing maneuverings.

"And there's a way to do that sort of calculation using fire?" Petra inquired.

"There is," Sorcha replied. She thought for a minute more, then realized she had a hand in the fire and withdrew it quickly, wiping her sooty fingers surreptitiously on her apron. She glanced up to find Negret watching the subterfuge with amusement. *Ah, well. What's seen is seen.* She risked flashing a rapid wink at him. *Our secret?* His smile stretched wider, and Sorcha's heart fluttered. "You asked for a tale with fire, Mr. Colophon," she said. "Would a fire-kenning do? A story of one," she clarified quickly.

"You mean you can't just up and calculate the impossible for us right now?" Antony Masseter asked, amused, as he lifted one of his cigars to his mouth and reached into his pocket for a match.

"No smoking in here, please, sir," Mrs. Haypotten said in a tone of faint reproach that nobody really thought was about the cigar.

"Apologies," Masseter replied smoothly, pocketing his smokes again and dropping into the chair at the little table between the sideboard and the window.

Sorcha leaned her chin on the hand that had been in the fire. "What impossible question have you got, Mr. Masseter?"

"I have a few," he said, his green eye glittering. "But I apologize. You weren't asking me, and I can manage my own calculations. For the most part."

He gestured to Negret, who said simply, "Yes, please."

"Very well, then." Sorcha leaned back against the side of the fireplace. "Let me just remember."

THIRTEEN

THE RECKONING

The Firekeeper's Tale

So.

There are any number of ways to do a *fierekenia,* as many ways as there are sorts of fires. And just as you might use geometry for solving one problem and the calculus for another, different types of fire work best for solving different sorts of reckonings. Some fires are for unriddling and computing; some are for when you want to do more than simply know. Some fires, some reckonings, can be used to manipulate results. And, since reckonings of this sort have repercussions, as I have said, manipulating results means — sometimes — manipulating reality.

Yes.

Some years ago, there was a maker of devices in Nagspeake, an inventor and engineer called John Ustion. He mostly dealt in navigational tools, but he also made calculating machines. And he was fire-savvy. He himself could do fire-kennings of all sorts, and other kinds of reckonings besides, and he dreamed of building engines just for those: small, portable things that could make reckoning easy. Or if not easy, easier, because again, no true reckoning can be done without consequences, and the inventor understood that not everyone could be trusted with the responsibility.

Still, to amuse himself, he went on trying to build a *fierekenia* mechanism, even though he knew he could likely never sell it.

Then, one day, a man came to see him. "I have been referred to you by Mr. Alphonsus Lung," said the man —

Oh, now, what an interesting coincidence that is, Mr. Reever! Though of course it can't be the same person, since your story was meant to have taken place in the faraway past, and mine must have been more recent. But I'm certain the name was the same. What a small world the city is. Or perhaps it's just that these old stories do always seem to connect.

Anyhow, the customer said, "I have been referred to you by Mr. Alphonsus Lung, whom I went to see about a calculating device. I'm sorry to say we had a disagreement about the specifics and cannot work together. But he was good enough to give me a few names of other craftsmen here in town who might be able to provide what I need, and yours was among them."

John Ustion knew Lung well, and the customer's story surprised him. It was hard to imagine anyone angering Lung to the point where he'd refuse a sale, but if someone did accomplish that, it was hard to imagine Lung still bothering to offer referrals.

"May I ask what the nature of the disagreement was?" Ustion asked.

"Certainly," the customer said easily. "I believe he doesn't trust me to have what I want to buy."

Well, that was interesting. I imagine some part of the engineer's mind must've warned him right then that he ought to refuse, too. If Lung didn't trust this man to the degree that he had declined to do business with him, then such a man simply wasn't to be trusted. And Lung's primary specialty was clockwork. What had this man wanted that a clockmaker couldn't trust him with? A clockmaker dealt in many things, of course, but chief among them was *time*, and after all, time was one of the few things in life that people, trustworthy or not, had some level of access to simply by existing. They might squander it, waste it, lose it, ignore it, or even kill it, but everyone did that to some extent. It was hardly for a clockmaker to refuse to sell someone the means to mark their time simply because . . .

Oh.

A different interpretation occurred to Ustion. The customer waited expectantly, watching the pieces come together.

"You went to him for a timepiece?" Ustion asked casually, when he thought he had it figured out.

"Yes."

"But not for *keeping* time. You could buy a chronometer anyplace."

The stranger inclined his head in assent. "Not for keeping

time, no, not as such. The device I want must be able to measure it, yes, but it must also do much, much more."

Captivated against his better judgment, Ustion showed the customer to a small table with a chair on either side. The two of them sat down opposite each other, and the inventor took pencil and paper from a drawer. "Tell me."

And Ustion proceeded to listen, fascinated, and take occasional notes as the customer described a mechanism he had once owned but that had somehow been lost or destroyed. When this stranger had completed a complicated array of figuring, calculating, and solving, he had been able to take his results and, using the mechanism, perform a second set of reckonings. This second set was of the sort that was purely manipulative, meant to alter the reality of time and space and probability, to carry the bearer not simply to a particular place and moment—though it could do that—but to carry him to the *right* place and moment for accomplishing a specific thing.

So that's why Lung wouldn't sell to you, Ustion thought. *He didn't trust you to be able to wield reality like that.*

"Correct," the customer said softly, as if Ustion had spoken out loud. "The question is, can *you* trust me? And if not . . . do you care?"

Ustion thought about this for a moment. "If Lung didn't trust you, I can't either," he said honestly.

The second part of the question hung between them.

The customer watched Ustion look down at the notes he'd

made. Finally, reluctantly, Ustion said, "You will have to commission your mechanism from someone else."

The customer considered him for a long moment. "But you could do it," he said softly, "if you wanted to." It was not a question, and Ustion didn't bother to answer. He'd already said he wouldn't sell to the customer, so to answer truthfully would be an unnecessary boast. But Ustion's mind was already occupied with working out the details, and not only did he think he could do it, he knew that as soon as the door had shut behind this strange customer, he would try.

"I'm very sorry," the inventor said, getting to his feet. "The city has plenty of artificers in it. I'm sure you will find the right person."

The customer rose and bowed. "Thank you for your time," he said. "I'm sure I will." He left, and John Ustion went to work.

. . . Just as the customer had known he would. Because this was not the first time he'd had this conversation since leaving Alphonsus Lung's shop, and in his wake he'd left a handful of fascinated, inspired craftsmen, all with different specialties and different interests and all of whom had refused to sell to him but all of whom he also knew were presently occupied with fashioning impossible devices exactly to his specifications. John Ustion was a jack of many trades, but he was fire-savvy and had been thinking for a long time about a *fierekenia* mechanism. So he instinctively turned to flame to solve this challenge.

The key to working with fire is knowing what kind to use.

Any craftsman will tell you the same. Ask a baker. Ask a black-smith. So the first thing John Ustion did was think of all the sorts of fire he knew.

There is lyke-fire, among the most powerful sorts, but also the most painful, and the most difficult to control. There is belluine, more powerful and more difficult still and sometimes needlessly destructive, and cald-fire, easier to manage but perhaps too playful for anything with stakes as high as time-working. Bone-fire requires too much fuel at too great a cost to build into any kind of machinery; seel-fire is easier to kindle but is better for obscuring than for revealing; hnappian is a lulling-fire; and to use either wax-fire or wane-fire requires using both, which would've meant a physically bigger device and seemed inelegant to Ustion's engineer's mind.

Tangle-fire, now ... tangle-fire has interesting physics under-pinning it that might do well when working with space and time. Fleugana is persnickety, but not impossibly so, and can be used to enable flight. Heed-fire and hodijana he considered, along with brumire and bruweiry and welking-fire. All had potential, but none seemed precisely right.

Then there is wheat-fire, which has nothing to do with grain but whose name comes instead from old names for whetting and honing, and a still older word that means *behold*. Sharpen and witness, that is what wheat-fire does ... and what it demands. It is a good fire for reckoning, but it is also heartless. Some fires are gentler and paint the things they reveal in kinder light, or arrange the skirts of their shadows strategically, but wheat-fire is brutal in its honesty. It is also shockingly simple to conjure for anyone with even a little fire-savvy; ask to be shown a thing, and wheat-fire obliges, come what may. The aftermath can sometimes be harder to reckon with. That is the fire John Ustion chose for his *fierekenia* mechanism: a fire for revelations, but a fire that has consequences and that demands its users face them.

Next he built a small calculating device composed of a line of brass dials set over a group of rods made of bone. All of them, dials and rods, were engraved with numbers and letters and symbols. Together, they allowed for thousands upon thousands of combinations that would identify a destination in time and space, and each turn of dial and rod would tighten by increments a spring. That spring would, in turn, regulate a pressure valve that would, when opened by a stopcock, release the precise con-centration of wheat-fire required to illuminate a passage to the looked-for destination. If the calculations were done correctly, the smaller reckonings would combine into a bigger one to guide the device and control the fire. And then, somehow — I don't know precisely how, but somehow — the fire would show the way into some other there-and-then.

It was a beautiful and terrifying device. Each time he turned a dial or twitched one of the rods into place, John Ustion under-stood why Alphonsus Lung had turned the customer away, and he knew he had been right to do the same.

But the contraption didn't work.

Ustion tried for weeks to get his device to do what he thought — what he knew — it ought to be able to do. He made notes, made adjustments, swapped out parts, tore it to pieces, and started fresh. Each time, he came back to the same design and the same fire. It ought to have worked — he *knew* it ought to work, but the mechanism just wouldn't do what he wanted. Something was missing. Still, he had a strong sense that, little by little, he was getting closer to figuring out what that something was. The mechanism persisted in not working, but Ustion became more and more convinced that it was just a matter of time before he solved its riddles.

A strange thing happened as he worked, though: he also began to feel more and more reluctant. He would set the parts aside for longer and longer between attempts. He would get new ideas but put off trying them. He would delay building pieces he suspected he needed, if he didn't already have them to hand. It wasn't that he'd lost interest — he longed to finish the device. But the closer he got to finishing it, the more he felt he simply . . . shouldn't.

And yet at the same time, he couldn't just walk away. A part of him — a part so strong, it seemed some days that it had a heartbeat of its own — needed to see the thing to completion. So his need and his conscience fought with each other as the weeks became months. Now and then he thought of the strange customer, and occasionally he considered visiting Alphonsus Lung and some of the others he suspected the customer might've gone to after Lung had turned him away. He wondered if they had been just as unable to let go of the beautiful, terrifying idea the stranger had put before them all. But he didn't seek them out.

Ten years passed, which seems like a long time but isn't really — not to someone working on the problem of manipulating time, anyway. At last John Ustion figured out what was missing from his design. Not *something*, but *several* somethings were still wanted to complete his time-working *fierekenia* mechanism. On the list he had compiled over the long years of testing and trial, there were four items: a spring with very specific properties that would convert the turns of the rods and dials into the right kinds of power and regulation; a key capable of tightening that spring and all that was to be wound up with it; a keyway that would allow the wheat-fire to not simply reveal a destination in time and space, but also open a door to it; and a box — or coffret; I hadn't heard that word before, but I like it quite a bit — to hold the lot.

That night, John Ustion slept badly. His dreams were all nightmares, each one a cautionary tale warning him to go no further with his *fierekenia* mechanism. In every nightmare, a different type of fire appeared and appealed to him not to finish the device, and when, each time, Ustion's pride and fascination drove him to declare that he would build it come hell or high water, whatever fire was there with him in the dream became a comet that consumed him with flame when it hit, so that over and over he woke up screaming in pain and panic, sure that he was being immolated in his own bed.

When at last, just before dawn, the wheat-fire came to him, it made no entreaties or threats. It said simply, *I will do it if you make me.* And then, without waiting for Ustion's defiant dream-reply, the wheat-fire consumed him with a touch. And, because what is revealed by wheat-fire can be so much more painful than its actual burn, the fire did not immolate him but merely showed him flashes of possibility, probability, and consequence. There were grim prospects, but also, surprisingly — or perhaps not; wheat-fire, after all, reveals nothing but the truth — there was the potential for great good as well.

It was the last dream of the night, and when he woke from it, Ustion went straight to his workshop. He took the pieces of the unfinished mechanism and the list of missing bits, and he locked them in a cabinet.

As I told you before, John Ustion was fire-savvy, and he was an artificier of the highest magnitude. He continued to perform reckonings himself when he needed them, and he built many, many wondrous machines. But he never opened that cabinet again.

Many decades later, just before he died, he told his granddaughter the story of the half-built device, and he asked her to take it from the cabinet and destroy it — a thing that he had never managed to convince himself to do in all the long years of his life. His granddaughter listened with the same fascination with which Ustion himself had listened to the specifications of the customer all those years ago, and she promised to do as he'd asked.

She put it off until after he was in the ground, telling herself there was plenty of time and that she couldn't bear to destroy anything of her grandfather's while he was still alive. Then she put it off again, telling herself now that he was gone, she couldn't bear to destroy anything he'd left behind.

At long last, after she'd had a good long think and a few glasses of courage, she went to the workshop and opened the cabinet.

There was nothing there — not the mechanism, and not the list.

She told herself her grandfather must've destroyed it himself. Perhaps he'd seen the ambivalence on her own face when he'd asked her to do it, and decided to spare her the temptation. Perhaps he'd done it years ago, but in the twilight of his life, he'd forgotten that fact, along with birthdays and the color blue and the songs he'd sung to her when she was a baby.

Either way, it was probably for the best.

"THINGS LEFT BEHIND are fascinating, aren't they?" Petra asked. "I mean, as an idea."

What on earth is she up to? Amalgam wondered. Amused and curious, he said, "Certainly. They can take on rather a life of their own."

From the chair by the sideboard, Masseter, too, watched her with interest, but his curiosity was beginning to solidify into an actual theory. It was for the sake of testing his theory that he said quietly, "The magic of that-which-remains."

Petra smiled at him, but the expression told him nothing. "You're very poetic, Mr. Masseter."

"Do you mean something like relics?" Negret Colophon asked.

"I don't really know what I mean," she said in a musing tone.

Yes, I believe you do, Masseter thought. *I think you mean something very specific.* But he couldn't quite be sure.

"Relics ..." Petra said dreamily. "The power of things left behind in memory ..."

"And left behind in reality," Negret put in. "Mr. and Mrs. Haypotten, you must be experts in things that are left behind. Surely guests are always forgetting things. I would imagine you have quite a collection."

Reever shot him an exasperated look, but his brother ignored it.

Mr. Haypotten nodded, looking studiously down into the teapot on the cart as if something very interesting had been left behind inside it. "Inevitably." His face was a little bit redder than it had been.

"Though we do try to return things," his wife added. "And a good many of our guests come back, so we manage it more often than not."

"There have been some notable exceptions, though." The innkeeper replaced the top on the teapot. "But you have me thinking about relics now. I believe I have a tale I could share."

FOURTEEN

THE PARTICULAR

The Innkeeper's Tale

IT WAS MADAME GRISAILLE'S STORY last night that put this tale into my mind — the bones of the hero, you know, and the mysterious box — and also my dear wife's, with the bottle of fog. Well, this is a tale my papa told me, which he had from his father. And Grandpapa always said he had this story from a fellow who knew the boy in it personally, so of course it must be true.

Much like my grandpapa himself, the boy in the yarn had emigrated from London during the years of the worst of the fogs, when he was about fifteen. His name was Hugo Bankcliff, and back home, he and his brothers had been linklighters, making their livings by lighting the way for people needing to pass through the fogs, which regularly came on so thick and dark that they could turn even the brightest noon to midnight. After he arrived in Nagspeake, where there was no need for linklighters, Hugo cobbled together a living doing odd jobs. He collected sea coal on the beaches where the Magothy Bay met the Atlantic; he patched sails in the Quayside Harbors; he collected orpiment and realgar and mispickel for the denizens of Ferrous Sanctus Monastery high up on Whilforber Hill. But piecing together all this work carried him all over the city, and at the end of the week, he was so tired, he would sleep away the Saturdays that were his chosen days of rest.

I myself heard Grandpapa say more than once that, as miserable as a proper London particular can be, especially to one who lives with pea-soupers day in and day out, he found himself missing the fog now and then. That was Hugo, too, at the end of his first year in Nagspeake. Despite all the coal fires the city burned, it didn't have the right geography for pea-soupers. Nagspeake's fogs were all of the ordinary kind, and they never made you have to light candles before noon. They didn't kill off the camellias or stain the brickwork, and they didn't require travelers to hire linklighters to find their ways through the murk, for it was barely murk at all. Nagspeake fogs were—and are still, for the most part—veils of gauze that lie gracefully between your eyes and the city; the true London fog is an oily velvet wrap thrown over your face, and just as hard to see or breathe through.

Even so, Hugo began to wish for a proper pea-souper,

both because he was homesick and because, even with all the assorted jobs he was working, he was barely living any better than when he'd been carrying pitch-topped torches through the streets of London. He'd look fondly at the fog glasses he'd worn practically every day in his former life but that had no use here, and he'd wish to wake up just once to a thick yellow pall over the whole watershed.

One morning he left his house in the Quayside Harbors with his shovel and rake as he did every Wednesday and went along the pier to wait for the boat that carried the sea-coalers down the Skidwrack to the Magothy and, beyond that, the Atlantic. When he got to the slip where the boat came, he found the other two sea-coalers bent over a mail-order catalog that the wind had blown onto the wharf.

"Hugo," called his best mate, another former Londoner, as he approached, "come help me try to stump the catalog here. If I think of something that isn't in it, Pete buys lunch."

"Can't be done," said the other boy, Nagspeake-born and feeling superior. "Deacon and Morvengarde have everything. That's the whole point of them."

"Fog," said Hugo instantly.

"Fog!" his Londoner friend crowed with delight as he flipped through the catalog's index. "I believe you've done it, Hugo. Well played."

"Be reasonable," the Nagspeaker boy protested. "It has to be something that can be bought and sold, obviously!"

"You said they have *everything*," the Londoner argued, turning pages. "You laid the conditions for this wager, not . . ." His words died away, and he lowered the book, and the other two boys peered down at the entry he'd found. Under the *F*s was the heading *FOG (*see *WEATHER, page 316.)*

Hugo's friend looked up at him. Then they both looked at the third boy, who was trying very hard to appear as though he'd already known that Deacon and Morvengarde were in the weather-delivery business. Then the boat arrived, and that was the end of it. The three of them gathered their tools and went off to break their backs for ten hours raking up coal. Surreptitiously, Hugo folded the catalog and stuck it in his bag. The Nagspeaker boy did not buy lunch.

Hugo didn't open the catalog at all until he'd gotten home, sweaty, aching, and tired from a day scraping black coal from the sands. On sea-coal days he usually paid extra at his rooming house for a bath; today, already thinking about other things he could do with that money, he scrubbed himself clean over the water basin in his room instead. Then, reverently, he took the catalog from his bag and opened it on his bed.

It had absorbed the salt air of the Atlantic, as did every bit of paper or porous stuff that made the journey to that stretch of sand. Turning to the index, Hugo could smell his especial beach, with its swirls of black coal and green sea lettuce and the snaking pale lines that were the record of the always-vanishing spume of the wave edges; the masses of gravelly piecemeal shells that broke up the sands here and there and the occasional flat, clear jellies without tentacles or stings that Hugo often failed to see until he was already stepping on them. But—was he imagining it?—there was another whiff of scent there, too, something that changed the combination and made it not exactly the same blend of odors that his clothes always carried home mingled with the sweat of a hard day's work.

At first he thought it was just the aromas of the catalog's specific paper and ink, but somehow he couldn't let the question go. Finally, Hugo picked up the catalog and riffled the pages before his nose, inhaling deeply. His heart leaped even as his chest constricted instinctively and prepared to cough to defend itself against the familiar viscous thickness, the chewy, oily yet abrasive air his body associated with that smell.

Because the smell of the fog was there. Right *there*, nestled in the pages. Hugo felt the pull of it like a yearning for food or sleep when he hadn't had any in a day or two. And just then, as the craving ache crested over him, the catalog fell open on his quilt, not to the index he'd been looking for, but to the weather section—as if the book itself had said, *I know what you need better than you know it yourself, so let's not waste time in searching.* There, on the center of the page and nestled in an ornate frame, was the entry:

FOG

Obscurities and effluvia of all varieties and opacity, including MISTS, MIASMAS, MURKS, GLOOMS, BRUMES, HAZES, SMOGS, SMOKES, SMAZES, GROUND CLOUDS, VAPORS, FUGS, SEA-FOGS and SEA-SMOKES and STEAM.

Please specify any particulates to be included (viz. water, carbonized matter, aromatics, chemicals — for available chemical options, see CHEMICALS, page 200), optimal visibility and/or density (Ringelmann scale or pencil smudge acceptable), and preferred levels of humidity, corrosiveness, conductivity, temperature, and tenacity.

If uncertain about how best to compound your preferred fog, we will be happy to advise you; you may also order by location and allow us either to recommend the perfect fog for your current circumstances or to replicate the fog you remember.

A wide variety of soots may also be purchased separately (see COMBUSTION, page 132).

For medicinal smoke, please see supplemental informational form at back of catalog (APPENDIX C: FORMS). May be purchased concurrently with a DIAGNOSIS (see MEDICAL, page 37); however, Deacon and Morvengarde assumes no liability regarding potential side effects. All panaceas are dispensed at the patient's own risk and responsibility.

As Hugo read the description, the scent of his fog curled deeper into his lungs, and by the time he had gotten to the pricing below, it wouldn't have mattered what a true London particular would cost. Hugo couldn't live without it, not now that he knew it could be had to order.

The price was high, but not impossibly so. It took him three weeks to save enough; then, on a Friday, he took his hard-earned money to the local offices of Deacon and Morvengarde and, with the help of the D&M representative, placed an order for his fog. He handed over his money and in exchange received a square blue receipt with gilded edges. Hugo carried the receipt in his wallet, afraid to let it leave his person. It had been a lot of money, after all; and the receipt itself was an attractive bit of paper, like one of the beautifully lettered prayers the church down the street handed out to parishioners each Sunday.

Hugo's attractive bit of paper said his fog would be delivered in a week, which meant the following Friday, which was a sail-patching day. Hugo spent all morning, then all afternoon, then all evening on the docks as he worked, watching and waiting for the distinctive oily yellow of the pea-souper to come rolling down the Skidwrack, his nose lifted in case it caught the first hint of the London fog before his eyes did.

But the fog didn't come.

At last, with his fingers bruised and his workday done, Hugo set off for home, torn between indignation that the famed Deacon and Morvengarde hadn't delivered on the day they'd promised and humiliation at having believed even for a moment that any sort of weather could be dispensed this way. He slunk into his lodging house and climbed the stairs glumly, cursing himself for wasting money on something so foolish.

There was a parcel waiting before his door.

It bore a blue-and-gilt label that exactly matched the receipt in Hugo's wallet. He picked it up gingerly. Something inside shifted, and there again was the smell: the exact, the precise, the very odor he remembered.

Inside his room, Hugo undid the parcel and found, nestled in straw and wrapped in tissue, a round box about the size of his palm, made of smoked glass. Except no — the glass wasn't smoked. That swirl was the fog itself, roiling against the lid in yellow and brown and gray and all the shades the London particular could take, its colors shifting and swirling like the blues and oranges of an opal. Except no opal could've been as pretty; not to Hugo, not just then.

He stared at the fog in its glass container for a few minutes, marveling at what he held. Then he glanced back into the package and found a small piece of folded paper that had been tucked inside the tissue. Unfolding it, he read:

> *Enclosed please find your purchase of one (1) genuine London Fog. Please take care when handling and do not attempt to contain fog in any vessel other than the one in which it was shipped. To release fog, turn lid widdershins; to recall fog, turn lid sunwise.*

*Please note that the box lid should never be fully
removed. We hope you enjoy your purchase and
will not hesitate to contact us if we may be of
further assistance.*

Yours,
Deacon and Morvengarde, Incorporated.
Purveyors of Goods, Services, and Expressage.
Trusted since time immemorial.

Hugo carried the box carefully to his window, which looked out over the river. His fingers tingled as he pushed up the sash. He made himself count to ten, then, leaning out into the night, turned the lid one rotation counterclockwise.

Instantly, a thick, smoky fug sifted out from under the glass, spilling free on all sides, so that the runnels of fog combined with the round dome of the box put Hugo immediately in mind of a strange, smoke-tentacled jellyfish. The sensation of the fog was heartbreakingly familiar as it poured over the sides of his hand: it really did have a *feel* to it, an actual thickness, almost a weight. It rolled down the side of the house to pool on the thin stretch of cobbled walkway, then overran that and flowed over the nearest bulkhead that separated the land from the water and onto the surface of the Skidwrack, where it settled in and began to spread.

Hugo watched this in wonder, looking from the river to the box in his palm and wondering how much fog the little glass container actually held. But it continued to pour out, and little by little, the mist on the river thickened, and the smell of the London particular began to overwrite the usual scents of the Quayside Harbors. As the level of it rose, the lights of the buildings out on the piers and the ships on the river began to dim until they were mere pinpricks. Then, one by one, they vanished altogether in the clotting dark of the fog.

Hugo leaned down close to the box and breathed deep, feeling actual pain as his lungs protested and a simultaneous but different kind of ache as his heart and memory absorbed the thing they had been craving. Then he put the box carefully inside his vest, pulled on his coat, stuffed one of its pockets with matches and an old shirt that could be torn into rags, and went out into the particular, the fog eddying around him as it continued spilling out of the vessel in his vest.

Hugo hunted in the alley behind his house for a bit of dry driftwood, nearly falling off the bulkhead twice before he found a suitable stick. He wrapped the top of it in his old shirt, clamped it between his knees as he lit a match from his pocket, and set the makeshift torch ablaze. *I'll need pitch for next time,* he thought. *This will burn too fast without it.*

The fog drowned the Quayside Harbors and its stretch of the Skidwrack in less than ten minutes, turning it into an entirely new and alien landscape. Though Hugo had lived there only a year, he had come to know the district well. But the fog made the familiar unknowable — so much so that twice he found people wandering lost in the miasma who probably knew the Harbors far better than Hugo did. And it could be more frightening than the darkest hours of the darkest night. Hugo helped the lost souls find their ways home until his torch had burned down to cinders, and although he tried to refuse the coins they offered in thanks, by the time he got home, he had enough to buy pitch to make a proper linklighter's torch.

He tossed the remnants of his driftwood stick into the river and went upstairs to his room. He shed his coat, took the glass box from his vest pocket, and, leaning out the window again, slowly turned the lid clockwise. As he tightened it, the fog flowed in just as it had flowed out, and by the time the lid was shut snugly, every shred of the particular had gone back into its container, leaving nothing behind but a vaguely sooty film on the window. *No more opening the box inside,* he decided as he put it on the crate that made a table beside his bed and shucked out of his now-filthy clothes.

The next day was Saturday. Instead of sleeping late, he woke early, his nose seeking and finding the scent of the fog instantly and rousing him out of dreams of London and home. Even though the murk had been in his room only once, its scent had permeated the threadbare curtains and sheets and lingered even in the clear bright light of morning. There on the bedside crate was the glass box. Hugo sat and stared at it for long minutes before he finally got up and dressed to start his day.

He found another shirt that could be sacrificed for rags and packed it in his bag, along with his matches and his fog glasses. Then he tucked the box carefully in his pocket and went straight to the Tar and Pitch Works, where he convinced the merchant to sell him a crock of leavings scraped from a broken barrel, enough to soak the rags and make a proper torch when he was ready. From there he headed for the water, pausing along the way to peer into each alley he passed until he found the perfect length of wood to make the handle.

Then, right at the edge of the pier, he hesitated. What to do with his fog?

He hadn't actually bought it intending to inundate Nag-speake for purposes of turning linklighter again. Something about that didn't feel right — pouring the fug over the city just to make money helping people get around in it. And he did remember that bad things could happen in the fog. There were thieves who posed as linklighters only to lead their customers into dark alleys and rob them. People drifted into the paths of horses. People wandered blindly off embankments and into the Thames to drown. People got sick — just a little sick if they were strong or lucky; deathly sick if they weren't. And to manage in a fog — just to move about in it without getting hurt, never mind finding your way to where you wanted to go — you had to know how to do it. You had to learn, which took time and experience. Even just pouring out a particular now and then could be deadly. What damage might he already have done, letting it loose the night before?

Hugo had been intending to find a boat to take him down the river to Bayside, where he could let the fog loose over the Magothy, but now he reconsidered. Bayside would be one of the worst places to unleash a particular. It had miles of water frontage, dozens of boats coming, going, and lying at anchor, and thousands of people staying there who weren't from Nagspeake at all and would be even more lost and helpless than the locals, who would be plenty lost and helpless themselves.

He had just decided to go inland along one of the Skidwrack's many branching creeks instead and see what a dollop of London fog would look like poured out in an abandoned bit of woods when a sailor heading down the pier elbowed past him with a sharp whack to the ribs, muttering "woolgathering landlubbers" in a not-specially-quiet voice as he went along. But Hugo didn't hear the words at all, because he had felt the crunch between his shirt and his vest. The sailor's elbow had cracked the glass box like an eggshell.

Immediately, rills of fog began to seep out of his pocket.

Hugo reached in, hoping against hope that the blow had merely knocked the lid open a bit. But he could feel the crack that spanned the glass dome and the cold, almost viscous smog that was issuing forth. He stumbled off the pier and into an alley, trailing fog behind him, and untied the kerchief from his neck. He folded the kerchief twice, took the box from his pocket, wincing at the break across the lid, and wrapped it tightly, even though he was certain that if three layers of cotton were nowhere near enough to keep a particular out (a thing he knew well from experience), they wouldn't be enough to hold one in, either.

And they weren't. The fog kept seeping free, and once it had escaped the confines of the round glass box, it pooled and began to thicken, rising like bread dough on the banks of the Skidwrack. Hugo cursed.

His instructions had warned him not to put the fog into anything other than the container it was in, but something more had to be done, and fast. He unwrapped the kerchief again and set it on the ground with the box sitting in the center. Trying ineffectually to wave away the pooling, thickening fog so that he could see what he was doing, Hugo opened his bag and took out the small crock of pitch. Reluctantly, he smeared a dollop of pitch tar along the length of the fissure, then tore a bit of rag from his old shirt and pressed the fabric against the tar, gluing it down fast. Then he rewrapped the whole thing and stood with the parcel in his palm to examine the results. The seep of fog drifting down had slowed, but it did not stop.

He cursed again, pocketed the wrapped box, and put his torch together as quickly as he could. Hugo struck a match and lit the pitchy rag at the top, then ventured out into the street again.

The particular was already spreading across the river and rolling up the banks. All around him, the busy waterside district was beginning to react to the sudden change in conditions, but so far the voices he could hear were more bemused than worried. The fog hadn't risen quite enough to turn the day to night; even before his desperate pitch-and-rag patch job, it had been leaching out of his pocket much more slowly than it had done when he'd opened the container properly the night before. But already the air was suffused with the fug, the daylight having to work hard to filter through the thickening yellow-gray, and if the particular behaved like it did last night, congealing and expanding, mounting to the heights of the houses and beyond . . . well, in that case, the midday darkness was coming, and then there would be panic.

Hugo took a moment to remember where he was and plan a route; then he navigated carefully to the Deacon and Morvengarde office where he'd placed his order.

He lost his way twice and detoured three times to help others who'd misplaced the familiar streets of the Harbors in the smog, so it took him an hour to get there. The air was thick and dark by the time he opened the door and stepped into the warmth and light of the office to find the same young woman who'd helped him place his order sitting at the desk.

The woman wore fog glasses, but they were pushed up on her forehead as she worked. Hugo pushed his up too and closed the door on the darkness.

"Can I help you?" she asked.

Hugo held up the broken box, from which yellow fog was still seeping. "The container is broken, and I can't put the fog back. How quickly can I get a replacement?"

The woman took the box gingerly and examined it. "We didn't ship it to you this way, did we?"

"Well, no. It was in my pocket and someone ran into me."

"I thought as much." The clerk eyed the miasma leaking sluggishly out and pooling on the office floor, then held out the box. "Take this outside, please, and I'll write up the order for you." And she named a price almost as high as the amount Hugo had paid to get the fog in the first place.

He stared, shocked. "I can't afford that."

"Then I'm afraid you can't have another container."

"But the fog won't stay in anymore! The city's drowning in it. These people aren't accustomed to this sort of fog. They'll go out of their minds!"

She made a condescending face. "Hardly *our* fault, as you admit you broke the container yourself."

He dredged up a memory of the enclosure that had come with the box. "But the paper in the parcel said not to hesitate to contact Deacon and Morvengarde if they — it — you — can be of further assistance!"

"Which you have done. Good on you." She coughed delicately, then again, but much less daintily. The fog he'd brought in with him was beginning to fill the room.

Hugo stared, then sputtered, "I'll — I'll tell them it came from you! I'll tell the papers, the mayor —"

The clerk shrugged. "We have no liability here. We only *sell* the fog. It's up to the buyer to be responsible with it. In fact . . ." She turned to a cabinet behind the desk and took a paper from it. "Yes, here's your original order. I believe you mentioned you wanted the fog for reasons of homesickness, which designates your particular fog as a panacea and makes this purchase a medicinal one. As you see here" — she held out his form and pointed — "you yourself signed and acknowledged that Deacon and Morvengarde is not responsible for unwanted side effects of medicinal products. I think," she said deliberately as she refiled the order form, "that if you were to step forward and admit that you let loose this fog on Nagspeake, things would not—*ahem* —go well for you."

From the sharp look that accompanied her words, Hugo couldn't be sure whether she meant things wouldn't go well for him with his neighbors in Nagspeake, or whether she meant things wouldn't go well for him with Deacon and Morvengarde. Or maybe that was just the miasma, obscuring her face and making it look more threatening than she meant it to. That was another thing the fog could do.

"Now," the young woman continued, folding her hands on her desk in a businesslike fashion, "I am *happy* to order you a replacement box, *if* you're able to pay. If not, please take that mess out of my office immediately." She waved a hand, half gesturing toward the door and half fanning the seeping effluvium away from herself.

Hugo, who well knew what a pea-souper could do even indoors, got an idea. "I'm not going anywhere until you order me another box, and free of charge."

"No," the clerk said, trying to stifle a cough.

Hugo shrugged and sat down in the chair opposite her desk.

"Deacon and Morvengarde has no responsibility—"

"I'm a customer," Hugo protested. "I'm unhappy with my purchase."

"That would perhaps count for something if you hadn't ordered and received exactly what you wanted," she argued, blinking hard as the level of yellow fog began to rise and the room began to fill. "And if you hadn't signed a form taking all responsibility yourself."

"And that," Hugo said, pulling his fog glasses down over his eyes, "might count for something if I wasn't willing to sit here and ruin your office until you fix things."

The young woman reluctantly pulled her own glasses on. "If you're unhappy with the service you've received," she said, climbing onto her chair and stepping from there onto her desktop in order to keep her chin above the level of the miasma, "perhaps you'd like me to escalate things to my employer."

There was an edge to her voice that made it sound less like an offer and more like a warning. Still, "Certainly," Hugo said, tying his pocket handkerchief around the lower half of his face and climbing onto his own chair just to keep them at roughly the same height.

The clerk glared at him as she tied a handkerchief over her mouth. "I'll call Mr. Morvengarde if you like," she said, her voice slightly muffled, "but I wouldn't advise it." And despite having to cough a bit as she spoke, it was perfectly clear this time that "I'll call Mr. Morvengarde if you like" was definitely a threat. He decided he emphatically did not want to meet the young woman's employer. Still, perhaps it needn't come to that.

Hugo nodded. "All right." Then he looked around the darkening room. The fog had risen over the level of the lamp on the woman's desk, and now what had been a bright and cozy light was muted to a dim glow, changed from a warm sun to no more than the hint of a faraway hidden moon on a cloudy night. It had gone from day to night in the office, just that quickly.

"How long will that take?" he asked quietly. "Is he here?"

"No," the young woman said at last.

"I can wait," Hugo said.

The two of them looked at each other.

She hacked up a series of coughs. Then she sighed. "All right." She climbed down, muttering. Then, louder, she said, "Ordering won't do the job, anyway. It would take another week for it to get here. And they'd take the cost out of my salary," she added mutinously. "But I can tell you where to find a new container here in town, if you'll just promise to leave."

Hugo heard her pulling open drawers, though he couldn't see anything at all. "But the instructions said never to put it in anything but the box it came in."

"I know that's what they *say*," the woman said, and there was the sound of a pen scratching on paper. "They say that because it's not good business to send you to our competitors for replacement parts." The woman's hand appeared out of the fug, clutching a piece of paper. "I'm fairly sure this is the right address, but honestly I can barely see two inches in front of my face."

Hugo took the page and read the words scrawled on it. *Feretory Street, Printer's Quarter.* "This is just a street."

"Anyone on that street can help you." The woman's hand appeared again, pointing desperately at the door. "Please go, will you? And if you tell them — or anyone — who sent you, I'll kill you myself."

Hugo went.

He avoided the river and cut through the woods that carpeted the hill to the northeast. It was certainly a very long route to take to get from the Quayside Harbors to the rest of Nagspeake, but the Skidwrack was twisty and shoaly under the best of circumstances, and he didn't trust anyone to navigate even their home waters in the kind of pea soup he was pouring out. Plus, although Hugo was trailing fog behind him, the woods and inlets ahead still had perfect visibility.

It took what felt like hours before he reached the outskirts of the artisan's district called the Printer's Quarter. He was thirsty and tired, but he didn't dare stop anywhere for even a moment longer than it took him to ask for directions. The quicker he moved on, he thought, the less fog he would leave behind and the longer it would take for it to congeal to fill whatever space he'd been in. Not to mention, with the particular spilling out as if something in his vest was on fire, Hugo was getting some strange looks.

He found Feretory Street as afternoon began to stretch toward evening. It was the street of the Reliquary Makers.

Now, a thing that Hugo, not being from Nagspeake, did not know, was that there had been a time when the city had been full of holy men and women, and then a time when a plague had taken them all. For some years after that, not long before Hugo had arrived, it had been the fashion to carry relics of those holy folk. But of course it would never have done to carry a charred crumb of a dead man's fingerbone about in one's pocket like a stray penny, and so reliquaries became all the rage: special purpose-made containers meant to house those precious miraculous bits and pieces. They could take any shape or style imaginable to accommodate any sort of relic, and they were crafted by jewelers, by clockmakers, by cabinetmakers and coffin builders, by glassblowers and potters and every kind of artist. Most of the reliquary makers eventually found workshops and studios on Feretory Street.

When Hugo arrived and started to read the signs that hung over the doors up and down the lane, he began to think he understood why he had been sent that way. Of course his replacement box would have to be a container made to hold something miraculous. Trailing his wake of fog, the boy headed for the nearest of the workshops.

This one happened to belong to a man called Gaz, who cast his reliquaries in silver metal set with windows of Roman glass for peeking in at the holy object inside. When Hugo entered, he found Gaz deep in conversation with a customer. Afraid of lingering too long, Hugo started to turn away and head back to the door with the fog swirling at his feet. But Gaz, who was perhaps eager to be finished with this specific piece of business, caught the boy's eye and held up a single finger. *Wait.*

While the maker of reliquaries concluded his business, Hugo roamed the workshop, peeking into display cases of reliquary jewelry — rings, pendants, pocket-watch cases — and glancing over the presentations of bigger objects — trinket boxes, curio cases, even bookshelves — made to hold larger relics. At last, as Hugo paused to peer down at a box the size and shape of a sarcophagus, the artisan raised his voice to a bark. "I tell you, sir, there is nothing to be done without the winder. I can work with the spring you've got here rather than the piece specified by the original plans, but it changes the works. I have explained it and explained it. If you still don't understand, you will simply have to take my word for it. If you don't believe me, you are welcome to take your requirements to a different reliquarist."

"We both know you're the only one who can assemble the device," the customer, a tall man with a single bright blue eye, said coldly.

"Then come back with a winder." The reliquary maker stepped pointedly around the counter. "In the meantime—" He coughed, frowned, and noticed for the first time the smog rising from the general direction of Hugo. "I have another customer who has been very patient."

The blue-eyed man took a deep breath—too deep, considering the worsening air quality in the room—opened his mouth to argue, and hacked up a lungful of fog instead. He collected a handful of objects from the countertop and stowed them in pockets around his person, then yanked a handkerchief from his breast pocket and held it over his nose and mouth as he stormed from the room, leaving Hugo looking helplessly at the reliquary maker as he observed the curling, clabbering fog with curiosity.

"Interesting," said Gaz. "Is this the relic that needs keeping?"

"I haven't got a relic," Hugo said. "I've got a particular. A pea-souper. A proper London fog." He took the cracked and pitch-wrapped glass vessel from his pocket. "It came in this box, but someone hit me and it was broken, and now I can't put it back or stop it spreading."

Gaz waved the boy over to the counter. He took a jeweler's glass from his pocket and fitted it to his right eye, then carefully unwrapped the kerchief and peeled away the pitch-stained rag. Immediately the fog began to pour forth in earnest. "Oh, my," the reliquary maker said with a laugh. He dropped the loupe back in his pocket, replaced the seal, then turned to a wall of cabinets behind him and took a jar of thick gold liquid from one and a small paintbrush from another. He uncorked the jar and, working rapidly, unwrapped the box again and painted a line of the gold substance along the crack.

"That will hold for a few minutes, at least," he said, corking the jar and setting the brush on top of it. He lifted the box, screwed the jeweler's glass back into one eye socket, and looked at the roil of fog. "I think you're wrong," he said at last. "If this isn't a relic now, it may ripen into one someday. But it hardly matters. Whoever sent you to us was right. Reliquary glass is what you want to hold the stuff. Unfortunately, I don't think I'm the man for the job." He coughed again. The sickly yellow fog had reached about the level of the countertop.

"Why?" Hugo asked. "The longer this takes, the more danger people will be in."

"I can quite imagine," Gaz said. "But you have come to an artisan quarter, and while it is true that anything may be a reliquary if it holds a relic, on Feretory Street we take a certain amount of pride in crafting the perfect vessel for each precious thing brought to us." He reached for a bell on the counter and rang it three times. "But don't worry. The person you want is my apprentice, Edita."

A moment later, a door opened to Hugo's left and someone began coughing. "What on earth happened in here?" a female voice said, and a moment later a girl about Hugo's age came wading through the particular. "This is . . . this is either disgusting or fantastic, and I can't decide which."

"Common difficulty when studying relics," Gaz explained. "Edita Skellandotter, apprentice reliquarist, please meet your first customer. He has brought us this fine London fog and needs a vessel for it." Then he appeared to remember that he hadn't asked Hugo's name.

Hugo introduced himself, Gaz lit a lamp, and Edita put on a pair of spectacles very much like Hugo's fog glasses, which reminded him to pull his own over his eyes. The three of them stared down at the broken glass. Edita looked up at her teacher. "Globe or case, do you think?"

Gaz smiled and shook his head. "That's for you to decide. With your customer, of course."

The girl looked at Hugo through lenses that were faceted like a fly's eye. "Does it need to open? Will you be wanting to take it out again? I could make this into a beautiful snow globe if you wanted." She blew at the fog swirling between them.

"Tiny pigeons instead of snow, maybe, flying over a city and a river, buoyed up by this fabulous murk." She was describing London. Hugo's heart leaped. Before he could say yes, however, Edita tilted her head. "Of course, a snow globe won't open," she added, coughing.

"Oh." He wasn't sure he ought to let it out again, but he didn't like not having the option. "What was the other thing? A case?"

"Wardian case," she explained. "A glass box for plants and little living things. Generally meant to stay closed, so the environment inside creates its own equilibrium. But you could open it." She looked at him closely through her many-planed spectacles. "I think that's what you want. A sort of . . . cloudarium."

"He does have to be able to put the fog back, if it's to be let out," Gaz cautioned.

Edita nodded. "I quite see that." She thought for a minute, then waved in the direction from which she'd appeared. "I think I have something." She vanished into the miasma. Hugo and Gaz followed, the reliquary maker guiding the boy across the workshop and into a back room.

The visibility in there was better, and Hugo looked around in wonder at the collection of glass objects that filled every surface. Since she'd mentioned snow globes, he wasn't surprised to see a shelf of sealed spheres holding all manner of particles suspended in a variety of liquids, many of which were swirling, even though presumably no one had shaken them. More glass spheres, these ones much smaller and clearly meant to be worn as jewelry, hung on chains from pegs on the wall. But mostly, there were glass boxes of every description. Some were fairly plain three-dimensional geometric shapes made of panes of glass and metal joinery, but most were works of architecture: houses, churches, lighthouses, castles of all shapes and sizes, even a tree-house built into a small but apparently living tree. Many of these had already been planted with flora. A door on the far side of the room stood open, revealing a connecting glass-walled conservatory bursting with greenery.

Edita looked over the baubles hanging from the pegs above the table and selected a small blown-glass sphere on a silver chain. "I think this will do the job. I think you want to be able to carry it."

She removed the cap that both closed the sphere and allowed it to hang from the chain, then took down a jar from a shelf, selected a single tiny white carved bird from a mass of similar pieces, and popped the bird inside.

"Hold this, please," she said, handing the glass ball to Hugo, along with a copper funnel she took from one of the worktable's drawers. "And hold this over the bauble. Now, who's got the box?"

Gaz had brought it with him. Edita took it and carefully turned the cap widdershins one rotation, then two, then three. Hugo held his breath as she opened it—the instructions, after all, had said to never fully remove the lid. But when she lifted the top away and tipped the lower part of the container over the copper funnel, the last bit of fog slid obediently into the sphere. The tiny carved bird swirled into motion, buffeted by currents in the confined murk.

"Thank you," Edita said, taking the sphere from Hugo and replacing its cap. As she turned it sunwise, the fog that was rising up around their shoulders now began to rush past them and into the pendant by way of the tiny crack of space between the glass and the lid.

It took her a long time to tighten it. A whole minute, then two. An impossible length of time, considering how very small the pendant's cap was. But of course, there was a vast amount of fog to bring back, and with every twist, more of it flowed through the vanishingly small crack into its new container.

At long last, after what seemed like hours to Hugo, the room began to clear as the final wisps of the fog trickled into the sphere. And then, finally, Edita raised her face, sooty and exhausted, and held up the reliquary.

"Sunwise to close, widdershins to open," she said in a cracked voice. They'd all been coughing quite a lot. "But you don't have to do it that way. Look." And she showed him how the cap also contained a tiny dropper, like a medicine bottle or something to dispense perfume. "You can measure out exactly how much you want, then just wind it in the same way when you're ready to, by twisting the cap."

Hugo watched the tiny bird swirling in the fog. It looked exactly like any of the thousands of pigeons he'd caught glimpses of in particulars back home, like tiny ghosts in the mist. "Thank you," he said in his own ravaged voice. "It's perfect." Then a terrible thought occurred to him. "How much does this cost?"

Edita smiled tiredly and reached for the long-forgotten, cracked glass box the fog had been shipped in. "Give me this," she said. "Reliquary glass, even broken, should never go to waste."

And so the deal was made and the city saved from the mysterious Nagspeake particular . . . though my father and grandfather both said that after that, very occasionally, there was a strange, oily yellow fog that came flowing down the Skidwrack when Hugo — or whoever possesses his reliquary these days — lets the particular out to roam for an afternoon.

~ INTERLUDE ~

"AT LAST," CROWED SANGWIN, "a merchant who isn't a nightmare!"

"Three of them," Tesserian said. He held out three saints to Maisie: a man calming a stormy, mist-shrouded sea; a young-looking girl holding two eyes on a plate; and a bald man holding a pair of massive keys. The castle now stood as tall as Maisie's shoulders.

"Do people really carry relics and reliquaries?" Maisie asked. "In the real world?"

"They do," Sangwin said, getting up from the table in the corner and passing her the marten he'd been carving. "You can go to Feretory Street yourself someday, if you like, and see some." He turned back to the table, swept up the pile of wood shavings, and, after a quick glance at Sorcha for permission, leaned carefully around Maisie, Tesserian, and the castle and tossed them onto the fire, where they sent up a quick flash of crackling sparkles.

Mr. Haypotten cleared his throat as he began to move around the room again, refilling glasses. "There is also one here in the inn." There was an uncertain, almost embarrassed tone to his voice. "My old friend Forel is a reliquarist. You know old Forel, don't you?" he said, turning to Reever Colophon, who happened to be the closest of the two brothers at that moment. "He's one of—follows the same—" He raised a hand toward the red-haired man's tattooed face, then arrested the gesture, flushing. He pivoted with his bottle, only to find himself under the scrutiny of Antony Masseter, who was watching this exchange with intense interest from the chair by the sideboard. Now his embarrassment was impossible to miss. Haypotten's face burned like the filament in a light bulb.

"He's a High Walker," Reever finished, smiling a little coolly. "As are my brother and I. Yes, we know Blaise Forel. You might say he recommended your inn to us."

"Knew," Negret corrected absently.

"That's right," the innkeeper's wife put in, looking at her husband. "He went missing years ago, didn't he?"

"A missing reliquary maker?" Masseter said. "I'd quite like to hear more about that."

"What's a High Walker?" Maisie interrupted as she balanced the marten on the pitched roof of one of the castle's gables. She was thinking back to the night before, when she and Madame Grisaille and Sorcha had danced with Reever and Negret. *They'll know your secret,* she had said to Madame, but the old lady had waved the worry away. *My dear, they already know. They have been in Nagspeake longer than anyone. The city has no secrets from them. Only people confuse them these days.*

Then, Reever, to Madame Grisaille: *You have always danced with us, so dance with me now.*

And she thought back even further, to Madame's story of the roamer-hero in the garden grave. *The iron has taken my coffret. It has taken it down, deep into the earth, below the tunnels under the city, below the land that lies beneath the tunnels.*

"Land," of course, could have simply meant exactly that: more earth, just down farther. But somehow that wasn't the way Maisie had understood it at the time. She had taken it to mean another *place.* Another city, perhaps: a city below, a place you could get to, as Jack had climbed the beanstalk to the land of the giants, if only instead of a beanstalk you had wild ironwork, and instead of climbing up, you went down. Down below Nagspeake, down below the tunnels that ran underneath it, down, and down, and down.

"What's a High Walker?" Reever repeated, his cool smile warmed by Maisie's open curiosity. "A High Walker is rare, nowadays—though there was a time when we were much more common in this place. You remember what the lady said about roamers? A High Walker is a sort of roamer."

"You have one of Forel's relics?" Negret asked the innkeeper. "He gave you one?"

Mr. Haypotten hesitated. "I . . . well, yes, to your first question, and not exactly, to your second." He had been filling Sangwin's glass, and he turned the bottle of spirits nervously in his hands. "I have been wondering if I ought to say something to you about it." He set down the whiskey. "But the truth is, it's been misplaced, and I couldn't bring myself to admit it."

"Misplaced?" Negret repeated in a cold tone that seemed entirely at odds with his usual good nature.

"Part of it, I should say. But — well, let me go and get what's here, and you'll see."

Captain Frost tapped his half-hour glass, turned it, and followed the innkeeper from the room.

"He left it here," Mrs. Haypotten said as the rattling of windows told them all that Frost had stepped outside by way of the inn's front door. "Mr. Forel, that was. He left . . . well, he left a number of things with us after his last stay. He often came here to work when he wanted a change of scene, you know. For years we kept a room, special for him, fronting the Skidwrack bend. You never knew when he'd show up." She looked at Reever. "The room you're in, Mr. Reever, in fact. That's the one he used to have when he'd come."

Reever and his brother exchanged a glance. Negret got up from his chair and began to pace the small bit of unoccupied floor between the hallway doors and the chairs before the fire. The others, variously embarrassed on the innkeeper's behalf and curious about this sudden change in mood, occupied themselves with drinks and quiet small talk.

The windows rattled again, and a moment later, Captain Frost came back. Mr. Haypotten returned only a minute or two after that. He held a roll of gray oilskin in one hand. "This is it. What wasn't lost."

He held the roll out to Reever, the closer of the twins. But Negret stalked across and took it instead. "His bookbinding tools."

"Those are all there," Haypotten continued nervously,

glancing from the twins to Masseter, who was watching with naked curiosity as Negret tugged open the knot in the leather tie that held the roll closed. "He only left a handful."

"Bookbinding? But I thought he made things for holding bits of holy people," Maisie said, spreading out before her the unused cards painted with saints. Plenty of them held books, but she didn't see how a book could be a reliquary unless you could somehow press a relic, like a flower or a butterfly, and preserve it between the pages.

"And so he did, but remember Mr. Haypotten's tale," Negret muttered, unrolling the oilskin to examine the instruments tucked in its pockets: styluses and awls; needles blunt, sharp, and curved; looped linen thread in a dozen colors; scoring tools and folders of bone and horn; sharp-ended scalpels and a tiny pair of scissors; minute vials of powders; and a round box he knew without having to look would contain a cake of beeswax. Then he rolled it back up and tied the leather lace closed again. "A relic isn't always what you think. Neither, therefore, is a reliquary." He looked up at the innkeeper. "That's what's missing, isn't it? A reliquary."

Mr. Haypotten red as a poppy now, opened his mouth. But before he could stammer out another word, Maisie spoke up. "Is it a book, then? The thing that's missing?"

All eyes turned to her. "Yes, it was," Mr. Haypotten managed.

"And that's what you've been looking for all this time?" Maisie asked Negret. "You've been searching the bookshelves."

The young man's tattooed face cracked into a smile. He

passed the roll of tools to his brother and crouched before Maisie. "You saw that, did you?"

Maisie grinned back. The words *Anyone would have seen* came to her tongue, but then she realized everyone hadn't, so she just grinned wider and said, "Yes."

Negret's smile broadened too. "And did you find it?"

"I found something," she replied cautiously. "It might be what you're talking about."

"Show me," Negret suggested with a conspiratorial wink.

Maisie got to her feet. "It's in my room." She glanced apprehensively at the Haypottens, wondering if she was about to be in trouble, but the innkeeper and his wife managed encouraging faces as she left the parlor, though their expressions faded back to nervous tightness the moment she was gone.

No one spoke this time. There were no sounds but the crackling of the fire, the soft creaking of Madame Grisaille's chair, a brief sizzle from the heating coils, and Negret's quietly pacing feet, until Maisie returned with a small bag made of dusty purple brocade and handed it over.

"Wherever did you find it, Maisie?" Mr. Haypotten asked, his voice thick with relief. "It's been missing these ten years, at least."

"There's a gap where the top stair on the way to the second floor doesn't quite meet the wall," Maisie explained. "It was in there, along with some little bones. I think they might've been a mouse once."

Sorcha stared, then laughed. "You did used to have that cat."

"That cat," Mrs. Haypotten groaned.

Negret ignored all of this as he picked open the tie closing the brocade bag and reached long, reverent fingers inside. "Aha." And he took out a very small book bound in buff-colored leather decorated with a pattern of charcoal-gray pinpoints.

Everyone in the room who was close enough to see it spotted immediately the similarity between the gray-dot pattern on the book and the patterns that lay scattered across the faces of the two Colophon brothers.

"That *is* a reliquary, then?" Maisie asked, peering into Negret's palm for a closer look.

"Or is it the relic?" Sangwin asked in a grim undertone. Then he winced, along with almost everyone else in the room, as Maisie plucked the book from Negret's hand.

Negret, however, merely nodded. "It's both. He made his own reliquary," he said as Maisie fanned the book open. "Not just anyone can do that."

Mrs. Haypotten muttered a near-silent prayer and crossed herself. She had long had misgivings about what sort of leather the little book was bound in, but by unspoken agreement, she and her husband had never discussed it. This, however, seemed to be confirmation of her worst suspicions.

Oblivious to the older lady's distress, Maisie turned page after page. All were blank. "But there's nothing in it!"

"Not yet." Negret gave her a conspiratorial wink. "Except that's not quite true." He reached out and flipped to a place where four ends of thread — it might have been waxed linen or fine gutstring — had been left uncut after having been used to tie two knots holding the pages in place. "And see here." He pointed to where the thick paper that had sandwiched the threads and knots held a visible pattern of impressions like a branching river, or the lines of a palm. "Thread your kitstring, then tie certain knots, leave certain lengths, press the pages, and sometimes you can divine your fortune. So perhaps there is something to be read here, after all."

"Seems late for telling *that* fellow's fortune," Masseter observed drily.

Negret lifted his shoulders. "Depends on what one wants to know."

"Could you tell our fortunes?" Maisie asked eagerly, handing the reliquary volume back.

Negret raised an eyebrow. "There's peril in telling a fortune. I'm not sure anyone here would risk it."

Maisie all but hopped up and down. "I would! Tell mine!"

A shadow passed over his face. "Another time, perhaps. You have to sew the stitches and tie the knots yourself, or it won't be your destiny that's written. And then of course the book has to be pressed. Fortune-signs are like photographs. They take time to develop."

He passed book and bag to his brother, who cradled them in his palms with all the solemnity of a priest holding a wafer. Then Negret crouched before the girl and her castle. "But speaking of stories yet to be told, we haven't heard a tale from you yet, Maisie." He took from his pocket the little book he'd bound the day before from scraps and Tesserian's spare aces. "What would you write, if you had a special book full of empty pages, a book meant to contain miracles?" He held it out, an offering.

Maisie looked at the little volume, then at the castle she and Tesserian had constructed. "I don't know."

Petra got up from the sofa and came over to sit on the hearth beside her. "Start one. See where it goes."

Hesitantly, Maisie took the handmade book and riffled the pages. "All right."

FIFTEEN

THE THREE KINGS

The Dancer's Tale

ONCE UPON A TIME, there were three kings. They were the King of Finding Things, the King of Opening Things, and the King of Tying Things. And they all lived together in a castle, watching over a kingdom made up of a thousand small islands in a huge green sea.

The three kings spent part of every year out on a journey, visiting the islands of their country, which were spread too far across the green sea for telegraph cables, visiting their people and the neighboring lands, and sometimes finding new islands and new people and introducing themselves and setting up alliances and trade treaties and embassies and that sort of thing.

At first they had thought it would be a bad idea to all go out voyaging at the same time, but they discovered they had to, because if the King of Finding Things didn't go, they couldn't find any of the places they wanted to get to, and if the King of

Tying Things didn't go, they couldn't tie up their boat when they reached a destination, and the King of Opening Things refused to be the one to stay home all the time because he said it wasn't fair. So they left a trusted person named Carol in charge when they left, and it worked all right.

One day, they were out sailing, and the King of Finding Things, who was up in the crow's-nest, spotted land through her spyglass. (She was a girl.) "Land ho!" she said. They sailed to the harbor, and although there was a nice pier with a sorbet stand on it (the shaved-ice sort of sorbet, not the other kind), there was no one in sight and nothing at all to see on the land anywhere, except for a big stretch of bushes that had been cut into a long, tall, very high wall.

The King of Tying Things tied up the boat with a very good knot that looked like a heart, and they all went ashore.

"This is strange," said the King of Opening Things.

"Very strange," said the King of Tying Things. And both of them looked to the King of Finding Things.

She strapped on her sword, which she didn't wear at sea because sometimes the sea was rough and that made sailing feel a bit like running with scissors. Then she nodded once and said, "If there's anyone or anything to be found on this island, I'll find it."

And together (but with the King of Finding Things in the lead) they marched up to the big hedge and started walking beside it. Before long, the King of Finding Things stopped. "Aha!" she said, and although neither of the other kings could see anything, she began to chop at the hedge with her sword until the branches fell away and there was a big wooden door with a big iron lock.

"Allow me," said the King of Opening Things, and he stepped forward. (He was very glad to have a way to be useful, because sometimes on these trips all he got to do was loosen stuck pickle-jar lids.) The door was locked, but of course that was no trouble. He had a set of picks to open locks without keys, and that's what he did.

Inside the door, they found a mess of a garden. It was almost more like a woods than a garden, actually. There didn't seem to be anywhere to walk, it was so overgrown.

But the King of Finding Things could see where the paths had been, and she could see where hedges and rosebushes that used to be separate had grown together. "It's not just a garden," she said as she found more and more clues. "It's a garden maze. It's just gone wild!"

The three of them worked together to find their way through. First the King of Finding Things would find the next correct part of the route, chopping a bit at the greenery when she had to. Then the King of Opening Things would make a path, and the King of Tying Things would tie the reaching and tangling plants to the side so they could all get through. And in that way, they got to the center of the maze, where they discovered a small castle with a single tower.

The three kings looked at one another.

"Is it possible?" asked the King of Finding Things.

"It would be a huge coincidence," said the King of Tying Things.

"There's only one way to find out," said the King of Opening Things. And he looked up at the tower and called, "Hey! Is someone in there?"

They waited, and then the window was pushed up and a girl leaned out. "Is that you?" she called, very surprised. And the three kings down on the ground looked at one another.

"I can't believe it," the King of Tying Things said.

"I can," said the King of Finding Things, who was used to huge coincidences with some of her finds. And this was a pretty big one. The person up in the tower was their sister: the fourth child of the family, the one who had been sent away. But she was not a king. She was . . . What is the other playing card in a pack, Mr. Tesserian? Not a king or a queen or an ace or a number or a jester or a saint.

Yes. A knave. The fourth child, the other sister, was the family villain, the Knave of Taking Things.

"What are you doing up there?" called the King of Opening Things.

"What do you mean, what am I doing up here?" the Knave of Taking Things called. "This is where you sent me!"

She couldn't be a king, you see, because a king shouldn't take things. A king ought to give. So her family had made her a knave, and when even that punishment wasn't enough to make her stop taking things, they sent her away, to a place surrounded by so much water, she couldn't reach any of the other islands in the kingdom. They said they'd send someone to look after her so she wouldn't be alone and wouldn't burn herself making soup. But then it rained too much, and no one came. So the Knave of Taking Things was alone for a long time.

But she had learned her lesson! She learned not to take things. As soon as she looked out the window and saw her brothers and sister, she called down and she promised.

"Come and get me," she begged. "Please! I'm ready to come home. I won't cause any more trouble. I won't be a villain anymore."

The three kings looked up at the castle window. "You really promise?" shouted the King of Opening Things.

"I do promise!" the knave shouted. "I promise never to take anything: never, never, *never* again!"

They looked at her with hard faces so she would understand how serious this was. "You'll have to pinkie-swear when we reach you," the King of Finding Things called back.

The knave promised that too, and down on the ground, the three kings began to make a plan.

The big gate door to the castle was easy: the King of Opening Things took care of that. Inside, they found a staircase leading up, but half the stairs were broken. On the bottom step, the King of Finding Things found an envelope sitting on top of a coil of rope. The envelope said, *Read me if you want to rescue the knave.* She opened the envelope and took out a note. *The stairs are broken,* it said. *To get up to the tower, you will need to climb, but this is the only rope and it has a spell on it so that it cannot be knotted.*

The King of Tying Things picked up the rope and started tying knots in it. But the note's message was true: none of the knots would stay. They untied themselves right away. It looked like a snake uncurling.

But the King of Tying Things had tricks for ropes like this. He had a sailor's tool that he could use to weave rope together if he wanted to tie something without a knot, and that's what he did. He wove the rope into a loop without a beginning or end, a loop he knew was stronger than any knot there was, a loop strong enough to bind monsters. But that day, the King of Tying things used it like a lasso, so that as they climbed, each time they reached a missing stair, he threw the rope around a piece of the banister beside the next part that was solid, and they all pulled themselves up that way.

When they reached the top, they found a door. "Are you there?" they called to their sister.

"Yes, I'm here!" she shouted. "The door is locked!"

But they already knew that, because the King of Finding Things had found another envelope propped up next to a Christmas cake on a table by the door. *The door is locked,* it said. *The key is the prize in this cake, but you have only one chance to cut a piece and find it.*

That made the three kings laugh, because every time there was a holiday and a cake with a prize, of course you knew who got it. The King of Finding Things had three false teeth made from pearls because she'd broken three of her own on all sorts of cake prizes: glass rubies and sixpences from England and tiny charm-bracelet bicycles. So she stepped forward, picked up the knife next to the plate, took a long, thoughtful look at the cake, and cut a triangle. She lifted the piece out and took a careful bite. She chewed, then reached into her mouth and took out a little package wrapped in wax paper. Inside the wax paper was a key, and she handed it to the King of Opening Things.

Her brother put the key in the lock. It took some jiggling, because it had been locked for a long time, but nothing that opened and closed could withstand the King of Opening Things. At last the door swung open, and the fourth sibling came running out and into the kings' arms.

"We love you and we missed you," they said. "We missed you so much!"

"I missed you!" she said, and, "I love you, too." And the Knave of Taking Things cried a little bit, because she had been a little bit afraid all that time while she'd been alone. Just a little bit. But then she was all right.

The knave made the pinkie oath she'd promised she would. Then they ate the rest of the cake, because they were all very hungry, and after that, they climbed back down the broken stairs and through the garden maze and back to their boat.

From then on, the Knave of Taking Things stayed home safely, the way she was supposed to, because she knew if she did, then one day, when she was grown up enough and when she had earned it, she might get to go on journeys with the kings too. But since she had learned her lesson and changed her ways and didn't take things anymore, she wasn't called by her old villain's name. Instead she was known after that as the Knave of Building Castles of Cards, because that's what she did while she waited for her brothers and sister to come back and tell her their tales.

INTERLUDE

MAISIE LOOKED AROUND, her face wavering between nervousness and triumph as her fingers worried Negret's handmade book. The adults in the room hesitated, torn in their own ways between surprise and sadness. It was Petra, on the hearth, who began resolutely to applaud, and after a heartbeat or two, the others joined in. The girl, who had begun to look worried, allowed herself to smile.

"But Maisie," Jessamy said from the sofa as the clapping faded to silence again, "no one would send a child away for taking things. You know that, surely."

"But they did," Maisie insisted. "They did! In the story," she added quickly. "But they did."

"Well, all sorts of things do happen in stories that would never happen in real life," Phineas Amalgam said, leaning forward in his chair in the corner and frowning.

Maisie's face was rapidly crumpling into distress. "It could happen," she said quietly. "People do take things."

"But a family would never send one of their own away for it," Jessamy persisted.

"They would," the girl said stubbornly, her eyes filling. "They did. In the story."

Jessamy, at a loss, got up from the sofa and came to sit cross-legged on the floor beside Maisie. She put an arm gingerly around her shoulder.

Amalgam stood, clearing his throat. "The thing about telling a story," he said, "is that one has to make choices. No story can contain every detail, so a storyteller has to decide what to put in and what to leave out. They have to pick and choose what to tell about what came before, what comes afterward, and plenty in between. It's part of the art, making those decisions, but just as it's very easy to leave too much in — and I am often guilty of that — it's often tempting to take too much out." He walked over to sit in the third, center chair by the fire, which had been empty for most of the evening. "And I think, if you don't mind a bit of constructive criticism from a man whose job it is to tell tales, you have taken too much out of this one."

Maisie wiped her eyes. "You think it should've been longer?" Her voice wavered. "I just wanted to get to the part where they took her home as fast as possible."

"I know," Amalgam said gently. "But still I think you have some missing pieces. Perhaps we can help you figure out what to put back. Would that be all right?"

The girl hesitated. She looked bashfully around the room. "I suppose so."

Amalgam clapped his hands on his knees. "Well, then. Here's one thing I always do when I'm figuring out whether I've told enough of the story: I tell it, just as you have done, to people I trust. Or at least," he added with a wink, "people I trust with the yarn." He looked around the room. "And then I say to them: I have told you this tale. What questions do you have?"

Maisie looked around at the faces in the room. She swallowed. "I told you this tale." Her voice was very small. "What questions do you have?"

There was a silence; then, "I have some."

Maisie turned, surprised to hear the first question come from Antony Masseter, at the corner chair by the sideboard. His eye patch was interesting, but apart from that, she had not paid much attention to him, nor he to her. "All right," she said dubiously.

"Very good." Masseter folded his arms. "You've told us the siblings of the knave left their home from time to time. Before the knave was sent away, did her siblings leave her at home when they went on these journeys?"

Maisie hesitated, then nodded.

"Did they tell the knave why she wasn't invited along?" Masseter asked. Maisie nodded again. "I am guessing," he said thoughtfully, getting to his feet, "that the reason had something to do with the sword the King of Finding Things wore, and the loop the King of Tying Things had learned to make that was strong enough to bind monsters. Perhaps their journeys occasionally took them into danger."

Reluctantly, Maisie said, "Yes, sometimes."

"I see." The peddler walked slowly, thoughtfully, toward the chairs surrounding the fire. "I think it's very important not to leave those things out. Or the part about how the knave came to be sent away." He leaned on the back of Amalgam's chair to look down at the young storyteller. "It wasn't simply that she took things *all* the time, was it?"

"No," Maisie whispered.

"I thought not. I found myself wondering—as I thought about the sword and the loop and the tools to open locks without keys—whether perhaps, it was *those* things she took. Not to *keep* them herself, of course, but simply to *know*. To know what the kings did when they left, and to know why those voyages were too dangerous for a knave to join. I wondered if perhaps she was a bit of a finder herself, and no matter how hard the others tried to hide their tools, the knave managed to find them. Perhaps she was given a lecture; possibly a lecture that made her feel quite a bit like she wasn't being taken seriously, or that they hadn't noticed how much she had grown up. She was told not to search; not to find; *not,* at all costs, to touch. But she couldn't help herself." He fixed his sharp green eye on the girl shrinking back into Jessamy's arm. "Could she?"

Maisie merely shook her head, her own eyes wide.

"Yes, this is all very important." Masseter looked down at the folklorist. "Wouldn't you say so, Amalgam?"

"I would indeed."

Masseter nodded. "I think it's vital to mention the reason why she took whatever it was she took the last time. Because I don't really think the knave was a villain, do you?"

"She took things," Maisie said helplessly. "They weren't hers, and she knew she wasn't supposed to do it."

"Yes, and she tried not to, didn't she? But then, you know,

she was also growing up. And I imagine at last she said to herself, *I'm not a child anymore. I can help. I can be useful.* So perhaps the final time she took — which was it, the last time?"

"The sword." The words were so quiet, they were almost inaudible.

"I see. Yes, I was wondering if perhaps, that last time, she took it intending to show the kings how careful she could be, and how responsible. To prove she could be trusted, even if she had to break a rule to demonstrate it." He and Maisie looked at each other for a moment. "Did she get hurt?"

"Yes," Maisie whispered. "It wasn't a sword, really, but a long knife, sharp on both sides. She — she didn't realize how heavy it would be."

"And after that, the kings sent her away. For her own safety, I imagine; probably just until some particularly dangerous encounter was finished."

Maisie started to protest. She pressed her lips together with a mutinous expression for a moment; then she sighed. "Yes."

The peddler nodded again. He scratched his head. "Those are all the questions I had. This is very helpful. I felt certain the knave wasn't a villain, nor was she just marooned without a plan to ever bring her back. Still, without all these details, one could easily get confusing ideas about it." He straightened unceremoniously and went to the sideboard to pour himself another whiskey. "It was a good story, I thought."

Maisie watched the peddler's back, awash with emotion and curiosity. "But how did you know all that?"

Masseter capped the bottle and tucked it back into its place. "What do you mean? I merely asked a few questions."

But Maisie was a girl, not a fool. "You didn't. You *knew*. You worked all that out yourself. Then you asked so I could tell you that you got it right. But how did you know?"

The peddler faced her again and took a long sip of his drink. "Because, my dear, the answers to the questions were already there. Your story fit a pattern — most things do. I merely connected the dots you left."

"I didn't leave any *dots!*" Maisie argued. "If there was a pattern, I'd know! It was my story!"

"Ah, well." Amalgam cleared his throat delicately. "Storytellers often don't know what the hell they're talking about, Maisie, my dear. A troublesome truth it's taken me a lifetime to come to terms with."

"By contrast . . ." Masseter took another drink — less a sip this time than a slug. He reached into his watch pocket and produced something small and gleaming from it: a silvery brooch in the shape of a flower, enameled in red and green and indigo, which he tucked into the palm with the firework scars without appearing to notice he was doing it. "By contrast," he said as he clenched and unclenched his fist against the sharp edges of the metal flower, "I am cursed to spot patterns and understand systems. I cannot *not* see them. And that, young lady, is how I caught the things you had left out, and knew how they would change your tale."

"Useful skill, that," Amalgam observed. "I wouldn't mind having a bit of that curse."

"You might think so," Masseter agreed, but his voice was grim. "Until you can see things in complete systems, you have no way of knowing how the smallest change in flow or sink will alter one, to say nothing of all the other intangibles that act upon things. So take this room, on this night. There's the rain and the tide working against the soil and rock and riverbed outside, yes. But." He nodded gallantly at Sorcha. "Also at work there is the particular geometry of the logs in a fire. There is the movement through the room of bodies around a house of cards." He glanced at Petra and raised an eyebrow. "There is the telling of a particular tale at a particular time."

"And what is this system you're describing?" Petra said with a grin.

"Well, that's so often the difficulty with them," Masseter replied with a bow of his head. "It's hard to know where one ends and another begins. Small systems feed into bigger ones like tributaries." His green eye flashed closed and open again, a strange, hard-edged wink. "They're rather like stories that way, in fact."

Petra stood and went over to refill her own glass. "I wonder. You know, it might be your turn, Mr. Masseter. Have you got a story to tell yourself?"

Masseter stood by as Petra reached past him for a bottle. "It's rather come to that, hasn't it?" he said quietly. "It's down to you and me." She smiled up at him in perfect innocence; there was a glitter in her eye that he thought was not from the fire. "Fine." He darted a glare across the parlor at Maisie. "The knave is not a villain."

"Hear, hear," Captain Frost pronounced from across the room, folding his arms across his chest.

"He's right," Tesserian whispered as he reached over to hand Maisie the queen of puppets.

She took the card in one hand, then remembered she still held the little handmade book in the other. "Wait." She offered it back to Negret.

But the bookbinding twin shook his head. "No, keep it," he said, taking Forel's roll of tools from his pocket and nodding at the stack of paper and the awl that already sat on the table beside his chair. "I can make another." Mrs. Haypotten pursed her lips hard, eyeing the sharp implements in the roll as Negret began straightening the papers into a stack, but she said nothing.

"Thank you." Maisie tucked the book in the pocket of her frock, then looked critically at the castle to find exactly the right place for the queen in her hand.

Masseter, meanwhile, waited at the sideboard until Petra had returned to her seat on the sofa. Then he took another long sip and two steps toward the center of the room. "Here goes, then."

SIXTEEN

THE GARDENER OF METEORITES

The Chapman's Tale

IN ANOTHER PLACE, in another time, there was a boy who could see the patterns.

All of them. And he nearly went mad with it.

Humans, like many creatures, are built to recognize patterns. It's a protection—a way to find what we need to survive, and also to see the dangers lurking in the shadows. It is how we recognize the things we sense, and how we understand the ways in which they fit into the world around us.

And patterns are everywhere. In the clouds. In the tides. In the red fruit, so like an apple, that hangs from the tree, just within reach, when you find yourself famished by the side of the road at high noon; in the creature whose face reminds you of a wolf's, the one you will now edge slowly away from. In the seedpods of pinecones and the nesting of spirals. In music, in speech.

In all these damned *stories*. Sequences. Series. Systems. Loops. Echoes.

This boy ... let's call him — no, not Pantin; though I imagine you haven't heard the last of his tales, Maisie. Anyhow, this boy wasn't from Nagspeake at all. Let's call him Foulk.

Foulk couldn't turn the patterns off. He couldn't stop seeing them, sensing them, anticipating them. The natural ones, the intentional ones, the accidental ones and coincidental ones; the meaningful ones and the ones that were there, unmissable, but simply didn't mean anything. The almost-patterns — oh, those were often worse: the ones that never quite manifested, or came close enough to meaningfulness to make him want to scream with frustration. Panes of window glass that didn't quite match. A sound repeated, its rhythm just out of phase with the order his brain expected. Torture on top of torture. And it was all constant. An assault, like voices screaming in his ears and pounding in his head all the time. Torchlight, directed straight into the eyes.

He dreamed of emptiness, and silence. A cloudless, birdless, colorless sky; a dark sea with no scent, no temperature, and no motion.

And then, one day when he was not quite fifteen, he had an idea. He decided the way to force all those patterns to fade into the background was to try to make himself look for one particular system among all the rest. Just one thread, one web in the forest of information. Because as he grew, as he became more and more accustomed to the constant barrage as one becomes accustomed to the needle-pain of freezing water or the sandpaper ache of smoggy air in the lungs . . . he had begun to become *aware* of something.

Not aware of the actual pattern, per se — not in the sense of being able to see it or smell it or touch it. But he thought he could perceive it. Perceive that it must exist, even if he couldn't spot it yet or pick it out of everything else. But he could feel it like pressure in his brain. All those years of inundation had made him unable to miss the hints of it, the moments he thought must be part of something bigger. They could not all be coincidence, nor all accidental. They could not all be meaningless.

Roads that lie strangely on the landscape. Springs that wind their devices in ways that physics cannot explain. Preternatural lights, unaccountable fogs, ice that freezes where it shouldn't, its crystals forming according to aberrant geometries with their own inexplicably deviative patterns. The uncanniness of some numbers, some fires, and the occasional lone blue stair.

Yes.

He began to search for more iterations of the data he thought might be part of the invisible pattern. And he began to find them, amid the noise of everything else. But these were like pieces of a puzzle that seemed they ought to fit, and simply . . . didn't. Or at least, if there *was* a means to make them fit, he couldn't find the right way to turn them.

There was one other pattern he looked for, and it centered around a girl. Her name was Jacinda, and in the rare moments when Foulk could stop the rushing of stimulus long enough to notice anything as more than a term in a sequence, he noticed her. He loved how she, almost alone among everything else in the world, could exist outside a pattern in his mind. Yes, she was part of a family, and also human, and also fit into any number of other taxonomies he could've named. But she seemed to shake them off as she walked. They trailed behind her, no more substantial than a shadow, or a cobweb. Outside the obscure, indiscernible pattern he sought, she was the only thing he actively tried to place. He loved her, and he ached to know where she fit into the set that also included himself.

Jacinda kept a garden in a field at the edge of town, a garden that was a miracle in its own way. It had not one but four meteorites in it that, according to local legend, had fallen from the sky on four separate occasions at some time in the unspecified past. One was smallish, pocked with golden and glittering crystals, and looked as if a pair of strong arms could lift it. The other three meteorites were iron, full of shallow pits and indentations that made them look as if hundreds of gigantic fingers had pressed into them all over, and varied from about the size of a large curled-up cat to that of a large curled-up sheep. And all around these, in the shallow remains of the craters they still sat in, Jacinda had planted tangles of flowers and vines and brambles.

But she was not a gentle, quiet horticulturist, this little gardener of meteorites. She was fierce, and she was brilliant. She knew the science behind those huge chunks of crystal and iron, and half the reason she planted things there was to attack with her fingers, her spade, and her gleaming curved garden shears the weeds that tried to choke them.

So Foulk looked for the obscure pattern he could sense but not see, and he yearned for Jacinda, and those two things held back the madness of the rest of the things he could not ignore, and time passed. The pattern still eluded him, but the search for it accomplished what Foulk had hoped: it drove the others into the scenery. Little by little, he forgot what it was like to see them all, hear them all, sense them all. They became a blur, a rushing in the background, like the landscape seen from a carriage or a train when your eye is focused somewhere other than on the window and what flashes by outside it. But it was still all there, ready to pop back into focus at any time.

One afternoon when he was almost sixteen, Foulk took a walk, looking for his pattern. He walked straight out of town on one of those old, old roads that crisscrossed the country. He ignored the infinitely repeating spirals and ratios in every flower head and he forced himself not to try to predict the movements of the flocking starlings or get lost in the wave action of wind across the wheat in the fields. Instead he looked for examples of the elusive system, and he let the road carry him deep into the countryside.

It had rained earlier that afternoon, but the sky had cleared, and now as the sun began to set with red and gold clarity, it reflected off the puddles that still lay in depressions in the rutted old roadway. He tried to ignore these, too; seeing the perfect mirroring of the world above in the road below at those uneven intervals was like sitting under a leaky roof that dropped single drips onto his forehead without predictable frequency. It was both system and nonsystem, and it hurt.

But then, because of course he couldn't totally ignore the puddles if he wanted to keep his feet dry, he saw something that made him stop: a puddle that reflected something it shouldn't have.

Reflections are predictable, mostly. They can be calculated. But mirrors, even the most ordinary of them, are uncanny. They all have a glaze of what Foulk would soon come to call the quality of *ferly*. Any surface that can become a mirror has the potential for bewitchment.

This puddle showed him a fingerpost, with two hand-shaped signs offset from each other by ninety degrees.

Foulk looked up and around himself, but of course, if he'd been walking toward a huge road sign, he'd have known it. There wasn't a sign. There wasn't even a crossroads. There was just this one very old, very rutted road, which he'd been following now for a good four miles without a single turning, and there were no intersections visible ahead, either.

But when he looked back down at his feet, Foulk found the crossroads still there in the puddle, plain as day. Or not, actually, because the sky over the reflected fingerpost was not the bright clear sunset of Foulk's own sky, but a deeply twilit one instead: dark enough that even when he crouched for a closer look, Foulk couldn't read the words on either of the finger-shaped signs. But he could see himself. There was a Foulk in the reflection, perfectly mirroring the boy's surprise as he looked out of the puddle.

"You can see it," said a voice, and another face appeared in the puddle.

It was ... well, it was Morvengarde, and it's impossible to describe the man until he's standing before you. But there he was. He was there in the reflection, and he was there still when Foulk turned away from the water on the ground and looked back at the real sky, looming over the boy and blocking out what was left of the sun.

It may surprise you, since Morvengarde and the company he founded are so much a part of Nagspeake history, to know that he has a place in the world beyond this city. But his shadow is long and his reach is broad—even so far as to lonely country roads in the middle of nowhere.

And when he appeared to Foulk on that lonely road, he was so instantly, obviously a part of the obscure system Foulk sought, and Foulk was so desperately relieved to have not one but two terms in the pattern—the reflection that did not reflect the world around it, and the stranger himself—that the boy almost completely failed to notice how terrifying the man was. At first, anyway.

"Yes," Foulk said, getting to his feet. "I see it. But where is it?"

"That particular crossing?" the man nodded down at the fingerpost. "Everywhere. Everywhere you are, anyhow. It's the crossroads you carry with you."

"I carry a crossroads even when I'm not at one?" Foulk asked, looking back down at the reflection.

"Oh, you're at one," the man said with a smile. Then he held out a hand. "My name is Morvengarde."

Foulk introduced himself, but he couldn't tear his eyes away from the puddle. "Why can I see it? Can everyone see their crossroads?"

"Certainly not," Morvengarde said, chuckling. "Most people would go mad if they had to be reminded constantly that their choices have consequences. You can see it because—and correct me if I err—you often see things others cannot. And what you cannot see," he added meaningfully, "you sense."

"The obscure system," Foulk said eagerly. "It's real, isn't it? This is part of it. *You're* part of it. Tell me what it is! Please. I've been looking for so long."

"It doesn't have a single name," Morvengarde said. "Different people have different names for it. The one I hear most is the Roaming World."

"The Roaming World," Foulk breathed. The relief was staggering. It reminded him of when he'd been much, much younger and had discovered that he was not, in fact, crazy, but that the number sequence and accompanying ratio he'd begun seeing everywhere were known phenomena and even had names: the Fibonacci sequence and the golden mean.

"It will come clearer over time," Morvengarde said. "The more you see, the more you look, the more you will find it. It hides in plain sight, but like many patterns, the overall structure becomes increasingly evident the more data you have."

"Is it really a whole world? And is it a whole *separate* world?" Foulk asked, looking down at the puddle. "Is there . . . is that some sort of portal? Or is this Roaming World just a system within this world?"

"Young man, philosophers have given entire lifetimes to that question. Perhaps someday you will be the one to answer it." Morvengarde reached into an inside pocket of his long coat. "It's a rare thing to encounter a roamer at the start of his wanderings. Allow me to give you a gift of welcome." And he took out a small magnifing glass like a jeweler's loupe. "This, I believe, will help you see."

Foulk took the glass. "What is it?"

"Look through it."

Foulk obeyed and peered up at the stranger. Morvengarde was suddenly outlined in vapor and astonishing color against the fields. It was as if he both wore a halo and was also generating glowing smoke that billowed away from his tall figure.

The boy yelped and pulled the glass away. The world returned to normal. He put it back, and once again Morvengarde was a thing of strange light and shadow.

"Is this how you see the world?" Foulk breathed in wonder.

"No, indeed," the stranger said. "Even among roamers, very few have the ability to see as you do, even when aided by a glass like that one. You have very special vision."

"What is it about you that the glass is showing me?" Foulk asked, too caught up in all this new information for tact or caution.

"Well, I couldn't say," Morvengarde replied, tucking his hands into his pockets. "Describe it."

Foulk tried, fumbling over words like *halo* and *nimbus* and *fog*, then *radiance* and *visible light* and *refraction* and even *foam* before Morvengarde, laughing, threw up his hands. "Enough. I think I can tell you what you're seeing."

We have heard from Mr. Haypotten about the makers of reliquaries here in Nagspeake, and the spectacular vessels they craft for containing the wondrous. But there is another kind of reliquary.

When do the remains of a miraculous person become miraculous themselves? A saint must — generally speaking — perform some number of miracles in life, but must also — again, generally — be dead before he or she can be given the title. But surely that's just formality. Some people contain the wondrous within themselves throughout their lives. How would they perform marvels in the first place, if there wasn't a core of the miraculous, some strange power already within them?

Mr. Morvengarde had a name for this quality. *Worden:* the quality of having a fate, a destiny, and he was always in search of those who possessed it. He also looked for those touched by a quality he called *ferly* — the strange and uncanny. Worden and ferly were revealed by a phenomenon Morvengarde called *weyward lumination:* weird light.

Objects that gave off weyward lumination he called relics, and *people* with worden or ferly—or best of all, both—he referred to as *reliquaries:* living, breathing, walking vessels for the miraculous. Foulk would very quickly discover, however, that not everyone is a saint who happens to be a reliquary.

"When you look at me," Morvengarde finished, "you are seeing both kinds of weyward light. Worden is the halo, and ferly is the mist."

Foulk stared down at the priceless loupe. "And I can really keep this?"

"Certainly. It's a gift." Morvengarde reached into his pocket again and took out a card. "I would be glad to hear from you sometime, Foulk. Write and tell me what the glass shows you. I will explain what I can. And perhaps you may return the favor in your own way."

"How?"

"I am a merchant by trade, in the Roaming World," Morvengarde said, presenting the card he'd taken from his vest.

MORVENGARDE
GRANDMASTER IN TOTO

DEACON AND MORVENGARDE, INCORPORATED

GOODS, SERVICES, AND EXPRESSAGE
TRUSTED SINCE TIME IMMEMORIAL

49 TRYSTERO WHARF, THE LIMEN DOCKS

"Should you come across relics in your wanderings, I will buy them from you. Or, in the case of a reliquary, I — or one of my chapmen — will offer to pay them very well now in exchange for their mortal remains being left to me when they die."

It began that simply. A boy who could see patterns, desperately looking for the one he couldn't quite see but that had to be there, and a lens that began to bring it into focus.

It wasn't precisely all around him, but the traces were more common than he'd expected. He took the loupe everywhere, glanced surreptitiously through it at everything, and began to learn to interpret what it revealed.

Ferly showed up through the lens as a sort of nimbus — a glowing mist around a particular subject that could vary in color, density, and concentration, not unlike all those fogs in the catalog listing Mr. Haypotten described. The uncanny comes in so many flavors, after all. A person marked with ferly could possess any number of varieties of it, and if you wanted to know what you were looking at, you had to look more than once, and carefully. Ferly doesn't only follow *people*. It follows objects. It can attach itself to places. It can arise from stories, dances, songs. It spreads sometimes, touching and transforming everything in its path. It is deeply complicated on many levels.

Worden seemed at first to be simpler. Through the loupe, it looked like a halo, just as Morvengarde had said. It was hard-edged, confined; it was usually immediately obvious to what or whom the worden belonged, which was not the case with the more nebulous ferly. And it was generally a binary thing: you had it or you didn't, and that was almost all the information the lens would show. Over time, however, Foulk would begin to be able to spot subtle differences in the halos he saw. You could have a secondary or tertiary or quaternary worden, a destiny linked to the worden of someone or something else. Worden could be modified almost endlessly by the shifting fogs of ferly. Or not. Most destinies, in fact, are not supernatural.

The lens of the loupe opened up an entirely new world of patterns and systems, and the boy was utterly ensorcelled. He was uniquely gifted to work out all the permutations of ferly, the subtle differences in primary and dependent worden, and to interpret the results when they layered over each other. And little by little, the Roaming World became his world, though it was some time before he wrote to Morvengarde, or encountered another roamer in person.

One day a few weeks after his meeting on that lonely road, he happened to be passing by Jacinda's garden in the field at the edge of town. She was pulling up weeds from around the flowers that grew among the meteorites. Foulk lingered, as he always did when passing there. And as he watched her weeding and humming to herself, some imp of the perverse made him take the loupe Morvengarde had given him from his pocket.

He fitted it to his eye, and gasped as the quality of the world changed before him. Jacinda's garden was roiling, absolutely *flooded* with ferly. He had never seen so much in one place.

He took the lens from his eye, wiped it clean on the edge of his shirt, and looked again. No, there was no mistake: the garden was positively alive with weyward lumination.

Of course, gardens often hide secrets; we have Madame Grisaille's tale from last night as an example. But Foulk didn't think there was much of a secret to the ferly he was seeing. This was, after all, a garden full of things that had fallen from the sky. One of them—perhaps more than one—was, in some way, miraculous.

He went home and wrote immediately to Morvengarde to tell him, and to ask him to come and give a valuation. Jacinda's family wasn't what you'd call poor, and he knew Jacinda would never willingly part with her meteorites, but he thought surely they'd all like to know if they possessed something as valuable as it seemed at least one of these sky rocks was likely to be. There might be an emergency one day, some reason they might need the money.

A week later, a blond woman turned up at Foulk's door with a tall, muscled man in smoked spectacles standing respectfully behind her.

"I have come from Morvengarde," she announced, presenting her own card. It was identical to the card the Roaming World merchant had given Foulk, except where the first had had simply the name MORVENGARDE in large copperplate followed by the title GRANDMASTER IN TOTO, this one read SELEUCIA DEACON, GRANDMASTER SECONDARIA. "I believe you have found something needing a valuation." The tall man in the smoked spectacles said nothing.

Something about the pair gave the boy the feeling of someone walking over his grave. But his fascination with the Roaming World had only grown since he'd met Morvengarde, and here were two more denizens, right at his door.

"It's a garden," he said. "A garden of meteorites. It belongs to my friend. It's — I think it's got a lot of ferly to it."

"Show me," the woman ordered, and together the three of them walked to the road that passed the field with Jacinda's garden. Jacinda was there, of course, her back to them as she cut long-stemmed flowers with heads the size of saucers and laid them in a basket.

Foulk reached into his pocket for his loupe, but Deacon had already taken a glass of her own from inside her coat. "Oh, my," she said, even before she had the glass fitted all the way into her eye socket. She looked for a moment, then passed the glass to the man who'd come with her. He tucked the loupe between his right eye and the smoked lens covering it, made a noise of surprise, then passed it back. "Very well, Foulk," Deacon said, pocketing the loupe. "You are absolutely right. Well done. Would you introduce us, please?"

Heart pounding, Foulk led them to a break in the garden wall, and they walked to where Jacinda was working. She looked up from her basket of flowers as they approached. Dahlias, they were, shaped like exploding fireworks. Red ones, yellow ones, dark purple ones like the late-evening sky he had seen in the reflection of his crossroads in the rain puddle weeks before.

Foulk could barely speak from nervousness, but somehow he managed the introduction. "Jacinda, this is Miss Deacon. I brought her here because she and her partner are merchants who specialize in . . . very valuable objects. She's interested in your meteorites and asked me to introduce her to you."

In the midst of this speech, both Seleucia Deacon and the man who'd come with her looked sharply at the boy. He fumbled but carried on, thinking they were reacting to his reference to her partner; he'd meant Morvengarde, of course, but perhaps they thought he'd been referring to the silent man, who seemed to be more of a bodyguard.

When he finished speaking, Jacinda looked to the newcomers. Her smile was friendly but wary, and Foulk realized he'd been a fool to think that Jacinda would be excited about the idea of selling her precious meteorites at any price. "It's very nice to meet you. I don't know if Mama and Papa will sell any of the meteorites, but they're home, so you're welcome to talk to them. This way." She tucked the basket of red, yellow, and purple dahlias over one forearm and motioned toward the house.

Before she could take a step, Seleucia Deacon put a hand on her shoulder. "Don't bother, my dear. These are too big for us to move. But thank you. Your flowers are beautiful. And thank you, Foulk. I hope you both have a lovely evening." And without another word, she and the bodyguard left the garden and disappeared down the road, leaving Foulk and Jacinda staring after them, and then staring at each other.

"That was strange," Jacinda said.

"Yes, it was," Foulk replied, but he knew his friend couldn't possibly understand just how strange it was. After all, if there was as much ferly in this garden as it had seemed, surely the size of the meteorites, troublesome though it might have been, wouldn't have stopped Morvengarde from acquiring them.

Then, "How have you been?" Jacinda asked. And Foulk forgot all about Deacon and Morvengarde and ferly and worden and all of it. They talked straight through until sunset, and when he left for home, Jacinda kissed his cheek, and the world rewrote itself, with new patterns bursting into existence everywhere he looked.

At some point between the time that Foulk left and the time her mother came out to call her in for supper, Jacinda disappeared.

Late that night, her parents came knocking on Foulk's door. They had seen the two of them talking in the garden and had hoped the boy might know where she'd gone. And even as he shook his head no, an idea started to take shape in Foulk's mind, and he began to feel sick to his stomach. Because there was a pattern here, impossible not to see, and he couldn't believe he'd missed it before.

When Deacon had looked at the garden, she'd agreed that there was a powerful source of ferly there. *You are absolutely right,* she'd said. *Well done.* But Deacon had not seemed particularly interested in the meteorites.

Morvengarde, when he'd given Foulk the loupe, had told him to watch out for both relics and reliquaries — *people* who were living vessels of weyward lumination. And Foulk understood that it could be very, very difficult to tell what the swirling fog that was ferly was actually attached to. When he had looked into the garden and seen it, he'd assumed it had been emanating from one or more of the meteorites. But Jacinda had been in there too, both times, working among the rocks.

What if *she* had been the source? What if she was a living reliquary?

Morvengarde, when he'd given Foulk his assignment, had said he offered reliquaries a good price to deed their mortal remains to him after they died. But clearly no one had had any sort of conversation with Jacinda's parents about their sixteen-year-old daughter's funerary arrangements. Foulk shuddered. The very thought of that conversation was horrifying to him — surely it would've been horrifying to her parents as well.

Was it possible Seleucia Deacon and the man in the smoked spectacles had just . . . had just *taken* her?

The next day, when Jacinda didn't turn up, Foulk went looking for Deacon and her bodyguard. No one in town had seen them. It was as if he had imagined them both.

He wrote to Morvengarde. The following week, he received a reply: *Deacon returned to HQ. Your assessment mistaken. Meteorites purely quotidian. We look forward to next find. M.*

Quotidian meant normal. Mundane. But *something* in that garden had not been quotidian. He wrote back again, and this time he asked the question he needed answered, point-blank: *Did she take Jacinda?*

The reply was brutally short and equally evasive: *Don't be ridiculous.*

Jacinda never turned up again.

A year later, Foulk left home. No one said it, but he couldn't miss the clues: the whole town thought he'd had something to do with Jacinda's disappearance. After all, he'd brought the strangers to her garden, and everyone knew there had been strangers, because he'd gone around the next day looking for them. He'd been the last person to speak to her before she'd vanished. His heart hurt, and he couldn't take the suspicion. He packed a bag and Morvengarde's loupe, and he took to the roads.

He hadn't contacted the merchant again, but it wasn't long before Deacon and Morvengarde tracked him down. Of course, they waited until the worst possible time, when Foulk had run out of money, gotten himself into five kinds of trouble, and could see that he was about to come to a sticky end. Seleucia Deacon swooped in with her big, silent bodyguard and rescued him. She didn't ask him to commit to working for the company, but she left the door open. And though he managed to resist it for years, inevitably, just before the American War Between the States broke out, Foulk wound up walking through that door. He tucked Morvengarde's loupe firmly into his eye socket and went in search of ferly and worden, wandering all the trails of the Roaming World.

Over time, Foulk became one of Deacon and Morvengarde's most profitable chapmen. And eventually, Morvengarde entrusted him with a unique and very special charge. You see, he turned out to have a certain touch of ferly himself: whether he'd been born with it or whether it was a matter of his constant daily interactions with it, the boy — now a young man — never knew. But along with his gift for recognizing systems, he turned out to also have a gift for spotting patterns and systems in *time*.

Time, of course, is as complicated as ferly. More, even. It can move in what seems like a line, can seem to be measurable by the predictable cascade of sand through glass, but that's mere illusion. The ability to see beyond the illusion to the truth of it is vanishingly rare, but Foulk could do it. It was a glorious challenge, like the hunt for the obscure hidden pattern that he now understood was the existence of the Roaming World. He had solved that problem, and so he turned himself to the question of time. And his employers bestowed upon him a device that helped him simplify the workings — the reckonings — it took to really see and anticipate the vagaries and interactions of time and space.

Because, just as he'd sensed with his glimpses of the Roaming World so long ago, Foulk began to see that there were brief points in time when the patterns and systems shifted. Loops could be broken. Whole new possibilities opened up. In those moments, great and even impossible things could be done — if you didn't *miss* the moment. For the most part, those junctures were impossible to anticipate; they were the confluence of so many factors that even Foulk's brain couldn't hold and calculate them all, and some came and went in less time than it took a heart to shudder. But Foulk could see how to do it. And with the aid of Morvengarde's device, he learned to calculate, anticipate, and use those moments.

As for Jacinda . . . it seems strange to say it, perhaps especially when talking of a man who was rapidly becoming something like an artificier of time and space, but . . . Foulk never looked back. At first it was that he couldn't bear to learn what he knew he would find, because it was impossible not to understand what happened when Morvengarde made a deal. Foulk learned that the Great Merchant never risked losing a relic. Yes, the terms of the deals he made were always that he would collect the relics after death. But no reliquary who made a deal with Morvengarde ever lived long after that.

Jacinda had surely been dead for a long time.

As the years went by, Foulk found another reason not to look back, or reminisce, or ask any untoward questions. He didn't want anyone to think he *cared*. And while he feigned carelessness, Foulk began to plan. Someday, he decided, someday he would go back for Jacinda. He would take his still-broadening skills and Morvengarde's mechanism, and he would reset her life, and save her from himself.

But he couldn't hurry. This was the kind of thing he'd have only one shot at, and there was every chance that, even if he succeeded, it would be the death of him. He had no idea what Deacon and Morvengarde had done with Jacinda's relics, but if he managed to save her, whatever parts of her they'd deemed valuable would vanish, and the merchants would be furious at the loss. He couldn't fail, and his likelihood of success went to zero if Deacon and Morvengarde doubted his loyalty for even a second. He planned, and he told himself he was waiting for the moment: that one juncture that was the singular true conjunction of time and opportunity for the saving of the girl he had loved when he was a boy.

And in the meantime, he did terrible things.

He did whatever they asked. He told himself this was to avoid any doubt they might've otherwise had, and he told himself when he went back to rescue Jacinda, it would all be undone. He told himself it would be as if all the dreadful things he had done had never happened at all — even though by then he knew that wasn't necessarily true. Time isn't like a strand you can tease out of a muffler or a knot and, simply by pulling on it, undo the whole. Foulk knew that. But he was also becoming incredibly good at time reckoning, and he told himself he'd find a way to undo Jacinda's death in a manner that would also undo all the rest of his crimes.

He told himself many, many lies.

All the while, the years spiraled around him. The War Between the States began. Foulk worked as a sutler, following armies and selling to soldiers, still seeking worden and ferly amid the hellscape of the Civil War in his own era, and in times and places beyond that. Battle had its particular set of systems, and so did time, but he saw all the patterns, quotidian and uncanny. He carried on.

It is . . . difficult to break from any orbit. He tried not to think of Jacinda, but when he did, Foulk thought of her garden and the meteorites that had broken free of all sorts of forces — more than he understood at the time — to land improbably in what would become her dahlia beds. He himself was feeling more and more like a satellite, flung in loops that changed in subtle ways even while bringing him back over and over again to basically the same place. He put off returning to Jacinda in her garden. There was always a reason, though never a good one.

There are some systems, some patterns, you can access only if you're willing to give something up. To really understand the deeper realities they reveal, some systems force you to make sacrifices. There is a property of multiplication, for instance, that states that three times four gives you the same result as four times three. But there is a kind of mathematics that's done with four-dimensional numbers called *quaternions*. It is the mathematics of rotation in three-dimensional space: the mathematics of orbits, in fact. If you want to do these kinds of calculations, you must first accept that A times B no longer equals B times A. And then there are eight-dimensional numbers called *octonions,* which require you to give up other fundamental mathematical properties. There are . . . well, *truths* that have to be tossed aside to understand these strange mathematics, which are also true.

It's not easy to let go of things you have always known to be true. But imagine finding that the patterns and facts you've held contain the evidence of a whole new reality you never suspected was there. And imagine that, to even begin to understand it, you have to question some things you've always believed. Bit by bit, you cast away little truths. *A* times *B* equals *B* times *A.* Or, *I am not the sort of person who would willingly allow another person to die.* Little by little, you give up everything you think you understand about the world. Oh, those certainties are still there, even still accurate in their way . . . but if you let yourself see them—if, in your confusion in the new and strange world you are exploring, you turn back even for a moment toward the old one—everything collapses.

This was Foulk, working for Morvengarde, trying to figure out how to break his orbit and waiting for the right moment to strike amid all the strange loops of his life. But late at night he tortured himself with questions. How many rotations, then, would it take? How many revolutions, how many spheres and rivers washing over him, how many perfect shuffles of spacetime, to return to where he started and who he had been?

And then, several things happened at more or less the same time.

Things one and two: Foulk failed an assignment, and he got Seleucia Deacon killed. That is a tale in itself, but the most amazing thing about it might've been that it did not get Foulk killed in response.

When he got over his shock, Foulk realized he'd likely been spared only because the one other person on Morvengarde's staff who could reckon with time as well as he could had been Deacon herself. After that, he decided it was time to stop putting off going back for Jacinda. After all, he'd unexpectedly been given a second chance after a terrible mistake. There wouldn't be another of those, and if he died before he hadn't at least tried to fix that first horrible error he'd made, everything else he'd done, all those other dreadful choices, would be for naught.

He decided to begin the reckoning he'd been planning for years.

The next thing to happen was that Seleucia Deacon's sister, Aniline, inherited her stock and became Morvengarde's new junior partner. It was Aniline who appeared before Foulk one day in the wilds of Georgia to present his next assignment. And at the same time, she gave him a gift.

"I am Grandmaster Secondaria now," she said without preamble. "And although I would gladly see your head on a pike, you are still of some value to this company. Therefore, I bring you a present of goodwill." And Aniline Deacon opened a box and showed him a very beautiful enameled flower in the shape of a yellow-and-red firework. "I heard from my sister that you like dahlias," the new Deacon whispered as she lifted the brooch from its wrappings.

Foulk had never so much as looked at another dahlia since leaving Jacinda in her garden the night she had vanished, so this could only be a reference to that incident, and meant for wounding. Sure enough, Aniline Deacon smiled and stabbed him over the heart as she pinned it on his vest. Then she gave him his next assignment, and then she vanished.

This is the last one, Foulk decided as he unbuttoned his shirt and pressed a handkerchief to the wound. *This mission, and no more, and then I will do what I must.* But he also knew he could not fail in this one. Aniline wanted him killed. If he didn't deliver on the job Morvengarde had set, nothing would save him, and if he died, his childhood sweetheart would stay dead too.

The assignment took him to Missouri, in another era that was not his own. And there, very much to his shock, he met a girl who was so like Jacinda that Foulk stumbled in his resolve. But in the end, he knew she was just one more sacrifice to be made so that he could undo it all.

And then, the unthinkable happened. Foulk failed a second time. Worse still, the device — the device that made everything possible — was broken.

There were no others in existence, as far as Deacon and Morvengarde knew. Seleucia had been the keeper of the only other similar mechanism in the company's possession, and it had been destroyed when she had been killed.

But once again, the merchants did not kill Foulk, because Aniline didn't have her sister's head for reckonings. *They couldn't kill him.* He was the only time-reckoner they had, and he was the only one with a true understanding of the device that had been lost. So instead of taking his life, they tasked him with rebuilding the mechanism, no matter how long it took, no matter how difficult the task.

And so he began.

Again the years spiraled.

And then, one day, the rain began to fall.

INTERLUDE

"**THIS INN . . .**" He rubbed the space between his eyes, hard. "It's like the old days. The days before I could shut out the patterns. Because the one I can't unsee — the one that drowns all the rest — that's the one that's everywhere here. It's *everywhere,*" he said savagely, glaring around the room as if they were all to blame. "Even without the loupe, the weyward lumination in this room is so bright, I can barely stand it. You . . . you *blaze.* Each of you. *Each of you* is a reliquary, and I can't take the glare." He took a halting pair of steps toward the fireplace. Amalgam lurched out of the chair between Reever and Negret, and Masseter dropped into it. With a shaking hand, he raised his glass to throw back the last of his drink.

Each of them? Maisie tore her eyes from the peddler and looked at the others, trying to see what he saw. Then she remembered the secrets she'd glimpsed herself, and it didn't seem so shocking a thing to say. *Then* she realized what he'd *actually* said, and she looked down at her hands. The cards Tesserian had passed her during Masseter's tale, the king of allsorts and the knave of gnomons as well as the queens of paquets, pennyfarthings, and secateurs, all drifted, forgotten, to the floor.

"Oh, yes," Masseter said softly, looking down at the girl sitting not far from his feet. "You especially, my dancing friend. And I think the others have seen it, even if you haven't. Certainly Tesserian there has, with his structures that won't fall until he grants them leave to do it. But *he* didn't build that castle. *You* did, my dear Knave of Building Castles of Cards. He's only been feeding you the pieces. And I think you would be just as dangerous a gambler as Tesserian if you chose to be. I suspect you read people as well as he does, if only you can convince them to dance. More, you can hear music the rest of us can't. You and the bookbinder, there," he said, nodding to Negret, who paused in the act of driving holes through his block of pages, one of Forel's awls twisting in his fingers. "The world sings to you, even in its silence. Someday it will tell you secrets, if it hasn't already. But I suspect it has. I suspect you have been a Queen of Finding Things yourself for some time now. Buttons, dragonflies, books . . ."

He hesitated, considering the shocked girl closely. "You have a worden and some sort of ferly on you too. Other knacks, other kinds of savvy you might not discover for years. Possibly the magic of that-which-remains." A flicker of regret crossed his expression, mingled with surprise; Masseter was not accustomed to feeling anything remotely like sorrow. "I would need the loupe to be certain." It was in his pocket, but he did not reach for it.

Maisie began to protest that she didn't understand, then realized that she did. Not everything, not by a long shot . . . but as she looked from the peddler to the castle, she thought perhaps she had an idea.

"I'm sorry," Masseter said, but the coldness had returned to his face and voice, and the girl turned instead to Tesserian, who managed a hesitant pat on her shoulder that didn't much help. Jessamy, still sitting at Maisie's side on the floor, shot a look of fury up at the chapman and tugged the girl into her arms. But there was nothing to say, because she could see the truth as clearly as Masseter: this was a child bound for the roads. Strange things would find her, even if she didn't go seeking them. She would stumble into them, just as she'd stumbled into this inn.

Meanwhile, Masseter turned to look thoughtfully at the Haypottens. "When you open your home and your place of business to roamers, other roamers will find it, each one tracking more of the dust of the old roads across your threshold. That sort of thing isn't so easily swept back out the door. It lingers. It clings to you, much like the residue of the uncanny fires built by the conflagrationeer who tends your hearth." He glanced grimly at Amalgam, who had backed up close to the corner table where Sangwin still sat. "The extraordinary calls to the extraordinary, doesn't it? So I suppose it isn't so strange that this house would see its share of creatures like us passing through." He threw out his arms to encompass the entire room. "But this many? This varied? And everyone pretending studiously to be human, even the ones who so obviously aren't. Why?" He nodded at Maisie again. "For her sake? Surely not. This isn't coincidence, all this weyward light in one place, and it isn't accident."

He pivoted slowly, meeting each of the fourteen pairs of staring eyes until his gaze fell on Petra, who, at some point during his tale, had perched against the riverward window where Sangwin had been smoking the night before.

"Me?" Petra grinned. She straightened and returned to her original seat on the sofa beside Sullivan. "Surely you're not suggesting I can control the rains and waters, Mr. Masseter."

"Maybe not," he said softly. "But you have controlled the telling, these last two days. Why?"

Petra shook her head as she sat, so that the dragonfly at her temple sent tiny flickers of reflected firelight around the room. "I believe these stories were Mr. Amalgam's idea."

"Maybe, or maybe we'll find that the two of you had a conversation earlier, perhaps at a meal, when the old traditions of storytelling came up. Perhaps you expressed that delightful, infectious curiosity of yours. Perhaps that's how he came to suggest it. But certainly since then, you've stepped in now and again to call forth certain tales. Not every time, not with every storyteller. But more than once. And," he added with a humorless chuckle, "I can't help but notice that, when you have, the tales that come forward out of your conjuring are tales of peddlers and men with one eye. Again: not an accident. *Not* a coincidence." The expression in his own eye chilled further, even as the rest of his face curved in a smile. "I know who you are. I know your name, and I know what story you're going to tell. *If* you tell the truth. You might as well just come out with it, beginning, if you please, with: *How?*"

The room held its breath. Some waited to hear the explanation for what they themselves had also sensed; others waited to see how this final act they'd been anticipating would play out at last. Three prepared grimly for battle; one prayed her hands would remain her own as she wrapped her arms tighter around the girl she held. One brushed fingers across the back of Petra's neck: *I am here, beside you, for whatever good it's worth.*

Petra herself leaned forward on the sofa, propping her elbows on her knees and looking thoughtfully over her interlaced hands at Masseter. "You know how. You said it yourself. There sometimes come moments when the patterns of time and chance and the endless moving pieces — people, stories, floodwaters — come into a particular configuration in which otherwise unbreakable loops can change. You didn't call the phenomenon by its name, but it has one."

"Kairos," Masseter said, his voice trailing into a hiss.

"Yes." Petra smiled thinly. "*Kairos.* The right moment for undertaking a particular action. And, as you have told us, the moment of kairos can be calculated, with the right sort of reckoning."

"That sort of reckoning is —" He shook his head, disbelieving. "Nearly impossible."

"Nearly," she agreed. "But not."

They stared at each other.

"How?" he asked again.

"Work," she spat. "Years of it. Years, training myself to see the patterns. Years, learning the mathematics, the probabilities and all the potential interactions and fluctuations of time and space, all the *millions* of variables that affect it all." She sat back, folding her arms across her chest. "And that's why we're here. This is the kairos moment, Mr. Masseter. For me. For you."

"For what?" he asked softly, dangerously.

"My turn to tell a tale, is it? Fine, then." Petra matched his tone to the precise murderous pitch. "Listen."

SEVENTEEN

THE SUMMONS OF THE BONE

The Orphan's Tale

L*ISTEN.*

The last time the waters began to rise, the first to die was Nell's father. The rain that had been falling for weeks made the bank slick, and Nell saw him go. She saw him lose his footing, saw him grasp for something, anything to hold to keep from plunging into the river Skidwrack. By the time she reached the embankment, he was gone, carried away by waters that just kept rising.

The waters took her sisters, too: the eldest in a sudden flood that caught her as she was chasing the family dog across a field, the youngest when lightning struck the tree the girl was sheltering beneath. Their mother was last and hardest, because when the waters of the river came lapping at the house and Nell knew they had to flee or be drowned, there was still time, plenty of time to leave. But Nell's mother refused, because she couldn't bear to leave the place where her eldest and youngest daughters were buried, even if it meant losing her middle child, too. She would not abandon the house, not even when the waters came rushing across the floor and drove them to the roof; not even when the waters filled the house like a bucket and the only thing left to do was grasp a piece of driftwood and hope safety still existed to be found somewhere.

When that happened, even then, Nell's mother would not go from the house. And when Nell finally dragged herself onto dry ground, she was alone. And still the waters kept rising.

She was fifteen, and she had nothing but her older sister's blue coat, which she had found caught on the branch of a drowned tree, for protection from the rain. As she hunted for the safety of higher ground, she encountered others like herself, set adrift by the waters, alone and afraid. Each time, they wondered what it would take to stop the floods. The rains kept coming; the waters kept rising. Soon, it seemed, the entire town — whatever was left of it — must drown.

One night, alone in a cave, Nell thought about an old bit of folklore she'd once heard. She was hungry and thirsty and had been awake for days, so perhaps it was delirium that made her decide to try it.

It took her a few days more to find a black cat, another few after that to find enough dry wood to boil water. When all that was left of the cat were its bones, she made her way to the river's swollen edge and set the bones on the surface. The frothing Skidwrack took all but one. The remaining bone spun gently, as if it were caught in the mildest of eddies. Then it slid against the plunging flow, upriver and out of sight.

A moment later, the figure of a tall man appeared at the bend in the river around which the single bone had disappeared. He strode upon the surface of the water as if it were a road, with a long, dark overcoat wrapped around him and a gray fedora keeping the rain from his head.

Nell watched with her heart in her throat, wiping drops from her eyes over and over as the strange figure approached. At last he stood before her with his coat whipping about his ankles and rain dripping from his hat. "I received your message," he said in a voice like thunder rolling far, far away. In the shadows under the hat's brim, a pair of searching eyes considered her curiously. "Put forth your question."

She folded her shaking hands and cleared her throat, and she saw the dark man smile very slightly, as if there was something endearing about her fear. "I want you to stop the water rising."

The man put his hands into the pockets of his coat. "That isn't a question."

"Please stop the water rising?"

"That is still not a question. It's a request with a question mark at the end of it."

"Well — can you stop the water rising?"

He smiled more. "You called me all this way to ask me a question I can answer with a single word?"

The girl realized her mistake and raised her hands quickly. "Wait. No. Let me think." And as she thought about her question, she realized she had a problem. She had expected to be allowed to make a request, but what the dark man had offered was something different. She could perhaps ask, *Will you stop the water rising?*—but even if he answered yes, that didn't mean he would stop it *now,* or at any time before her town would be wiped off the coast. She could not think of any way to ask him to solve the problem of the rising water.

At last she asked the only question she'd come up with. It didn't accomplish what she'd wanted to accomplish from this meeting, but it was the best she could think of. "How can I stop the water rising?"

"Ah. Now, that is a good question. Before I can answer it properly, you must tell me why it falls to you to ask this thing."

He listened as she told him about how the water had taken her family, one by one. She told him how, as she had sought a way to stop the flood, she had seen other parts of the town deluged, other families rent apart by the swamping of either their lands or their people. He listened to the pain in her voice, and he listened to the rain as it fell ever harder, as if it wished to drown her words until it could drown the girl herself.

Then he pointed with a long hand to the river water rushing past the small spit of muddy ground upon which they stood. "Your message to me was in the form of a single bone."

"The one that floated upriver," she whispered.

"Do you know why this is so, that a single bone exists in the whole of a cat that can do this, and why that bone alone may be used to summon me?"

She shook her head.

"There is a sort of magic called orphan magic," he said. "It is the magic of that-which-remains, of that-which-is-alone. It is, in many ways, the magic of desperation, but it is never the magic of chance. When one remains, it is the one that was meant to remain. It is the one that is special; it is precious because it is unique; it is powerful because that is how it survived." The man took something from his pocket, and she recognized it as the white bone she had set adrift on the river an hour before. "There is one bone in a cat that may call me, but it must be separated from the others to do its work. It has potential when it is connected to the rest, but when it is sundered away, its potential becomes power."

She nodded, trying not to think of what she had had to do to the cat to release that one tiny bone's orphan magic.

He lifted his head just a fraction, just enough for her to catch the glint of his eyes through the drops cascading from his hat brim. "You have been sundered from your people by violence. You are the last to stand, an orphan. You are the bone that will float upriver."

"I don't understand." But that wasn't quite true. She understood just enough to be afraid.

His expression became sympathetic. "I know. And I cannot explain it to you in a way that will make you understand, not fully. But you are the orphan bone. Just as one bone was sufficient to call me, you will be sufficient to stop the water." He stepped to her side, put one arm around her shoulder, and pointed upriver with that long hand. "There are great forces in the middle country, and at the source of the river is the reason its waters keep on rising. If you wish to stop them, you will have to confront the source of the waters. And you will likely not survive," he added. "However, it is equally likely you will be able to stop the rising and keep the town from being drowned completely."

"How?" she asked with a shaking voice. "How will I find the source in time? How will I know what to do?" She tried not to think about what he had said about her not surviving.

"Finding it is the easy part. Because of the orphan magic, the Skidwrack will take you upriver if you ask it to, just as it carried the cat's bone. Knowing what to do . . . You will simply have to hope you are clever as well as an orphan. The magic may well help you accomplish what you set out to do, because what else is magic good for? But magic won't make you clever. Magic won't tell you what to do, or how."

"Can't *you* tell me?" she asked desperately. "That's what I asked, after all!"

"You asked how you could stop the waters rising, and I tell you: you can stop it by letting the river carry you to its source to confront what waits there. I tell you orphan magic will carry you upriver, and orphan magic will help you accomplish your task. But one magic bone isn't worth all the answers in the world, even if I had them." He pushed his hat back and leaned down so they were eye to eye. He was handsome beyond imagination, and his eyes were worse than any nightmare. But there was nothing but honesty in them as he added, "And I don't have all the answers in the world, Nell."

He spoke her name as if he'd said the word *goodbye* instead, and she knew there was nothing more to learn from the man who had answered the summons of the bone. So she nodded and looked down at the river at their feet.

His arm was still around her shoulder. "Would you like me to help you into the water?" His voice was gentle, muted by the rain, and it was as if he had asked for a dance. She nodded, and he swept her into his arms, and, without appearing to have a care for his expensive-looking suit, he stepped down the muddy bank and into the Skidwrack with Nell held tight against his chest.

His dark coat fanned out across the surface. "Don't fear the river," he whispered. "You are that-which-remains. It will carry you, if you let it."

She held her breath and closed her eyes as the strong arms released her into the current. At the very last moment, she felt him tuck something small and thin into the fingers she clenched over her stomach: the bone that had called him in the first place.

The dark man stood in the surging river and watched her disappear upriver with the slender bit of bone in her hand. Then, with a very small frown of regret between his eyes, he took hold of a tree root and climbed the muddy bank.

For Nell, being carried by the river was strangely peaceful. Fear seemed beside the point, and she was too tired for it anyway. She was exhausted. She ached with sadness. The sensation was like being swung in a hammock, which was good, because her mind was in chaos. She could not begin to imagine what waited for her, or what would be expected of her, or how she would accomplish what needed doing. She did not know if she was clever, or merely desperate.

There's no need to worry before it's time, the river said as it rocked her. *Sleep. You will need your rest. I cannot give you much, but I can give you that.*

I am hallucinating, she thought. *My river doesn't speak.*

The Skidwrack merely burbled and laughed. The day was fading, and there were stars overhead. She watched them pass slowly as the river chuckled and murmured.

And then, without warning, two hands grabbed her shoulders and jerked her roughly out of the water and up onto dry land.

It was a sharp, harsh action, and it made the water splash and froth. Her head dropped beneath the surface for a moment, and for the first time since the stranger had lowered her into it, Nell tasted the river. She choked and sputtered and rocks scraped her back through her drowned sister's coat as the unseen person hauled her up onto the bank. She fought free from the hands, rolled to her side, and coughed up more water than she had realized she'd swallowed. At last, Nell wiped her eyes clear and looked at the person who'd interrupted her journey.

The look of concern on his face was at odds with his gaze. At first she thought this was just a trick of the water she was still blinking away, or a function of the fact that one of his eyes was a delicate orb made of tin, with an iris enameled the same cold blue as his right.

"Are you all right?" he asked.

"I was until you grabbed me," she snapped.

"Was I supposed to leave you in the water?" he asked, surprised. "I was passing on the road, and I saw a body in the river. You didn't look dead. What should I have done?"

Something about his tone was wrong, just as something about his eyes was wrong. *Here is a lie,* Nell thought, though she couldn't work out where in those words the lie crouched.

"Yes," she said, "you should have. We have business, the river and I."

The mask of concern fell away, and for a moment, the face that considered her was nothing but pure, cold calculation.

"Did he tell you that you had to do it?" the stranger asked. "The man who answered the summons?"

Nell, who had been about to stand and wade back into the river, faltered. "How could you know?"

"I know." Like the man in the black coat, this fellow had terrible eyes. In his blue-and-tin gaze, however, there was no emotion to be read. "I also know he lied to you if he told you that sacrificing yourself was the only way to stop the water's rising."

"He didn't say it was the *only* way," Nell said cautiously. "I asked how I could stop it, and this was his answer."

"Ah." The stranger nodded. "That was your mistake. So much depends on phrasing, doesn't it?"

The river lapped at Nell's foot, and she scooted a little ways farther up the bank. Already the water had risen another couple of inches. Why had she bothered to move? She and the river had work to do. She'd only be returning to it. *Unless,* a tiny voice protested. *What if this man really does know another way?*

He nodded as if he knew her thoughts. "I do, you know. Have another way." He crouched beside her and rested his elbows on his knees. "I, too, have been sundered. In a sense, I, too, am all that is left. And I have something you don't: I know why the waters are rising. I know what crouches at the river's source. The other way is: I go and you stay."

Nell's heart leaped. "You would do that?"

He smiled, and if only something of the smile had reached his eyes, it would have been like sun breaking through the clouds. "I will. I only need the bone." And together they looked down at the slender pale thing Nell still held clenched in one hand.

"Orphan magic?" Nell said, opening her hand between them.

"Orphan magic," the man confirmed. His fingers twitched as he held them over the bone. "May I?"

Nell hesitated. "You'll really do it? You can? You will?"

"I can," he said. "And I will," he added. Something about it felt like an afterthought.

"And you'll hurry?" Already the waters of the river were toying with her feet again.

"The only thing I'm waiting for is the bone." His voice was kind, encouraging, patient. But his face was stiffening into irritation.

Nell took a breath. She lifted her palm in offering, and the stranger plucked the precious thing from it. "Thank you, Nell." He tucked it in a pocket in his waistcoat and stood. "And now I go." He strode into the water without another look at her.

Nell held her breath as he lay back in the Skidwrack, his coat spreading over the surface like a slick of oil. *If he's lying, I'll know,* she thought. *The river won't take him. If he's lying, it'll sweep him away in the other direction.*

The stranger rotated once in the water in an eddy that spun him gently a full 360 degrees. Then, slowly but surely, he began to drift, just as she had, upriver against the current. Nell stood. She watched him disappear with his hand cupped protectively over the pocket with the bone in it. Then, with a very small frown of regret between her eyes, she took hold of a tree root and climbed the muddy bank.

When she reached the top, she discovered there was no road. The road was on the *other* side of the river; here there was nothing but forest. It was only the first lie she would catch him in. The much bigger lie was still to be uncovered. For what Nell didn't know was that half a mile upriver, the blue-eyed stranger would climb from the water, wring the wet from his clothes, and strike out on foot. *Away* from the rising waters. Away from what was left of Nell's town, which a few days later would be washed totally from the world, left to live in Nell's tortured memory and the occasional scrap that washed up on the freshly drawn coast or at the edges of the floodplain when the flooding finally ran its course and the river calmed. Away from the promise he'd made. And all for the sake of the bone in his pocket, and the strange magic it contained.

ꙮ— INTERLUDE —ꙮ

As Petra stopped speaking, her eyes came to land, confidently, heavily, on Antony Masseter.

Masseter met Petra's gaze with his single bright green eye.

For a moment, the only sounds were the crackling of Sorcha's fire and the drumming of the rain on the roof. Then Mr. Haypotten made a brusque noise. "I say, now, it's getting quite late. Who'll finish the toasted cheese, before we all go our separate ways for the night?"

No one answered. Everyone's eyes were on either the young woman on the sofa or the peddler facing her from his chair opposite the hearth.

Then Masseter reached up to his firelit face. With one hand, he stretched the flesh away from his eye. The rest of his face twisted as with the other hand he reached in, took hold of his bulging right eyeball, and delicately pulled it out of the socket.

Or at least, that's how it looked, and if Petra had been a different sort of person, she might have gasped in horror. But she wasn't a different sort of person, and she merely watched with an expression of something like disdain as Masseter tossed a clear, curved bit of glass, colorless except in one circular space where it was tinted with golden green, onto the floor between them. Jessamy snarled in protest as it shattered not far from Maisie, though the girl herself didn't so much as flinch.

Then the peddler flipped the patch up onto his forehead to

reveal a gleaming silver hammered-metal orb with a laquered iris of the same cornflower blue as the eye that had worn the false lens. The blue-enameled metal contracted around the pupil as if to adjust to the light in the room.

Petra looked down at a shard that had slid across the floor to rest at her feet. Without standing, she reached out her left heel and ground the yellow-green colored glass to powder.

Masseter chuckled, and it might've sounded genuine enough to anyone who wasn't also able to see the brittle coldness in the blue eye that had been hidden under the green.

"Petra," he said. "Short for Petronella, I think. But I would never have recognized you, Nell, not if you hadn't tipped your hand with all your little machinations. You changed your hair."

"I'm also fifteen years older," she said. "Sometimes time just passes normally, a pattern you seem to have forgotten. You, of course, look exactly the same."

The peddler crossed one ankle over his knee. "What do you want?"

Petra's disdain sharpened into anger. "You didn't keep your word. You lied."

"I lie when I need to." His face hardened. "And when I feel like it."

"You lied," Petra repeated, "and you let my town die. There's nothing left there but rooftops."

"Saved you, didn't I?" he asked, baring his teeth. "That's something."

"No. I was *willing*. I had made up my mind to be a sacrifice if that's what was needed to save the town. You stopped me," she snarled. "You didn't *save* me, you *stopped* me. You promised me you could save my *home*. And then you didn't. Did you lie about knowing how to stop the flood, too?"

"Of course I did," Masseter retorted. "Don't be ridiculous."

"So condescending." Petra shook her head. "Just because you've popped in and out of a dozen lifetimes doesn't mean you've lived a dozen of them."

He grinned. "Perhaps not, but I am something of an expert on time and how it passes. And I've endured about as much as I plan to endure of whatever *this* is, so I'll ask again. What is it you want from me?"

"Give me back the bone."

The peddler shook his head. "No."

"You took it from me under false pretenses. You took it in a lie."

"But I took it, and I'll keep it. Your anger is . . . understandable. And impressive. But it matters far, far less to me than the consequences if I don't manage to finish what I've started. Your bone is part of that, and it has properties I need."

He reached into a pocket and took something out: a hunk of metal about the size of a palm. The filigreed box, bought for an eye in the hollow-way and fitted with a paper keyway taken from a homicidal room in a house that could not be mapped, containing rods and dials and gears and valves designed by a fire-reckoner and assembled by a maker of reliquaries.

The peddler undid a catch on the side and opened the box.

"It's there, you see?" he said softly, holding it up for her. "Along with the adit-gate from Fellwool House and John Ustion's *fier-ekenia* mechanism, all nestled into the hollow-ware man's coffret, which cost me dearly, but I had precious few options by that point."

"You stole my great-grandfather's device?" Sorcha demanded. Then, more shocked still, "And you *finished* it?"

"I had to, when it became clear he wouldn't," Masseter snapped. "A dozen artificers I set to work on the problem. None of them would sell to me after Lung sent me on my way, but I knew none would be able to resist the challenge. A dozen artificers, a dozen secret tries, eleven total failures. Only Ustion's came close, and then he walked away from it. So I took it, yes. He never knew, so don't bother staring at me like that, and it sounds like your mother was just as happy to find it gone."

"But how did you finish it?" Sorcha persisted. "You're not fire-savvy."

"No, but I know someone who is. Someone across the Tailrace. I took him the pieces, and he gave me instructions. He told me what to look for, so that I could then take it all to the reliquarist, who assures me that now only one piece remains." He sucked in a mouthful of air. "That's all. Just one piece, and I'm finished. It will all be finished."

There was nothing inside that looked like a bone. Nothing, that is, until Petra remembered Negret Colophon's story of the peddlers and the whalebone spring. Then she saw it: the tiny, delicate whorl of pale yellow.

"How did you even manage that?" she asked. "A cat's bone isn't pliable. It's nothing like whalebone."

"Yours was magic, if you recall," Masseter said. "And the thing is so nearly complete. I regret to disappoint—"

"Yes, yes, your grand task is nearly finished," Petra interrupted. "And I know what you came here for."

He fell silent and looked at her without a word, as if he longed to be able to wish her dead.

"It's how I knew you would come," she continued. "Especially once the waters started to rise. You couldn't risk this place being drowned like my home was. You might never have found it again."

Still he said nothing. The young woman reached under a throw pillow beside her on the sofa. Then she withdrew her hand and showed him the gold-and-ceramic music box, the one from Madame Grisaille's room, which lay at the crossroads of the lines in her palm.

"Your machine will want winding," she murmured, looking down at the scene painted on its lid. "And for that, you will need a very special winder-key that can coil more than metal." Then she looked up at him. "I think I am right in guessing that a winder that can coil time is rarer even than cat-bone springs."

The peddler's face had drained to the color of dry china clay. "Give that to me."

"No."

He made a move as if to dart forward out of his chair. Once again, just like the night before, there was a well-intentioned but belated impulse on the part of a number of the guests to try and intercede as things suddenly lurched toward physical violence. But even as Sangwin, Amalgam, Captain Frost, and Mr. Haypotten got moving, Masseter himself stopped cold in his tracks. He fell forward onto his knees before the card castle with a grunt of pain as the very nails in the floor pulled themselves loose and lengthened into grabbing fingers that held his feet immobile.

Maisie allowed herself to be pulled farther out of the way, then wriggled loose from Jessamy's grip and watched, fascinated, as the grasping iron flexed and tightened its grip on the peddler's shoes.

Petra looked coldly down on Masseter from her place on the sofa like a queen looking down from her throne. "I have had fifteen years to prepare for this moment."

"Learned a few things, have you?" the peddler grunted as he shoved himself to his feet. The iron fingers lengthened as he stood, twisting to entwine about his calves.

"I made some friends." She nodded to Madame Grisaille, sitting like a monarch herself in her seat in the corner. The old lady raised one hand off the arm of her chair and curled her fingers into her palm, and the iron that bound the peddler's legs tightened, grinding the bones in his feet against each other.

"The lady declares that you will stand where you are," Reever said from the chair to Masseter's right. "She prefers that her city not be drowned for the sake of your device." In the chair to Masseter's left, Negret said nothing, but he twirled the long, needle-sharp awl he'd been holding in his fingers, and suddenly it was no longer a bindery tool, but a weapon.

The peddler ignored the brothers and stared at the woman in the rocking chair. "So the iron does walk abroad."

"When she must," Madame said in her thrumming voice. The peddler shuddered, as if he could hear her words resonating through his own skeleton.

"Now." Petra held out a hand. "Give me my bone. Then I am going to do what I can to stop this flood."

"Why?" the peddler snarled. "You're going to try out your supposed orphan magic now, after all these years? It won't work."

"Maybe not," Petra said. "But I'll have tried."

Masseter looked at the box in her palm. "Give me the winder, and I'll give you the spring."

Petra's eyes were hard. "No. Not until I've done what I have to do. Then you can have it."

Masseter's mismatched eyes bulged in confusion and anger. "When you've done what? Gone to the source of the river? Drowned on the way? Died on whatever fool errand awaits you if you arrive? Am I to follow you to the middle country and take my spring and my winder from your corpse?"

"Neither one of them is yours," Petra spat. "And yes, you could do that. Or you could follow me to the middle country, help me do what needs doing, and have the spring and the winder when you've made amends for what you did to my town."

"What does the winder matter to you, anyhow?" the peddler argued. "You'll be at the bottom of a river, either way."

"It matters because you don't get to lie and kill a whole community and still keep the thing you came for," she snarled.

"Vengeance?" the peddler said in disbelief. "You'll keep the thing just so I can't have it?"

"Yes!" She calmed her voice. "If you like. You have your choice. Make amends and have the spring and the winder with my gratitude, or lose both."

Masseter put his hands in his pockets. "Or I could kill you and take them."

To his right, Reever Colophon barked out a laugh. "No," he said, leaning back comfortably in his chair and watching in amusement as the iron twisted its tendrils more tightly around Masseter's legs. "You could not." To Masseter's left, Negret tapped the stiletto-shaped awl silently against one knee.

"And if you try," Madame added, "I will carry you from this place, and when the waters fall, the people will discover a new statue somewhere in the city, a statue of a nameless man with mismatched eyes. And as the years pass, the statue will grow legends. They'll say it cries out in desperation, and they'll say on the right kind of night, you can almost hear the words. As if — impossible, of course — but as if there were a man imprisoned within it, begging for his freedom from an unknown but vengeful queen who put him there for his sins."

"Suppose I say yes," Masseter said quietly, his eyes on Petra, "and when we have gone up the river together, when we have gone beyond the reach of the unknown queen, suppose I kill you then?"

Sullivan spoke from Petra's side. "You'll have to go through me."

"Well, now it's a party," Masseter retorted, rolling his eyes. "Happily, friend."

Petra ignored him. She gave Sullivan an apologetic smile and shook her head.

The seiche smiled back, his eyebrows arched. "If you don't want my company, that's fair. But you aren't the only one who has restitution to make, so don't be a martyr, Petra." His voice changed. "Let me come with you."

The quality of Petra's smile shifted a fraction. "I can't ask that of you."

"You don't have to ask." The eye with the scar below it flashed a wink.

Masseter sniffed. "I could kill you both for that scene alone."

"I'm sure you could." Petra stood and walked to him and actually patted his cheek. Masseter bore the condescension without flinching, but fury radiated off him in waves. "But if the stories are true," Petra said, "you haven't killed yet in the course of building your new device. You've let plenty die, but you haven't taken a life with your own hands. I think there's a reason for that. Possibly that reason has a name."

"Jacinda," Maisie said quietly from the hearth. She picked

the queen of secateurs up from the floor, stood, and put the card into the peddler's palm, the one marked with the little spray of scattered scars. He crumpled the card in his fist with a snarl and raised his hand as if to strike the girl, then just as quickly dropped his hand again and thrust it into his pocket, the queen still clenched in it.

Meanwhile, Petra unscrewed the winder from the music box and put it into her watch pocket. She handed the box to Mrs. Haypotten and smiled thinly at the merchant. "Make your choice."

For a long moment, they looked at each other. With his scarred hand, now empty again, Masseter reached into his own unfinished device, the one contained in the filigreed box. Carefully he plucked out the spring. Petra held out a palm, and the peddler put the spring carefully into it.

Maisie stretched herself up on her knees, craning her neck for a look at the curl of bone. Words and figures had been carved into its flat surfaces, but they were minute, and she would have needed a glass to read them.

"The calculation is inseparable from the consequence," Masseter said, watching Petra closely as she, too, inspected the spiral. "Not magic, perhaps, but something one should never walk through time without remembering. Something you should perhaps remember, as well,"

"Thank you." Petra put the spring away with the winder. She glanced to the iron queen, and immediately the nails unwound themselves from Masseter's legs and feet and eased themselves back to their original places in the floor. "Shall we go, Mr. Masseter?"

He closed the box and returned it to his pocket, then bent and rubbed his shins. "I am at your service."

"Remember it," the iron queen said grimly. In his chair, Negret gave the awl one more tap on his knee, then turned its point with fierce and deadly precision on the stack of papers.

Petra, meanwhile, opened the French doors between the riverward windows and stepped outside. The rain whipped in, and the surface of the water was now mere feet below the porch's tiled floor.

Masseter followed her with curious eyes. "Shouldn't we go and get . . ." He gestured vaguely back inside.

Petra glanced over her shoulder. "What? Our tooth powder?"

"Anything?"

The young woman took a deep breath. Then she laughed. "I imagine we can find what we need along the way. I don't know what that's likely to be."

She walked to the gap in the railing that showed where the stairs led down to the river, then stepped down onto the blue stair and from there onto the surface of the water. It bore her feet up as surely as if she were standing on rock. She laughed again, the rain slicking her bobbed curls into a sleek, chestnut-colored cap.

The seiche strode past the merchant and through the open

door. "I suppose you can walk on water, too," Masseter muttered.

Sullivan said nothing, just stepped down onto the floodwater beside Petra. The two of them looked back at Masseter. Petra reached up a hand. The one-eyed merchant squared his shoulders, crossed the porch, and allowed her to help him down onto the surface. Whether because Petra still possessed some lingering orphan magic or because the river understood what was being asked of it, his feet did not sink.

As the three of them turned away from the inn, Maisie shook herself and ran to the French doors. "Petra!" she wailed. Out on the water, Petra turned and waved but didn't stop walking.

Jessamy Butcher and Madame Grisaille followed Maisie onto the porch, each with a hand at the ready to restrain the girl if she tried to follow. "Where is she going?" Maisie choked on her words and on the rain, her chrysanthemum shawl whipping in the wind.

"Into the wilds of the middle country," Madame Grisaille said, drawing her gently back into the shelter of the parlor. She took Maisie's shawl from her and passed it to Jessamy, then unwound a wrap from her own shoulders and swathed the shivering girl in it. "But look, my dear, she isn't going alone."

"But she's going without us," Maisie protested. "Why would she go with *them?* They're not her friends."

"I think Mr. Sullivan would take issue with that," Jessamy observed drily, hanging the girl's shawl from a corner of the mantelpiece. "But Maisie, she *isn't* going without us." She returned to the door and crouched at Maisie's side as they watched the trio walking on the water toward a bend in the river, nearly out of sight. "Just imagine. Imagine our friend. Days from now, when she and her companions reach the source of the Skidwrack. And imagine it isn't a spring, but a crossroads."

"Why?"

"Because I'm telling this story," Jessamy said softly. "And because my stories are all stories of crossroads."

Maisie sighed and nodded.

"So let me tell it properly. Listen." She glanced over her shoulder into the parlor. "*Listen.* That's the way to begin, isn't it, Mr. Amalgam?"

Phineas Amalgam inclined his head as he left the corner table and settled once more into the vacant chair by the fire. "Tell it however you see fit, my dear. May we stay?"

"If you like." Jessamy turned back to the river, and to the girl who watched it, searching for moving silhouettes in the darkness.

EIGHTEEN

---◆---

THE CROSSROADS

The Headcutter's Tale

*L*ISTEN. DEEP IN THE MIDDLE COUNTRY, there is a crossroads. Perhaps it is a literal one, a place where two roads intersect; perhaps it is one like the boy Foulk saw reflected in a puddle. Either way, they will come to a crossroads, these three. And at that crossroads, who will our Petra find there but that same man in his long coat and gray fedora, the one she met so many years ago on the night she sent a cat's bone upriver."

Jessamy could have described that crossroads from memory, and the fingerpost that stood there, one arm pointing off in the direction of the river that would twist and turn its way to Nagspeake and the others pointing, perhaps, to even stranger places. It would have looked very much like the scene painted on the music box that, without its winder, could no longer perform the one song the Devil himself could not play. (And in fact, months from that day, Mrs. Haypotten would remember that the box with the crossroads was missing its winder. When she fitted it with a new one, the innkeeper's wife wound the box and lifted the lid, only to frown as the first notes of "Riverward" began to tinkle out. "I could've sworn it was the kite-shaped box as played that one," she murmured. "This one played . . ." But for the life of her, she couldn't remember what tune she had expected to hear. The song danced out of reach, refusing to be remembered even as it refused to be forgotten.)

But now: "She'll meet that man again," Jessamy said to Maisie. "And she'll walk up to him, her feet sure and confident from miles of walking on water, and she'll say, 'Take the waters from my river.' And the man in the fedora will smile at her — the smile of someone who doesn't quite understand what's about to happen, but thinks he knows, and thinks he has his world safely in his own hands."

Maisie, who had seen that very expression on the face of Antony Masseter in the moments before Petra had shown him the music box, nodded. But her wide eyes did not leave the Skidwrack.

Jessamy leaned closer to Maisie's ear. "And the man will say, 'I will make you a bet.' He will whisper it, because only fools who are bluffing shout their wagers." She glanced over her shoulder, back into the parlor. "Isn't that true, Mr. Tesserian?"

Cross-legged by the hearth, Al Tesserian nodded. "That's the way of it, in my experience."

"And Petra's two companions, standing at her back, will

share a look between them then. The seiche who never believed he could love anyone, who did not think he deserved to love or be loved after the things he's done but who loves Petra, and would gladly make bets with the Devil for her sake; and the one-eyed merchant who cannot afford to see her fail. The look that passes between them, however, is not one of worry, because they have walked with her on the river for days now, and they have shared enough adventures to know better than the Devil what he is about to tangle with."

Maisie gave a tiny, conspiratorial smirk.

"'Not a bet,' Petra will say. 'A contest.' The man in the fedora will grin again and show his teeth, because now that the challenge has been made, all he has to do is accept. 'What shall the contest be?' he will ask, still thinking he can afford to give away such advantages as choosing the conditions. And what do you think Petra will say?" Jessamy glanced at the old, gaunt lady standing at Maisie's other side. "Madame?"

Madame lifted a hand, as if the answer could not be more obvious. "Surely Petra will say, 'We shall dance.'"

Maisie's smirk widened.

"Petra will say, 'We shall dance,'" Jessamy repeated, taking one of Maisie's hands in hers and turning the girl in a circle and drawing her away from the open doors. Far away on the river, three tiny figures disappeared around a bend and into legend; back in the parlor, a young girl laughed as a woman wearing gloves and stigmata spun her again, faster.

"Can the Devil dance?" Maisie asked, reeling.

"Mr. Amalgam, you know the lore," Jessamy said. "Is the Devil any good at dancing?"

From his chair, Amalgam replied, "The Devil's good at whatever he needs to be good at."

"So the Devil can dance," Jessamy continued, "but he bears the burden of too many secrets — every secret kept out of malice, every secret kept out of fear, every secret kept out of ignorance the Devil carries with him, in case they might be useful to him someday. And as you know," she said, touching Maisie's shoulder with one gloved finger, "a person cannot dance with all their soul while holding tight to secrets, even if they're someone else's. Still, he won't think he needs to dance with all his soul, not to beat an ordinary woman, so the Devil won't worry overmuch about that.

"Then, 'Give us light,' the Devil will cry, and a ring of flame will surround them all." Jessamy turned, her eyes seeking Sorcha and finding her standing by the hearth, hands clasped at her back. "What sort of fire will that be, Sorcha?"

"Not true hellfire, surely," the firekeeper said, smiling. She reached up and took down one of the fancy paper matches she and Maisie had made earlier that day. "Flamedry, perhaps, or some other sort of border fire." She reached the spill into the flames. When it caught, she touched the burning end to the palm of her empty hand, then drew her hands apart again. Strung between the spill in one hand and her opposite palm like the strands of a cat's cradle was a gleaming thread of fire hung with individual flames that burned downward, fluttering like dangling flags.

Maisie stared in shock. Sorcha laughed again; then, as the paper match burned rapidly down to nothing, she flung her arms sharply wide, and the flaring flags flew to pieces like fireworks.

"So they will have their fire," Jessamy continued as sparks rained down in the parlor. She tugged Maisie's hand to reclaim her attention. "'Give us a jury,' the Devil will call, and the air around them will seem to thicken as spirits emerge out of nowhere, illuminated by the flames just as the ghostly sailors were revealed by the light of a storm bottle in the captain's tale." She turned to nod at Captain Frost in his chair by the display cabinet. "All come to determine the winner. And, 'Give me a song,' he'll shout, and all the musicians who ever lost a headcut-ting with the Devil will find themselves there at the crossroads, their hands bound to do his bidding when he calls until their days are done and they surrender their souls at last." Jessamy's hands in her borrowed embroidered gloves twitched as she spoke, but her voice stayed clear and strong as wide-eyed Maisie turned to her to hear the rest of the story.

"And then the headcutters will play," Jessamy continued, "and the Devil will dance. And a lesser person would despair, because even dancing without his entire soul, the Devil is a whirlwind. But—" She paused. "This will not be a lesser person who stands before him, waiting her turn. And so, although the seiche boy who loves her might reach for her hand, and although she might squeeze his hand back, Petra won't despair. Because she will have two things the Devil doesn't know about. So when his dance comes to an end in a whirl of dust and nightmare, the Devil will bow and offer his musicians to Petra. 'Give the girl a song,' he will order."

She held up a finger. "But Petra will refuse. 'None of your songs for me,' she'll say. Because the first thing Petra will have is a song already in her mind. The only song that beats the Devil." And Jessamy glanced over her shoulder at the twin who sang under his breath when he thought no one could hear and who was at present stitching the binding on a book covered with swirling blue and gold and green paper. "Isn't that right, Mr. Negret? I know you know it. Whistle a bit for us now."

And Negret smiled apologetically, for Jessamy Butcher had been the one person he had not wanted to overhear him singing this song. But there was no anger in her face, so he tied a knot and bit off the thread, stood, and delivered the finished book to Sorcha, along with a brief kiss on her cheek. Then, perching on the arm of his chair, he began to whistle the song that the music box with the crossroads scene would never play again, and Maisie's heart leaped into motion just as it had when she'd heard these same notes played the day before.

Jessamy's heart did a different kind of lurch, but she forced herself to ignore it. "And the second thing she will have is even rarer than the gift of that song," she said, compelling warmth into her voice. "And that is *nothing*. No secrets left to keep, nothing to lose, nothing held back, and nothing she wants more than to beat the Devil. And so she will dance." She held out her hands to

Maisie, and, when Maisie reached back with her own, Jessamy lifted her right up off the ground and twirled the girl in her arms again. "I don't know for certain that there is any dance the Devil cannot do, and I no longer lay wagers myself. Still, if I did, I would bet that if there is a dance outside his capability, it's this kind." She bent the laughing girl back in a dip. "A dance of nothing: nothing hidden, nothing held back—nothing, perhaps, but joy. And if Petra had forgotten how to put those sorts of steps together—many of us do, you know, as we grow—you will have taught her again yourself."

Maisie sighed with happiness, even though she knew Jessamy had it exactly backwards. The right dance would be *everything*, not *nothing*—but perhaps that was how the same steps done by different people could look so very dissimilar while still being technically the same dance. Or the same story told by two people could seem like such entirely different accounts, like the two versions of Amalgam's tale of the enchanted house in the pines.

"And when she is finished," Jessamy continued, spinning Maisie back down onto her own two feet, "all the dead and dark things of the jury will declare the winner they have chosen unanimously. 'The lady takes the game,' they will say in voices like the tomb, like the wind, like the groan of ice against the hulls of ghost ships—voices with an arcane music to them that will make poor Mr. Masseter's head, always tortured by patterns, ache for days. But he will cheer through it. And the Devil will rise in a fury, because although he is bound to abide by the rules of his own wagers, there's no law that says he's got to be a gentleman about it. But when at last he has finished venting his fury, our friends will be left standing tall at the crossroads. And someday, someone will tell their story, as I have told it to you."

"But differently," Maisie put in, "because it will have happened."

"Yes." Jessamy nodded, then tilted her head as she considered. "Or perhaps the truth is more complicated. If, as Mr. Masseter told us, time is not a single thread, then perhaps, somehow, in some way, it already has happened. Or perhaps it's simpler still. Perhaps in some way it already has happened, merely because I've told it."

Maisie nodded. She looked out at the Skidwrack through the dwindling rain for a long time. The adults in the room behind her waited, none of them quite willing to walk away, just in case, in spite of everything that Jessamy had said, in spite of the music Negret was still whistling, the girl broke her reverie and darted out to fling herself onto the river.

At last, Sorcha came to stand beside Maisie at the door and took her hand. "Think of the stories she will have when she comes back."

Maisie sighed and turned back toward the parlor, and the dissatisfaction on her face reminded Amalgam of the strange blend of gratification and discontent that occasionally seemed to follow even his best-told tales. Because sometimes the better the story, the greater the restlessness that comes when it ends and the listener has to go on, imagining the story continuing some-where, but untold and out of sight.

Then: "I'm hungry," Maisie announced, and the spell was broken.

"Come on, then," Mrs. Haypotten said briskly, crossing the room and holding out a hand. "Let's find you an apple."

"Cake," the girl specified, correctly guessing that, in this moment, she could've asked for a marzipan turtledove in a spun-sugar tree and gotten it.

"Cake it is," the innkeeper's wife agreed.

As Maisie crossed the room to claim her dessert, Tesserian cleared his throat from the hearth. When she looked over, he nodded at the castle that now stood almost as tall as Maisie her-self, with all her wooden creatures peeking from its windows and doors and porches and balconies.

"Shall we?" he asked, pointing to a card that made up part of the very top of the cupola.

Maisie grinned and all but pranced over to the castle. She reached out and plucked the card the gambler had indicated from its place. The others watched curiously; surely it would've been more effective to topple the structure by taking a piece from the foundation. But when Maisie removed the queen of puppets from its place, the castle exploded outward in all directions, including upward, as if that single queen had been anchoring the entire assemblage to the ground.

The cards rained down as the sparks of Sorcha's border fire

had done. Except, somehow they never quite fell all the way. Caught, perhaps, in some sort of vortex, the cards swirled like confetti in the air, and Maisie twirled again, dancing this time with scores of assorted kings, queens, knaves, jesters, and saints, and a tiny menagerie of wooden beasts that paraded through the air as if they were nothing more than paper themselves.

Jessamy watched all this from beside the glass doors, her attention divided between the child and the river. Reever Colophon came to stand beside her.

"Are you all right?" he asked quietly.

"I wish I could have gone too," Jessamy said. She looked down at her gloved hand, which lay against the glass of one of the French doors. "But there's no knowing how long these hands will do what I ask them to."

Reever said nothing, but he held out his own palm. Jessamy considered, then put hers into it.

"Still yours?" he asked.

She nodded. He interlaced his fingers with Jessamy's and glanced over his shoulder, to where Negret sat on the arm of his chair, still whistling the song that was everything and nothing, but laughing now in between lines as he watched Maisie twirl with the cards and creatures that somehow still refused to fall to the ground.

"Will you dance, Miss Butcher?" Reever asked. When she didn't answer right away, he leaned close to her ear and added quietly, "I promise I'll keep your secrets."

She let out a long breath. "All right."

So one High Walker danced with the Headcutter as the other whistled the only song the Devil cannot play, and the folklorist ordered chapters in his mind and the printmaker imagined how he would carve the scene. The gambler watched his cards parade, and the captain forgot to turn his glass, and the innkeepers held hands and smiled as the Queen of Building Castles of Cards reached a hand out first to the firekeeper and then to the lady who was the avatar of the city's wild iron, and she pulled them into the dance too. The flames in the hearth sent a flurry of sparks up like tame fireworks to illuminate the parlor as the three dancers, the youngest and the eldest of the storytellers, spun each other round and round, laughing.

So they danced away their secrets. Outside, unnoticed, the floodwaters of the Skidwrack began to fall.

A NOTE ABOUT
THE CLARION BOOKS EDITION

Many of you will already be familiar with *The Raconteur's Commonplace Book* from *Greenglass House* and *Ghosts of Greenglass House,* in which a mysterious guest at the Pine family's inn shares the book with Milo during the winter holidays. I first encountered *Raconteur's* and its author, Nagspeake folklorist Phineas Amalgam, back in 2010, while working on an as-yet-unpublished book called *Wild Iron,* the first story I ever wrote that was set in the Sovereign City. I'm delighted to present this new edition of *The Raconteur's Commonplace Book* to you, complete with beautiful original art by Jaime Zollars and Nicole Wong, who have brought Amalgam's book and The Blue Vein Tavern in Nagspeake circa 1930 to life as beautifully as anyone could wish.

In the writing of *The Raconteur's Commonplace Book,* which would become his most famous work, it's likely that Amalgam was inspired by Charles Dickens' 1855 book, *The Holly-Tree Inn,* which shares a similar structure: guests at an inn pass the time during inclement weather by sharing tales. The combination of tales and interludes incorporates a wide range of folklore—not merely legends, myths, and fairy tales but also superstitions, riddles, ballads, dance, fortunetelling, folk art, and so forth.

Phineas Amalgam was both a collector and a creator of lore, and in *Raconteur's* he uses a combination of his own stories and older Nagspeake tales of more mysterious provenance. The gambler's tale, "The Ferryman," is probably derived from a poem in *Aunt Lucy's Counterpane Book* ("Crossing, Crossing"); "Three Kings" is recognizable as a version of Griffin Walter's story of the same name, occasionally anthologized in other collections of Nagspeake lore; and "The Devil and the Scavenger" is believed to come not from Nagspeake at all, but from the itinerant peddlers who have passed through the city since time immemorial. Nagspeakers will recognize the protagonist of "The Unmappable House" as half of the inseparable pair from the anonymously authored *The Tales of Troublewit and Pantin,* but as far as we know this is the only Pantin story in which the boy appears without his shape-shifting iron sidekick. (This story, by the way, has been the root of a number of scholarly feuds over the years. One bar near City University still has a line painted down the middle of the main room thanks to a decades-old feud between scholars who can't agree over what it means that Phineas Amalgam wrote himself into the book as a guest at the inn and then proceeded to have his character tell a Pantin story rather than any of the tales in the book that are more recognizably his own inventions. Some believe this was his admission that he is the author of *The Tales of Troublewit and Pantin.* Other folklorists will hit you in the face with whatever object's closest for even suggesting this, as almost every one of them has a pet theory about the true identity of the *Troublewit and Pantin* author.)

In editing this edition, I did make one significant departure from the version Milo would have read. In my research into Phineas Amalgam for *Wild Iron*, I came upon a manuscript version of *Raconteur's* dated 1932 in which the stories were arranged in a slightly different order than they were in the "slim red volume" Milo had been given. I have a pretty good idea why Amalgam rearranged them for that edition, but there's evidence in his letters that suggests he regretted it. I've restored the 1932 order for this version. I hope you'll enjoy it as much as I did.

Finally, I would be remiss if I didn't acknowledge the great debt I owe this collection for the influence it's had on my own works set in the Roaming World. If you'd like to know more about the characters here and where to follow their trails in my other books, here are just a few suggestions. Find the man who sees the patterns in *Bluecrowne* and *The Kairos Mechanism;* in *Bluecrowne* and *The Left-Handed Fate* you can sail again with Melusine and Lowe (whose name, I'm sorry to say, Mr. Frost may have misremembered). You will find more High Walkers in *The Broken Lands* and lurking in the background in *Bluecrowne;* in *Bluecrowne* you will also meet an ancestor of Maisie's and a few familiar peddlers. To find others like Jessamy, along with more tales of crossroads, read *The Boneshaker* and *The Broken Lands;* or pair *The Broken Lands* with *Bluecrowne* to meet others like Sorcha. Nagspeake's self-aware iron is everywhere in the city, of course, but it's most visible in *The Left-Handed Fate* and *The Thief Knot*. And lastly, many of my books are set in the Sovereign City of Nagspeake, but for peak exploring-the-place reading, you may enjoy *The Left-Handed Fate* and *The Thief Knot* most.

Kate Milford
Creve Coeur, Nagspeake, 2021

ACKNOWLEDGMENTS

The Raconteur's Commonplace Book might represent the most fun I've ever had writing a book. I've never *not* had fun writing a book, but *Raconteur's* required the most puzzle-work I've had to do while putting a thing together, and since "short" is not my forte, writing all the individual tales was both a challenge and a delight. But this book took a lot of bandwidth, and I wouldn't have been able to do it without the help and encouragement and support of a truly wonderful network of people.

Firstly, always, most of all, all my gratitude and love to Nathan, Griffin, and Tess (and the auxiliary Milford team of Ed, Maxy, and Maz). I love you with all my heart. And Griffin, you were only four at the time, so you may or may not remember the night at a fancy-pants restaurant when you started to tell me about the King of Finding Things, the King of Opening Things, and the King of Tying Things, but thank you for telling me they existed and inviting me to write about them. The idea of bookbinding as fortunetelling became part of this story after Zane Morris (whose company Cradle makes notebooks from discarded materials and uses the proceeds from their sales to fund music workshops), showed me the beautiful branching thread patterns hidden in the center pages of his books. The reliquaries of Gaz of Feretory Street were inspired by actual objects made by an artist named Stan Gaz who I once met many years ago in New York. I've had the idea of a maker of reliquaries kicking around in my brain ever since. Dhonielle Clayton gave me the name of the inn almost a decade ago, back when we were in a critique group together. Thank you all for the inspiration. Thank you also to Chelsea Youss and Rayhan Youss, Kate Compton, Alice Mackay, and Tova Volchek for helping me find the time to do all the work of writing and revising and traveling and all the other oddball tasks that go into bringing a Nagspeake tale to life (and for occasionally taking over when, say, a cake needs to be iced). And to Gus and the very special folks at Emphasis Restaurant, Coffee RX, and Cocoa Grinder in Bay Ridge, thank you for giving folks like me in the neighborhood such great places to get stuff done. But there wouldn't be stuff to get done without the folks who heard me talk about this oddball book I wanted to write and thought, "Hey, that sounds like a fun project," and then proceeded to handle the business end of things. So thank you always, always, always to Lynne Polvino for taking a chance on another leap into the Sovereign City of Nagspeake with me; to Jaime Zollars for another staggeringly beautiful cover and another bit of architecture I wish I could live in forever; to Nicole Wong for bringing the tales to life so fantastically; and to Sharismar Rodriguez and Celeste Knudsen for assembling it all into such a beautiful object. Thank you to Barry Goldblatt, Dana Spector, and especially Tina Dubois for managing all the stuff that makes this career possible. Tina, I still reread your in-flight email from Thanksgiving whenever any shred of worry starts to creep in. Thank you so, so much.

I have spent ten wonderful years working alongside the wonderful folks at McNally Jackson Books, and it's hard to put into words how grateful I am to have been part of the family. Thank you to Sarah, Doug, Cristin, and all of my dear, dear friends. Thank you for letting me sling books with you. Thank you for all that you do. I am also hugely grateful to all the other wonderful bookstores, schools, and libraries who've helped my books find their readers over the years. Thank you for making me feel so welcome, and for all the work you do every day.

And to all the readers who've come back to Nagspeake and the Roaming World over and over to join me on these weird adventures, I simply can't thank you enough. To share these tales with you has been a joy and a gift for me. Roam well, my friends, until we meet again.